PENG

Welcome to th

Welcome to the Neighbourhood

JANE FALLON

PENGUIN BOOKS

PENGUIN BOOKS

UK | USA | Canada | Ireland | Australia
India | New Zealand | South Africa

Penguin Books is part of the Penguin Random House group of companies
whose addresses can be found at global.penguinrandomhouse.com

Penguin Random House UK,
One Embassy Gardens, 8 Viaduct Gardens, London s w 11 7bw

penguin.co.uk

Penguin
Random House
UK

First published 2026
002

Copyright © Jane Fallon, 2026

The moral right of the author has been asserted

Set in 12.5/14.75pt Garamond MT Std
Typeset by Six Red Marbles UK, Thetford, Norfolk
Printed and bound in Great Britain by Clays Ltd, Elcograf S.p.A.

The authorized representative in the EEA is Penguin Random House Ireland,
Morrison Chambers, 32 Nassau Street, Dublin D02 YH68

A CIP catalogue record for this book is available from the British Library

ISBN: 978–1–405–95109–8
TRADE PAPERBACK ISBN: 978–0–241–54114–2

Penguin Random House is committed to a sustainable future
for our business, our readers and our planet. This book is made from
Forest Stewardship Council® certified paper.

*Dedicated to my friends at the amazing charity
All Dogs Matter for their tireless work rescuing dogs
(and the occasional cat. They helped Pickle find her way to me).
Like all charities, they need volunteers and donations:
https://alldogsmatter.co.uk*

PART ONE

I

Growing up, Kitty always knew her life was destined to be special. She had it all planned out: a glittering career in the arts (not performing, that wasn't her, but behind the scenes somewhere. Arts-adjacent), a Shoreditch loft, a cool inner circle of glamorous, witty friends. Parties. Dinners. First nights. Lovers. She could picture it. A Big Life. Nothing like the dull suburban surroundings of her upbringing.

And then she'd met Gethin. And got a job in an office processing customer complaints. And a half-share of a little house on an estate of identical little houses.

And before she knew it, the future was all mapped out with trips to Asda and episodes of *Strictly* on repeat until she died.

Or, at least, until she did something about it.

Although that might have been a bit of a mistake, looking back.

At first it had felt like an adventure. A bold, brave new start. A promotion to the London head office had come up out of nowhere and it had seemed like too good an opportunity to miss. London was immersive galleries and quirky museums and bubble tea shops (not that she knew what those were, really, but they sounded like something she would enjoy). It was fashion shows and tasting menus and gangs of girlfriends giggling on night buses. She had lived most of her adult life in a fug of FOMO, coupled up, settled down. In reality it was almost certainly a mid-life crisis, she can see that now. She was pushing forty, seventeen years into the life she had never meant to have with Geth. Stuck in a relationship that was cosy and comfortable and safe and predictable. And utterly dull.

She'd felt old before her time, spending night after night at home, just the two of them or on boring couples' evenings with other boring couples. Listening to anecdotes about trips to the garden centre or a discourse on the virtues of hiring a postnatal doula, and wondering if standing up and throwing a glass of wine – or even a well-aimed fork – might be the way to put an end to them. She had accepted the job before she'd even had the chance to consider where she might be able to afford to live or how she might explain what the hell she was thinking to her fiancé. It was a purely reactive decision.

Her relationship with Geth was over as soon as she'd hit send on the email saying yes, she would love the position. She'd tried to let him down kindly. She'd tried 'It's not you, it's me', and 'You'll meet someone better', but he'd been obtuse to the point of making her wonder if he was doing it deliberately to wind her up. 'I just can't stand it any more,' she'd shouted in the end. 'I'm dying a slow death one fucking quiz night at a time.' (Quiz nights at the pub featured heavily in their life together. Other plans were made around them. So, she'd known it was a low blow.) Finally he'd cried, quiet tears that he'd tried to wipe away before she saw them, in typical considerate

Geth fashion, and she'd felt like the worst person ever. He was a nice man. He just wasn't her nice man.

'We could have a baby,' he'd said later with hope in his voice, and Kitty had almost laughed, because really if that one sentence didn't perfectly illustrate the way they were on different life paths, then she didn't know what did.

Afterwards she'd written a list: the pros of moving, the cons of her life now. Under pros she'd written *New job! New house! New friends! Culture! Fun! Excitement! Life!!* Under cons she'd put just one word: *Atrophy.* Then she'd worried that if she dropped dead suddenly no one would know what she was talking about, so she'd added *Routine, Suburbia, Boredom!!*

She'd wanted her choice validated, so she'd tried to justify herself to their friends. But no one had bought it. No one had even thought she was doing the right thing. Or had been afraid to tell her she wasn't, come to that. Especially not her siblings. She already thought of herself as the family sad case, both her brother and sister having found themselves glittering careers and fulfilling relationships decades ago. Conveniently in faraway towns. Kitty had always been the accidental plodder, stuck in the slow lane. And, if she were being honest, she knew they both had always hoped she would be the one to remain in close proximity to their parents as they aged, thus letting them off the hook except for duty visits at Christmas and for birthdays.

She's at her desk by eight. Still in Customer Complaints, only now she's in charge of a small part of it. She had started her new position just as everyone regrouped after the pandemic and hours were a free-for-all – the company considering themselves lucky if anyone came in at all at that point – and she had requested that she work from eight till four. It was summer and she'd loved to watch the city waking up. The fresh new day full of potential and promise. Now, every morning as she fights the alarm at six, she wants to go back in time and strangle that person.

She had thought it would be clever to go for the biggest property she could afford, anywhere where she thought she wouldn't get murdered on the way to the shops, and so she's ended up in the middle of nowhere, ten minutes from the bus that will take her to the nearest tube station for the long trek to work. A sensible long-term strategy, she had told herself, not quite able to fully throw off all the shackles of responsibility. She hates it.

In all her rash bravado she hadn't factored in how hard it would be to integrate herself into a strange city as you sailed into your forties. In books, when strangers rock up in a new town they inevitably bump into someone in the first few days who tuns out to be their soulmate. By page twenty-five they have a whole new social circle of quirky locals who are immediately available – and willing – to hang out day and night. Who will bail them out of the inevitable scrapes that follow. One or more will probably propose. Of course, real life is not like that. Of course, most people Kitty's age were happily settled down with their social diaries exactly as full as they wanted them to be. She had no idea what other middle-aged incomers did – join a choir or a book club? Take up salsa dancing? Assemble a crew of other friendless work colleagues? None of it was appealing. In fact, the thought of any of those options made her break out in a cold sweat. She had thought maybe she'd find a kindred spirit somewhere amongst her neighbours, but, despite the fact that most of them were kind and friendly, they were also mostly the wrong side of eighty. She tended to cross the road to avoid another interminable chat about parking or the state of number 5's bins. Although, to be fair, number 5's bin management was pretty shocking.

She had paced the city on her days off, a running commentary in her head. *Look, there's Tape. Is that the Groucho Club? I'm outside a gallery opening on the Kings Road! I'm walking past Chiltern Firehouse!* She had no idea how to cross the divide from observing to taking part. In the evenings she would steel herself, smile into the mirror until it hurt (she had read somewhere that smiling released endorphins that, in turn, made you actually feel like smiling, although the results were not always noticeable – to her, at least) and then phone home. '*Guess where I went today!* Her mum would lap up the details, anxious for good news. She would ask who with and Kitty would rattle off the name of one of her work colleagues, trying to keep the lie as close to home as possible. In bed at night she would blush when she remembered the conversation.

Occasionally, at first, she had forced herself out of her comfort zone: a birthday party for one of her team where no one was over twenty-six or in possession of their original lips. They were actually all nice people, but she had been afraid to drink in case she made a fool of herself and couldn't show her face in the office on the Monday. A walk-social designed to bring neighbours together where only she and the man who had organised it turned up and

7

he threw a strop in the car park when he saw the turnout and went home without even saying goodbye. A volunteer event to help plant trees in the park. All the others had seemingly known each other already and had viewed Kitty with suspicion while they asked after each other's children and partners with the ease of old friends.

London was impenetrable.

After a few months she had thought seriously about giving up and moving back to Bedfordshire with her tail between her legs. She felt exhausted, sad, lonely and scared that she'd blown everything she had. She had detonated a bomb under her perfectly adequate life – a life that was fine, it was acceptable, it was tolerable. It was a life that a lot of people would probably aspire to. Maybe tedious was the new black. But she couldn't face Geth. She didn't need to see his 'I told you so' face, or the pitying expressions of their mutual friends, most now fully paid-up members of Team G. Kitty was the one who had walked out on a – so they all, apparently, thought – perfectly happy relationship. Never mind that it was stale and tired and soul-crushing. She had opened the Pandora's box we all have in our head and out had come the intoxicating promise of freedom. It had threatened all their cosy Sunday lunches and matching pyjamas and framed prints of the word 'love' in cursive pink over the bed. It had showed them there was another life out there and that terrified them. She could hardly admit that that other life had ended up being just as unfulfilling. Just as routine and mundane as the one she'd thrown away.

She had to find a way to make it work.

Forest Streets Residents' WhatsApp Group:

Mrs B Martin: Please note food caddies are collected on Saturdays in Ashdown Close. Please do not put them out with the rubbish and recycling on Wednesdays. None of us want to trip over your half-eaten KFC for 3 days each week. You know who you are.

It's not an easy achievement, getting to the age of forty-three and having no friends. No social life. No life at all, really.

But here she is.

It's an exaggeration, of course. Kitty has friends. In the middling-sized town in Bedfordshire, where she grew up. Scattered around the country from uni or other past lives. She just doesn't have any here in London. No one she can hang out with just because they feel like hanging out. No gang, no girls, no bestie.

Except, that is . . .

We all have one. That friend we have nothing in common with. Who is just there because of circumstances, or proximity, or, in Kitty's case, lack of a viable alternative. The life raft that you cling to when you're desperate and you don't know how to climb off when you're not.

Meet Grace.

Grace who considers a gap in a conversation a challenge.

Who likes to fill any silence with the random contents of her brain. Who is incapable of crossing the road without saving up the details for later.

Grace who likes Wordle and loves Adele and knows how everyone in the royal family is related and the names of all their children. Who fills her evenings watching the soaps and reading overblown romances featuring swarthy men with wild hair and floaty shirts open to the navel. Whose life is a holding pen until her dreamed-of future happy ending materialises.

Grace who can sometimes be blindsidingly kind. Who always buys the *Big Issue* and says keep the change and probably cries when she watches videos featuring sad cats who need homes.

Grace who is desperate to have someone in her life to take care of.

But let's face it: Grace who Kitty would trade in if anyone else would have her.

Kitty knows that a big part of her irritation with Grace is that she's not the friend she would ever have chosen. They're a marriage of convenience. They have little in common, few shared interests. They're friends because at a particular point in their lives they had no one else in a big scary city, and somehow they're still stuck in that situation. And the truth is Kitty needs one friend, however imperfect; if nothing else, just to bear witness to the fact that she exists. She's a tiny tree in a huge forest and someone needs to hear her if she falls.

It seems to her she spends half her life avoiding Grace's calls and the other half throwing just enough scraps so that their friendship won't wither and die completely. She's on permanent resuscitation duty. A walking, breathing defibrillator. She forces herself to call her while she chops tomatoes, onions and carrots for soup. She holds her breath, hoping Grace won't pick up.

Of course she answers.

'I'm on a train home from my mum's,' she says. Kitty puts her on speaker. 'Honestly, you would not believe the day I've had . . .'

She listens for long enough to make sure there's nothing wrong. Sometimes she worries Grace will tell her some devastating news and Kitty will say something like 'Oh good' or 'That's great' because she will have tuned out and missed something vital. Not today. Grace embarks on an interminable story about a man who tried to chat her up when she was on the bus with her elderly mother. Grace always has a story about being hit on. In Grace Land there are queues of men falling over themselves to meet her, begging for her number or some other crumb from her table. Kitty doesn't believe a word of it. Not because Grace isn't attractive. She is. She's small and slight with an angular face, cheekbones Kitty would die for and huge grey eyes under an admittedly frightful self-dyed bixie cut and giant, unflattering, black-framed glasses that could start a forest fire if she stood too close to a tree on a sunny day. But, because Grace is so desperate to find love and settle down, Kitty doesn't think she would be dismissing all these would-be lovers out of hand if they existed. She's been single ever since Kitty has known her. They both have. That was how they met. A speed dating event. One of Kitty's increasingly rare forays into 'making an effort'. She had wondered, briefly, if what she needed to do was to find a new partner, if only so they could introduce her to their friends. In the end, neither she nor Grace left with a date, but they spent the evening chatting (or at least, Grace did) and ended up friends by default. Two singletons who needed to cobble together a social life out of nothing.

They're from a similar demographic. Two years apart in age, no kids (Kitty by choice, Grace by her husband's choice: her divorce was in part kick-started by her discovering he'd had a sneaky vasectomy a couple of years previously and all their trying for a baby had been for show). Both from nice nuclear families. Both recent incomers to London after their lives elsewhere fell apart. Good if uninspiring jobs. They were definitely each other's types on paper.

'Well?' Kitty hears her saying. 'Are you still there?'

Kitty pauses, knife in the air. 'Of course.'

'Don't you think that's odd?'

No idea. Pick a side. 'God, yeah.'

'He didn't even acknowledge it. I mean, you would, wouldn't you? Say sorry or something?'

Kitty closes her eyes and leans against the fridge. 'Definitely.'

She's half drifting off when she hears a noise outside. Voices. She walks over and peers out of the front window. The next-door house has been on the market for months, despite several price reductions. It's not exactly an area people are falling over themselves to live in. Most would rather be a bit closer to the action. Or further away, in the countryside. Not this weird semi-suburban no-man's-land. It's a quiet road, only four pairs of semi-detached houses on each side. It's mostly old people who have been here forever with a couple of young families starting out who are ticking off the days until they can afford to move somewhere more exciting. The house in question isn't Kitty's mirror twin. (That belongs to Sam and Linz and their three children, all of whom seem to like to shout at once while watching the TV on full volume and playing football against the shared wall. Kitty can't get cross because she hears Sam and Linz yelling at them to pipe down every thirty seconds or so, but the kids, it seems, have not yet grasped the concept of authority. Neither has Muffin, their yappy, growly, arsehole of a dog. Linz is always trying to invite Kitty over for a 'cheeky vodka' or, occasionally, if Sam is on kid-wrangling duties, a 'cheeky Nando's', but saying she's too busy is a hill Kitty is prepared to die on.) It's the one separated from her by the alley that leads to their small back gardens. Today there's a self-drive removal van out front. Kitty peers round the half-blind. Grace is still in full flow in the background – something about her neighbour who is selling up because she's realised that the fact her front door is directly opposite her balcony door is bad feng shui, and should Grace be worried about her own situation – so she figures she can leave her unattended for a moment. There's a woman about Kitty's age patting down her pockets as if looking for keys. She's wearing a pink pea coat and faded jeans. Clumpy black lace-ups. Her long hair is dyed a stark jet black. She looks way too cool to be moving to Ashdown Close in Kitty's humble opinion. She says something and a man joins her. Similar age. Dark hair. Neat beard. Wearing a Levi's trucker jacket and chunky framed sunglasses propped up on his head. He looks as if he could chop down a tree with his bare hands but make you a dirty chai latte while he was doing it. He smiles at the woman, and she flashes him a wide grin back. Kitty feels a lump in her throat watching their shared moment of connection although she doesn't understand why.

She picks up her phone and cuts across Grace's voice. 'I need to go, sorry. Talk to you soon.'

'Oh. OK. Are we still on for Thursday night?'

Kitty's heart sinks. Thursday-night drinks. A semi-regular horror in her calendar that allows her to kid herself she has a social life. She lives in a vibrant, bustling metropolis of nine million people and the highlight of her diary is Thursday nights eating soggy fish and chips in the pub with Grace. In the early days of their friendship, they used to try to get out more, to enjoy what the big bad city had to offer. But there were only so many times Kitty could pretend to be excited about sitting through *We Will Rock You* or watching Aled Jones crooning churchy classics. And Grace had zero interest in Kitty's love of weird museums (the more random the better – the Museum of Human Disease in Sydney is a long-held ambition) and outsider art exhibitions. So, in the end, they agreed to disagree and just stick to drinks and meals. 'I don't think I can this week. I'll let you know.'

She hangs up before Grace can respond.

She watches out of the window again as the woman with the black hair grabs an orange tote bag from between the front seats. She looks like every cool friend

Kitty imagined she'd make when she decided to move to London. Kitty feels a bit giddy at the prospect of a bit of new life in the street. She doesn't really think the woman moving in next door is about to become her new best buddy, but you never know. And it's time she made some changes.

The couple start to wrestle a retro-looking sideboard from the back of the van. It's a struggle with just the two of them. Kitty grabs her keys.

It's time for her new life to begin.

3

She makes the mistake of looking in the full-length mirror by the front door before she opens it. At her pale pink pyjama bottoms, her fluffy Ted Baker sliders, her lank unwashed hair. She hesitates. Then she hears raised voices and the Watsons from number 7 appear, all smiles, and pitch in. Kitty hears the four of them laughing about something and then, minutes later, the sideboard safely deposited inside, the Watsons continue on down the road waving goodbye.

'Come over for a drink when you're settled,' Judy? Julie? calls out. She and her husband (who Kitty thinks is called something blokey and solid like Pete or Steve), the other younger couple in the Close aside from Sam and Linz, go to the pub at the end of the road every Saturday night at exactly six thirty to play darts. That's the only thing Kitty really knows about them. That and the 50/50 shot at their names. They're hand-holders, their fingers perennially entwined, which should be sweet but somehow comes across to Kitty like an aggressive act of possession by both of them. They make her uneasy for some reason. They strike her as the kind of people who are too friendly in that way that makes you feel if you all had a couple of drinks and then you didn't agree to go on holiday with them, you'd end up with a glass in your face. She has no solid evidence for this, by the way. It would not stand up in court.

Two armchairs, a coffee table and a pale cream 1960s arc floor lamp later and the show's over. Kitty waits for a moment, disappointed, hoping for an encore. She gets dressed without showering and takes herself out for a run. Back home she FaceTimes her parents as she does most days. It's sometimes easier for her mum to recognise a face rather than a voice, although their moments of connection are becoming fewer and farther between, and Kitty sometimes feels she's stressing her out, forcing her to talk to a stranger. Kitty's idea of dementia before her mother started showing the obvious signs was sweet, almost comical confusion, more distressing for the rest of the family than the sufferer. She hadn't reckoned on the panic, the terror, the crippling anguish that would enmesh her mum as she tried to make sense of a new world where she often recognised no one. Today, though, is a good day. There are moments – long moments – when they're mother and daughter again. For Kitty that almost makes it more painful. Her mum is in there somewhere, just out of reach. Her heart breaks with the loss of her all over again. But she puts on a brave face for her dad, as she always does. At one point her mother looks at her father in surprise, a huge open smile lighting up her face. 'Oh,' she says, and she reaches out a hand to gently stroke his cheek. Kitty swallows a huge lump in her throat and makes excuses that she has to get on.

She hoovers the living room and puts two loads of washing on. She spots the new couple from next door heading in the direction of the shops, the woman now dressed in a cute pair of paint-flecked overalls, like a 1940s poster girl, and then sees them later, coming back, takeaway coffees in hand. The man drapes an arm round the woman's shoulder and she leans in. Kitty watches until their front door closes.

Sam and Linz have a shouting match in their garden because one of them has forgotten to add the BBQ coals to the Ocado order and their friends are coming round and they have a whole tray of salmon fillets from Tesco and no way to cook them and it's all your fucking fault because you were supposed to remember (*You have an oven inside*, Kitty thinks. *And a hob*. Maybe she should pop round and remind them). Judy/Julie and Pete/Steve unload a startled-looking faux bronze deer from the boot of their car and carry it round to their back garden. The old man at number 4 leaves his house smart in a tie and suit trousers, carrying a bunch of daffs. Kitty smiles at the thought he has a friend to visit.

Still, by Sunday evening she's actually looking forward to going into work. She loves her weekends but sometimes they can seem just a beat too long.

She's a team leader. Her team being one third of the Customer Service department of a budget airline based in Acton. Basically, her job is to listen to people complain to her about the people complaining to them. She enjoys it, but the company is a disgrace. Booking a bargain-price flight essentially leaves you sitting on the floor drinking water out of the toilet if you're lucky. Anything and everything else that makes it possible for you to actually take that flight requires a second mortgage. The Customer Service department is rarely quiet and understandably so. Their mandate is to deny, deny, deny and, if backed into a corner, give vouchers. All the while being unfailingly polite and sounding – even if not being – helpful.

She checks everyone in her team of five is OK. Does the rotas for next month, which takes approximately thirty seconds because everyone has their preferred shift and it just so happens they all fit together perfectly: Evie and Ross like 8 to 4, same as Kitty, Mark and Jacob want 12 to 8 and Jade always chooses the swing shift that covers the busiest time, 10 till 6. Then, she spends the rest of the morning doing her favourite part of the job – compiling and checking for patterns in the past twenty-four hours' complaints. Anything with more than a couple of hits gets flagged up. She saves the one-offs into a file for future reference and a sub-file of the most entertaining: *Yesterday at 16.12, customer on the 171 to Malaga could not eat the hummus and vegetable sandwich (cucumber and roasted tomato only. They had removed the spinach pre-boarding because it looked 'icky') they had brought on board as the gentleman behind had taken his shoes off and put his foot on their armrest, and they could see his hairy toes.*

Good work, Kitty sends to Ross whose report it is. *I particularly like the detail about the sandwich.*

He sends back a smiley face. *Yes, I was proud of that too.*

Kitty chuckles. Obviously it's highly unprofessional to make fun of the clientele, but sometimes the only strategy to get through the day is to find a way to entertain yourself.

She spends way too much time gazing off into space and speculating what her new neighbours' names might be and whether calling round to say hello is worse than not calling round to say hello. Maybe it was better to hope it happened organically. Maybe she can somehow time her trips to the shops with theirs and accidentally bump into them on the street.

It happens sooner than she'd hoped.

She's trudging back from the bus stop after work, running through what she has in her fridge, silently debating the virtues of ramen noodles versus baked potatoes, when a voice startles her.

'Hi.'

She jumps. Look round. The couple from number 8 are on their doorstep, a small, elegant whippet bouncing round them excitedly, jaws round its lead.

'Oh. Hi. You've moved in.'

She's stunned at her own banality. *Way to go, Kitty.*

'Just.' The woman smiles and pushes a strand of hair away from her face. She has porcelain pale skin and bright blue eyes. A dusting of freckles. 'We're still in chaos. You're next door, aren't you?'

Kitty nods. 'Kitty.' She points at herself as if the other woman might otherwise think she's calling a passing cat.

'Sian. And Rich.'

Kitty repeats the names as if she's trying them out for size

Rich steps forward and offers out a hand for Kitty to shake. The dog does that thing where it decides it's essential to sniff your genitals right there and then with no formal introduction. Kitty reaches down to pat it and try to steer it away at the same time.

'Dante,' Sian says sternly. 'Sorry, he's got no manners.'

'He's lovely,' Kitty says, because crotch sniffing aside, he really is. 'Have you settled in?'

'God, no,' Sian says with a laugh. 'Mayhem. Shit, we need to get going if we're going to get back in time for Ocado. Nice to meet you, Katie.'

The thing about people having a dog is that you know they're going to have to walk it, at least occasionally, and Kitty soon gets used to seeing Sian and Rich passing her house with Dante after work. Sometimes a van with THE DOGS BOLLOX! emblazoned on the side pulls up and a young woman lets herself in to number 8, piles Dante into the back with a barking kerfuffle of other dogs and drives off towards the park, and Kitty realises she's a little disappointed. She hasn't felt as if she could ambush them (she can't get past the panic in her head about how she's going to correct Sian when she calls her by the wrong name again. She should have said something straight away, laughed it off), so she still knows no more about her neighbours but, in her head, Sian is some kind of designer. Jewellery, maybe, or bags. And Rich works for a start-up. Something techy but ethical. How they ended up here in Ashdown Close is beyond even Kitty's imagination. They're around her age, she thinks. No sign of any kids until one Friday evening a skinny boy of about eighteen or nineteen arrives with a bulging holdall. From the ease between them and the joy in Dante's step when they walk past later, Kitty assumes he's their son, home from uni for the weekend, dirty washing in tow. As if to prove her right, there are tiny waisted jeans and indie band T-shirts flapping on the washing line in the morning.

Kitty has never wanted children. Could never see the appeal in giving her life over so completely. She's always found interacting with kids – small ones anyway – baffling. She tries way too hard to get them to like her and it's as if they can sense her desperation like sharks with blood particles in the water. Still, she's sometimes wondered if she's missed out. If she could have somehow got through the early years, it might be pretty great to have a teenager around now, although, of course, there's no guarantee they would be speaking to her. Just her luck to devote all her time to parenting for years on end only for them to announce they were divorcing her at fifteen.

Sian, Rich and – what should she call him? Statistically he was probably called Jack or Oliver. Either of those would probably be a safe bet. But Kitty likes to think Sian and Rich would have swum against the tide, so maybe a simple Joe or a statement like Iggy. Anyway, Sian, Rich and whatever-his-name-is are clearly not on the brink of divorce. It's a beautiful weekend and she sees them sitting around together in the back garden chatting and laughing. Iggy Joe throws a ball for a near hysterical Dante. At about half past two he and Rich wave their goodbyes to Sian as they head off somewhere.

'Oat milk!' Sian shouts as they leave by the garden gate. Grocery shopping then.

Kitty takes her tea outside and sits with her face to the sun. She ignores two calls from Grace. She hasn't spoken to her all week. She doesn't know if this means she's ghosting her because she's had the sniff of a better offer on the horizon. She tells herself she's just backing off. Cooling things down between them. Hoping that Grace will find herself another friend to latch on to. Hoping, obviously, that she might too. But, like with all good dumpings, she doesn't want to jump until she's lined up the alternative. So, when Grace calls again, she answers reluctantly. She pulls her sunglasses down over her eyes and leans back, in for the long haul.

'God! There you are! I've been trying you for the last week. Did you not get my messages?'

'Sorry, I've been busy . . .'

'I was thinking you'd had a terrible accident. I almost started calling the hospitals.'

'No. Just . . .'

'I've been dying to tell you what happened at work . . .' And she's off with a story about one of her colleagues and their quest to get their office painted something other than regulation pale green. Sometimes Kitty finds it almost comforting, like those white-noise apps you can use to help you sleep.

'I saw Harry Styles in the Co-op in Friern Barnet Road yesterday,' she says at one point to amuse herself, when she spots a gap in Grace's flow. 'Buying crumpets.' Grace doesn't even break her stride. Kitty hears what sounds like a snort from next door's garden. She holds the phone away from her ear and realises Sian must be able to hear every word. Kitty feels a little glow of pride that she's made her laugh. She thinks about making another smart-arse comment, but decides it'll look too try-hard.

Next door have two sets of visitors while Kitty lies there. First Mrs Martin – Betty – from number 11 who, from the snatches of conversation Kitty can hear through the open kitchen door, has come to fill Sian in on the many street rules, most of them made up by her. (*If you have visitors, please ask them to park in front of your own house if they can't fit on your drive. Please don't put your bins out until the morning of collection because of foxes. Please try not to order parcels unless you'll be home to receive them as it attracts thieves if they're left outside regularly.*) Ashdown Close is a friendly enough place – at least on the surface – but Betty is the obligatory street curmudgeon. She's also the scourge of the local residents' WhatsApp group – comprising Ashdown and the two parallel roads either side – chi-chi Sherwood Avenue with its big, detached houses above and Dean Road, which is made up of identical semis, the same as Ashdown, below, along with the sections of the two scruffy main thoroughfares either end that connect them. Fifty-odd households in all out of a possible hundred and fifty or so belong. It's mostly conversations about bins and parking. Thrilling stuff. And the occasional video of a completely harmless-looking person going about their business with a message like *Be wary! Saw this man in a hoody walking up and down Dean!* or *Anyone know what this woman is up to?* along with an innocuous Ring video of a delivery driver leaving a package. WhatsApp paranoia. Betty only stays a few minutes, but she uses the time like an MI5 pro, so by the time she leaves Kitty knows that Sian and Rich have moved from a flat in Balham, that he works doing something with security systems (Betty doesn't ask what Sian does, being apparently from the heartland of the 1950s), that Rhys (Rhys! Not anywhere on Kitty's list, but she likes it) is in his second year at Brighton Uni and that he and his father are currently at Planet Organic in Muswell Hill.

She hears Sian sigh the second time the Ring doorbell chimes on her phone. Hears her get up and walk towards the back of the garden, rather than the front door. 'Hi?' Kitty makes out her saying. She gets up and ambles aimlessly towards Sian's voice, looking at the ground as if she's trying to spot weeds. (Her garden is actually all weeds. Without the weeds it would just be bare earth, so she doesn't dare pull any of them up.)

'It's Julie and Pete from number seven.' (Julie and Pete! Kitty tries to commit the names to memory.) Julie's hopeful voice squeaks from both Sian's phone and the front step. The volume coming from the phone plummets halfway through the words as, Kitty assumes, Sian stabs at the controls. 'We just brought a little bottle of something round to say welcome.'

'How lovely,' Sian says in a stage whisper. 'We're actually out all afternoon, but I'm sure if you leave it on the step, it'll be fine. Thanks so much.'

'Fancy sharing it this evening?' Pete booms, all matey-matey.

'Oh. Damn. We can't. Our son's home and we have plans. Another time, definitely.'

'No biggie,' he says. 'We're always around.'

It goes quiet for a few moments. Kitty hovers, not wanting to give herself away. She feels a rather pathetic sense of triumph at Sian's rejection of Julie and Pete. *Grow up*, she tells herself.

'You definitely did not just hear that, Katie,' a voice floats over the fence.

Kitty starts. 'My lips are sealed,' she says, laughing.

Sian's head pops up above the trellis. Kitty feels as if she's been caught lurking. 'They're full-on round here, aren't they?'

Kitty smiles at her. 'It'll die down. You'll just have to go and play darts with them a few times, maybe a couple of drinking contests . . .'

Sian raises her eyebrows. 'Keys in a bowl on the table, I hope.'

Kitty is still thinking of a hilariously witty riposte when Sian's head swings round towards the house. 'Oh good, the boys are back. See you.' And she's gone.

Kitty stands there replaying the moment, hoping Rich and Rhys will come out into the garden and they can continue the chat. She definitely likes Sian. And it's a ballsy move to risk your neighbours clocking the fact you're hiding from them. It's definitely behaviour Kitty aspires to.

4

'Why don't you pop round for a drink later? I'm in all evening.'

She has no idea how the words found their way out of her mouth. She was just on her way back from work via the local shops – fabulous if you need a burner phone or a key cut or a large, unidentifiable, aggressively fibrous root vegetable, but pretty much useless for anything else – carrying a bag containing some instant noodles, a head of broccoli and a bottle of pinot grigio, when she bumped into her new neighbours, on their way out with the dog. Somehow in the exchange of pleasantries her offer slipped out. She tells herself they'll say no. Everyone's preferred default is no, right? She sees Rich shoot Sian a look with a raised eyebrow. Sian smiles.

'That'd be great. What time?'

'Um.' Kitty looks at her phone; it's just after five now. 'Half six?'

'Lovely,' Sian says. 'We're just taking Dant for a quick walk. See you later.'

And, just like that, they stroll off down the road, leaving Kitty standing there wondering what she was thinking of.

Shit. Fuck. Bollocks.

Her house is tidy. Living on your own either makes for extreme mess or extreme clean and thankfully she's in the latter camp, but it's far from visitor ready. She grabs up the board her jigsaw is on and takes it upstairs to her bedroom. No one needs to see her half-completed Moomins. God knows what signal that would send out. She heads back down and shoves a half-eaten bag of mini Mars bars into a drawer. Surface crap gone, she admires the Abigail Ahern lamp, the single Aria chair she bought from Soho Home, the Andrew Martin cushions. The beautiful things she saves up for that no one ever sees. That don't even really feel like her. She checks the fridge for booze. She has the wine she bought and some vodka. A full bottle of tonic. She runs back upstairs and changes into her most faded, softest jeans and a short-sleeve icy blue jumper. She puts shoes on then takes them off again and sticks her feet into her silver FitFlops, admiring the raspberry pink polish. She slaps a bit of Vaseline on her lips and drags her fingers through her hair. By five to six she's already sitting at the kitchen table, fingers drumming, waiting. Should she eat something? Or can she wait till they go? Maybe she should put some nuts in a bowl, although that would look like she was trying way too hard. She tells herself to calm down, she's being ridiculous. It's just that it's so long since she had anyone other than family round, she's forgotten how to do it. At four minutes past half past the doorbell rings.

Sian hands her a bottle of Prosecco as soon as she opens the door. Rich follows up with red wine.

'We weren't sure what you liked,' he says.

'God. Lovely. Either. Both, thanks. Come on in.'

'I've been wanting a chance to apologise anyway,' Sian says. 'For you having to hear my blatant lie-telling the other day. To Julie and Pete from number seven. I'm not usually so rude.'

'Not rude at all,' Kitty leads them into the kitchen. 'Terrifying, how convincing you were . . .'

Sian laughs.

'She's good, isn't she?' Rich says, throwing an arm over his wife's shoulder. 'I mean, I should be worried, really.'

'I felt awful . . .'

'Only because Katie had caught you out,' Rich says. 'Be honest.'

'OK. Maybe. Shit, does that make me a terrible person?'

'Awful,' he says indulgently. Kitty envies the way they are with each other. There's a playfulness that's somehow way more intimate than any amount of PDA. She and Geth were never playful, not after a while anyway. It was all business: the mortgage, the weekly shop, whose turn it was to go on top. Everything equitable. Nothing spontaneous.

'I just couldn't face it. I mean, I'm sure they're nice enough . . .'

'They're like vampires,' Kitty says with a smile. 'Just don't invite them in or you'll never get rid of them.'

'Are you sure they didn't hear? I'd hate for them to feel slighted.'

'I don't think so. Pete's like a bull in a china shop and he would have probably said *I can hear you round the back* and blundered on through if they had. They're just excited about someone new moving in who's not eighty-five. I don't think they'll be turning up every five minutes.' Even as she says it, Kitty is not entirely sure this is true.

'Thank god,' Sian says. 'It's just that weekends feel so precious, you know.'

'Don't feel you have to justify yourself to me,' Kitty smiles. 'You're talking to the person who hides behind the sofa with all the lights out every Halloween. I once told the woman who used to live at number six I was going away for the weekend to avoid having to go to her birthday do and then I couldn't go out for two days in case she saw me. I couldn't even order Deliveroo and so I ended up eating frozen fish fingers every meal.'

Sian and Rich laugh as if she's joking, even though she's actually not.

'That reminds me,' Rich says. He shoots Sian a look. 'From what you've just said, this is probably your worst nightmare, so feel free to say no and we absolutely won't be offended –'

'Totally not . . .' Sian interjects.

"But we thought we'd have a little housewarming drink on Saturday week. Just so we can say hello to all the neighbours in one go . . .'

'And it might stop all the random visits. But obviously don't feel you have to.'

Definitely, Kitty thinks. *I will bite your hand off for a bit of non-Grace-related entertainment.* 'No, I'd love to. Thank you. It's Kitty, by the way.'

They both look at her blankly.

'Me. I'm Kitty. Not Katie.' She feels herself turning red.

Sian lets out a loud snort. 'Fuck! Have I been calling you the wrong name? Oh my god, I am so frickin' sorry. How rude is that?'

'It's fine . . . people are always doing it . . .'

'Too late. You're Katie to us now,' Rich says with a surprisingly booming laugh. 'Once Sian gets something in her head it's impossible to convince her otherwise.'

Sian swipes at him. 'You were doing it too.'

'You know what I think? I think she told us her name was Katie. I mean, two of us can't be wrong . . .'

'Ha!' Kitty says. 'You've discovered my secret.'

The ice is broken. Kitty can feel her nervousness gone. 'Fizz or red?' she says.

Sian asks Kitty about work, and she manages to make them both laugh with tales from the most entertaining complaints file. She wheels out an all-time favourite: *The woman next to me had an emotional support dog and, when I looked away to speak to my husband who was across the aisle, it ate my chicken korma. When I asked for another meal I was told I would have to pay an extra £7. I asked the woman whose dog it was to pay, and she told me she'd brought a packet of ham for the dog, and I could have that if I wanted. I declined. The dog then produced tremendous wind for the rest of the flight.* Sian and Rich beg her for more and she dredges up a couple of other gems: *It was really stuffy in there, and I wanted some fresh air, but I didn't know how to get the air thing working, and the magazine in the pocket in front of my seat had already been read by someone else who had drawn a penis and two testicles on a photo of Elon Musk.* 'I particularly liked the fact they specified the number of testicles,' she adds, and both Sian and Rich guffaw.

They talk about everything. An actual three-way conversation where everyone gets to contribute. Sian, it turns out, is a Spanish teacher, just started at the local secondary school, covering maternity leave, but hoping it can turn into a permanent position.

'Boring as fuck,' she says. 'But I basically can't do anything else that pays, and I've just sort of stuck with it. It's destroying my will to live one verb conjugation at a time.'

'How have you ended up here?'

Sian lets out what sounds like a sigh. 'Rich's firm moved to Borehamwood. Balham was just too far. And, I don't know, we thought it would be good to still be in London.' Rich tells Kitty his work sucks his soul dry. 'He's a brilliant sculptor,' Sian says, with a tinge of regret. 'But, you know, who makes a living at that?'

'Wow,' Kitty says. 'I'd love to see your stuff sometime.'

Sian shoots Rich a look. 'He doesn't do it any more.'

Rich shrugs. 'It was a hobby, that's all. And we don't have the space really. Besides, I wasn't that good.'

'He was great,' Sian says.

'How about you?' Rich says, obviously keen to change the subject. 'You don't feel like your typical Ashdown Close resident.'

Kitty tells them about Geth and her impulsive upending of her life. She doesn't usually open up so soon, or so fully, but there's something about Sian that makes Kitty want to confide in her. Rich too, but Sian feels more and more like the friend she's been looking for.

'It's a nice place though,' she says. She doesn't want them to regret their decision and sell up. 'But you need to like small children and very old people, I'm just saying.'

'Ha!' Sian splutters into her drink, sending it up her nose. 'At least you're here.'

Kitty feels a glow so warm she imagines you could see it through her chest.

5

Forest Streets Residents' WhatsApp Group:

**Vernie at Number 3: I baked too many scones again! If anyone
would like some let me know. Raspberry and white chocolate or
peanut butter. The foxes love my peanut butter scones!**

Kitty follows Sian around the exhibition, clueless, buzzing
with the idea that they're having a play date. Sian texted
her this morning and asked if Kitty would go with her
because Rich couldn't make it after all. Kitty had delved
into her overfull bank of excuses. But then she remembered her new resolve. New Kitty would make the effort
with someone she felt an affinity with. New Kitty would
force herself out of her comfort zone. What was the
worst that could happen. She took a halfway step. *Might
be able to. What time are you going?* As if she had plans of her
own to consider.

*The tickets are for 11 so need to leave 10.15 ish. We're going to see
Rich's mum and dad but not till later this afternoon so we could have
a quick lunch after. Or not. Up to you.*

If she was ever going to try to cultivate a friendship
with Sian, now was the time to say yes. She'd texted back
before she could talk herself out of it. *Perfect. I'll come
over 10.15.*

She doesn't even quite know where she is. Dalston, or

Clissold Park maybe. She doesn't even care. She's out out. Just going to an art installation with a friend. No big deal. It's in some kind of warehouse space, and Kitty is a bit confused about the timed tickets because it's hardly the Royal Academy and there's not exactly a stampede outside. Sian told her on the way over that the artist was someone she used to work with. The chat in Sian's battered old car was easy. Sometimes you just click with someone and there are no awkward silences. Or one-sided information overloads. It felt natural, and Kitty relaxed enough to consider that she might actually be having a good time. Inside they're pretty much the only punters, but Kitty realises that the reason for the timed entry is that there's some kind of performance art element that involves a woman (Celine, the artist herself, Sian tells her) dressed like a drowned Victorian, delivering a tortuous monologue at the top of each hour. She wills the ground to swallow her up. Is she allowed to laugh? Maybe the whole thing is a double bluff, and she's supposed to. She doesn't want to offend Sian, or Celine for that matter. She keeps her eyes firmly on the paintings – huge mystical landscapes that actually do have a certain charm – while Celine flits around opining like a possessed Kate Bush. Kitty daren't look at Sian because she can only assume Sian knew exactly what they were in for and still signed up willingly. A couple of people arrive late and Kitty sees Celine break character and give them a furious eye roll. She rubs her hand over her mouth as if she's deep in thought to hide a laugh. There's not even a coffee shop they can disappear into and, even if there was, she assumes they're expected to stay for the whole performance. Finally, Celine stops abruptly, just as Kitty and Sian shuffle towards the last few paintings. Everyone claps earnestly.

'Please enjoy,' she shouts.

'What do you think?' Sian asks in a low voice, and Kitty is saved from having to answer by the appearance of Celine right behind them. She notices Celine has a card machine in her hand, which slightly ruins the illusion.

'Brilliant, Cel,' Sian says, embracing her. 'You have such a unique style.'

Celine looks at Kitty for some praise. 'Wonderful,' Kitty says.

'This is Kitty, my neighbour.'

'Thanks for coming,' Celine says with a strong West Country burr.

A young girl hovers nearby with some plastic flutes of wine. Kitty wouldn't usually take to drink before lunchtime on a Saturday, but needs must. It's warm and a bit sweet and utterly revolting, but she downs it anyway.

'There's such a strong sense of mythic fantasy,' Sian says, and Celine preens. 'Arthur Rackham meets Kit Williams. Don't you think, Kitty?' Kitty freezes, no idea what the correct response might be. She assumes yes, as Celine definitely looks pleased by the comment. And then she sees the corner of Sian's mouth lift in a smirk. At first she thinks Sian is laughing at her and her obvious discomfort. Her heart drops. Has Sian just brought her here to show her up? And then Sian gives her a subtle wink, and she realises with relief that she's in on the joke.

'Absolutely,' she says. 'Very strong sense of that.'

'Well, they're all still for sale,' Celine says, seemingly as comfortable in salesman as artist mode.

'Sian and Rich have been looking for a piece for their new living room, haven't you?' Kitty raises her eyebrows at Sian and sees her almost crack and turn it into a cough.

'I should take a brochure,' Sian says when she recovers. 'But I think these may be a bit big for the space, sadly.'

Celine wafts off to her next victims on a cloud of praise, a job well done. 'Oh my god, let's get out of here,' Sian says as soon as she's out of earshot. She grabs Kitty's arm, and they hustle for the door. 'You owe me lunch for that.'

'Actually, I think you'll find you owe me lunch for bringing me here in the first place.'

'Point taken. Where shall we go?'

'I don't care. Wherever you can park.' She browses the brochure as Sian drives. 'That was fifteen hundred quid, that last one,' she says, incredulous. 'Do people buy them?'

'God knows.' Sian fiddles with the glove compartment and finds some chewing gum. Kitty takes a piece when she offers it. 'Unlikely, I think. Not at that price.'

'Where did you work with her?'

'Wickes,' Sian says. 'We were twenty-two. She used to steal all the paint samples.'

'I hope she didn't think we were taking the piss.' Kitty suddenly feels guilty.

'God, no. She's wonderfully deluded about how good she is. It's like armour. She'll just be thrilled we went.'

They find a parking space outside a fake-flower-adorned café and order cheese stuffed baked potatoes and salad.

'So, Kitty Harbinson, tell me all about yourself,' Sian says once the food has been delivered. Kitty is momentarily confused that Sian knows her surname. She has no idea what hers is yet. 'They delivered a letter for you to ours,' Sian says as if she realises. 'I stuck it through your door yesterday.'

'What's your surname? You and Rich?'

'Selway. And Rich's a Price. We're married but I've never got that name-change thing. Are you single? I mean, I know you live on your own . . .'

Kitty nods. 'Never been married. Geth and I were engaged. That's the boyfriend I told you about. I don't think I could ever live with someone again.'

'If you don't want to, why should you?' Sian grinds pepper on her potato until the whole thing is covered with black flecks. 'Good for you.'

'I should probably be less inflexible . . .'

'Bollocks. If you can't find a relationship where you can be yourself, then it's better not to be in a relationship at all, don't you think?'

'I do, actually. But it's not always easy.'

'You'll meet a man one of these days who adores you but would rather live in an eight-by-eight prison cell with no running water and giant cockroaches than live with you, and then you'll both be happy ever after, I guarantee it.'

'Well, he sounds like a catch,' Kitty says, laughing. 'I wonder why he's single.'

'You know what I mean.'

'I do, but seriously, I'm not bothered if it never happens.' She almost stumbles as she says this. For the first time she wonders if it's true or just something she tells herself. Watching Sian and Rich together has reminded her that relationships can actually be fun. 'How long have you and Rich been together?'

'Twenty-one years. Can you even imagine? Married for nineteen.'

'What's he up to today, by the way?

Sian spears a chunk of tomato with her fork. 'Nothing much, I don't think. He's been to enough of Celine's shows over the years to know what he's missing. I think his exact words were "Tell her I've died if that's the only way to get me out of going."'

'Ha! So, you roped me in.'

'Rookie mistake,' Sian says. 'You said yes.'

'Where did you meet? You and Rich.'

'One of my friends married one of his friends and they sat us on the same table at the reception. They divorced after a year, and we ended up together. Like the plot of a nineties romcom. Except now two of our best mates don't speak to each other. I think they left that part out of the movie.'

'Did they both come to your wedding?'

Sian laughs. 'Yes, but we had to agree to put them at opposite ends of the room. Even after all that time. They'd both split up from other people too by then, so you think they'd have had bigger grudges to bear.'

'I couldn't care less if I saw Geth or not. Sit him next to me or don't, I don't think I could summon up the energy to get worked up about it. Is that bad?'

'How long ago did you separate?'

Kitty pushes her plate away. Wipes her hands on a paper napkin. 'Four years. But I don't think I'd have been that fussed after a couple of months. That was us all over. No passion.'

Sian raises an eyebrow. Thick. Dark. Enviable. 'Have you not had a relationship since?'

'Nothing serious. I don't think I could do serious any more.'

'I like the whole living-together thing,' Sian says, leaning back in her chair. 'I don't know, I like all the mundane stuff. Arguing about whose turn it is to fill the dishwasher and negotiating who gets to have the first shower.' She suddenly laughs. 'Your face!'

'Go home at the end of the night and give me my own space,' Kitty says with mock horror. 'I get to have the first and only shower every morning, and don't even think about touching my dishwasher.'

'I think I'm a bit of a traditionalist underneath it all,' Sian says. 'Although that's not necessarily something I would admit to in public.'

'Well, Rich seems like one of the good guys. I mean, if you absolutely have to co-habit with someone.'

Sian smiles. 'He is.'

Kitty is home by half one, the blissful long afternoon stretching out in front of her. Sian and Rich are on their way to visit his family in Kent. ('They're gorgeous. Dream in-laws. Unlike my own mum. I don't really bother any more.') On the way home Grace calls and Kitty turns her phone to silent and lets it ring out.

Sorry, out and about, she texts a few minutes later. *Call you soon.*

6

Forest Streets Residents' WhatsApp Group:

Mrs B Martin: If anyone finds a green rubber gardening shoe, size 5, please return it to me. I believe the local foxes (who seem to think Ashdown Close is an all-you-can-eat buffet, due to certain people feeding them) may have stolen it.

She wakes up on Wednesday morning with a feeling of work dread. Some days she just can't face it. It's nothing specific. It's the long commute, the hours of more of the same, the overwhelming desire to change into more comfy clothes and slouch. She emails the team telling them she's going to be working from home insofar as her Wi-Fi can cope. They all do it occasionally, and for the most part it seems to work OK and not bother anyone. She makes a tea and takes herself back to bed for a precious extra hour. She wonders how many people actually spend the mornings they work from home working in bed. She's done it herself. But today she forces herself up and into the shower at half seven. She grabs a coffee and a slice of toast and peanut butter, and she's sitting at the little desk she's set up in the spare bedroom, logged into the system, by eight.

After an hour or so she realises, as she always does, that what she didn't want was to work from home, what she wanted was a day off. Working from home is the worst of all worlds because all the triggers you're surrounded by are telling you to relax, do some chores, read a book, but in reality you have to sit on an uncomfortable chair in your back bedroom refreshing your Wi-Fi all day. She punctuates the morning with trips up and down the stairs for snacks and drinks, and peers out of the window at Sian and Rich's garden, knowing they won't be around to witness her admiring their bright yellow vintage Weber barbecue or the two orange deck chairs that flank it. If she cranes her neck, she can see a slice of their living room where a white egg chair is positioned to soak up the sunshine. The dog drapes across it elegantly. Kitty wastes the best part of an hour googling vintage furniture shops and local dog rescue centres. At lunchtime she forces herself out to walk for ten minutes and then she falls asleep on the sofa and only wakes up when Evie rings to run through a formatting issue in the database. She sees through Kitty straight away, picking up on the grogginess in her voice.

'Were you asleep?' she says, with a smile in her voice.

'No! I mean, OK, yes, possibly. A little.'

'Ha! I knew it. Good for you.' Evie starts talking Kitty through the problem and Kitty heads upstairs to her desktop to try to access the page, but she's down to two bars. They chat about nothing much while they wait. Eventually, Kitty tells her she'll call her back when her reception perks up a bit. She stands up and stretches, still laughing at something Evie told her about a woman she met on Zoe last night. ('She told me she did PR for Dua Lipa, but then she let slip she had to go to Bolton for work today, so I said, "Isn't she playing Milan tomorrow night? Why would she be in Bolton?" and this woman tried to bluff something about setting up some local press event. She picked on the wrong person to tell that lie to. I could probably recite the whole of Dua's schedule verbatim if pressed.'

'Oh, so she's just Dua now? You're on first-name terms?' Kitty had said.

'We definitely would be,' Evie had said without hesitation. 'If she knew I existed.')

A sudden movement outside catches Kitty's eye. There's a person in Sian's back garden, moving away from the house. A woman. She looks around and then makes a dash for the side gate and lets herself out into the shared alley.

Kitty freezes. Should she go round and see what's going on? She keeps watching. Once through the gate, though, the woman does something odd. The only way out is onto the road, but she stops dead. Instead of running, she starts to edge along the side of the wall cautiously. Kitty runs to her bedroom at the front to watch her emerge. She needs to at least see which way the woman goes. She's surprised to see Sian's car is in the drive and Sian herself unloading something from the boot. For a moment she thinks, *Oh great, Sian's home, she can check everything's OK,* and then she wonders if the strange woman is planning some kind of practical joke and she's going to leap out at any second shouting 'Boo!' Nothing happens. Kitty runs to look out the back again. Nothing. Then she dashes back to the road side so she doesn't miss anything. Sian has finally manoeuvred a card table out of the rear of her car and is slamming shut the boot.

Kitty watches as she carries the table to the front door. Unless she's missed something, the stranger is still somewhere in the no-man's-land of the twenty-eight-foot-long side alley, home to a row of wheelie bins and not much else. Should she go down in case Sian is in danger? She decides against it because a) she's a card-carrying coward and b) what could she even do? She's better off here waiting with her finger hovering over her phone's nine key. She opens the top window a little so she can hear if there's any shouting. She hears their front door slam as Sian lets herself in, and almost immediately the woman shoots out into the street and, with a quick glance back, walks off casually past Kitty's house as if she doesn't have a care in the world. Kitty waits to see if Sian comes flying out of the front door, looking for whoever has been inside, but all is quiet. Hopefully, Sian's return disturbed her before she did any real damage. She certainly didn't seem to be carrying anything.

Kitty turns back to the direction she went in just as the woman beeps a car unlocked outside number 15. She should take a photo, Kitty thinks, and she holds her phone up, capturing a blurred image of the silver Fiat 500, just too late to get anything of the person getting into it except the back of her blonde hair and a flash of a faded blue blouse. It's a nice car for a burglar. She's obviously good at her job. Kitty decides she'll pop round later and show Sian the picture, just in case it's of any help, although she could kick herself for not thinking of taking one when she could have got a clearer shot. The woman was wearing pedal pushers, Kitty remembers. Pale yellow. Hardly standard attire for housebreaking. Late thirties or forties, she would guess. That's as much intel as she managed to gather.

She leans over to close the window just as she hears their front door open again. Maybe Sian has finally discovered something missing or a broken window and is coming out to investigate. Kitty waits. She hears a laugh. A man. Sian steps out, followed by a flustered-looking Rich. Kitty takes a step back. So, he was already at home. Sian and Rich walk over to the car and both grab a few items from the back seat: Kitty can see a chrome table lamp, a box containing what looks like a classic 1970s mustard-yellow and brown tea set, an ice bucket. 'I thought I might as well pick them up. I'm going to finish early every Wednesday, I think . . .' Sian is saying. These do not look like two people traumatised by a recent home invasion. Kitty sits down on the arm of the chair behind her. What is going on?

She completely forgets to call Evie back while she runs through possible scenarios in her head. It's a friend of Sian's and she and Rich are planning a birthday surprise. Obviously, Kitty has no idea when Sian's birthday is, but it's plausible. She's his estranged sister come to borrow money without Sian knowing. She's a client of his who's planning a state-of-the-art safe room and needs anonymity (Kitty is fully aware that she's clutching at straws). She steadfastly avoids considering the obvious until it takes up so much space in her head that she can no longer ignore it. That Rich might be having an affair. That his and Sian's happy, easy, enviable relationship might be a lie.

7

See, Kitty thinks, *this is what happens when you decide to make new friends.* Obviously, she can't go to the party. Not because she's judging – she barely knows them and Rich is an adult, the choices he makes are entirely up to him and none of her business, she tells herself – but she can't face Sian. Whatever Rich was up to, he didn't want her to know about it. His car wasn't even on the drive, Kitty realises, as if he was trying to hide the fact he was home at all. Birthday surprise aside, any other option she can come up with makes her feel uneasy. She can't hang out with them knowing one of them is keeping a big secret from the other. And that she's a party to it.

She should have just stayed in her lane. She's fine on her own. She's happy. Now she's going to have to start avoiding bumping into Sian and Rich in the street or sitting in her garden when they're sitting in theirs. She might have to move house. It's possible, she thinks, that she has a tendency to catastrophise.

It's right at that moment that she gets a text from Grace asking if she fancies an after-work drink. Actually, what it says is: *Drinkies? Please say I can tempt you.*

Kitty responds without hesitation. *Sorry, I'm at home. I didn't go in today.*

She's barely hit send when there's another ping. *Spoilsport. I can come up to you. I can finish early today. 6 in the Market Arms?*

It's hard to argue with someone offering to traipse across London to save you the trouble. Plus taking no for an answer is not one of Grace's strong points. And, truthfully, Kitty could do with a distraction. In a moment of weakness, she finds herself sending back *OK*.

She walks the long way round to the pub to avoid going past number 8. Ashdown Close is a ladder rung between two major roads and she turns left out of the house instead of right. It adds a good six minutes to her journey, but the alternative is less appealing. She passes the smiley elderly couple from number 3 – Vernie and Malcolm – shuffling up the street, her hand looped over his arm, and they give her a cheery hello. She arrives at the pub before Grace and nabs a table by the windows at the back, bypassing the bar. Now she's torn between risking giving up her prize by going to get a drink, losing whatever possessions she leaves marking her territory to an opportunist thief (who wouldn't want her Matalan coat as featured in their Autumn/Winter 2018 collection? It's practically a vintage heirloom now), or waiting, drinkless, until Grace arrives. She chooses the latter. Luckily, she doesn't have to wait for long. Grace is talking before she's even in hearing range of a bat. Kitty can see her mouth moving as she walks towards her. Her heart sinks.

'Oh. You haven't got a drink,' Grace says as she gets close enough that Kitty and half the pub can hear. 'I'll go. Oh, I got you these.' She hands Kitty a brown paper bag and Kitty peers inside and sees fresh dates. That's the thing about Grace, she's unfailingly kind. Kitty once told her she had a thing for fat, sticky dates and ever since then, if Grace sees any particularly appealing-looking specimens, she buys Kitty some. 'Oh, fab. Thank you. Don't let me eat them all at once.' Grace turns on her heel and heads for the bar. Kitty knows Grace will get a bottle of white and two glasses, and that's fine. Even though Kitty quite fancied a gin and tonic.

'So,' Grace says when she returns, plonking the bottle down. 'Where have you been? You've been very elusive these last few weeks.'

Kitty opens her mouth to answer, not sure what she's going to say, but Grace doesn't even leave space for a breath. Kitty doesn't know why she never learns her lesson.

'I had a fight with some woman on the bus because she wouldn't pick up her bags and let me sit down . . .'

'Does this end with her asking you out?' Kitty says before she can stop herself. Grace doesn't miss a beat, just pauses briefly to roll her eyes. Kitty takes a long sip of wine, actually enjoying being out. People-watching. Her attention is caught by the door opening and two people walking in. Sian and Rich. She feels herself blush as if the three of them have a secret, and then she remembers that only two of them do. Sian is, she assumes, clueless. She looks down at her drink before they see her. She can't face them. She'll accidentally blurt out something she shouldn't.

'Kitty!'

Great.

Grace's head whips round like it's coming loose. 'Who's that?'

Kitty waves a weak hand at Sian and Rich. 'My new neighbours.'

Grace beams at them and beckons them over. 'Join us. I'm Grace, Kitty's friend.'

'Oh,' Rich says as they approach the table. 'Well, we don't want to muscle in on your evening . . .' He looks at Kitty. She forces herself to smile at him. 'No. Do. Absolutely.'

'If you're sure?' He introduces both himself and Sian to Grace, who seems thrilled to have a new captive audience. 'I'll get some drinks.' He sees their bottle. 'Are you OK?'

'Actually, I'd love a G and T,' Kitty says. This is going to take something stronger than wine.

'It's nice in here,' Sian says as she shrugs off her army surplus jacket to reveal wiry arms in a soft grey T-shirt. 'It's the first time we've been in. We just moved in about a month ago,' she adds as an aside to Grace.

'Oh. Amazing.' Grace starts an interminable anecdote about the time she moved house and the removal men went AWOL with half her stuff. It starts off as a pretty funny story, in fact, something about her discovering they'd gone to entirely the wrong house and unloaded all her worldly goods onto a stranger's lawn, but it just goes on and on, and the level of detail would shame even the most fastidious forensic scientist. At one point Sian raises her eyebrows at Kitty in a gesture of solidarity, and Kitty can't help but smile. It's a bit schoolyard. A bit *Mean Girls*. But she figures what Grace doesn't see won't hurt her. And besides, Sian needs her.

'I saw Harry Styles in the Co-op the other day buying crumpets,' Sian says quietly enough that Grace might not be able to make out the words over the sound of her own voice. Kitty snorts and turns it into a cough. Damn. She really likes Sian. She really hopes Rich isn't doing anything he shouldn't. Thankfully, Rich returns at just that moment and Kitty uses the momentary lull to ask how Rhys is getting on back at uni. She can see Grace's mind working overtime, trying to think of an in. Her mouth opens and shuts a couple of times like a goldfish looking for food. Kitty watches Sian and Rich, trying to analyse if anything between them feels different to the way it did when she last saw them together – the evening round at hers – and the answer is a resounding no. Not that she knows them well enough to really tell, but they finish each other's sentences, they share conspiratorial glances, they lightly touch each other's hands and legs when they're interrupting or making a point. There's no nervousness to Rich. No edge. He looks like a man who loves his wife as much as she loves him.

Grace spots an access point. Rhys has apparently just spent a weekend seeing a friend in Salisbury, and she once went through Salisbury on a train, which is seemingly enough for her to crowbar in an anecdote about getting stuck in a Great Western Railway toilet. Sian and Rich laugh along.

'You should come to our little housewarming, Grace,' Sian says, once the story is finally over. Why do people do that? Take the risk and extend an invitation to a random friend of a friend who, for all they know, could actually be an enemy of a friend. Grace and Kitty could have been meeting up to discuss how much they hate each other. Kitty raises her eyebrows at Sian, but Sian doesn't seem to pick up on the hint. And anyway, it's too late. Grace has dived on the invitation like a seagull on an ice-cream cone.

'I'd love to! When is it?'

'Saturday.'

Grace turns to Kitty. 'You're going, yes?'

'Um.' Shit. She hasn't come up with an excuse yet. 'I think so. I'm just waiting on Derm. My brother,' she adds, turning to Sian and Rich. 'I might have to go down there.'

'Really?' Grace says sceptically. She must have taken in the information that Kitty and Dermot don't exactly get on somehow. By osmosis, Kitty imagines.

'And it's only a small thing, isn't it?' Kitty's starting to sound desperate. 'For the neighbours, really.'

'And a few of our friends,' Rich chips in.

'You have to come, Kitty,' Sian says. 'I'm relying on you to help me fight Julie and Pete off.'

Kitty makes what she hopes is a non-committal noise.

'And I can't go if you don't go,' Grace says petulantly.

'I'll let you know,' Kitty says as firmly as she can. And then she gives them all a smile to, hopefully, mitigate how harsh that must have sounded.

Sian and Rich, thankfully, have a table booked in the restaurant upstairs at seven. They try and persuade Kitty and Grace to join them. Grace is clearly tempted, but, when neither of them is looking, Kitty gives her a glare that would freeze vodka and Grace stops talking mid-sentence. Mid-word, in fact. It's as if she's found Grace's off switch.

'Next time, definitely,' Kitty says. 'I just . . . if I hadn't left the chicken in the oven . . .'

Grace shoots her a look. They've never discussed Kitty cooking for Grace. Kitty has never invited her over. She's always thought Grace was the kind of person who would turn up out of the blue on a random Saturday just on the off chance that Kitty was in and at a loose end, if she knew her exact address, and so she's kept that barrier up. Luckily neither Sian nor Rich seem to realise she's bluffing. They trip off towards the stairs hand in hand.

'I didn't know you were cooking. That's so nice . . .'

Kitty frowns. 'I'm not. There is no chicken. I just didn't fancy it, that's all.'

Grace fiddles with the stem of her glass. 'You don't like them?'

'No. I do. It's complicated.'

'How?' Grace takes a sip while Kitty thinks how to answer. 'I had some neighbours once, when I lived in Ealing,' she starts, clearly finding the silence unbearable. 'This mother and daughter. Meg and Sienna. Anyway, we all got on fine for a bit . . .'

Kitty tunes out, preoccupied with the problem that is Sian and Rich. There's no way of knowing if her suspicions are right, or if she's condemned her friendship with them because of a stupid misunderstanding on her part. If living next door to them is going to become unbearably awkward for no reason. She finds herself wishing she could get some clarity, a different perspective. And then she remembers that she's actually sitting here with another human being.

'Grace,' she says.

'. . . the same one as they had when they used to live in Wapping . . .'

'Gracie!'

Half the pub looks round. Grace stops in her tracks.

'Can you listen for a minute? I want to talk to you about something.'

You know when you hide a dog treat in your hand and then you open your fist and there's nothing there? Utter confusion. That. 'OK.'

Now Kitty's scared she's worried her. Grace is looking at her as if she's in for a telling-off. 'It's no big deal, I just want to ask your advice about something. About Sian and Rich.'

That perks Grace up. 'I knew you weren't sure about them. I liked them. And it was nice of them to invite me to their party. I mean . . .'

'Could you just listen for a second?' This is a mistake. She doesn't know why she's even bothering to try. Grace frowns, but she goes quiet.

'I saw something, the other day. I want your take on it.' Kitty manages to get through the whole story. Grace, once she realises she's potentially being let in on a juicy piece of gossip, listens, wide-eyed.

'You think they're having a thing, right? Rich and the woman?' she says, as soon as Kitty finishes.

'That's what I think. And Sian's so lovely . . .'

'What a bastard.'

'I know. I mean, maybe I'm wrong, but something's not adding up.'

'So, that's why you don't want to go to the party! I get it now, but surely, it's even *more* reason to go.'

Kitty rattles around in the paper bag and comes up with a plump date. She doesn't offer one to Grace because she knows Grace thinks they're evil. 'It's the stickiness,' she'd said once, when Kitty had first declared her love for them.

She had gagged theatrically like a toddler tasting broccoli for the first time. 'I can't . . .'

'Why?' Kitty says now.

'Maybe he'll get drunk and give something away.'

Kitty feels herself scowl. 'It's none of my business. I just want to keep right out of it.'

'OK, maybe I'll still go,' Grace says lightly.

'No. What? You can't.'

'Why not? They invited me. I'm sure I can work out which house they're in if I wander up and down Ashdown Close a few times.'

Damn. Kitty had forgotten that Grace knows the name of her street even if not the number of her house. 'Seriously, though, I think I just need to back away from being friends with them. It makes me uncomfortable now. Like I'm lying to Sian too.'

'If you're right.'

Kitty nods. 'If I'm right.' They run through all the other explanations they can think of – basically the same ones Kitty came up with the other day plus a couple from Grace: she's his AA sponsor and Sian doesn't know he has a problem (actually possible, although Kitty says to Grace that he seems very comfortable around alcohol. 'Drugs, then,' Grace says authoritatively), or he's converting religion and she's giving him secret instruction.

'He doesn't strike me as religious,' Kitty says, dismissing that one out of hand.

'Think about it,' Grace says, after Kitty has got them another drink. 'You either cut yourself off completely for what might turn out to be no reason and miss out on having nice neighbours you can hang out with, or you try to find out what's going on and then decide what to do. It would be crazy to stop being friends with Rich because he's decided to join the Salvation Army.'

'Oh, I don't know,' Kitty says. 'I think that would be a deal breaker.'

'Let's both go to their party and see if we notice anything. He might have left something lying around . . .'

'Not if he's trying to keep it a secret from Sian.'

'True,' Grace says. 'But he might let something slip. Come on, what else are you doing that night?'

Kitty considers. Comes up with nothing. 'OK. Let's do it. But don't say anything to either of them, will you?'

'Of course not,' Grace says as if she's affronted that Kitty has even suggested such a thing. As if the idea of Grace running her mouth is ludicrous.

Plan made, she settles back into Grace mode and Kitty sits back and lets it wash over her. She knows Grace is right. She needs to give Rich the benefit of the doubt until she has reason to do otherwise. And besides, how bad can a couple of hours with her neighbours be?

8

By Saturday afternoon she's wishing she hadn't let Grace talk her into going to the party. She thinks about feigning illness or a family trauma, but she knows Grace will see straight through her. They can just make an appearance, she decides. Show their faces to be polite and then make a quick escape to the pub.

Grace shows up at a quarter to seven, just as Kitty is walking around the house with a different style of shoe on each foot, trying to decide which to wear. Kitty lets her in and limps down the hall in front of her. 'Flats or heels?' she asks, and Grace wastes no time saying 'Flats. You don't want to be worrying about your feet hurting all evening. I once went to a party and my shoes were so painful I took them off and hid them behind a pot plant and when I went to go home, they'd gone, and I had to get on the tube barefoot . . .'

Sometimes Kitty thinks if she just lets her ramble on her batteries might run flat eventually. It hasn't happened yet.

'Oh, this is lovely,' Grace interrupts herself. Kitty stands back and lets her go into the living room first. 'I have a rug just like that. I'm ready to go if you are? I just need the loo. Shall I use the one down here or is there only one upstairs? I've brought a bottle of wine.'

Kitty closes her eyes. She's exhausted already.

'Hold on a sec,' she calls out a few minutes later as Grace is marching towards the front door. A woman on a mission. Grace stops in her tracks. Kitty ducks into the kitchen and squints at number 8 through the side window, trying to make out if there are people in there yet. 'I don't want to be the first.' Just as she's saying it, Julie and Pete appear along the street, either side of old Mr Millman from number 4. 'OK,' Kitty says. 'Let's just wait for them to go in.'

They give it five minutes. Grace uses the time to find an open bottle of white in the fridge and pour them both a small glass, which they neck standing by the sink.

'Oh, thank god,' Sian says when she opens the door. 'Hi, Grace, nice to see you again.' She grabs Kitty's arm. 'You have to save me. They've asked us to join the darts team already.'

'And, of course, you've said yes.'

'We're going to have to find another pub to drink in.'

Sian pulls her into the living space. Grace follows. Kitty is curious to see what they've done to the house. Their stylish décor puts hers to shame – the G Plan sideboard, the arc lamp, the egg chair, along with a turntable, a glitzy cocktail cabinet, polished parquet and fluffy white rugs. All original by the look of it. They've knocked the wall through from the kitchen too, something Kitty knows she should have done years ago, and the light floods in from both sides.

'It's gorgeous in here,' she says. 'So much lighter than mine.'

'It's not even a supporting wall. Just take a sledgehammer to it. We'll help.'

'God, do you think I could?'

'What's the worst that could happen?'

'My house falls down? While I'm trapped underneath it?'

Sian shrugs. 'And?'

As well as Julie, Pete and Mr Millman, there are a few other familiar faces. Sam and Linz seemingly without the kids. Kitty finds herself wondering who the lucky babysitter is. And if they charge extra for danger money. Betty. Vernie and Malcolm. The others, she assumes, are Sian and Rich's friends. Too cool for school in their tufted corduroy jackets and fighter pilot moustaches. God knows what they make of their old friends' new social circle. 'Hip' being a word that is generally only used around Ashdown Close in conjunction with 'replacement'.

'Where have all the beards gone?' Kitty whispers to Grace.

Grace snorts. 'It's all about the moustache now. Keep up.'

'I feel as if I'm in a seventies porn film.' Kitty waves and smiles at her neighbours. She spots Rich, who is shaking cocktails over by the kitchen island. Sian is holding out two glasses for him to fill, which, Kitty assumes, are for her and Grace. She really doesn't want to get pissed. If the oldies are all drinking spirits, it'll be a bloodbath by eight.

The drinks are cranberry pink and delicious. And probably lethal. Sian drags Kitty and Grace round, introducing them to strangers whose names Kitty forgets immediately. They're all friendly enough, but she doesn't think they have more than a passing interest in the local residents. They probably view them as an exhibit for one night only. Grace strikes up a conversation with each and every one of them and, to a man, they make their excuses and move away after a few minutes of being talked at.

'We need to remember why we're here,' she says to Kitty when she spots her leaning against a sideboard, taking it all in.

Kitty raises an eyebrow. 'To have a nice time?'

'Intel,' Grace says meaningfully.

'And what have you found out so far?'

Grace downs her cocktail. 'Well, nothing. But it's all groundwork. I think that one likes me,' she says, nodding at a burly, bespectacled man who Kitty thinks was called Frederick and who seems to have done nothing to indicate his interest in Grace except for a vague glance in their direction.

Julie and Pete suddenly appear beside them, slightly tipsy already. Pete slings an arm round Kitty's shoulder, and she feels herself tense up. 'How's Miss Kitty Kat?'

Kitty doesn't even dignify that with an answer. 'This is my friend Grace. Julie and Pete, number seven.'

'Lovely, isn't it?' Julie says. 'We should have these get-togethers more often.'

Over my cold dead body, Kitty thinks.

'Sian and Rich seem lovely, don't they? And how they've done it in here? Lovely. Don't you think, Grace?'

'Lovely,' Grace says, and Kitty has to hide a chuckle by turning it into a cough. Grace does have her moments.

'More drinks, anyone?' Rich wanders over rattling his shaker and they all hold out their glasses like obedient children. 'Actually, Kitty, could I borrow you for a moment? Sian asked me to grab you.'

'Oh. Sure.' She's not entirely certain she wants to spend time with him alone, but she can hardly say no. 'Oh, Grace, tell Julie and Pete that story you were telling me the other day about that guy at your work. It's hilarious,' she adds. It almost feels too cruel. Rich leads her over to the back of the room where the patio doors are open on to the garden even though it's not really warm enough to go outside. Sian is chatting away to Vernie and Malcolm. They're a sweet old couple, always together like a pair of gnarly bookends. They both give Kitty big smiles when they see her. Vernie reaches over for a hug. 'Did you want me?' Kitty says to Sian when she escapes Vernie's voluptuous clutches. You don't know you've lived till you've had your face in your octogenarian neighbour's cleavage.

'I thought you might need rescuing,' Sian says conspiratorially. 'Didn't Grace come with you? Should I go and get her?'

'Oh. She's fine, I think.' Kitty doesn't really want to bitch about Julie and Pete in front of Vernie and Malcolm. They could be best friends with them for all she knows.

'Vernie was just telling me that Pete can be a bit much,' Sian says, as if she's read Kitty's hesitancy. 'So, we thought we'd send the cavalry.'

'That's me, apparently,' Rich says with a wry smile. 'I've been called worse. Oh, hey!'

They all look round to see who he's greeting. Someone is making their way across the room, arms outstretched in greeting. Kitty hears herself catch her breath. It's her. The woman she saw sneaking out of Sian and Rich's house. The woman she saw hiding in the alley.

The woman who was desperate that Sian didn't know she'd been home alone with Rich.

9

Sian swoops the woman up into a hug. 'Lottie, meet Kitty, Vernie and Malcolm,' she says as they separate. Kitty realises she's staring. She sneaks a look at Rich and sees he is smiling at the new arrival, not a trace of anxiety showing. She looks for signs of excitement, but there's none of that either. He's the same Rich as he was two minutes ago. Relaxed, having fun with friends old and new. Lottie – Kitty recognises the platinum-blonde bob, but today Lottie is wearing a vintage-looking tea dress and bright red lipstick – smiles at them all, revealing tiny, neat teeth.

Kitty scans the room for Grace and finds her right where she left her, yabbering away at Julie and Pete. They look a bit shell-shocked, but they both seem to be valiantly trying to join in, so the image Kitty sees is like three squabbling birds pecking away at each other over the last worm in the feeder. She needs to get Grace's attention so, while Lottie tells the others an admittedly funny story about her journey up, she dashes off a quick text. *She's here!!!!!* Grace will know who she means so long as she actually looks at the message. Kitty hears her phone beep from the other side of the room, over the soft sounds of Joni Mitchell. She definitely hears it, because Grace's text alert is someone shouting 'Help help!', which she thinks is hilarious, but Kitty finds slightly disturbing. In fact, everyone looks round for a split second, which, thankfully, means Grace can't pretend the thing didn't just go off in the first place. She reaches into her pocket and holds it up apologetically. The room dissolves into laughter. She catches Kitty's eye, and Kitty raises her eyebrows in a way she hopes says *Read the fucking message*. It must work, because she sees Grace look down at her phone, a frown on her face.

'Grace is hilarious,' Rich is saying. 'How do you know her?'

Kitty tells them the speed dating story, all the while willing Grace to take on board the significance of what she's sent her and come over.

'Have you done it again since?' Sian asks, the bamboo straw from her cocktail still in her mouth.

'God, no. One Grace in my life is enough.'

Sian laughs. 'A colleague at my old work met someone at a naked speed dating event.'

'No,' Kitty says. 'Just . . . No.'

'I hope they wiped the seats down in between,' Malcolm says and Vernie chuckles heartily, as she always does whenever he makes a joke. They're a lovely couple. Kitty reminds herself she should make more of an effort with them.

'I don't even want to know what that's about,' Grace has appeared at her elbow.

'Don't ask,' Kitty says. 'Oh. Who hasn't met Grace? This is Vernie and Malcolm from number three, and Sian and Rich's friend *Lottie*.' She gives Grace a subtle kick on the ankle for emphasis, when she says Lottie's name.

'Kitty was just telling us how you met,' Rich says.

'Best date ever,' Grace says, and Kitty feels a little jolt of affection for her and then a rush of guilt about the way she's been avoiding her. Grace looks at Lottie. 'So, how do you three know each –' She's stopped from asking what was almost certainly going to be the first of many unsubtle questions by Sian saying, 'Oh, there's Andrew.'

They all look round as a wiry, tanned man makes his way across the room. He hugs both Sian and Rich and then snakes his arm round Lottie's shoulders. Kitty side-eyes Grace who raises her eyebrows back.

'Hi, I'm Kitty from next door,' Kitty says, hoping he'll elaborate on how he fits in. He obliges.

'Oh, Sian's told us about you. I'm Andrew. Lottie's husband.'

Grace digs a nail into Kitty's arm and Kitty tries not to flinch.

'Lottie and Andrew are old friends,' Sian says. 'We've known each other, what? Nineteen years?'

'Something like that.' Lottie smiles at her and Kitty's heart lurches out to Sian who is beaming away. Oblivious. 'Me and Sian a bit more. We met at antenatal classes when we all lived in Balham.'

Kitty feels a fierce wave of protectiveness that almost knocks her off her feet. 'Oh, you have a kid the same age as Rhys?' she asks. Because isn't that pretty much the ultimate betrayal? Two mum friends?

'Archie,' Lottie says, nodding. 'And a seventeen-year-old. Harry. Harriet. So, yeah. We go back a long way.'

'I'll get you a drink,' Rich says.

'Oh god, not the cosmopolitans!' Andrew smiles. 'Can I get a beer instead?'

'Whatever your heart desires,' Rich says and Kitty almost scowls at him. He moves off towards the fridge.

'So, Lottie, tell us all about yourself,' Grace says, with all the subtlety of a member of the CID. Kitty is actually thankful for her no-filter interrogation skills, but she wills her to keep quiet long enough so they can get the answers.

Lottie tucks her hair behind her ear. 'Oh. Well. Um. I have a shop. A little vintage clothes place in Crouch End. People bring me their stuff. To sell. You know.' She speaks in short, staccato sentences as if she's nervous to commit to the whole thought.

'She's underselling herself,' Andrew interrupts. 'She's an amazing seamstress and she fixes them all up like new, and she makes stuff, too.'

Sian flaps at the sleeve of Lottie's dress. 'Is this one of yours?'

'It is.'

'It's gorgeous,' Grace says. 'I wish I could do that. The last time I made anything was when we had to do sewing at school and I ended up making a pair of trousers for my mum, but the first time she wore them they split right up the back because I hadn't left enough seam allowance. She was at church . . .' Sian, Lottie and Rich all laugh loudly. Kitty sees Grace, thrilled by her new captive audience, open her mouth to elaborate further. 'She . . . ow.' She glares at Kitty, who just poked her hard in the side of her ribs to remind her what they're there for. 'Anyway,' she mutters sulkily.

'Lottie made my wedding dress,' Sian says. 'I'll show you a picture.' She heads over to the G Plan sideboard and rummages in a cupboard. The room is crowded now. Twenty-five people or more. You could sort the neighbours from the friends with one hundred per cent accuracy on looks alone. The neighbours are the only ones dressed in clothes from the current century. The conversation babbles around them like the hum of traffic. Only the sound of Rich's cocktail shaker cuts through the chatter.

'For *our* wedding she altered her grandmother's dress,' Andrew says with an affectionate look at Lottie. 'It was stunning.'

'You would not believe how small people were in the fifties,' Lottie says. 'I had to source more lace and basically expand in every direction.'

Sian produces a framed picture with a flourish and holds it up for inspection. She looks stunning in it. They both do, her and Rich. But it's Sian who stands out with her big, kohl-rimmed doe eyes and her messy up-do.

'Wow,' Kitty says, 'you looked incredible.' The dress is fitted, deep, rich red lace. Plunged at the neckline with rough-edged straps. She looks like Vampyra but in a really good, not overdone way.

'Isn't she clever?' Sian says, smiling at Lottie.

'She is,' Kitty says through gritted teeth. 'But it's the way you carry it off . . .'

They're interrupted by a knocking sound just as Rich arrives back with his full shaker and a beer for Andrew. Everyone stops talking. Pete is rapping on the kitchen counter with some kind of utensil. 'Quiet, everybody,' he booms.

'Oh, please god, no,' Kitty says under her breath to Sian, who snorts.

'I'm sure we'd all like to thank Sian and Rich for inviting us over tonight and to welcome them to their gorgeous new home in Ashdown Close. Especially if they keep on making us drinks like this.' He holds up his pink-tinged glass. People titter half-heartedly. Kitty looks at the sideboard where Sian has now placed the wedding photo. The sheer happiness on Sian's face as she looks up at Rich infuriates her. She feels breath on her ear and starts as a voice mutters, 'Isn't that gorgeous? One of hers.' She looks round to see Lottie leaning in. She can smell her floral perfume. 'The painting. Oh. Isn't that what you were looking at?' Kitty looks back and sees a dramatic abstract framed on the wall. Thick swirls of red and yellow like a sea on fire. It's stunning. 'Really?' she says to Lottie, forgetting her distrust for a moment. 'It's amazing.' Pete is still droning on about the virtues of Ashdown Close. (*Oh, and if you ever forget where you've parked your car, just ask Betty. Always up to date with everyone's comings and goings is our Bet.*) Lottie nods emphatically. 'She's ridiculously talented. Wasted doing what she's doing.'

'I thought Rich was the artist.'

'He is too. But Sian's better. Not that I'd admit to that in public, obvs.'

Kitty doesn't know what to say to that, so she turns her attention back to Pete who, thankfully, seems to be wrapping up. 'Seriously, though, they seem like a lovely couple and they're a welcome addition to the neighbourhood. We're a friendly bunch. At least, most of us are. Not so sure about you, Betty. Haha! Only joking.' Kitty grimaces at Sian and Grace. Betty looks daggers. 'Anyway, me and Julie would like to raise a toast to them and I'm sure you'd all like to join us. To Rich and Sian!'

Everyone obliges by lifting their drinks. 'Rich and Sian,' they all parrot.

'Who put him in charge?' Kitty says under her breath. They're all still looking over at Pete as if they're waiting for Act Two. Kitty turns her head towards Grace, intending to give her a big Pete-induced eye roll, but her gaze lands on Rich and the fact that he's whispering something into Lottie's ear, while resting a hand softly on her lower back. She catches Grace's eye and sees that she sees it too.

'When's your birthday, Sian?' Grace says. Kitty shoots her a warning look. 'I just wondered what star sign you were. I'd have you down as a Taurus, so it must be soon.'

Sian doesn't seem to have noticed Rich and Lottie. 'December. Sagittarius. I know nothing about that shit, though, to be honest.'

Grace looks pointedly at Kitty. She might as well say, 'I told you so.'

'I fucking hate cheaters,' Grace says as they stumble over Kitty's doorstep. The word has the shock value absent when used by a habitual swearer. 'Fucking hate them. Bastards.' Grace was cheated on by Hal multiple times, Kitty knows. The vasectomy was not his only betrayal. The thrill of the early days was what he thrived on. The classic love-bomb stage. Why he had married her, Grace had told her, she still had no idea. Perhaps, she'd sometimes speculated, he had wanted to change, to grow up, but all the talk of having kids had freaked him out. She'd forgiven him over and over again. Taken him back. Tried to make it work. All for the sake of the babies she thought they were trying for that it turned out they were never going to have. She clearly still can't let it go. Her views on infidelity have always been black and white.

They're the kind of drunk where everything is still OK. Kitty knows they haven't disgraced themselves, but she also knows it'll get messy in a bit when their bodies have had time to catch up with the quantity of spirits they've put into them. Thankfully she'd had the sense to realise she was starting to feel brave, starting to feel as if she might just tell Rich exactly what she thought of him if she stayed, and she'd got out of there in one piece. The dancing had started – usually Kitty's cue to leave anywhere – and, even though she was tempted to stay and watch her neighbours misbehave, she knew it was only a matter of time before she did something she'd regret. She'd hugged Sian for way too long as they left, Grace still protesting that she had space for another cocktail.

'I'll tell you all the goss tomorrow,' Sian had said. 'I don't think some of this lot are used to drinking.'

'Water or another drink?' Kitty says now, knowing they shouldn't.

'Both. No more vodka, though.'

Kitty drags herself to the kitchen and finds a bottle of brandy in a cupboard. 'Just a small one,' she says, more for her own benefit than Grace's because she doubts Grace can hear her. She pours them both a glass and takes them through, intending to come back for the water. She's actually looking forward to the debrief. She's pretty sure her instincts are right. There was definitely a moment there between Rich and Lottie when they thought no one was looking. 'If it's true, what are we going to do?'

There's no response. Kitty peers round the living room door. Grace is passed out asleep on the pristine white sofa, face down in a cushion.

Forest Streets Residents' WhatsApp Group:

Linz B: First time in years I've been up half the night for fun and not because one of the kids was playing up! Few too many cheeky cosmos though!! Thanks Rich and Sian at number 8. Actually not sure they're on here to see this, lol!

Grace spent the night in the living room. Kitty poured the brandy away – her own too – took off Grace's shoes and found a throw to cover her with. She thought about trying to manoeuvre a pillow in between Grace's burgundy lipstick and the cushion fabric, but she wasn't sure how it might look if Grace woke up and Kitty was manhandling her. She left a large glass of water on the coffee table and placed a bowl on the floor in case Grace felt sick and couldn't get to the toilet. Then she crawled up the stairs and threw herself into bed fully clothed. She couldn't sleep, though, thoughts of Grace drooling on the soft furnishings or, god forbid, throwing up on the carpet, buzzing round inside her head like a swarm of bees.

She's woken up by the smell of bacon frying. Groaning, she feels around for her phone to check the time. It's after ten. She can't remember when she's ever slept this late. She runs through the shame checklist: did she make a fool of herself? No. Does she remember leaving the party? Yes. Was everyone else as drunk as she was? Definitely. Almost certainly more so by the time they eventually staggered home. Satisfied, she tries to sit up, but her head is pounding so she gives up and lies back down. There's a tap on her door. Shit. Grace. Kitty manages to grunt a response. Grace breezes in with a tray. Looking fresh and awake. How is this possible? Kitty briefly wonders if she's missed a whole day, and Grace has had time to recover. She was definitely in a worse state than Kitty. Kitty can't imagine the horror show that is her face at the moment, and it must smell like a rat-infested brewery in the stuffy bedroom.

'I thought you might like some breakfast,' Grace says. 'I hope you don't mind, but I took your key and went to the shop.'

She offloads a coffee and a glass of water onto the bedside table and puts the tray on the bed beside Kitty.

'Thanks,' Kitty manages. On the tray is a plate with a beautifully greasy-looking bacon sandwich: white bread, crispy bacon, a little bowl with tomato ketchup. 'Oh god, that's heaven,' she says gratefully.

Grace fishes a sachet out of her pocket. Alka Seltzer. 'Put this in your water. I'll leave you to it. If I were you, I'd eat and then sleep it off for a bit. I've got an Uber coming.'

'Thanks. God. Sorry.'

'What are you sorry about? I passed out on your couch. Thanks for covering me up, by the way. I assume that was you?'

'I think so. Don't you feel bad?'

'Awful,' Grace laughs. 'I just want to get to my own bed. I'll call you tomorrow.'

'We have to discuss.'

'Absolutely. But not now. I can barely string a sentence together.'

'That's not like you,' Kitty says, and Grace laughs hoarsely, like a fifty a day smoker.

'Anything else you need before I go?'

'A liver transplant?'

'Go back to sleep,' Grace says firmly. 'But eat first.'

Eventually (two p.m. Two p.m.! She has somehow managed to sleep for four more hours), she drags herself into the shower and emerges feeling almost human. It's been very quiet in the Close today. Eerily so. Kitty imagines all her neighbours are chucking up into buckets and wondering how they can ever face each other again. The thought cheers her up. She decides to walk round the block before it gets dark again and she's missed the whole day. She might bump into one of them emerging and find out when it finished and just how messy it got. There's nothing that beats a hangover more than knowing someone else was worse off than you. She can go to the Polish supermarket and treat herself to some sticky chocolate-covered plums, she decides. The thought makes her mouth water. She gingerly approaches her living room, expecting a bomb site, but it's as tidy as it was before they went out last night. Tidier, in fact. The throw is folded on the arm of the sofa. Kitty examines the cushions for signs of make-up or worse but, apart from a slight dampness where Grace has obviously scrubbed at something, they're spotless. The bowl is back in the kitchen, the washing-up done.

As she passes Malcolm and Vernie's house, it occurs to her that she should check up on them, see if they need anything. Calling round uninvited is not something she has ever done. But someone needs to check they're in one piece.

Vernie looks like one of the walking dead when she opens the door. 'Oh, Kitty,' she says when she sees who it is. 'What did we do? Come in. Come in.'

Kitty hovers. 'I'm actually just on my way to the shops, but I thought I'd check if you were both OK and whether you needed supplies. If you feel anything like I do, you might want some comfort food.'

'Do you feel bad too?' Vernie says, holding herself upright in the doorway. 'Thank goodness. I don't mean that like it came out. I just mean I'm glad we're not the only ones. Malcolm's gone back to bed.'

'Well, I've only just got up, if that's any consolation. I think everyone was pretty hammered by the time we left.'

'They just kept filling our glasses up.'

'Drink lots of water. Do you have paracetamol?'

Vernie nods. 'It was fun, though, wasn't it?'

'It was,' Kitty says. 'So, do you need anything? You should eat stodge.'

'Don't talk about food.' Vernie pulls a face and then she suddenly says, 'Chips! Is that too much to ask you to stop at the chip shop?'

'Definitely not. I have to pass it anyway. What do you want with them?'

'You're an angel. Nothing with them. Just lots of chips. Three portions. Or four. Here.' She picks up her handbag from a side table and roots around, coming up with a twenty-pound note. Kitty waves it away.

71

'My treat,' she says, feeling magnanimous. 'I might get some for myself too.'

'You should. You need fattening up.'

'See you in a few minutes.'

She carries on towards the main road and then she starts to feel guilty about Betty. She's miserable at the best of times, so it's hard to imagine what she would be like with added drinker's remorse, but, Kitty thinks, *What if that was my mum and no one checked up on her?* Maybe she should call in on all the oldies. Start being a good neighbour. She doubles back and walks past her own house, along to number 11. Betty looks in a similar state to Vernie when she answers the door, and she eyes Kitty warily.

'Kitty. From number ten,' Kitty says in case Betty's memory is fuzzy.

'I know. What can I do for you?'

'I'm just checking up on how everyone is doing after last night. Do you need anything?'

'That's very kind of you,' Betty says formally. 'But there's nothing I need.' She starts to close the door in Kitty's face, but she's not quick enough before Kitty see a glimpse of Mr Millman from number 4 on his way down the stairs, wearing nothing but a towel round his waist. Ah. OK. Kitty is actually glad Betty has got some pleasure in her life, but she thinks her OAP good deed services might have closed for the day. They're having a better time than she is. It should be them checking up on her.

'Hi, Mr Millman,' she calls loudly as the door slams shut.

Greasy packets of chips delivered (and one eaten by herself – actual heaven), she sees Rich walk past with the dog and she sends Sian a text. *Ashdown Close will never be the same again!* She adds a load of laughing emojis. *Seriously the whole place is one big collective hangover. You OK?*

A few minutes later she gets a reply. *Actually dying. What were we thinking? The last ones didn't leave till 4 a.m. Julie and Pete, obviously.*

It was fun, Kitty sends. *But I'm glad I left before I saw Betty and Mr Millman getting it on.*

There's a beep. *No!!!!!!!*

Yes!!!! That's your fault haha!

Oh god, Kitty reads. *They're all going to hate us.*

Are you kidding? This is the most excitement we've ever had. Your friends seem nice btw. Andrew and Lottie.

She watches her phone, waiting for an answer. She imagines Rich sneaking off on the pretext of exercising Dante and making sneaky calls to his lover. *I could barely keep my hands off you last night you looked so hot.* The pair of them breathing heavily down the phone.

They're the best, Sian says. *They loved you too. We should all get together.*

Definitely, Kitty says, before she can think better of it.

She calls Grace and settles in for the long haul.

'Rich or Andrew?' Grace says, once they've dissected the evening fully and come round to Rich and Lottie once again via a five-minute story about a friend of Grace's whose wife got pregnant by the gardener. Kitty honestly never knows if Grace's stories are even true because isn't that essentially the plot of *Lady Chatterley's Lover*? Once Grace told her a story that Kitty would swear was the plot of *The Shining* but had basically happened to her on the bus on the way to work. 'If you had to.'

'OK. So, I can't imagine what circumstances those are, but for argument's sake definitely not Rich.'

'You don't think he's good-looking?'

Kitty considers for a second. 'No, he totally is, but it's all a bit too perfect. No rough edges.'

Grace laughs. 'Perfection is bad?'

'In sexiness terms, absolutely.'

'So, Andrew then,' Grace says as if that's now decided. 'It would be Rich for me any day. I mean, just on looks, obviously.'

Kitty lets out a dismissive 'Pffft.'

'It's definitely true, by the way, if you ask me,' Grace says after a moment, serious now.

'I know. I think so too. They were looking very cosy.'

'All that stuff about being best mates and bringing up their kids together. It's gross.'

Kitty lets out a long sigh. 'I guess that's me staying out of their way from now on then, too complicated.'

'What are you going to do?'

'I'm not going to do anything. What *can* I do?'

'You can't just let him keep doing it to Sian,' Grace says, outraged.

'I barely know them. It's awful, and I feel desperately sorry for Sian, but I don't think I can get involved. For all we know, she knows and it's fine so long as they keep it behind closed doors.'

'Yeah, right.'

'Well, either way, it's a mess I don't want to involve myself in. Not without proof, anyway.' Nothing can be gained by blundering in with hearsay and half-formed theories and blowing up Sian's whole life, even though

Kitty's heart is aching for the friend she made so easily and unexpectedly.

Grace huffs. 'You can't just do nothing. You witnessed that little moment between them at the party, right? Him running his hand down her back. We both saw that.'

'I don't think he was stroking it. It was just there. That's hardly conclusive. So, they're affectionate. Lots of friends are.'

'Not like that.'

Kitty cuts the call short. She can't be bothered to argue any more. Later, of course, she'll wish she had. That she'd tried a bit harder to talk Grace round to her way of thinking.

Forest Streets Residents' WhatsApp Group:

Magda Wroblewska: Helluva party at 8 Ashdown on Saturday night for neighbours and friends! Thanks to Rich and Sian for their generous hospitality. I bet some of your 'friends' appreciate how attentive you are as host, eh, Rich? Especially one pretty lady!

What the actual fuck?

Kitty reads it again.

It definitely says what she thought it said. And there's a winky face at the end, just to ram home the point.

Magda is a new arrival to the group. Kitty can vaguely remember spotting the welcome message yesterday, but she barely takes notice of new members unless they say they live on Ashdown, because the flats on the two main roads seem to have an ever-changing population of temporary tenants who bombard the group with messages about borrowing carpet cleaners or offering dog-walking services for a few months and then disappear without so much as a goodbye. Some of the long-termers, irritated by the coming and going, formed a subgroup a couple of years ago, strictly by invite only, from which the short-term renters are excluded. It's all a bit unnecessary, and Kitty tries her best to stay out of the politics. So, now she's just paranoid that the secret group – which she declined to join – are all talking about her behind her back. She scrolls back though the feed to see if Magda has posted before but there's no action until she hits group admin Shirley Howard Martin's *Please all say hello to new member Magda!!! Magda has moved into Summerdown Court!* post. A few people engaged: *Hi, Magda!* and *Nice to meet you, Magda!* Bunches of flowers emojis, waving-hands emojis. Magda sent a smiley face in response to each one. Nothing else. And now she's posted a random shade-throwing comment about Rich. Just like that. Out of nowhere.

It can only be one person.

Kitty hasn't spoken to Grace since their conversation about Rich and Lottie where Grace made it clear Kitty's lack of action was a disappointment to her. Now, it seems, she's on some kind of self-righteous mission to expose Rich and avenge Sian, people she barely even knows.

Kitty sends a text. *What the fuck??*

What? Grace sends back innocently.

You know what. WhatsApp!

Haha! You've seen it. Has it got pulses racing in Ashdown Close?

She's not even denying it. Kitty hits the button to call her number. 'What are you doing?' she says when Grace answers.

'What? No one's going to know what it means except Rich. And you, of course. It's not like I've put a poster up saying "Rich is shagging his best friend's wife." Or even "his wife's best friend".'

'So, let me get this straight. You joined my local WhatsApp group just so you could post this? How does that even work?'

She hears Grace sigh. 'You should tell them not to put a poster up in the pub inviting people to join if they want to be exclusive.'

'Residents. Inviting *residents* to join. Did they not even check who you were?' Kitty can't remember how she first found the Forest Streets group. Shirley put a note through all their doors, she thinks, asking them to provide their phone numbers if they wanted to be added. Kitty doesn't think she ever imagined major security would be needed to protect the group from cyber-crime. That there could be fakers lurking on there listening in on the conversations about whether the parking bay in front of the barbers is really allowed to be occupied day in, day out by the same music-blaring BMW 3 Series. (Kitty had been gratified to see that someone named Ad had replied, *Because otherwise we'd have to hang around the park to buy our drugs* with a shrugging emoji. Although he'd never posted since, so he may well have been murdered for being a snitch.)

'Not even slightly.'

'Can you delete the comment?'

'Not possible.'

'It must be. What if you leave the group?'

'I have no idea, but I don't think my past comments would leave with me. And anyway. No. He deserves to know he's not getting away with it.'

'It's. Nothing. To. Do. With. You,' Kitty spells out, emphasising each word. 'And by the way, he's not even in the group. Neither of them is.'

'You can't just sit back and watch while he does this to Sian. I could have saved years of wasted time if someone had been brave enough to let me know how Hal was treating me. Not to mention all the humiliation I could have been spared. Have you got any idea how that feels, to know that people have been pitying you behind your back? Probably laughing at you too. I found out after that my colleague Sharon had seen him out with some woman at a restaurant . . .'

Ah, so it's struck a nerve, Kitty realises. This time it's personal. Grace's voice is getting higher and higher pitched.

'. . . holding hands across the table, but she was worried I'd shoot the messenger if she told me! Can you imagine? That was two years before we finally split up. Two years! I could have fallen in love with someone else and got pregnant in that time. So don't tell me it's wrong to get involved or whatever . . .'

'Grace,' Kitty says.

'It's all right for you because you want to live on your own. You have no idea what it's like to have someone kiss you goodbye in the evening, moaning about the fact they have to work late and they'd much rather spend the evening vegging out with you, and then you find they've actually been sneaking off to meet someone else. Or telling you how desperate they are to have kids, and it'll happen eventually, but secretly having the snip to make sure it never does. I mean, how did he think I would never find out? What if I'd insisted we go to get fertility help? What then? And imagine if . . .'

'Grace. Just shut up for a second. Please.' Kitty hears Grace take a breath and jumps in before she kicks off again. 'It's awful what Hal did to you. I get that. I really do.

But it's got nothing to do with Rich and Sian. You can't make this your own personal revenge on faithless men.'

'Oh, fuck off, Kitty,' Grace says, and the line goes dead.

Kitty stares at the phone in her hand for a moment wondering what just happened.

Kitty can't work out whether it's worth drawing attention to the Magda comment by asking Shirley Howard Martin to take it down, assuming that's even possible, or to maybe verify Magda's existence, or if it would be better to let it sit there, for the most part, ignored. And there are already several messages below it. *Has anyone got a good babysitter? My phone got stolen – this is my new number. I've got a couple of oak side tables I'm going to skip unless anyone wants them. What was the reason for the police presence on Sherwood Avenue at 2 a.m.?* Kitty is momentarily distracted. What *was* the reason for the police presence on Sherwood Avenue at 2 a.m.? There are no responses as yet. She'll check back later, she decides. See if the Magda comment has had any traction too. Decide what to do then. Meanwhile she needs to clear her head and stop worrying away at things that don't concern her. She changes into her running stuff, plugs in her headphones, turns left out of the front door and heads towards the little park at a slow jogging pace, avoiding the cracked and bevelled paving stones that the Forest Streets group get very aerated about. It's a beautiful spring evening, light now that the clocks have sprung forward. Kitty wouldn't run here otherwise. Too many creepy corners. Too many creepy lurkers. But on a night like tonight there's a parade of athleisure-encased bodies shuffling or sprinting round the paths. Some gliding effortlessly, barely breaking a sweat. Others, like herself, huffing and panting, hair frizzing, faces red. The worse she looks the more good it's doing her, is what she tells herself.

Out of the corner of her eye she sees a pale grey blur and realises that up ahead Dante is running towards her on the other end of a lead held by Rich. She almost freezes on the spot. Rich is the last person she wants to bump into. It's too late to turn back and, besides, he might catch her up, he's going so much faster than her. So, she speeds up a little and fixes her eyes on the concrete in front of her as if she hasn't seen him. Dante's not having it. He's met her before. That means they're practically best friends in his eyes. He lunges at her excitedly and she jumps and accidentally catches Rich's eye.

There's nothing she can do but stop. 'Oh. Hi. I didn't see you.' She can hardly look at him, can feel the disapproval coming off her in waves.

'You were in the zone,' he says with a smile.

'I was concentrating on not having a heart attack. It still might happen.'

'I didn't know you were a runner.'

She pulls her scrappy ponytail tighter. 'I think that's overstating it. I occasionally go for a very slow jog. There's a difference.'

He indicates the dog. 'I bring him so if I get knackered I can slow right down and pretend I'm just taking him for a walk.'

'Clever. I should get myself one.'

'You can borrow this one any time you like. No amount of walks will ever be enough for him.'

'Oh,' she says, remembering she needs to act as if it's business as usual. 'Thanks for the party, by the way. I had a blast.'

He pulls one foot up behind him in a stretch. 'Any excuse.'

Kitty flaps a hand up ahead. 'Well, I should . . .'

'I might just do another lap with you,' he says and she almost shouts 'No!' but she reins herself in.

'Sure,' she says. The sooner she gets this over with the better. But Rich, it seems, wants to chat.

'It's actually really nice, this park.'

'Mmmm. The drug dealers think so. It's their favourite.'

He laughs. 'How did you end up living round here?'

'Same as you,' Kitty says, breathing heavily. Running is bad enough, but running and talking is nigh on impossible. It should be an Olympic discipline. She makes air quotes. 'A sound financial decision.'

'Do we all just reach an age and agree to become our parents? I feel as if that's happening to me.'

Kitty stops herself from saying *Why? Did your parents shag around too?*

He seems totally relaxed. Even with the running. As if he doesn't have a care in the world. Either he's very practised at this or he has no idea he's been rumbled. Kitty feels herself scowl.

'How's Sian?'

'Great. Getting used to the new school, I think.'

'I don't know how she does it,' Kitty says, trying to slow the pace. She doesn't want to spend any more time with him than she has to, but she doesn't want to do herself an injury either. 'All those kids. All that noise.'

82

'She doesn't have that full a timetable. It's not a compulsory subject.'

'I bet they love her.' Kitty stops on the pretext of retying her shoelaces. 'The hot teacher and all that.'

He pulls a face. 'I'm not sure I want to dwell on what a load of fourteen-year-old boys think about my wife.'

She forces a laugh. 'You're living their dream.'

They're nearing the end of the loop, back to where they started. Kitty is pretty sure she can make her excuses and leave once they get to the point where the paths cross. She slows to a halt again.

'Anyway, she'd love you to come over again. I mean, we both would. Any time.' He gives Kitty a warm smile. She would trust that smile, she thinks. She would fall for his shit.

'We should have that dinner with Lottie and Andrew. It'd be nice to get to know them a bit better.' Why did she say that? She doesn't know what's wrong with her that she can't just leave it alone. She's as bad as Grace. Because she wanted to see his reaction, she thinks, just as Dante jumps up at her leg excitedly and reflex makes her look down and she misses it.

'Yeah, let's,' Rich says, having had the time to compose himself. 'We'd love that.'

12

It's Jade's birthday. Kitty waits for Mark and Jacob to arrive for the midday shift and then breaks out the Colin the Caterpillar and cheap Prosecco she traditionally brings in to mark any member of the team's big day. They put the phones on out of office (strictly forbidden), sing one chorus of 'Happy Birthday' and toast Jade's good health, before Kitty and the other eight-to-fourers take their lunch break. She heats soup in the microwave in the little staff kitchen and tucks herself into a corner of the break room, her head in a book. That's the other thing about doing the early shift, you get to have lunch before the one o'clock rush, so her only companion is a woman from accounts who always brings her own food in too and who, although Kitty is on smiling terms with her, has somehow entered into an unwritten contract that says they stick to their own lanes and give each other space. Ross and Evie have gone out to the pub on the corner. Kitty's little team are all twenty-odd years younger than her, and without exception, lovely. It's a starter job. None of them stay long. They always invite Kitty out with them, though, and she's sometimes tempted, but she knows they're only duty-asking. They'd probably be horrified if she said yes. And hanging out with a load of twenty-three-year-olds, crying into her wine about how tragic her life has become, is not a good look for the boss. Nor is it the answer to her problems.

It's been two days since her fight with Grace. There have been no messages since the morning after, when Grace sent *I'm so sorry. I'd had too much to drink xx*. Kitty ignored it, still smarting with irritation. Since then, nothing. From either of them, just to be clear. Kitty hasn't exactly been falling over herself to get in touch with Grace either. She's actually desperate to tell Grace about her upcoming dinner with Lottie and Andrew – to tell someone – but she's not sure if she can trust her any more. And besides, Grace was the one who hung up on her. She's the one who should be going into overdrive to make amends.

She's been avoiding Sian too, for which she feels terrible. But knowing a secret about someone is a toxic burden that poisons every communication you have with them. What Kitty thinks she knows about Rich and Lottie is burning a hole in her brain. She feels as if Sian could read it in her face. They've texted a few times, so it's not as if it's awkward, and this morning came the one Kitty had been dreading and looking forward to in equal measure. *Dinner tomorrow night at ours with Lottie and Andrew? 7.30? Hope you can both make it.*

She's momentarily confused when another message appears almost immediately. *How lovely! Yes, I'll be there.* It's from Grace. Too late, Kitty sees the tiny '2 people' written at the top of the thread. Sian must have sent the invitation to both of them. She didn't even realise Sian had taken Grace's number.

As if she can read Kitty's mind, a WhatsApp appears from Grace: *Are we still speaking?* Kitty ignores it. But she knows she can't leave the loose cannon that is Grace to go to dinner with Sian and Rich alone – and besides, Grace wouldn't even have been invited if it wasn't for Kitty, why should Kitty have to be the one to miss out? – and so she sends Sian an acceptance, ignoring the group chat with Grace.

Grace messages her again. *You are going to the dinner, aren't you? I already said yes.*

Kitty tries to distract herself by posting a few things on the street WhatsApp group, just to push Magda further back into history. *Did anyone ever find out what the police were doing in Sherwood the other night?* and *Thinking of getting a cleaner one morning a week. Any recommendations?* She's not, and anyway, someone once told her that 'cleaner' on these forums is often a euphemism for something completely different, which leaves her slightly alarmed for all the genuine cleaners and cleaner-seekers out there. But it fills up a bit of space. Magda's message has still had no responses. Kitty tells herself to let it go. Sian and Rich will never see it.

She makes a tea to take to bed, still not having responded to Grace. She's about to plug her phone in to charge on the kitchen counter when she sees a WhatsApp notification. She's curious about who's up at this time and engaging, so, stupidly, she looks. Her heart almost stops. It's Magda.

Hi Kitty! I do cleaning for several people locally. I have some free days.

Grace. Kitty messages her privately. *What the hell are you doing? Get off my WhatsApp!!*

Well, you're not speaking to me, Grace writes back. *How else am I supposed to get your attention?*

Kitty paces up and down the kitchen, the tiles cool

under her feet. She assumes this is just Grace being Grace, not anything more sinister. She's just trying to get Kitty's attention; she's admitted as much.

Delete that profile, Kitty writes back. *It's freaking me out.*

OK. But can we be friends again? I miss you.

Kitty grimaces. What is she, eight? Grace follows up with a picture she's found god knows where of a big-eyed puppy with a carnation in its mouth. Kitty turns her phone face down. It beeps again and she sighs and picks it up. This time Grace has added the words 'Pwetty Pwease' to the photo. Despite herself, Kitty laughs.

Only if you stop sending me that godawful shit.

Deal! Hooray!

I'll call you tomorrow, Kitty sends. *Behave.*

Lottie and Andrew are on the doorstep when Kitty shows up, bottle in hand. Lottie is in another tea dress, this time in yellow with green sprigged flowers. She's curvy, soft to Sian's lean. Maybe that's the attraction. Twenty-one years of being together poleaxed by a bigger pair of tits. A tale as old as time. Kitty tries to rearrange the glare that threatens to take over her face into something softer. Andrew is casual in jeans and a faded brown T-shirt with The Bonzo Dog Doo-Dah Band emblazoned across the chest, a freebie, Kitty assumes, from Lottie's vintage collection. He's in good shape. Toned in that farm fit way of someone who works hard rather than works out. Kitty has forgotten what he does for a living, but it must be something physical. He's tanned, so maybe outdoors. The main thing she notices about him is how smiley he is. Even when he's not actually smiling, the lines that feather from his eyes give him away. He's very attractive, she realises. Not in an obvious way, but he gives off a kind of energy that makes you want to look twice. Not for the first time, she wonders if Lottie has considered what she's risking. He scratches at something on his arm and the sleeve of his T-shirt rides up, revealing the bottom of a tattoo that looks like an old-fashioned Popeye anchor. If there's one thing Kitty is a sucker for, it's tattoos. Within reason, obviously. Not on faces. Or all joined together with no room left for skin. And distorted portraits of babies are a definite turn-off. As are spiders' webs, pictures of your dear old dad, and mindfulness soundbites. But a single, tasteful image on a well-toned arm? Sign her up.

They all swap hugs. Lottie smells of roses. Soft, feminine. Kitty greets Andrew more enthusiastically, without meaning to be so obvious. Sian isn't the only victim here.

He runs a hand over his cropped hair. 'Just you?'

'She's on her way,' Kitty says defensively. She feels a bit affronted, as if she's not enough without Grace, the life and soul. She had tried to persuade Grace to cry off at the last minute, citing a migraine (on the pretext that Magda proved Grace was a loose cannon and not to be trusted), but Grace was having none of it, so instead Kitty had delivered a lecture on the importance of being on her best behaviour and Grace – to give her credit – hadn't told her to stop being patronising but had meekly agreed not to say anything provocative.

'We're just observing, that's all,' Kitty had said, ramming her point home. 'Don't shoot your mouth off.' They still hadn't seen each other since their fight.

'Well, we're happy to see you,' Lottie says now. Which is nice of her, Kitty has to admit.

Rich opens the door wearing an apron, and the smell of garlic and expensive candles follows him. He holds his arms out wide. 'Hey.'

Kitty watches him grab Lottie into a hug. She sneaks a look at Andrew, whose smile doesn't drop. She thinks he's as clueless to what's going on as Sian is. She proffers up her bottle of Sancerre when it's her turn, held in front of her as a kind of barrier. Keep Out. No hugging. Now she actually finds herself wishing Grace was here beside her. She needs safety in numbers. They all troop into the kitchen where Sian is stirring something on the hob, big glass of red in one hand. Her long hair is piled up on top of her head and secured with a clip, and she's wearing a pair of baggy grey dungarees with a vest top underneath, rolled up at the legs to reveal tanned bare feet and bright purple toenails. She accepts a kiss on the cheek from each of the guests, spatula held wide in one hand, wine in the other.

'I'm pretending I'm cooking, but really Rich has done everything.'

'You're chief stirrer,' he says. 'I'll get drinks.'

'It smells incredible.'

Something rich reddish brown and fragrant is bubbling away in a large saucepan. There's a Pyrex dish of mash keeping warm in the oven and garlicky bread ready to go under the grill. Under a cloche on the table there's a bowl of mixed salad. 'Sausage and mushroom casserole,' Sian says, looking at Kitty. 'Rich's speciality. No one will touch the salad. It's there for show.'

'I might. I'm starving.'

Sian shakes her head. 'No one's ever managed it yet. The lure of the carbs is too great.'

'Can I do anything?'

'Absolutely not. I can leave it for a bit now anyway.' She gives Kitty an unexpected hug. 'I'm so glad you could come.'

'It's really good to see you,' Kitty says in return. The doorbell rings again and Andrew makes a trip back to let Grace in. Grace beams when she sees Kitty and makes a big show of hugging both Rich and Lottie. Kitty feels herself relax.

They each take a glass of wine and settle in the living area, Lottie and Andrew on the sofa, Rich and Sian on the Parker Knolls, Kitty on a metal-framed white-pleather armchair and Grace perched on a footstool, ankles crossed daintily. Dante peers in sadly from the little sunroom at the back. 'Not to be trusted,' Rich says with a laugh, seeing Kitty looking. 'We'll let him in once we've eaten.'

'I'll save him a sausage.'

'He's had three already. Don't let the poor abandoned skinny stray act fool you.'

'How's school?' Andrew says to Sian. 'On the scale of one to scary.'

'Terrifying. Soul-destroying. Mind-numbing. But not as bad as it could be, actually. I have one absolute little shit in Year Ten, but the rest of them are pretty cool.'

'How big is it?' Kitty asks, and they slip into a comfortable chat about their respective work.

Kitty gives them a few from the archives. (*I arrived a*

couple minutes late because I was trying to choose between Tom Ford Ombré Leather and the Johnny Depp one for my husband, and I needed to find a shop assistant to try them both, so I could see what they would smell like on a man before I picked, but all the male ones were at lunch so I had to wait, and then they refused to let me board because the doors had already been shut.)

'She went for the Tom Ford, by the way,' she adds. 'Liked the umami undertones, apparently.'

Andrew, it turns out, has a landscaping business, hence the tan. 'Oh,' he says out of nowhere, looking at Sian. 'I can start your planting this week if that works.'

'He's doing us a huge favour,' Sian says, turning to Kitty. 'He usually does massive projects where they've ripped up a whole beautiful garden to build a McMansion and Andrew has to put it back together and make it look as if it's been growing there for a hundred years. We're just having a couple of acers and a few ornamental box hedges.'

'Will either of you be here?'

'Depends what day it is,' Sian says. 'I don't have classes on a Wednesday afternoon, so if you come then I can throw snacks your way. Otherwise, we'll have to arrange for the gate keys and stuff. I could hide them somewhere, but . . .'

'Wednesday afternoon is perfect. I'll text you about the time.'

Rich jumps up and prods at the casserole. Kitty can't help trying to pick up on any nuances between him and Lottie. Little looks or accidental contact, but so far they're behaving like two old friends with no other agenda. She imagines they must be practised at it by now; the four of them seem to spend a lot of time together.

'Where's your shop again, Lottie?' she asks, making an effort.

'Crouchie. On the Hill. You should come in sometime. I've got some stuff you'd look gorgeous in.'

'I'll bring them over,' Sian says. 'One Saturday.'

'Do you live up that way too?'

'Highgate now. Not the posh bit. We moved from Balham. When the kids were little. We wanted to be in spitting distance of places like there and Hampstead. For Andrew's business.'

'Of course,' Kitty says. 'Rich people's gardens.'

Lottie laughs. 'Exactly.'

'It was my dad's business originally,' Andrew says. 'In suburban south London. But when I took over I wanted to expand up here. Bigger opportunities, you know.'

'Ah, so you're a nepo baby,' Kitty says and then feels about ten feet tall when they all crack up.

Rich slides the tray of garlic bread under the grill. 'Ready to eat in about five?'

They all make enthusiastic noises. Sian slips a record out of its sleeve and the dulcet tones of Karen Carpenter fill the air. This is the kind of evening Kitty imagined having when she first moved to London. Cool friends and good food. Flowing chat and easy laughs. Easy listening on the stereo. There would be less of the affairs, ideally. Less of the feeling that's it's all going to implode some-day soon. 'Sit anywhere,' Sian says, plonking her glass on the table. Kitty hovers, unsure where she should put her-self, and then decides it really doesn't matter. She takes a chair on one side and busies herself filling everyone's water glass from a green glass jug. Kitty had thought she'd be intimidated being a newbie among a group of such old friends, but the conversation is light and inclusive. If one of them strays into an anecdote that means nothing to her, one of the others takes time out to explain who they're all talking about and the backstory. They're a nice bunch of people. Apart from You Know What. She mentally curses Rich and Lottie for ruining everything so spectacularly.

'You're quiet tonight,' Sian pipes up, looking at Grace. 'Are you OK?'

'Absolutely,' Grace says, flashing a big smile. 'I'm just taking it all in.' Kitty almost laughs. It's such an un-Grace-like thing to say. She can see her twitching, aching to chip in with an anecdote, but she's obviously taken Kitty's lecturing literally and is desperately trying to prove she can be trusted.

'Grace just got a promotion at work,' she says, throwing her a bone. It should be a safe enough topic.

'Really? That's brilliant. I don't think I even know what you do,' Sian says and Grace exhales like she's an over-blown-up lilo that has finally had the valve removed just before it pops. 'Patient admin in a hospital. It sounds really dull, but I actually love it.' She goes on to explain in minute detail what she does every day now compared to what her role entailed before she went up a grade. It mainly seems to involve not having to do her own filing any more. Kitty catches Sian's eye and winks.

Rich carries weighty-looking dishes of casserole and mash and waves at them all to help themselves. Lottie goes in immediately, piling her plate high and digging in with her fork without waiting for anyone else.

'This is amazing, Rich,' she gasps. She oohs and aahs

with appreciation with each mouthful in that way some people have of making eating feel like foreplay. Kitty can't work out if it's an act for Rich's benefit or if she's always like this. 'Oh god, this mash,' she purrs, heaping more onto her plate. Kitty gets irritated then. It's definitely a performance for one person's benefit only. A live sex show.

Rich watches with an indulgent smile on his face. 'Nothing better than someone appreciating your cooking.'

Kitty holds in a scowl.

'You were right about the salad.' She serves herself a handful just to make a point, trying to bring the conversation round from indulgent, sensuous carbs to cold, frigid lettuce leaves. No one is getting off watching someone else eat rocket. Lottie is not to be distracted, though. 'The casserole is to die for. So *unctuous*. Oh. My. God.' Kitty half expects her to start banging the table in a re-enactment of the famous climax scene from *When Harry Met Sally*. 'Mmmm.'

Rich reaches over and squeezes her arm. 'Thanks, Lotsie,' he laughs. 'Most appreciative customer ever.'

'Are you like this in restaurants?' Kitty asks, trying to keep the scepticism out of her voice and the frown off her face.

'Only if the food is really, really good.' Lottie slugs down a big gulp of wine. 'And this is really, really good.'

'Have some more,' Rich says, spoon hovering over the casserole. Kitty looks away. She feels as if she's intruding on something. Grace catches her eye, nostrils flared, like a bull about to attack. Kitty risks a frown that she hopes says *Aren't they gross?*

Now Kitty is attuned to it, she keeps seeing Rich and Lottie exchange little looks. When Lottie asks whether the four of them need to talk about who is taking what on the holiday to Santorini they have planned in August (to Kitty: we used to go away together every year for a while, but things got complicated when the kids got old enough to have an opinion. We thought we'd give it one last hurrah before Harry goes off to uni and we're all empty nesters crying into our wine) and she spirals off into a story about the time they stayed in an Airbnb in Portofino, and they had no towels because none of them had read the fine print. When Rich tells her about the time they all stayed overnight at the Natural History Museum in New York and Rhys, Harry and Archie wandered into an off-limits area and triggered all the alarms, Kitty wonders if these memories hold special secret meanings for Rich and Lottie. Stolen moments. Snatched kisses. How long has it been going on?

Andrew leans back in his chair with a wry smile on his face, arms crossed in front of him, a hand on each shoulder. Kitty accidentally catches his eye while she's watching for his reaction, and then she has to pantomime looking at each of them in turn as if she was just casually observing.

'We have pudding,' Rich announces once they're all stuffed with casserole. They each protest and then accept a slice of Key lime pie. Lottie practically creams herself when she takes a mouthful. (*Oh, Rich! Oh my god! You've excelled yourself. Oh god! Oh!*) Kitty's eyes almost pop out of her head with the effort she has to exert to stop herself from rolling them at Grace. The other three all look at Lottie adoringly. It seems to Kitty that there's always one person in any friendship group who is like the indulged baby. They're granted puppy rights: aren't they cute? Isn't everything they do adorable? Usually, in her cynical opinion, they are fully aware of this fact, and they play up to it. Lottie is one hundred per cent in that camp, she thinks. She swallows down her irritation with her (delicious) pie.

Food over, they all help pile up the dishes and Rich clanks plates into the dishwasher while the rest of them settle back on the comfy chairs nursing amarettos. Lottie and Andrew sit on the sofa, she with her tiny pink-toenailed feet tucked up under her. Iron & Wine has replaced Karen Carpenter. Kitty drifts off for a moment and, when she tunes back in, the conversation has somehow come round to WhatsApp groups and whether there is one for the street. Kitty fumbles a bit. Shit, she really should have talked to Shirley Howard Martin about Magda. She shoots a glance at Grace, who at least has the decency to look mortified.

'I almost never go on there,' Kitty says. 'It's just people moaning.'

'I need to drum up some more private tuition,' Sian says. This is clearly why the topic came up. 'Because my part-time state-school teaching job pays about as well as you might imagine. I had six regulars in Balham, but none of them want to schlep up here, and only one fancies Zoom.'

'Nextdoor might be better. It covers a wider area. I'm not sure how many kids in your age range there are just in this bit.'

Sian stretches her arms above her head, revealing a

ghostly pale snapshot of stomach. 'I could teach any age, though. They don't have to be studying it already. But you're probably right.'

'Yeah,' Kitty says, seizing on that. 'It would definitely get to more people.'

Lottie's eyes are starting to close. 'I'm so sleepy,' she says in a baby voice, followed by a big yawn.

Rich laughs. 'She always does this,' he says to Kitty. 'She'll be flat out in a minute.'

'So not true,' Lottie says, rubbing her eyes. A streak of inky black liner edges down her cheek. 'Actual slander.'

'Wait. Let me show you that jacket before you conk out,' Rich says. 'I saw it in the window of an Oxfam shop,' he says to Kitty and Grace. 'I think it might be quite old, but I thought Lotts might know.'

Lottie unfurls herself slowly. 'Oh yes, show me now while I still have my critical faculties.'

Kitty looks from one to the other. Are they really going to do this? In plain sight? She watches them leave the room. She wants to say *Just bring it down. Surely Lottie can look at it in here.* She looks over at Sian to see if she's even noticed, but she's chatting away to Andrew and Grace and, beyond a cursory glance, barely even seems to notice them go.

'I need the loo,' Grace announces, standing up. Kitty looks at her, panicked, but it's quite possible Grace really does need to pee. She should probably trust her. Still, it's an agonising wait for her to come back. She distracts herself by asking Andrew more about his business. She's always thought gardening seemed like a wholesome, stress-free way to make a living if only she knew one plant from another and wasn't constitutionally unsuited to any weather that wasn't mild and sunny.

Grace comes back in first, just as Andrew is telling Kitty and Sian a story about a client who kept changing their mind about the position of a large new magnolia and made him move it so many times it gave up and died, and who is now refusing to pay for it. Kitty whips round to look at her and Grace gives her a hard stare, eyebrows shooting up under her fringe, that definitely means *I have news*. Shit.

Rich and Lottie are only seconds behind, all smiles.

'Nineteen forties,' Lottie says. 'Bespoke for someone.'

'Lotts thinks she can move the buttons and shorten the sleeves without ruining the lining. It must have been made for an orang-utan.'

'Long arms,' Lottie adds as if they might not have understood. 'Easy to fix.'

'Fab,' Sian says. 'You can wear it to Dido and Edmund's wedding. Are you coming to that?' she says, looking at both Lottie and Andrew.

Lottie shakes her head. 'Not invited.'

'Thank god,' Andrew says.

Sian snorts. 'I'm sure it'll be fun. It's at a big old pub near Cambridge. If nothing else, the countryside'll be pretty.'

Kitty can hardly concentrate for wondering what Grace is about to tell her. Rich and Lottie look happy, so whatever she did, it went undetected. That's something at least.

'Do you remember that time we got locked in that pub, Lotts?' Rich turns to Kitty. 'These two had gone outside but Lottie and I both needed the loo and when we came out someone had locked the door through into the bar because it was closing time and they didn't want anyone sneaking in the back way.' He chuckles. 'We were both hammering on it with our fists, but they'd put really loud music on while they were cleaning and no one could hear us.'

'There was no phone reception because we were in the middle of nowhere,' Lottie laughs. 'In the end Sian and Andrew got worried and came back in looking for us. The staff were very apologetic.'

Kitty fakes a laugh along with her. 'How long were you locked in for?'

'Oh, god knows,' Lottie says wide-eyed. 'I thought we'd still be there next morning. I was looking around for where we might sleep.'

Kitty sees Andrew flick a look at Sian. And then it hits her.

Andrew suspects.

13

It makes her feel a bit better. Not for Andrew, obviously. He must feel wretched. But the fact that Rich and Lottie aren't fooling everyone. That the responsibility for whether or not Sian finds out no longer lies solely on Kitty's shoulders. Her's and Grace's. Because Kitty is still sure that Sian has no idea. Sian adores Rich. She adores them both, him and Lottie. But at least Andrew can be the one to decide when the right time is to tell her. He knows her a thousand times better than Kitty does. She wonders, briefly, whether she should let him know that she knows, so that he can have someone to offload on if he needs to, but she's only met him twice; it would feel like too great an imposition.

As she and Grace say goodnight, leaving the four of them to it at half eleven – stumbling slightly as she stands up from one too many digestifs – Sian follows her to the front door and asks Kitty if she fancies going to lunch in the Hertfordshire countryside with her, Rich and Dante on Sunday. Kitty is tempted for a moment, but she knows she can't spend any more time with the two of them. Not together. So, she makes up an excuse about seeing her parents and promises to text Sian after the weekend. Maybe they can go somewhere just the two of them. Somewhere distracting like the cinema or the theatre so there's not too much time to talk. Kitty doesn't trust herself. But maybe if Andrew has worked it out, it'll all blow up soon and she can, at least, be there to help Sian pick up the pieces.

Grace grabs her arm. 'Can I come in and get that book you borrowed before my Uber gets here?'

'Of course,' Kitty says. She practically pulls Grace towards her house, waving a hand at Sian.

'What's up?' she hisses as soon as the front door shuts behind them.

Grace leans against the wall. 'OK, so I didn't follow them deliberately. Well, I did a bit, but I really did need to go to the bathroom. And I may or may not have gone to the one upstairs just in case I stumbled across anything, but anyway . . .'

'What? Jesus, Gracie, just tell me.'

'It's all true. I saw them . . .' She pauses for effect. Kitty has to stop herself from screaming at her to spit it out. 'I crept up there so they wouldn't hear me coming. Just in case, you know? And they were in one of the bedrooms with the door slightly open . . .'

'Honestly, I love you, but you are really doing my head in right now . . .'

'Snogging,' Grace says quickly. 'They were snogging.'

'Are you sure? I mean, one hundred per cent.'

Grace nods. 'One hundred per cent. I wish I'd taken my phone up now. I could have got a picture.'

'Shit.'

'So, we have to tell her. Well, you do probably. We can't not, Kit.'

'Oh god,' Kitty says, putting her head in her hands. 'Why did you have to go up there?'

'Me going up there isn't the point. They were still

doing it whether I saw them or not. And Sian needs to know what her husband is like. And Andrew deserves the truth too.'

'I think he might know something's up.'

'Wait. What? When did this happen?'

Kitty wanders into the kitchen and opens the fridge. They might as well have another glass of wine. She's pretty sure Grace hasn't actually ordered her Uber yet. 'When they were telling that story about being stuck in a pub together. I don't know, there was something about the way he looked at them.'

'Poor bloke.' Grace pulls two glasses from a cupboard.

'I thought maybe I could keep out of it now. He'll say something to Sian and then . . .'

'Or maybe he's waiting to know for definite. Maybe we could help now we have actual proof.'

Kitty sighs. 'I barely know him. I need to sleep on it.'

'We can't pretend we don't know now, that's all I'm saying.'

On Wednesday, when Kitty gets home from work clutching a no-longer-frozen M&S lasagne that's been dripping all over her legs since Euston Road, leaving a damp puddle on the floor of the 134, there's a pale grey van parked on Sian and Rich's drive, with HART LANDSCAPING written in green along the side. From her upstairs window she sees Andrew manoeuvring a skinny hedging plant into position next to a line-up of lookalikes on the inside of next door's fence. She heads down to the garden before she can talk herself out of it and shouts hello across the low gate. Despite Grace's insistence, she has no intention of saying anything to him about Lottie and Rich. But she might be able to sound out if he truly does have any inkling. If she can dare to hope he might do the dirty work for her by letting Sian know. She likes him, but it's Sian she cares about. He jumps, then laughs, embarrassed.

'Jesus. You nearly killed me.'

'I am so sorry. I saw you out here and thought you might fancy a coffee while I'm making myself one. But maybe caffeine would tip you over the edge, heart wise.'

He leans on his fork in a classic gardener calendar pose. 'I'm already wired. Sian's been drip-feeding me hot drinks.'

'It's looking good. Will that all grow together and form a solid hedge? I know nothing about gardening, obviously.'

'That's the idea. I mean, it'll take a while.'

'I should do mine,' Kitty says, looking around at her sad garden. It's mostly dirt, no grass, with deep borders that should provide the greenery but actually look a bit empty and, even at this time of year, half dead. Sam and Linz replaced the middle section of their fence a few months ago, after the old, rickety one finally crumbled under a relentless assault from their son Kyle's football, and it glows a neon orange never seen in nature. 'It'll weather down eventually,' Sam had said to Kitty as they wrestled it up, but there's no sign of that yet.

'Really?' he says with a wry smile. 'I thought maybe radioactive was a new gardening trend I'd missed.'

'Ha!' Kitty snorts. 'I think I always thought that planting things that wouldn't look their best for a few years would be like accepting that I'd still be living here when they did.'

'How long ago did you move in?'

She grimaces. 'Four years. I know what you're going to say.'

He holds his hands up. 'Far be it from me to point out how beautiful it could be looking by now. You don't like it here, then?'

'It's not that. I mean, it's OK. It's just not my dream home, you know?'

'I'm not sure any of us are living in those. It's nice round here, though.'

She flaps away a honey bee. 'Definitely better since Sian moved in. How's Lottie by the way?'

He smiles what looks to her like a genuine smile. 'Good. Busy.'

'That was nice the other night . . .'

'It was. You know, I often have leftover plants that I don't know what to do with. I'd be happy to let you have some if you don't mind taking pot luck on what they are.' OK, so he's not biting. He's hardly going to confide in her, though, he barely knows her.

'Oh. Wow. That's really nice. I would only kill them within days, though.'

'Not if they're planted up properly and you water them occasionally. I don't mind bedding the odd thing in myself if I'm around.'

'No. God. I couldn't ask you to do that . . .'

'I mean, it would have to be a bit piecemeal, but if you don't mind me climbing over your garden gate occasionally, when I have something . . . it just might make it a bit more cheerful, and I can use it as an excuse to get out of the washing-up if we're hanging out next door.'

Kitty laughs. 'OK, well, put it this way, I won't stop you. It really is unnecessarily kind of you.'

'I'm sure one of the others would help.' He massages a hand into the back of his neck.

Kitty panics suddenly that she's become the local charity case. 'If I'm home I'll muck in, obviously. I don't want to put anyone out.'

'You'd be doing me a favour,' he says, which makes no sense to her. An image flashes up in her head of him and Lottie crowded out of their own home by plants that Andrew can't get rid of. Little Shop of Horrors with privet. She wonders briefly if their home is a shrine to the 1940s. A perfectly curated style museum of Lottie's making. It's odd, she thinks, that Lottie and Andrew seem to be living in different centuries.

'What do you usually do with the leftovers?'

He pulls an apologetic face. 'I quite like a bit of guerrilla gardening . . .'

'No! Tell me! Where?'

'Anywhere that looks a bit unloved, really. I've stuck a few perennials round an estate at the end of our road, and there's a kids' playground . . .'

'No way. I love this. OK. I can't believe this wasn't the first thing you told me about yourself. "I'm some kind of gardening superhero."'

His tan deepens as he blushes. 'I don't get to do it as much as I'd like. I did put some herbs in the planters outside the hospital the other week. I don't know if anyone will work out what they are and use them, but they smell nice. Oh, and a couple of little apple trees in a grass verge up near the station. I have a bit of a thing about thinking councils should plant things people can pick and eat for free, but they never do.'

'Oh, my god. This is absolutely brilliant. Now I'm thinking I'd be taking freebies away from people who need them much more than me.'

He rolls his eyes. 'At least I can do yours in daylight. I won't have to be creeping around after dark.'

'Why has Sian never told me about this?'

'I . . . I mean, they know I've done it a couple of times, but not quite the extent of it. I've got a bit obsessed if I'm being honest. Maybe don't . . .'

'I won't bring it up,' Kitty says. 'But I would like to say I think it's fantastic and commendable, and all those things.'

'Middle-class guilt,' he says. 'You could be forgiven for thinking I'm doing it to make myself, rather than other people, feel better.'

'Even if you are, you've brightened up someone's environment. That's more than I ever do.'

He shrugs. 'Anyway. It really is no big deal. If there's any time you'd rather not find a semi-stranger poking around in your back garden, let me know. My mobile's on the company website, you can just send me a text.'

She finds herself slightly blown away by both the offer and what she's discovered about him. Lottie's crime hovers at the edges of her brain and she has to bite her tongue. 'Well, I should leave you to it.'

'Unless you want to help. I'm absolutely up for some exploitative free labour.'

'I can if you want. I mean, it's not as if I've already done a full day's work or anything.'

He chuckles. His laugh lines crinkle. 'Any good ones today?'

The answer is no. Nothing even slightly amusing. But he doesn't have to know that. She dredges around in her brain and comes up with something from the day before yesterday. *'One of the gentleman air hostesses had a very loud laugh, which ruined my enjoyment of the film I was watching on my laptop.'*

'They actually said "gentleman air hostesses"?'

'Hundred per cent. The film was *Cats*, apparently, and, you know, it'd take a lot to ruin that.'

He snorts. Kitty hears a window open and looks round to see Sian leaning out of the top floor. 'Kitty Harbinson, get round here for a glass of wine right now. We can sit in the garden and heckle Andrew.'

Andrew stretches. 'Sorry to spoil your fun, but I'll be knocking off in a minute.'

Kitty is just thinking she might accept when Sian says, 'Oh good. Rich is on his way home. Five minutes, he says. Can you both stay?'

'I've got a Zoom yoga class,' Kitty interrupts, looking at her phone as if to check at what time that could possibly be. 'At half five. Shit, I'd better go.'

'Come over later if we're still out there,' Sian calls. Kitty gives her a thumbs up, thinking, *No chance.*

'And I need to get going . . .' Andrew says as she starts to walk away. Is he avoiding Rich too? She can't tell. Reading people is clearly not in her skill set. She bats away a thought about how disappointed Grace is going to be with her lack of progress. Grace probably would have come straight out with a question like 'So, are Lottie and Rich close?', or 'Do you trust your wife with your best friend?', but Kitty can't just crowbar herself into their lives like that, consequences be damned. It's just not her.

'Good to see you, Kitty,' he calls after her. 'Don't be surprised if you find a rogue hydrangea in your garden sometime soon.'

Grace has a date. Whereas Kitty gave up all attempts to meet someone after one too many disastrous experiences, Grace has speed-dated, blind-dated, blindfold-dated, silent-dated (that one nearly killed her and she eventually got thrown out for breaking the rules) and even pheromone-dated (where you sniff people's smelly old T-shirts and then decide which fragrant potentials you'd like to meet), and now, MAFS inspired, she's signed up with an old-fashioned matchmaker. Thursday-night drinks are cancelled because tonight is her first introduction. Julian (Poor Julian, as he is already known to Kitty in her head) is a divorced father of two, according to his very brief profile. Kitty can hear Grace's biological clock ticking Captain Hook-like as Grace tells her. She's forty-one, but she can't let go of her dream and it's not up to Kitty to remind her of the statistics. The truth is Grace would be a great mum. It breaks Kitty's heart, really. Still, maybe Julian and his two could fill that void. Or maybe he has to wrestle them from the arms of his ex every third Friday and deliver them back by four on the dot on the Sunday afternoon and doesn't get to play any other part in their lives except through lawyers.

'What does he do again?' Kitty asked when Grace told her they had found her a victim.

'No idea. They match you on more sort of esoteric things, apparently. Values and morals, stuff like that.'

'Who's going to sign up and then tell them they have terrible morals and questionable values?' Kitty had scoffed.

'You fill out endless psychological profiles. It's a science.'

'Definitely not a science. It's like those quizzes in magazines where you know which answer you have to choose to get the result you want, whether it's true or not. No one ever ticks the extremes. You always choose b or c.'

'I have to try, Kitty,' Grace had said, and Kitty had felt bad that she couldn't just keep her mouth shut. Grace would find out for herself soon enough if he was a good match or not.

'Stranger things have happened,' she said, softening her approach a bit. 'I'll keep everything crossed.'

'We have to commit to three dates, whatever we think. That way we give each other a chance.' Kitty must have accidentally let out a snort because Grace had snapped her head around.

'What? What if he has halitosis? Or slurps when he eats? Or he says something awful to you?'

'Three dates. That's the deal. I think it makes sense.'

'And what if you don't?'

'Two strikes and you're out. They won't match you with anyone else.'

'Where are you meeting him?

'At the Corinthia. The bar. His choice. Which is good. Classy. Then I choose the next one and we agree on the third.'

'And you know what he looks like?'

'No. Their ethos is that you shouldn't be put off by the cover. You need to actually get to know the person.'

'Jesus,' Kitty had said. 'It gets worse.'

'Same for him as for me,' Grace had responded, which, Kitty supposed, was true.

'Yeah, but you're gorgeous. He won't believe his luck. How will you know it's him?'

'Because he'll be sitting at the table he's booked in his name. It's hardly rocket science.'

'OK.' Kitty had exhaled loudly. 'Well, text me when you get home so I know you're safe.'

Now she sends Grace a message from the dank chill of the bus. It's a beautiful day, but icy cold out. A ten-degree drop in temperature that has catapulted the world back to winter, the daffodils shivering with frost on the grass verges. *Have fun tonight!* She feels weirdly envious. Not of the date. She has no interest in dating anyone. But of the different experience. The new restaurant. A reason to dress up.

Ten minutes after she gets in, she sees Sian return home on her own in the car. Impulsively Kitty sends her a text. *Fancy a coffee?*

She combs her hair and puts on some lip gloss while she waits. She hasn't seen Sian for a few days. Not since they briefly crossed paths in the garden. Kitty's guessing nothing's changed, that Andrew has kept any suspicions he might have to himself. But, who knows.

Absolutely! If we can combine it with walking Dant. He's desperate!

Perfect. The café in the park. Meet you outside in 5? She

doesn't want to give Rich a chance to return and want to join them. Their friendship has to be strictly the two of them now. No Rich. No Lottie. Kitty can keep what she knows to herself so long as she doesn't have to spend time with either of them. Let it all play out courtesy of Andrew (hopefully). Be there to mop up the pieces.

She steps out and has to go straight back inside to find her gloves.

'What's going on?' she says as she sees Sian, swaddled up like a baby in a variety of brightly coloured shawls and scarves encasing the whole of her upper body. Dante is smart in a fleecy coat.

'Fuck's sake,' Sian says. 'Every fucking year. Why don't we learn?'

'It's lovely though,' Kitty says, hugging her. And it is. Sunny. Crisp. White tips shimmering on the grass. They walk towards the park, Dante pulling at his lead like a demented sled dog. 'How's things?'

'Good. That was fun the other night, wasn't it?'

'Fab. Thank you. Oh. While I remember . . . I have a spare ticket to Sufjan Stevens at the Royal Festival Hall in a couple of weeks. The friend I was meant to be going with can't make it any more. You don't fancy it, do you?'

This is all a lie, obviously. Kitty had never even heard of Sufjan Stevens until she was rifling through Rich and Sian's vinyl collection at the dinner and spotted several albums and then sought them out on Spotify. But it's the kind of gig she has always imagined herself going to in her cool London life with her cool London friends, except that up till now she would have had to go on her own because Grace refuses to see anyone who smacks of indie. She likes the pop classics and she likes to see them murdered by middle-aged beer-bellied ex-boy banders. Her taste in theatre only extends as far left field as *Hamilton* (which Kitty adored, but it's hardly subversive). Trying to get Grace to go to *The Book of Mormon* would be, Kitty imagines, like it must have been trying to persuade your granny to see *Hair* in the 1960s. In the early days Kitty gamely did solo theatre trips, but it made her feel too sad, too desperate. Isn't half the point of those things sharing the experience? But she's been listening to Sufjan on repeat for the past few days like a panicked pre-teen trying to keep up with the hip kids. Truthfully, she actually doesn't have the tickets yet, but she did browse the site a couple of days ago and there were a few left.

'Are you kidding? We love him . . .'

Kitty grimaces. 'I only have one spare, sorry . . .' No way was she going to risk Rich ruining the evening.

'Did Grace not want to go?'

Kitty pulls the tiniest of faces. 'I didn't tell her about it. I love her to bits, but she can be a tiny bit clingy sometimes. I knew it wouldn't be her thing at all, but she'd have said yes anyway if I'd asked. Is that awful?'

'Not at all. Anyway, I'm in. Rich can babysit Dante. What night is it?'

Kitty fills her in with the details, feeling a warm glow in her chest.

'What's he up to today?'

'Five a side. Him and Andrew and a load of other dads all having a mid-life crisis together.'

That sounds about right, Kitty thinks. 'Andrew seems like a nice bloke.'

Sian pulls one of the scarves up over her nose, which has turned pink. 'He's lovely. Really, like a properly good person.'

'He said he might let me have some plants for my garden.'

'Oh, he's great like that. Definitely take him up on it. Let me know when he's coming in case I'm around.'

'I will.' Kitty changes the subject. Tells Sian about Grace and Poor Julian.

'Maybe that's the way to do it,' Sian says as they reach the gates to the park. Dante thrashes around like he's possessed until she unclips his lead. 'If you want longevity, I mean. Take all the passion out of it, because that's going to die off anyway eventually and it'll be what's left that matters.'

'Is it that inevitable, do you think? God, that's sad.'

'It's not, though. It's the other stuff that's real. I don't mean there's no . . . you know . . . but you can't sustain that high-octane first flush forever.'

Kitty thinks about her own relationship with Geth and how they went from wanting to rip each other's clothes off twenty-four hours a day to barely noticing if the other one undressed in front of them at breakneck speed. Almost overnight. Maybe it should have felt comfortable, but it didn't. Maybe that's how you know you're all wrong for each other. The mundane feels just that. Mundane. 'Yeah. You might be right. Let's hope Rich feels the same?' She tries to make it sound like a light, throwaway comment, giving a wry eyebrow raise that she hopes says she's joking. Does she imagine the slight hesitation in Sian's response, though? Does her laugh sound forced?

'Yes, let's hope so. I'd be fascinated to see the criteria they base it on. Grace's thing,' Sian says, leaning down to pick up a stick and throwing it.

'I know. Like if you say to them being funny is important to you, how do they define that? You could end up with someone who just makes dad jokes all the time.'

'It's all percentages, I assume. They probably have an algorithm that pairs people up on the number of answers in common. Did she have an interview?'

'Two. So, I think they're thorough. They should be. It's costing her a fortune.'

'I hope she finds someone lovely. She deserves it.'

'She does,' Kitty says, feeling bad for the way she sometimes is with Grace. 'I mean, she drives me insane, but she has a heart of gold.'

Sian waves her right arm to indicate they should take the path towards the café. Kitty tells her about Grace and Hal and the way he deceived her. Sian listens, eyes growing wider. 'Jesus Christ, some people are shits. Fuck.'

'She can't get over the fact that one of her friends knew – not about the vasectomy, the other stuff – and didn't tell her. I can't decide what I think about that.' *Shut up, Kitty*, a voice inside her says, but apparently not loudly enough. 'I mean, what would you do?'

Sian doesn't hesitate. 'You'd have to say something, wouldn't you? If it was your friend. I mean, they might just shoot the messenger, but what choice do you have? I'm on Grace's side on this one.'

'Really? What if you weren't sure? If you thought you'd seen something, but you might not have done? Like something that could be completely innocuous.'

'Still yes. Girl code. All that shit. Speak first and work out the details later.'

'However small?'

Sian nods exaggeratedly. 'However small.'

Kitty sees Julie and Pete up in the distance coming their way. Sian must do too, because she raises a hand to greet them. Kitty knows she can't miss her moment. If she doesn't step up now, Sian will never forgive her if – when – she finds out about Lottie and Rich, and that Kitty knew all along. She stops Sian's hand in its tracks. Julie and Pete are still oblivious.

'Sian . . . come over here a sec . . .' She leads her off the path. She can't risk starting this and then being interrupted. Sian gives her a small frown but follows her anyway. They sit on a bench out of sight of the path, Kitty wishing she'd waited till after they'd got coffees, so she'd have something to do with her hands. The dog runs circles around them, panting foggy clouds.

Kitty breathes in slowly, trying to slow her heart. She attempts to form the first sentence in her head. She has to do this properly; she can't just blurt it out. She breathes in slowly to steady herself. And then Sian does something she wasn't anticipating. Something that changes everything. She looks Kitty straight in the eye, with such an intensity that Kitty can't look away.

'Kitty,' she says quietly. 'It's OK. I know.'

14

Kitty is momentarily stunned into silence. Sian knows? She reaches for something to say. Finds nothing. So, she reaches for Sian's hand instead.

'How?' she stutters.

Sian gulps and then momentarily shuts her eyes. 'I found something on his phone. The other day. A message from Lottie. I mean, I suspected . . .'

'I'm so sorry.' Kitty exhales noisily. 'Are you sure?'

'It was pretty conclusive. Explicit. He's deleted it now and there haven't been any others since that I know of. It's hard to look.'

Kitty is desperate to ask what it said, but she doesn't want to seem as if she's just looking for the gossip. 'Shit. That's so awful.'

Sian dabs a finger lightly under her eyes. Sniffs. 'You knew, though?'

Kitty screws up her face. 'Not really. Not definitely. That's why I was so . . . I saw Lottie sneaking out of your back garden the day you came home from work early with all those bits of furniture in the car. And then, I don't know, I've just been watching how they are. And then Grace saw something at your party. Them together . . .'

Sian frowns. 'She . . .?'

Kitty reaches out a hand and puts it on hers. 'But it's not like I had any evidence. Anything I could show you.'

She remembers something. 'Well, I took a photo of her getting into her car just in case she turned out to be a burglar, but it was hardly damning. I only realised who she was later, obviously. And then, well, I didn't know what to say.'

'It's OK. It's good to finally have someone to talk to about it. Shit, you had to listen to me bang on about how he's the perfect husband. You must have thought I was so stupid.'

She starts crying properly now and Kitty's heart feels as if it's going to break. 'Of course I didn't. I just can't believe they'd do that.'

'Me neither,' Sian says with a grim smile.

'Does Andrew know? I wondered.'

Sian rubs at her eyes. 'Kind of. I told him I had suspicions. I had to tread carefully, because I knew he wouldn't want to hear it, and, to be honest, he doesn't really believe it.'

'He doesn't want to.'

'Exactly. I mean, neither do I. It feels surreal. Like a dream. A nightmare, obviously. Tell me what Grace saw. I need to know everything.'

So, Kitty tells her exactly what Grace said. She can't look at Sian as she says it, can't bear to be the confirmer of bad news. When she gets to the end, Sian nods. 'OK' is all she says.

A little brindle Staffy runs over, tail wagging, and Kitty absent-mindedly reaches down and strokes its head. Dante looks affronted and clambers up on the bench and onto Sian's lap.

'She's my best fucking friend. And she has it so easy

pottering around in that stupid little shop that has about three customers a year. Sorry, that sounds really bitchy.'

'I think you're entitled to bitch about her a bit at this point . . .'

'She just doesn't need to steal my life, that's all. She has an enviable one of her own.'

'Have you said anything to Rich yet?'

Sian shakes her head. 'Once I say anything, that's it. There'll be no going back.'

'What? You're not going to just let them get away with it?'

'OK. The real truth is I didn't get a chance because we were at his mum and dad's, and then the next time I looked the message had gone. If I say anything now, he'll deny, deny, deny, and then what?'

'You don't think he'd come clean?'

'That's not what he's like, Kitty. I love him, but sometimes he can be a bit . . . you don't know what he's like. He'd just tell me I was imagining things, make me feel stupid and irrational for even thinking it . . .'

She tails off. Kitty tries to imagine Rich – easy-going, seemingly devoted Rich – manipulating Sian's emotions like that, and she feels a surge of fury on her friend's behalf.

'I'll back you up . . .'

'No!' Kitty jumps as Sian cuts her off. 'Don't say anything. Please. Let me handle it my way. I just need to wait until I find concrete proof to show Andrew. And then me and him can confront them together.'

'Of course. It's not as if you won't find something if Rich has no idea you're on to him.'

'Will you help me?' Sian suddenly looks about twelve years old with her eyeliner smudged with tears and her sleeves pulled down over her hands mopping them up.

Kitty doesn't even hesitate. 'Absolutely.'

And then she thinks: *Grace is going to love this*.

15

Forest Streets Residents' WhatsApp Group:

Mrs B Martin: Would the person who failed to clean up after their dog outside number 11 Ashdown Close kindly return to deal with it.

'Not my type.'

They're heading for lunch in the airy café at the back of the Wallace Collection, rain hammering on the glass roof. They've whizzed round the Canalettos, Landseers and Rembrandts for culture's sake while Grace told Kitty about her date. Kitty is saving telling her about Sian and Rich until they've ordered.

'Start from the beginning. Every detail,' she had said as they stood in front of *The Laughing Cavalier* admiring his moustache. This was obviously music to Grace's ears, and after the first two minutes or so Kitty had had to interrupt and tell her that she actually didn't need to know what make of car Grace's Uber was, or the reason she chose to wear her grey jacket rather than the blue (a more neutral colour, in case anyone is interested. No political connotations). 'Was he there when you arrived?'

'Yes. And I was early, so that was a point for him. But I knew as soon as I saw him: no. I mean, nothing wrong with him, but I wouldn't have looked at him twice if I met him at a party.'

'Isn't that the whole point of this thing, though?' Kitty had managed to say before Grace started off again.

'He's blond and I've never fancied a blond in my life. Big. Too tall. Drippy-looking. Like if you made a totem pole of Prince Edward.'

Kitty snorted. A woman admiring a Rubens shot her a filthy look.

'Terrible suit that didn't fit him properly. Limp handshake. I don't want to sound horrible, but I actually thought about walking straight out. But they do have a brilliant track record, so there's obviously a reason they put us together. (*They couldn't find anyone else on their books*, Kitty thought. *Or they found a perfect match but he's in the middle of three pointless dates with someone else.*) So, anyway, he was perfectly nice. Polite. He's a chartered surveyor. Lives in Kingston. Divorced from Petra. Two grown-up kids. Fifty-two. Likes playing golf. Just a bog-standard man really. Dull. Stiff.' She ran out of steam, deflated.

'As opposed to?'

Grace sniffed. 'Someone I might fall for.'

'I bet you asked for trustworthy and kind and reliable . . .' Kitty said.

Grace shrugged. 'I suppose. I'm going to ask them why they matched us.'

'I'm pretty sure everyone does that after the first meet-up.'

'*He* won't. He liked me, I could tell.'

Ah, the old Grace bravado was back. Kitty raised an eyebrow. 'What's not to like? So where are you taking him on the next date?'

'I don't know. I don't care. I really thought this would be different.'

'It still might be. Take him somewhere where he has to loosen up a bit. Give him a chance. Remember why you're doing this.'

Grace huffed. 'Somewhere we don't have to talk and I don't have to look at him.'

'That's my girl,' Kitty said. 'Give it all you've got.'

'What's up with you anyway?'

Kitty grabbed her arm. 'Let's go and get lunch. I need all your concentration for this.'

Grace's first reaction when Kitty told her that Sian knew about Rich and Lottie was relief. Once you had all the info, once you could accept what was happening to you, you could start to take back control of your life. She totally understood Sian's desperate need to find proof and to bring the whole thing to a head, to be the person in control for once. And, ever since her own marriage had imploded so drastically, Grace had promised herself that she would never not go to the aid of any woman trying to expose a cheating partner. She felt almost evangelical about it. She would never behave like her so-called friends had behaved.

She'd known there was something wrong between her and Hal for a while, of course she had, but she'd put it down to the stress of trying to get pregnant. She'd thought that he was as devastated as she was by the time it was taking, by watching her crumble every month when she realised it hadn't happened yet. He'd started going out for a drink after work more, something she couldn't begrudge him. He had moved to a different hospital, and he was trying to bond with his new colleagues, that was all. All marriages went through tricky patches. Grace knew that. Hal was just letting off steam. But she'd mourned the loss of her charming, gregarious partner. She hadn't realised that he hadn't really changed at all; he'd just changed around her. Outgoing, charisma-oozing Hal still existed, just not at home. Still, she'd tried to engage him, saving up funny anecdotes to tell him later. Manufacturing one if nothing much of note had happened. Practically begging him not to fall out of love with her.

It still hadn't even occurred to her that he might be cheating. That was one of the things that most irked her still when she thought about him. Her blind faith. The way that she'd enabled his behaviour by believing everything he'd told her without questioning it.

So, she didn't hesitate for a second when Kitty told her that Sian needed their help.

A week later they meet at the clock tower on The Broadway in Crouch End. Ten a.m. on the dot. The first properly hot Saturday of the year. People are actually smiling. Sunglasses are out. Grace is like an excitable puppy on its debut walk, bouncing around, tail wagging. 'Gritty!' she says the moment she sees Kitty. Kitty waits for an explanation. 'That's the name of our detective agency. Grace and Kitty. Get it?' Grace has always had an ambition to work as a private investigator, mainly because of her love of Hetty Wainthropp peering round garden hedges with a suspicious look on her face when she was growing up. For some reason she has the idea she would be a natural, despite the fact that Kitty has pointed out her complete lack of ability to stay quiet for more than a few seconds at a time.

'Brilliant,' Kitty says now, drily. 'Can I be the surly troubled one?'

'Only if you have a heart of gold buried deep underneath,' Grace says. 'Which I believe you do.'

Kitty scoffs. 'Don't hold your breath.'

Grace ignores that. 'If I distract her by picking out stuff, you can sneak out the back and have a nose round.'

The cover story is this: Grace has her second date with Julian tonight and she's feeling in a rut, clothes-wise. She's hoping Lottie's shop might give her the inspiration she needs to jolt herself out of her comfort zone. Grace's dress sense is conservative, to say the least. Neat separates. Matching bag and shoes. Matching finger- and toenails. Nude tights. No loud prints. Blue and green should never be seen. She and Kitty once had a conversation about what they would wear to the Palace if they ever got given an OBE and Grace had basically told Kitty that if she didn't wear a hat, according to convention, then Kitty was a horrible, disrespectful person and would probably be ejected, and quite rightly so. 'Dress codes exist for a reason,' she'd said, and Kitty had said, 'What reason? Why does Charles get to have a say in what I wear? I'm not sending him a note saying don't wear that jacket with the gold epaulettes, it looks ridiculous.' So, the idea of Grace suddenly wanting to rock a vintage look is laughable, but they're hoping Lottie won't question it.

'I thought you were doing the snooping? You'll be the

one out the back for hours trying stuff on . . .' Kitty says defensively.

Sian has told Kitty that the changing area is basically a cubicle off the little room at the rear. The room where Lottie leaves her bag all day, and probably her phone, although there's no chance Kitty and Grace will be able to get into that without the password.

'My way works better. She won't be suspicious of you. She might wonder what I'm up to back there if I take too long. Just offer to make us all a coffee and have a quick nose round.'

'Grace, no.' They walk the rest of the way in a huffy silence, Grace's shiny black court shoes clicking on the pavement reproachfully.

Kitty is the first to break it. She can't bear an atmosphere. Memories of Geth gazing at her judgementally as she packed her bags, the air heavy with his disapproval. Her crumpling under the weight of his disappointment rather than because she was sad to leave. Him taking her tears as a sign she had regrets.

'You're hopeless at being on your own,' he'd said somewhat desperately. Gethin wasn't a bad person, he had never been cruel – compared to Hal he seemed like an actual saint – but he had been a douser of bonfires. His response to her telling him she was trying something new was always a negative one – he didn't think she'd enjoy it/ be good at it/be safe. He couldn't help himself. She knew now that it had been born of his own insecurities. His fear that she'd outgrow him and their relationship. And, ironically, it had turned out he'd been right to worry, although she never could have imagined that at the time.

'What are you expecting me to find?' she asks Grace now in a hoarse whisper as they arrive at Memory Lane Vintage Clothing. 'Pants with the word "Rich" sewn into them?'

Grace ignores her. A bell tinkles as she pushes open the door.

The shop is tiny, with that faint smell that follows old clothes around. Racks bulge with a rainbow of colours, dresses on one side, everything else jostling for space on the other. Further in there's a display of VINTAGE INSPIRED! items that must be the ones Lottie makes herself, and a little glass counter, topped by an old-fashioned till. Boxy handbags sit like tiny works of art underneath. There's no sign of Lottie or anyone else.

'Hello?' Grace calls. Kitty busies herself rifling through the general rack.

'Coming!' She recognises the voice. A toilet flushes. 'Sorry, just having a wee . . . Grace, how lovely! Kitty!'

Kitty forces a smile onto her face. 'Hey. Well, this is gorgeous.'

Lottie is in full-on 1940s mode in a polka-dot swing dress, scarf tied round her hair, bright red lipstick. She looks cute, Kitty has to concede.

'What brings you up here?'

'This,' Kitty says, waving her arms around. 'Grace needs an outfit.'

'Ooh! What for?'

'A date with someone she doesn't like,' Kitty says.

'For the theatre,' Grace adds. She has chosen an immersive courtroom drama for date two, where audience members are dragged into the action whether they like it or not.

Lottie gives her an appraising look. 'I have so many things that would look fab on you. Any preferences? Dress? Trousers? Skirt?'

'Surprise me,' Grace says. She gives Kitty a meaningful look as Lottie turns to rummage through the racks. Kitty ignores her. Lottie pulls a pair of faded flared jeans from a hanger and looks at the label.

'These would look incredible on you, Kitty. What are you? A twelve?'

'I don't need anything,' she says defensively, although they do look cool.

'Just try them on,' Lottie says. 'While I make a big pile for Grace.'

Grace raises her eyebrows at Kitty so hard they almost leave her head. Kitty knows what she's trying to convey. *Do it.* 'Honestly, we're probably going to be ages going through stuff, so you might as well.'

Kitty snatches them from Lottie's hand ungratefully and stomps off towards the back room. She thinks about just waiting it out and then returning to say they don't fit, but then she hears Lottie shout, 'Come and show us when you've got them on.' She casts a look around the space. There's a table piled with junk – a laptop and pile of paperwork jostling with a kettle and a mini fridge, racks of clothes, bulging cardboard boxes stacked in a teetering heap. She spies Lottie's phone peeking out from under the paperwork. Maybe it's full of incriminating messages to Rich, but Kitty is never going to find out because a) she doesn't know Lottie's password, b) she's scared of getting caught and most importantly c) she doesn't think she could ever keep food down again if she subjected herself to Lottie's sexy baby talk in text. She jabs at it anyway, just in case it's password-free, but it asks for face recognition so she drops it back on the table and jumps backwards as if it might take a sneaky photo. She steps into the little cubicle and pulls the curtain across. The jeans are soft and snug. Slightly too long, but possibly the most flattering thing her arse has ever encountered. Fitted on the thighs with the kick of a flare below the knee. She has no idea if flares are in. She doesn't care. She doesn't think the rigid rules of fashion count if something is vintage. She loves them. Lottie clearly has the gift. Kitty shuffles back into the shop space self-consciously.

Lottie's jaw drops. 'You are so buying them. Oh my god. I can take them up.' She grabs a pincushion full of pins and kneels on the floor before Kitty can even answer. 'You want them for flats, right?'

'I suppose so. What do you think?'

'Definitely,' she says. 'They look amazing.' She offers to throw the alteration in to the already greatly reduced sale price, and the next thing Kitty knows she's waving her card at the contactless machine. It's a blur.

Grace, meanwhile, keeps throwing her meaningful looks. She can tell Grace's heart is not really in the clothes-buying thing – Lottie is gamely holding pieces up to her and appraising while, Kitty assumes, waiting for some kind of reaction, and Kitty starts to feel guilty that Grace is basically being rude by not engaging. So, she does what she always does in circumstances like this and overcompensates, gushing over every offering. Grace flicks her head at the back room manically every time Lottie's attention is elsewhere and Kitty pretends she doesn't notice.

'I see a kettle out there . . . maybe you should make a coffee, Kitty,' Grace says pointedly.

'Oh yes, do if you want,' Lottie says. 'Or I can do it while Grace is trying stuff on.'

Kitty can't do it. What did they really think they were going to achieve? She wants to help Sian, she really does. But now they're here the whole thing seems ridiculous. She picks up her bag. 'I saw a little café a couple of doors down. I'll go and get us a decent one. What do you both want?' She almost freezes in the chill of Grace's glare. She leaves without even changing, pins clipping against her ankles.

When she returns with two skimmed lattes and an oat cappuccino, Grace is in the fitting room. Kitty can feel the fumes of Grace's anger with her radiating through the atmosphere, a black, heavy cloud. Lottie is tidying away some of the rejected offerings. 'It was lovely of you both to come.'

Kitty hands her a coffee. 'Well, Sian mentioned you had a sale . . .'

Lottie waves a hand at a chair. Kitty moves the pile of hangers from the seat and sits down. Lottie unearths another one for herself. Prises the lid off her coffee and takes a sip. 'Mmm,' she says, but Kitty feels as if it's not so performatively sexy without her preferred audience. If Rich was there, she'd be licking the lid and contriving to leave a ring of foam around her mouth. She hears a huff, and the curtain over the fitting room billows as Grace wrestles with an outfit. She's desperate to be able to report some progress back to Sian. She needs to at least talk to Lottie about Rich and try to gauge her reaction, or this will have been a completely wasted trip. She fumbles about in her brain to come up with a leading question.

Grace's voice pipes up from next door. 'This one fits, but I look ridiculous.' Kitty looks up as she emerges from behind the curtain looking drop dead gorgeous in a pale pink shift dress. Bare legs, no shoes. She looks about ten years younger, not that that should be a thing these days now we're all embracing our grey hairs, but, you know, it's still the compliment we all want.

'Jesus, Grace, you look incredible,' Kitty says. She really does.

'Stop it,' Grace says, but she blushes, so Kitty can see she's pleased.

'Wow,' Lottie adds. 'That could have been made for you.'

'I feel silly. It's not me. No offence, Lottie.'

Kitty suddenly feels really sad for her. Stuck in her frumpy comfort zone. Too afraid to try anything different.

'It could be,' Kitty says. 'Why not?'

Grace opens her mouth to say something contradictory, but nothing comes out.

Kitty's not finished. 'Who's it for if not you? You look amazing in it so therefore it's for you.'

'Start a possibles pile,' Lottie says. 'Try something else but, honestly, that'll be hard to top.'

'She's right,' Kitty adds emphatically. 'Actually, Lottie,' she says, trying to throw Grace a bone. 'Maybe I should let you pick some stuff out for me given you're clearly so brilliant at it.' If she can occupy Lottie down at the front of the shop, Grace can do whatever she wants out the back.

Lottie jumps up, grabbing her coffee. 'With pleasure. Come and have a look.'

Kitty gives Grace a hard eyebrow raise of her own as they leave, and pulls the door closed. Not completely, that would be too obvious. But just enough. Lottie heads for the racks nearest the door and Kitty follows, blocking the view as much as she can. Hopefully Grace will have the sense to slip into a different outfit before she starts poking about, just in case Lottie suddenly decides to go back there for something.

'What's Andrew up to today?' Kitty says as Lottie starts rummaging. There's a haze of colour and pattern.

'Work. He's doing a garden in Temple Fortune. Big job.'

'So, do the pair of you just get to see each other on Sundays?'

Lottie gives a rueful laugh. 'Pretty much. And evenings, obviously. Although I sometimes end up staying here till late sorting stuff out that I can't get done in the day.'

Kitty can't imagine she's ever run off her feet. There hasn't been the sniff of another customer since she and Grace arrived. As if Lottie can read her mind, she says, 'I've got a kind of side thing going on where I source stuff for one of the hire houses. For films and TV. You know. That kind of thing. I'm trying to do more of that.'

'Where do you even start?' Kitty is actually interested. She has a morbid fascination with niche careers that people have carved out for themselves seemingly out of nowhere. It's some kind of fantasy wishful thinking, she knows that. Imagine if she could stumble across an unfulfilled gap in the market that satisfied the unfulfilled gap in her soul. If only she had any skills. Or passions.

'House clearances mostly. I mean, people bring stuff in. Obviously. But that's a drop in the ocean.'

'And you know what —' There's a crash from the back room and Kitty raises her voice to cover it. Lottie doesn't seem to notice — 'you're looking for?'

'I do lots of research. My degree was History of Fashion. That was a long time ago, though. Clearly.' She holds skirts and dresses up against Kitty as she talks, throwing them into one of two piles. Kitty is actually starting to get curious about what Lottie is selecting for her. It's a bit like being set up on a blind date. You finally see the way other people view you.

'Do you have any help?'

'Two days a week at the moment. So, I can go off and do other things. If I need to. You know.'

I bet, Kitty thinks. She's sure it must be easy enough for Rich to sneak out for a few hours on the pretext of meeting a client. Just seeing to their security needs. Checking their vulnerable entry points.

'Sian helps me out sometimes if I'm really stuck.'

Kitty's about to say something when Grace pops out from the back in a cream trouser suit that screams Bianca Jagger. If Kitty didn't know it was her, she would barely recognise her.

'Yes!' Lottie says. 'Wait. You need shoes.' She scrabbles around. 'What size?'

'Six?' Grace says as if it's a question. Kitty can't stop staring at her. She looks fabulous. 'I don't know about trouser suits, though.'

'What are you talking about?' Kitty gasps. 'You look incredible. Forget Julian, you need to buy this whatever.'

'Try these.' Lottie hands over the most beautiful pair of

nude Louboutins Kitty has ever seen and Grace wrestles a foot in.

'Oh my god, you're so buying that,' Kitty says just as Lottie says, 'Perfection.'

Grace grimaces. 'When would I wear it, though?'

Kitty rolls her eyes. 'Wear it to the pub, who cares? Wear it to Tesco's. You look fabulous.'

'I'll keep going,' Grace says, retreating. Kitty tries to catch her eye as she goes, but Grace gives her nothing. She wonders if Grace has got Stockholm syndrome at this point. If she's actually become more interested in the fashion than the fact-finding.

'How do you feel about combats?' Lottie says to Kitty.

'I mean, I don't know. Maybe. Melanie Blatt looked good in them.'

Lottie throws a khaki green item on to the yes pile. 'Exactly. Original nineties. Channel All Saints.'

'How often do you see Rich and Sian?' Kitty asks, admittedly out of nowhere. If Lottie wonders why she's jumped to such a non sequitur, she doesn't flinch. 'It must be lovely to have couple friends like that where you both like both of them equally. I could never stand most of my ex's friends' partners.' This is not strictly true. Some of them were OK. Until they all abandoned her after the event, of course.

'God. No. We lucked out. I think we were all so relieved to find each other when we were having our first babies and had no clue, you know.'

Kitty nods. 'Still. To stay so close all of this time. You must really care about each other. And Andrew and Rich, are they as close as you and Sian?'

'Definitely. Best buds. How about this?' She holds out a pale blue tiered skirt.

'Why not?' Kitty knows she's getting nowhere and she's starting to get bored. Thankfully Grace appears at the door, now dressed in her own clothes. 'That's it,' she says. 'Just those two possibles, but I don't think either of them are quite right. You try yours on now, Kit.' She gives Kitty a hard stare. 'I left a dress in the changing room that might suit you.' What? Kitty almost says it out loud. Nothing that fits Grace would fit her. Grace opens her eyes wide and glares at her.

'I'll just clear out the rest of your stuff,' Lottie says, heading for the back.

Grace looks panicked. 'No! I've brought it all out, look.' She turns and grabs a pile from the table and thrusts it at Lottie. Kitty takes her cue and picks up the items that Lottie has put aside for her.

'I won't be long,' she says.

'I'll help you put these away,' Grace says to Lottie as she pulls the door to.

'I'm going to persuade you into that trouser suit,' Kitty hears Lottie say.

She has no idea what Grace has found or how she intends to show it to her. She casts an eye around the room, but nothing has changed. She decides to dump her haul in the fitting room, although she doesn't really have any intention of trying any of it on. Grace was definitely trying to tell her something. Inside the little room there's a folded green dress on the bench and, wrapped in it, a piece of paper. Written in biro is *Look in the tiny inside pocket of her red bag!*

Her heart starts pounding. She doesn't know if she can do this. There are two bags, both seemingly bursting with crap. A stiff black patent leather with a gold clip that is a long way from being done up, and a larger red half-handbag half-tote hanging from the chair. Kitty can hear Grace chattering away, and she peers round the door. She's up the front of the shop with Lottie, both holding hangers. They seem to be getting on like a house on fire. Kitty grabs the red bag and takes it into the fitting room, and then she panics that Lottie might come in and wonder why it's there, so she takes it out again and crouches down on the floor close enough to return it to its perch if she thinks she's in trouble. She pulls out lipsticks and a purse, Tampax, tissues, a book, a random pile of papers, a scarf. She remembers Grace said to look in the little pocket, so she shoves all that back and digs her fingers around inside. There's a zipped compartment containing various store cards and screwed-up receipts, a wrapped maxi pad, a single key. She doggedly checks every receipt, trying to discover what Grace found that was so revealing. She can't work out what relevance the fact that Lottie bought truffles at a fancy grocer's in Hampstead or paint samples from Farrow & Ball could have on anything. She concentrates on listening and realises the chatting has stopped. She tugs at the zip on the pocket and scrabbles back to the fitting room. She'd forgotten her own advice. She needs to be seen to be trying something on if Lottie appears. She decides the combats are the easiest option, ditches the jeans and slides them over her hips, not even bothering to notice if they fit. She creeps back out, hears Lottie laugh. Another quick look round the door tells her they are still rehanging Grace's items. But the pile is almost down to nothing. She has to get a move on. She grabs the bag again and pulls it wide open. There's an even smaller pocket on the other side from the one she just looked in. The only thing in there is a piece of paper. A sheet torn from one of those notepads they leave by the bed in posh hotels. THE MARYLEBONE. There are just six words written on it. *Booked. My name. Tues. 2? Rx*

16

She sits back on her heels, the wind taken out of her sails. Is this it? Is this proof? An arrangement to meet? She curses herself that she left her phone out in the shop, but she's safe in the knowledge that Grace will almost certainly have taken a photo of the evidence. She stares at the note, trying to commit it to memory just in case, and then stuffs it back in the bag. Half of her is bursting with pride that she and Grace have pulled this off. The other half feels sick at the prospect of having to report back to Sian that it looks as if they have more confirmation of her suspicions. Kitty is desperate to get out of there now, so she grabs her jacket and walks out into the shop.

'Oh, those look great,' Lottie says. Kitty has completely forgotten that she's still wearing the combats. She tries to style it out. Slings her jacket over her shoulder.

'They're good, right?' She has no idea. She hasn't even looked in the mirror. 'Grace?'

Grace, who wouldn't be seen dead in jeans, let alone combats, and don't even mention joggers, gives her a forced smile. 'Very you.' This does not sound like a compliment.

'Maybe next time. Are you nearly done?' Kitty notices for the first time that Grace is back in the trouser suit and Lottie is pinning a dart in the waistband. 'Where did you get changed?'

'Behind that clothes rail. We locked the door.' Grace laughs and her whole face lights up. She's enjoying herself.

'You're buying it then?'

'Yes. I should, shouldn't I? Should I?'

'A hundred per cent. It looks amazing.'

'It won't be ready for tonight, obvs. But Lottie's going to drop it off with you next week if that's OK?'

Lottie takes a pin out of her mouth. 'Or with Sian. I'm seeing her on Tuesday. I'll bring your jeans too.'

'Great,' Kitty manages. She's not sure she wants Lottie anywhere near her house. 'I should . . .' She flaps her hand back towards the fitting room.

'Nothing else take your fancy?' Lottie says.

Kitty thinks of the pile of untried-on clothes.

'Not really. Gorgeous stuff, though.'

'I must be losing my touch,' Lottie laughs.

Grace suddenly fixes Kitty with an intense look, as if she's remembered why they're here. 'Did you find everything you needed, though?'

'Absolutely,' Kitty says, keeping eye contact. If Lottie wonders what they mean, she doesn't react; she's busy tidying away her sewing box.

'There,' she says to Grace. 'All done. You can take them off now.'

'You can have first dibs at the changing room,' Kitty offers. 'Actually, just let me get all those clothes out of there first.'

'Oh, leave them,' Lottie says. 'It'll give me something to do. I'm not exactly run off my feet. Are you sure you don't want those? They look great on you.' She steers Kitty in front of a mirror. She's right: they suit her. *They look like something Sian would wear*, Kitty thinks. She thinks of Grace and her rigid rules, and the fact she's allowed herself to be talked into something way out of her comfort zone. She looks at the handwritten tag hanging off one of the belt loops, the figure crossed out and a considerably smaller one written in.

'Go on then.'

Lottie claps her hands and squeals like an excited sea lion. For the life of her, Kitty cannot imagine what Rich sees in her.

Kitty and Grace laugh in that uncontrollable, unstable way teenagers do when they've got away with something that had the potential to irreparably ruin their lives if they'd been caught. They both know it's not funny. Nothing about it is funny. But they need the release. Grace grabs onto Kitty's arm, tears pouring down her cheeks. Kitty can't catch her breath. Without either of them saying anything, they head back to her house, neither wanting to be on their own. Kitty makes Grace walk round the long way from the bus stop, to avoid going past number 8. She needs to pick her moment to report back, and she certainly doesn't want to see Rich, her face would give her away.

She makes a salad for lunch with the random leftovers she has in her fridge – hummus, a nub of Cheddar, some leftover salad. She slices the rock-solid end off a semi-hard baguette. 'It must be from him, right?' she says, for probably the fourth time. She and Grace have gone round and round the issue countless times, trying to establish that what they found is what they think they've found.

'Show it to Sian and let her decide,' Grace had said the first time Kitty had asked the question. They were sitting on the bus, their hysteria fit over. The post-euphoria low settling in. 'Maybe that hotel means something to them.'

'Maybe "R" is "Rachel" or "Rebecca" and they were meeting for coffee.'

'Kit, just let Sian decide,' Grace had said again. 'She asked us to look, and this is what we found.' Now she picks up a slice of cucumber and nibbles on it. 'You need to get her on her own.'

'Let's talk about something else,' Kitty says, as if she wasn't the main offender for the endless repetition. 'Have you decided what you're wearing tonight?'

Grace lets out a big sigh. 'I think I might just cancel.'

'You can't, because you'd just have to rearrange.'

'Well, I'm not going to make an effort.'

Kitty spears a tomato. 'Lucky old Julian.'

Her phone beeps. She digs it out of her pocket. Sian. She holds it up to show Grace.

How did it go?

'I don't want to tell her by text,' she says. 'What if Rich sees? Shall I invite her round?'

Grace shrugs. 'Might as well.'

Interesting. Grace is here now if you fancy a coffee. 'That's vague enough, isn't it? If he reads it, I mean. Obviously, we might end up with both of them coming round.'

Grace pulls a face. 'I think she'll ditch him if she thinks we've got something to tell her.'

'OK. I'm sending. Do you want anything else to eat? I'm still hungry.'

Grace shakes her head, clears her plate away. Kitty pokes

around in a cupboard and comes up with a half-full packet of Hobnobs. She takes one out, folds the packaging over and refastens it with a pink clip, puts it back in the cupboard and then repeats the whole process again because she's kidding herself if she thinks she won't end up wanting two.

'What do you think she'll do . . . ?' Grace says as the doorbell rings.

Kitty closes her eyes. 'Here goes.'

Sian is on her own, looking wired. Kitty grabs her in a hug.

'Tell me,' she says into Kitty's shoulder.

'Grace is in the kitchen,' she says, and Sian follows her in. Then Grace gives her a grimace that looks like the face of a nurse about to tell someone their loved one has died, so if Sian hadn't already worked out there was bad news coming, she will have now.

Kitty doesn't even bother to offer her a drink. She just wants to put her out of her misery. She finds the photo on Grace's phone and holds it out in front of her. 'Grace found this in Lottie's bag. It looks like . . . I don't know . . .'

Sian peers at it. Kitty notices she has dark shadows under her eyes. She crumples her face up in concentration. 'The Marylebone Hotel? I mean . . . it's his writing . . .'

'Are you sure?' Kitty asks, clutching at straws.

Sian nods. 'I'd know it anywhere. And he always joins up his double Os like that. Like they're eyes.'

'It looks like a plan to meet,' Grace says helpfully. 'In a hotel,' she adds as if she hasn't quite hammered it home.

Sian looks up at Kitty and her expression is so vulnerable Kitty feels tears prick at the back of her eyes. 'Why would he give her a note?'

Kitty and Grace have already shared their theories about this. 'We think because it doesn't leave a trace. No incriminating texts, no record of him calling her just in case that might look odd. No having to whisper when you and Andrew aren't looking. He just slips a note into her bag and they probably have an agreed place where she could leave one for him.'

'But that message I found was in his phone.'

That's true. Kitty had forgotten that. 'In a text?'

'WhatsApp.'

Grace lifts a finger as if she's asking for permission to speak. 'Maybe she sent that early days and then they decided it was too risky. But he couldn't bring himself to delete it for a while.'

Kitty looks at Sian. 'That could be it.'

Sian closes her eyes for a second. 'What happens if they have to cancel, or something comes up?'

Kitty feels as if Sian is looking to her for a get-out clause. 'I don't know. Maybe they have a code word they text each other that means abort. Something that wouldn't look suspicious if you or Andrew saw it, whereas sending details of hotels and dates and times would.' Sian stares at the photo as if she's hoping it might give up more answers.

'That's a posh hotel. Should we ring up and ask if they've got a record of either of them?'

'I don't think they'd tell us. And besides, if they're going to these lengths, I don't think they'd use their real names. I'm really sorry, Sian.'

'What are you going to do next?' Grace says quietly.

'I need to speak to Andrew,' Sian says. 'Maybe he'll believe me now.'

*

Grace eventually leaves at four, giving herself nowhere near enough time to get across London, get ready and meet Julian at seven. Kitty has had a weirdly enjoyable day despite everything. Sian veered between being inconsolable, angry and euphoric that at least she now knew what the truth was. 'Feeling stupid is the worst,' she'd said at one point. 'Feeling as if you just don't know what you're up against.' And then she'd cried. 'How could they do it? Either of them? Our kids are best friends . . .'

Kitty and Grace had told her they'd be there for whatever she needed them for. 'Even if you just need somewhere to escape to for five minutes,' Kitty had said. 'Any time.'

Eventually they'd helped her get it together enough to go back and face Rich. He was on his way to collect his elderly parents for the night, it turned out.

'I'm going to have to play happy families,' Sian had sobbed. 'And they're lovely. They don't deserve to get dragged into any of this.'

'Shit,' Kitty had said. 'What a mess. I'm so sorry.'

Sian had managed a smile. 'Knowledge is power, right? I really appreciate what you did today. Both of you.'

'Kick him where it hurts,' Grace had chipped in. 'Hard. Really hard. Don't let him get away with it.'

Once she'd gone, Kitty and Grace had flopped on the sofa and both promptly fallen asleep like two new parents whose baby has finally gone down after an all-night screaming session. Julian, Kitty thought, should count himself lucky Grace woke up at all. Or maybe he'd have counted himself luckier if she hadn't. The next thing Kitty heard was Grace banging stuff around shouting things like 'bugger' and 'damnation'. 'Bugger' is ten on the Richter scale for sober Grace, so Kitty knew something was very wrong.

'I'm booking you an Uber,' Kitty had said as Grace stumbled around gathering up her stuff.

'Why am I going on this stupid date?' Grace had muttered, stuffing what looked like Kitty's phone into her bag. Kitty had retrieved it and then she'd checked the app. 'There's one four minutes away. Calm down. What do you need to do when you get home?'

'Everything!' Grace had said dramatically.

'You don't care about this date anyway, so just have a quick shower, throw anything on and maybe eat a sandwich. You're not eating later, are you?'

Grace had screwed her face up. 'No way.'

'There you go then. Sit down for one second.'

She did as she was told.

'Deep breaths. It's all under control. Text me later when you get home, remember? And try to be nice to Julian.'

Kitty steels herself for another long night in. Tells herself it's what she wants: Deliveroo, a film she can't really be bothered to watch. She wonders what Andrew and Lottie are doing right now. How good he is at pretending. If he's giving her the benefit of the doubt, clueless about the bombshell coming his way.

17

Forest Streets Residents' WhatsApp Group:

Vernie at Number 3: I baked a pistachio and passionfruit sponge cake! Malcolm is only allowed one slice due to his high cholesterol. I need to get it out of his sight! Any takers?

There's a man in Kitty's garden. She arrived home from work early because she decided to give herself an hour off. She couldn't concentrate anyway. She spots the parked Hart Landscaping van and a little line of green leafy soldiers leading up to her house from along the road and feels momentarily a bit irritated that she might have to make polite conversation if Andrew spots her. Her plans were actually to flop on the sofa in a heap. Still, she reminds herself, he's doing her a huge favour and he's also good company and a man who is going through a shit time, whether he knows it or not. She drops off her bag in the kitchen, flicks on the kettle and heads for the back door. Andrew is digging over a spot next to Sam and Linz's fence. He waves when he sees her.

'I'm meeting Rich for a beer, so I thought I might as well get here a bit early. Is that OK?'

'More than OK,' Kitty says. 'Did you climb over?'

He gives her a guilty-as-charged look. 'None of the plants are that big, so I thought . . .'

She laughs. 'What's going in?' She studies his face. Does he look like a man who's just had his world shattered? On balance she thinks not. She wonders if she can sneak back into the house and call Sian: *Did you show him the note? Does he know there's no doubt now?*

'I've got a few pyracanthas left over,' he's saying. 'So, I thought I'd put those in along that bit of fence here. They'll fill in together eventually, so they'll disguise all this . . .' He waves a hand at the orange horror. 'Although the worst of it will have faded by then anyway. And they're prickly so, good for security.' One of Sam and Linz's kids squeals at sound barrier-breaking levels. 'And give it time, it should create a bit more of a noise screen too, although I'm not sure anything could block that out completely.'

'It already looks ten times nicer out here.'

He looks around. 'I've got enough to do this middle section, anyway.'

'Whose lorry did they fall off the back of?'

He laughs. 'My own. I over-ordered.'

'Well, I appreciate your mistake. I'm making coffee. Do you want one?'

He puts a hand on his lower back. 'Oh god, yes please, then I can take a break. I'm too old to do this myself. I usually have an underling. I just point and they dig – I like to swan around and do as little as possible.'

Somehow, Kitty finds that hard to imagine. There's a nervous energy about Andrew that makes it hard to picture him slacking. Inside she dials Sian's number, but it goes to voicemail. Of course, she'll be teaching.

When she takes the coffee out, he's patting down the soil around the third plant. She wasn't lying when she said the garden was starting to look better. Even a tiny injection of green has brightened the whole place up. She puts his mug on the grubby little metal table. 'There you go.'

He looks round. 'Aren't you joining me? I need an excuse to take a break, like "the client wishes to discuss the ongoing progress."' He flaps ironic quote marks round the sentence.

For a split-second Kitty wonders whether he's flirting with her a little, but she quickly squashes that thought. He's one of those people who is just easy company; personable and open, quick to make friends. Funny. Good-looking. She checks herself. That is not a road she wants to go down. Really, she should claim busyness and drink her coffee inside, but she tells herself she's an adult and she's entirely capable of chatting to someone she thinks might be attractive without turning it into a flirtfest. 'Back in a sec,' she says before she can change her mind.

'Three more to go and then I'm out of your hair,' he says, when she re-emerges with her mug and sits down on one of the uncomfortable white wrought-iron chairs that she thought looked so stylish and Parisian when she bought them but which are now collecting rust. He sits on the other one. 'Gosh, you really don't want to spend much time out here, do you?'

'Bad decision. Looks over practicality.'

He peers down. 'They have looks?'

'Not any more. You don't regularly over-order on patio furniture, do you?'

'Ha! Sadly not. You're on your own there.' He tips his face up to the sun and Kitty finds herself studying him. What is it that makes Lottie think she can do better? She knows it's not that simple, obviously. It's not a binary sort: this person or that person? With a list of comparisons and a clear-cut decision. There are micro aggressions to negotiate and near subliminal irritations to take into account. You can love someone but realise one day that if they say 'Aaah' after they take their first sip of tea one more time you will probably murder them in their bed and not even feel sorry. Love is complicated. But still.

'What would you change, if you could change one thing about your life?' she asks. She's curious to know if he's dissatisfied. Not that he's likely to say 'I think Lottie might be cheating on me', but he might give something away. Andrew leans back in the chair, arms reached out in a stretch over his head. Kitty finds herself staring at the tanned flash of stomach as his T-shirt rides up. He's one of those people who seems very comfortable with his physicality. She wonders if he climbs or does circus skills or parkour. He looks like the type.

'Honestly? Not a lot. Is that nauseating?'

'Pretty much. And enviable, obviously.' He doesn't know. He can't.

'I mean, nothing's . . .'

'Mate . . .'

Kitty jumps. Rich is peering over the gate. She's thankful that she's facing away, so he didn't catch her gawping at his oblivious friend. Andrew clutches at his heart dramatically. 'Shit. Don't do that. Why is everyone creeping up on me lately?'

Rich laughs. 'Just letting you know I'm home. Hi, Kitty.'

Kitty squeaks a 'Hi' back. She can't look at him, though.

Can't watch him being all buddy-buddy with Andrew as if there's nothing wrong.

'I've got two more to bed in. I'll be over in about fifteen minutes.'

She grabs up their mugs. 'I'll leave you to it. Thanks so much again.'

She somehow forgets that Lottie is coming over on Tuesday. She's spent a good part of the past couple of evenings peering round the curtains like the street busybody, whenever she hears a noise from next door, desperate for news. She's spotted both Sian and Rich in the street, accompanied by a grey-haired couple in matching tracksuits, his in grey, hers in teal. Sian looks to be doing an incredible job of acting as if everything is business as usual, but Kitty can see the effort it's taking. Rhys arrived on Sunday afternoon with a huge holdall and left in the evening with the same huge holdall, so she's guessing he combined seeing his grandparents with laundry. She sent Sian a text this morning just saying *You OK?* And Sian texted back a heart. So, Kitty is none the wiser. Luckily, she's had the ongoing saga of Grace and Julian to take her mind off things. Grace, who is now thinking of throwing herself into a relationship with Julian for the sole reason that he let slip he's desperate for another baby.

'You don't even like him,' Kitty had said when Grace told her this. Kitty was still in bed, with tea and toast, having a Sunday lie-in.

'I can grow to like him. Or who even cares? This might be my only chance.'

Kitty couldn't believe what she was hearing. 'You told

me he was boring. Do you want to have a boring baby? It'll say its first words and you'll be stifling a yawn.' She was only half joking.

'Stop being stupid.'

'Grace. I get it. I do. Just . . . do you want to be tied to Julian for the rest of your life? You barely know him.'

'All I'm saying is that I'm going to give things a chance. I'm not jumping into bed with him tomorrow and trying to get pregnant.'

'Just the day after,' Kitty said, with, she hoped, enough lightness in her voice not to piss Grace off more.

Grace gave a small laugh. 'Exactly. Next week at the latest.'

Kitty didn't know what to think. Maybe having a baby with a dull, steady man would be just what Grace needed to give her life meaning. Maybe it wasn't the most stupid idea ever.

'Go for it,' Kitty said. 'I can be godmother with special responsibility for humour.'

'That is a deal. Anyway, he was quite game at the theatre thing. They made him go on stage and be a member of the jury and he went along with it. He was wearing this awful stripey shirt, though, like a city boy from the eighties. I'm going to have to talk to him about his dress sense . . .'

'I'm sure he'll be grateful,' Kitty said, sarcastically.

'. . . and his aftershave sucks the air out of the room. I had to tell him.'

'And he still wants to see you again?'

Kitty could practically feel her shrug. Why wouldn't he?

'So, when's date number three?'

'Friday. Horse riding in Hyde Park.'

Kitty actually splutters her coffee. 'I didn't know you could ride a horse.'

'I can't. Neither can Julian. We thought we should do something both of us were new to. It's a real test of character.'

'Fucking hell, Grace. Why would you put yourself through that?'

Grace ignores the question. 'I need to work out what I'm going to wear.'

'Jeans. You're going to wear jeans. You'll be sitting astride a half-ton animal, probably in the pissing rain . . .'

'I'm not wearing jeans. This is a date.'

'OK. Well, a ballgown then . . .'

'Scoff all you like. The matchmakers advise you to put yourselves out of your comfort zone for date three.'

'So, jeans it is then.'

'Maybe I should find some jodhpurs . . .'

Kitty snorts. 'That would be like turning up for your first day's training as a barrister in the wig . . .'

'I was joking. Remember that? I need to buy some athleisure.'

She says 'athleisure' like she's naming a particularly gruesome skin condition she's been diagnosed with. Kitty raises a sceptical eyebrow. 'Good idea. That I can help you with. Is Julian ready for some camel toe?'

Grace guffaws. 'You're gross.'

This afternoon Kitty got home to find her pyracanthas had been joined by some low-lying greenery on the side that borders her garden with Sian and Rich's. She'd wandered outside, ostensibly to investigate, but really in the hope of finding Andrew skulking in the bushes. Not that there was any chance anyone could be in her garden and not be in plain sight. She'd felt a stab of disappointment that she'd missed him. She's back to doing a bit of light general spying when she sees a taxi pull up. Lottie emerges from the back. Shit. Kitty ducks down. Hopefully Lottie will just leave the clothes with Sian and Kitty can collect them at her leisure. Lottie gathers three dust bag-covered hangers from the back seat and gives a glance at Kitty's kitchen window. Luckily Kitty is upstairs, so Lottie doesn't spot her peering round the curtains, although, she realises, Rich's parents who are staying in Rhys's room at the front of the house could well. She takes a step back. She needs to decide what to do. If Lottie rings the bell, is she going to pretend to be out? And then will she have to sit here all evening with the lights off if Lottie sticks around?

She runs her fingers through her hair on the way down the stairs. Rubs at any stray mascara under her eyes. Wishes she was wearing something more original than yoga pants. Whatever she thinks of Lottie, she doesn't want to be dismissed out of hand as having no style. She hears Lottie squeak a greeting as she must see Sian approaching from next door. She forces a smile onto her face and flings open the front door to find them both standing there.

'Hey!'

Lottie thrusts the dust bag at her. 'Ta-da!'

'Fabulous, thanks.' Kitty takes it from her. 'Do you want a drink or . . . ?'

Lottie surprises her by grabbing her into a hug. 'Nice to see you, Kitty.'

Kitty looks at Sian over her shoulder and pulls a face. Sian shrugs.

'You should try those on,' Lottie is saying. 'Just in case.'

'They'll be fine,' Kitty says. 'I really appreciate it, thanks.'

'No time for a drink, sadly,' Sian says. 'We're taking Barbara and Ray to the Globe. *Much Ado About Nothing*.' She grimaces.

Kitty peers at the sky. 'Isn't it going to rain?'

'Probably,' Sian says glumly. 'Do you want to come? I'm sure there'll be tickets.'

'Absolutely not,' Kitty laughs, but she's definitely not joking. 'Thanks, though.'

She hasn't managed to speak to Sian since Saturday. They've texted back and forth, surface, banal things. They both know how easy it is to get caught out by message now. But she hasn't been able to ask her the big question – has she talked to Andrew yet? Clearly Lottie is still oblivious and happy – the cat that got (and fake-orgasmed over) the cream – so, Kitty assumes either she hasn't had the chance, or they've decided to keep it to themselves for now. There has definitely been no confrontation.

'Oh,' Lottie says. 'I was thinking. Kitty has to come to the Salon. Sian, when's the next one?'

Kitty looks between them, confused. Does her hair need doing? Her nails? Sian sees her confusion and laughs. 'It's the wankiest name ever for the best nights. We get together and talk about books we've read or exhibitions we've seen. Or shows. Whatever. It's basically a cool bunch of women talking about art. And eating and drinking.'

'Mostly eating and drinking,' Lottie interjects.

'We use a room at this little members' club in Soho, just so we can all feel as if we're at the Algonquin. Same core group of people and occasionally someone new. People drop in and out. There's no obligation to, you know, go every time. It's fun, honestly.'

Lottie is looking at something on her phone. 'Next one's the nineteenth of June. That's a Thursday.'

It's also the day Kitty and Grace have a long-standing date to try Gymkhana. It took forever to book a table. Grace hasn't stopped talking about it since. She's already picked out what she's having from the tasting menu. Kitty can remember having to listen to a long one-person debate about the virtues of the salmon tikka over the quail kebab.

'Sounds fabulous.'

Kitty basks in the promise of a night out that's not just her and Grace talking about Grace's love life or the merits of Michael Bublé's new album. Of a whole new plugged-in social world. It's a shame that Lottie will have to be there, but her days in Sian's orbit are numbered, of that Kitty is fairly certain.

'Andrew would literally rather do anything else,' Lottie says. 'And, on this occasion, "literally" is being used correctly.'

Sian leans over and slaps Kitty's arm. 'You'll love it. Please say you'll come.'

Kitty is hit with a hot blow of guilt. 'Should I invite Grace?'

Sian pulls the tiniest of faces. 'I'm not sure. It's a bit . . . you have to kind of fit in. It probably wouldn't be her thing.'

'Got it. No worries,' Kitty says with, she realises, relief. She's done her duty, she's asked. 'Count me in.

'How *is* Andrew?' Kitty says, trying not to instil the words with any meaning beyond a polite enquiry. 'I'm really grateful for the plants.'

'Great. Working. Mill Hill. Footballer.' Sometimes the way Lottie speaks is a bit like watching someone with hiccups. Kitty has to resist the urge to tell her to drink a glass of water backwards.

'It's their wedding anniversary next month,' Sian says pointedly. 'Seventeen years.'

Kitty tries to keep a straight expression. 'Oh. Amazing. Are you doing anything special?'

'Dinner probably. Maybe with these two.' Lottie jerks a thumb at Sian.

'And how does it feel? Seventeen years?'

'A bit like sixteen did.' She laughs. 'It's just a day really, isn't it? And we'd been together years by the time we actually got married. Besides, Sian and Rich will be married for twenty in August.'

Kitty can't compute being with the same person for twenty years. Twenty minutes is a stretch these days. And then to find out you're not married to the person you thought you were after all. 'Amazing. You should have a party, Sian,' she says, giving Sian a sly attempt at a wink.

'We'll be in Santorini. Our anniversary is one of the reasons for the big trip. That and Harry's eighteenth.'

Of course, Kitty thinks, *the holiday. How is that going to work?* 'Lovely,' she says, because she can't think of anything better.

They're interrupted by a phone. Lottie's.

'Oh, do you mind?' she says. 'It's a work thing.'

Kitty waves a hand towards the living room. 'No, of course. You can go in there.'

She and Sian watch Lottie walk away. They're both silent for a moment and Kitty knows Sian is making sure Lottie is telling the truth. If she's speaking to Rich in code, it's a very complex one involving long stays, poke bonnets and 'the shelf'. It's definitely clothing-related.

Sian leans in towards Kitty. 'I told him yesterday. About the note.'

'And he believed you?'

In the background Lottie is discussing something that sounds like 'reticules'. 'Teeny-tiny bags,' she says, clarifying to the person on the other end, 'that they tied round their wrists.'

'He kept coming up with justifications for what it might mean. I felt awful trying to convince him there was no other explanation . . .'

'Poor bloke. What did he say about the WhatsApp she sent?'

Sian shakes her head. 'Rich came home. I didn't get the chance. I should have started with that really. Then he'd have understood why I'm so certain.'

Lottie is winding the conversation down. Sian flicks a look at her. 'He might ask you about it. The note. So, you can tell him about the message if you want. Otherwise I will next time I'm on my own with him.'

Kitty nods quickly. 'And then they decided not to go after all,' she says loudly as Lottie comes back in. 'Can you imagine?'

*

Andrew is on her doorstep. Somehow ashen despite the tan. Sian, Rich, Lottie and Rich's parents piled into a black cab about half an hour ago, on their way to the theatre, Barbara and Ray dressed up in their finest and laden down with big puffer coats and umbrellas just in case. Kitty had flung open the front door without even thinking who might be out there, ignoring her own advice about charity scammers and home invaders, and there he was. She opens her mouth to speak, but it's so obvious this is not a normal social visit that she can't find any words.

'Can I come in?' he says.

Kitty steps back. 'Of course. Is everything OK?' Shit. She thinks she knows what's coming. 'They all left already. I thought you were working. Do you want a glass of wine? I'm having one.' She's blathering now. She doesn't know what to do if he puts her on the spot.

'Sian told me,' he says, following her into the kitchen. 'About the note.'

Kitty grabs two glasses and a bottle from the fridge. She pours them both a large measure without checking again if he wants one. 'I know. I'm so sorry. I didn't know whether to say anything to you. Maybe there's an innocent explanation.'

'Could there be? You saw it . . .'

'I don't know. No.'

He nods. 'It's a lot to take in.'

'Come and sit down.' She hands him a glass, and he follows her over to the table.

'An arrangement to meet, right? At a hotel. That's what you think?'

157

Kitty nods. 'Grace took a photo of it. I can get her to send it to me now, if you want. I guess you haven't seen it.'

He looks pained. 'Can you just tell me what it said. I mean, I know, but exactly.'

The words are burned into her brain. ' "Booked. My name. Tuesday. Two?" And then signed "R".'

He shuts his eyes. 'And it was on a headed bit of paper?'

'The Marylebone. Sian says he was doing a bit of work near there a while back, so our guess is that he went in and booked it in person and wrote that at the same time.'

'Where did you even find it? I mean, to know it was for Lottie?'

Shit.

Fuck.

She has no idea what Sian has actually told him. Or what valid reason there could possibly be for her rifling through Lottie's things.

'Um. It fell out of her bag. We were at the shop, me and Grace, and Grace was trying to put her coffee down somewhere while she tried stuff on, and she moved the bag and . . . well, Sian had already told us she had suspicions about them, I think she told you that too . . .' Shh, Kitty. Quit while you're ahead.

Luckily Andrew seems to have taken what she's saying at face value. 'She made a comment the other week and I suppose I've been trying to watch them together. And there's . . . I don't know. Lotts has gone out a couple of times and been a bit vague about where. I just didn't think it could be true, though. I still don't.'

'Sian told you what Grace saw? At their house?'

He nods. She waits for him to say something, but he just stares at the floor.

'Have you looked at her phone? Just in case ... I mean ...' She's pretty sure he wouldn't find anything now if he did, but you never know. Maybe Lottie hasn't been as cautious as Rich.

'God, no. I feel as if once I go there we're done anyway, aren't we?' He suddenly leans forward and buries his head in his hands. 'I can't take it in.'

She feels so bad for him she doesn't know what to do with herself. She stretches out a hand and pats his arm gently, which feels both woefully inadequate and overly intimate.

Here goes.

'Um. OK. Well, there's something else,' she says nervously. She wishes she didn't have to be the one to deliver more bad news, but he needs to know. 'Sian saw a message. WhatsApp. She was going to tell you, but ...'

He huffs out a breath. 'Go on.'

'I haven't seen it myself. From Lottie to Rich.' She closes her eyes briefly, steeling herself. 'Explicit, that's what she said, but I don't know the details. You'd have to ask her.'

He rubs at his eyes. 'My wife and my best friend. Fuck. What a cliché.'

'Don't think like that.' But he's right. It's the ultimate betrayal by both of them. 'What are you going to do?'

'Do you know what's really tragic,' he says, ignoring her question. 'Lottie texted me earlier and said we should have a party for our anniversary.'

'I suppose that implies that she thinks that's something to celebrate ...' Kitty says, quietly. 'Maybe it's all been a moment of madness. A glitch. And she's regretting it already.'

He looks at her. 'Making arrangements to meet in hotels? Booking rooms? It hardly sounds as if things just got out of hand for a second. I didn't even know they'd spent any time together just the two of them, so they were already keeping secrets.'

Kitty doesn't know what to say to that. They sit there in silence for a second, and then Andrew exhales loudly.

'Harry has her A-levels any minute. I can't let anything fuck that up for her. In answer to your question. And then it's her eighteenth . . .'

'So, you're not going to say anything? To Lottie or to Rich?'

He shakes his head. 'Not yet. I can't. I've asked Sian not to either. I can't let it all blow up now. What difference is another few months going to make? It's either happening or it's not. And it'll give us time to really make sure it's not just all a big misunderstanding. Once we throw those accusations, there's no going back, really, even if it turns out we're wrong. I mean, I know that's unlikely . . .' He tails off.

'Can you do that? Keep it in? I'm not sure I could.'

He gives her a weak smile. 'We'll soon find out.'

'Sian's ready to kill Rich, I think.'

He reaches for the wine bottle, holds it up to her. 'Do you mind?' She shakes her head, and he fills up their glasses. 'Her and me both. I'll understand if she can't hold it together, obviously. I'm asking a lot.'

Something Sian said occurs to Kitty. 'Aren't Rhys and Archie best mates?'

Andrew exhales through tight lips as if he's trying to control his reaction. 'Yep. Nice, huh?'

'God, what a mess.'

'Not what you expected when you met us all, right?' He gives her a crooked smile. Even though he's anything other than happy, his eyes crinkle at the edges, a pattern formed by years of laughter. His eyes are a bright pale grey against his tan. Kitty catches his gaze for a second and then looks away quickly, an unfamiliar feeling gripping her insides. She chastises herself. *Now is not the time to decide you have a bit of an inappropriate crush on Andrew, Kitty.*

'I'm sorry you've ended up caught up in all this,' he says. He slides his wine glass backwards and forwards in a repetitive motion. 'I'm embarrassed that I'm even having to have this conversation with you.'

'God, no, don't be. I'd be the same. You just want to know the truth, right? So you know what you're up against.'

'What an idiot,' he says. 'You know when I said the other day I wouldn't change anything about my life . . .' He shakes his head.

'How long do you think it's been going on? Do you want to eat something?' she adds as an afterthought. She's just realised how hungry she is.

He shakes his head. 'I should get out of your way.'

'Not at all. I'll order a pizza and then if you're still here when it arrives you can have a bit.' She finds the Deliveroo app. Orders a marinara while he talks.

'I've been thinking about that. Maybe it's been years. Maybe our whole life has been a lie.'

Kitty leans back. 'I don't think so. Lottie doesn't seem like the sort of person who could keep all that hidden.'

'You could say she doesn't seem like the sort of person who could do this at all . . . but people aren't always what they seem, apparently.'

She tries to keep her visceral dislike of Lottie to herself. All the performative eating, the moaning and groaning and licking her lips and her fingers makes sense now.

'Mmm,' she says, non-committally. 'Don't torture yourself looking for the details. It'll all come out in the end.'

He does that thing he does where he rubs his hand over his head. There are traces of dirt under his short nails, so she assumes he's been hands-on earth moving today. 'You're right. Let's talk about something else.'

'Good idea.'

Of course she can't think of anything else to talk about, and neither, it seems, can he. They sit in a heavy silence.

'What sunscreen do you use?' Kitty says, suddenly. God knows where that came from. She thinks from the fact that his skin looks pretty healthy for someone who spends every day outdoors.

He looks at her, confused. And then a smile lights up his face. 'What . . .?'

'Indulge me,' she says. 'It's the best conversation topic I can come up with at such short notice.'

Andrew laughs loudly. 'Well, in that case. Green People do a good one. Cruelty free. Would you like me to recommend a moisturiser?'

'Absolutely,' she says. 'Go for it.'

'I can't. If my skin's feeling dry, I just stick my finger in whatever Lottie is using . . .'

They both go quiet again at the mention of Lottie's name, the moment broken. Andrew picks up his mobile. 'I should probably get going . . .' He jabs at the Uber app. 'There's one two minutes away.'

'The pizza will be here in . . .' she checks. 'Well, it still hasn't left the restaurant, but soon. The driver is there waiting, look . . .' She holds it up. She doesn't really want to send him off to an empty house to sit around waiting for Lottie to come home. Imagining the secret moments she and Rich might steal in plain sight: a brush of a hand, a whisper. Poor Sian trying to keep up appearances in front of his parents.

'It's OK. Thanks. Look, I'm sorry for just turning up. I don't want you to feel you're somehow involved. You've only just met us all and now you're part of a soap opera.'

'God. No. it's fine. Any time, really. If you just want someone to talk to . . .'

'Thanks.'

'Is Sian OK? I haven't had much chance to get her on her own.'

He sighs. 'As OK as she can be, I imagine. I mean, raging, obviously, but devastated mostly.'

'You have to wonder what they're thinking, don't you? How it crossed that line.' She sees a black car pull up outside. 'Wow, he really was close by.'

Andrew takes his glass over to the sink and rinses it. 'I can't,' he says. 'I can't bring myself to picture it. I don't want to imagine the details; it makes it seem too real.'

18

She can tell that Sian is wishing she hadn't accepted the offer of a Sufjan Stevens ticket. She doesn't want to leave Rich to his own devices, and she doesn't want to be seen to be the sort of person who spends an evening with a friend worrying about what her husband is up to. Kitty is almost tempted to offer her a way out by claiming illness, but she actually thinks it will do Sian good. Not to mention their burgeoning friendship. And if Rich is going to sneak around and meet Lottie, he could do that any time. The note they found proves that. In the cab on the way down to the Southbank, Sian tells her that sticking to her agreement with Andrew to keep her suspicions to herself is killing her.

'I can barely look at Rich,' she says. 'But I have to keep remembering Harry. Rhys was a basket case during his A-levels. The stress is horrendous without adding all of this on top. That's why we're not saying anything yet . . .'

'Andrew told me. I totally get it.'

Sian momentarily stops applying mascara, using her phone's camera as a mirror. If Kitty did that in a moving vehicle she knows it would not be pretty. 'You saw Andrew?'

'He came round. He wanted to hear about the note from the horse's mouth, I think.'

'Right. When was that?'

Kitty fills her in. 'I don't think he can take it in. That they're capable of it.'

'Yeah. It's a mind fuck,' Sian says. 'He's in denial, I think. I don't know what he needs to convince him it's really happening.'

'Are you really going to go on the Santorini holiday?'

Sian sighs. 'Andrew thinks we should. It's Harry's eighteenth. He thinks we shouldn't blow everything up till after that. The boys had a brilliant joint eighteenth. It's a huge deal when you're that age. It was Harry's idea for us all to go away for hers.' She snorts. 'And Rich's and my anniversary, obviously, so that'll be fun. I'm thinking maybe I can claim Covid a couple of days before and leave them all to it.'

'You can't leave Andrew alone with the lovebirds.'

'I know. I won't really. I know! You should come!'

Kitty thinks how much she would have loved this invitation a few weeks ago. A gang of friends to go on holiday with. 'I think I'm washing my hair that week.'

Sian snorts. 'I don't blame you.'

'That's a long time though,' Kitty says. 'To put up with it all, I mean.'

Sian screws up her face. 'I know. Waiting for the exams to be over was one thing . . . but, listen, I'm happy to be guided by Andrew. The kids have to come first, right?'

'Of course.'

'I'll just use the time to work out what happens next.' She suddenly has to blink back a tear. She closes her eyes briefly and then gives Kitty a smile that's so vulnerable Kitty has to look away. 'It'll be OK. Don't worry about me.'

Somehow, they have fun. They drink bottles of beer, balancing them precariously under their seats, and let the music wash over them, surrounded by the coolerati. For the first time Kitty feels a part of things. Sian visibly relaxes, especially after Lottie sends her a photo of her and Harry in matching bathrobes and face masks with the caption 'Girls' night in!'. Assuming it genuinely is from tonight (Kitty doesn't raise that caveat with Sian), then there's no chance Lottie and Rich are having a sneaky assignation. At one point, between songs, Sian reaches out a hand and squeezes Kitty's. 'Thanks for this,' she says. 'I don't know what I'd do without you.'

'You'll get through it,' Kitty says quietly, engulfed in a warm glow. 'And I'm always around if you need me. That's what friends are for, right?'

19

Kitty can hardly think straight.

This afternoon.

Something.

Happened.

It's nearly three weeks since Kitty and Grace found the note. Sadly, despite Grace's best efforts to snare him and his fertile, willing sperm, Julian decided to cut his losses after date three, unmoved by the shared experience of teetering on top of an elephant-sized pissed-off animal who would rather have been at home in his nice warm stable than negotiating Hyde Park Corner with a nervous novice kicking him in the sides every few seconds. Grace had found it funny, but it turned out Julian had no sense of humour where his own discomfort was concerned. She's currently waiting on a new perfect match. At the debrief she let the matchmakers know all the ways in which they'd got it wrong ('too dull, too boring, too blond, no sense of humour, no style, no class'). Kitty was sure they'd been thrilled.

'Lucky escape,' Grace said, when she told her. Kitty was painting her toenails, phone on speaker.

'You wanted to have his baby a second ago,' Kitty said.

'Well, I changed my mind,' Grace snapped back, conveniently forgetting that it was Julian who called things off. Kitty knows she's more upset than she's owning up to, though. She knows it's all bluff.

She's been spending most of her free time with Sian. Evenings at the pub when Rich is playing football, a Saturday afternoon at the Courtauld, a night at the Royal Court. Between trips out, Sian has taken to hanging out at hers to put a bit of distance between herself and Rich, and they've established an easy no-need-to-fill-every-silence way of being around each other, watching a film or listening to music. Kitty has missed Thursday drinks with Grace two weeks in a row and hasn't managed to make time to see her in between either. Grace has been grumpy on the phone – a couple of times alluding to *Your new best friend* in a slightly churlish way, but Kitty hopes she understands that Sian needs the company at the moment. Of course, Kitty could invite her along, but she feels as if her new friendship needs careful nurturing without Grace stomping over it with her endless anecdotes.

'Do you have a plan yet?' Kitty had said to Sian one afternoon when they were sitting on a bench in the park, Dante between them. She'd been trying not to ask too many questions about the future, partly because she knew Sian was still trying to process what was going on, but also because she knew the strain keeping up appearances was causing her, and she didn't want to make that harder by encouraging her to imagine her post-Rich life. But it was also worrying Kitty that Sian might be burying her head in the sand a bit too deep. Her and Rich's life together was going to take a lot of unravelling. She needed to think about things like what they were going to do with the house, for example. Where she might live.

'Not really.' Sian stood up, leaning over and throwing

her coffee cup into the bin. 'Let's walk,' she said, effectively shutting the subject down.

Last Wednesday Kitty came home from work to find Andrew digging about in next door's garden again. She was impressed that he was still thinking about their box hedging given everything that had happened, but maybe he just liked being able to keep an eye on Rich. She had noticed Sian's car parked out front when she walked past, so he had company if he needed it. She watched him for a minute or so. Given the choice between him and Rich, Andrew would definitely be her type any day – it was true what she'd said to Grace. Not that she'd been thinking about it more since. Rich was too self-consciously metrosexual. Too groomed. Too considered. Too having-an-affair-with-both-his-wife's-best-friend-and-his-best-friend's-wife. Obviously, everyone's tastes are different, but she couldn't imagine what Lottie saw that made her want to throw it all up in the air, apart from something shiny and new. Kitty would bet that Rich didn't have an anchor tattooed on his bicep. She stared a second too long, of course. Andrew's spidey senses kicked in and he looked up, straight at her. Shit. She waved a hand and then got the hell away from the window before he'd even had a chance to complete his wave back. Her blush could have toasted marshmallows.

She changed into her running stuff and got out of the house to sweat off her crippling embarrassment, chiding herself in her head: What must he think? A pink-faced forty-something woman gawping at him like he's a pumped-up *Love Island* wannabe. She wasn't even sure how long she'd been standing there. Too long, that was for certain. She might as well have been holding a tub of popcorn.

It took two circuits of the park for her scarlet shame face to be replaced by her scarlet exercise face. She slowed to a walk and tried to regulate her breathing. She was overreacting, she knew. But that also told her something. She liked Andrew. Not in an *I want to marry him and have his babies* kind of a way, but something much more primal. And she one hundred per cent knew she would never have allowed herself to go there, even in the privacy of her own head, if he had been a happily married man. It was as if Lottie's betrayal had given her permission to consider it. It was just good old-fashioned lust, and she was pitifully unused to it. It would pass.

Of course Andrew was loading up his van when she got back to the house. Just as she was too close to turn round and make herself scarce again without being seen, he appeared from the side alley with a spade in one hand and some kind of lethal-looking cutting tool in the other. Kitty literally jumped.

Andrew rewarded her with a big, spontaneous smile and all her inappropriate feelings came flooding back. 'Hey.'

'Oh. Hi.' She gave a half-hearted attempt at flattening down her hair although, to be fair, flyaways were probably the least of her worries. She felt a drop of sweat take up residence on the end of her nose and wiped it off with the back of her hand.

'I've just been for a run.'

No. Shit. Sherlock.

'I kind of guessed,' he said with a laugh. 'How's things?'

'Oh, you know. How's the garden?'

'Finished,' he said.

'I sort of didn't expect you to show up again,' Kitty said, quietly enough that if Rich was home he wouldn't hear.

Andrew slung the tools in the back of the van. 'Business as usual, remember. Besides, I made sure he wasn't going to be here.'

Kitty grimaced. 'How are Harry's exams going?'

'They start next week, so she's holed up revising with her friend.'

So, the clock was finally ticking. Kitty could only think that must be a relief for everyone who knew what was going to happen after.

'And you,' Kitty said, lowering her voice even more, 'how are you doing?'

He looked off into the distance for so long Kitty wondered if she should nudge him back to attention. She was about to say something when he spoke so quietly she could only just make out the words. 'She has form, you know. Lottie.'

Kitty almost thought she misheard him. 'She . . .?' She lowered her voice again. 'Really?'

He looked around as if Lottie might appear at any moment. 'About five years ago. We got through it. It didn't go on for long. She realised she'd made a mistake pretty quickly. Everyone can fuck up, right? That's what I thought.'

'Yeah. I think so too. Once.' She hears Grace in her head: *Absolutely not. Once a cheater, always a cheater.*

'I believed how much she regretted it. Totally. If I

171

hadn't, I wouldn't have . . . She did everything to try and make it up to me. And we've been great ever since. That's what I thought, anyway. But the bottom line is I know she's capable of it.'

'Shit.'

'And Rich knew how devastated I was. That's one of the things that hurts the most. He was the only person I told, and he saw the way it practically broke me. I confided everything in him. His advice was that I should leave. Get out while I could. I've been wondering lately if that was because he was into her then.'

Kitty stays quiet. It feels important to let him say what he's trying to say.

'Sian doesn't even know about it. I made Rich promise not to tell her. I didn't want her thinking badly of Lottie. Not once I knew I was going to stay with her. I wanted to protect her. Even after everything.'

'That's understandable,' Kitty said, thinking that Lottie had got off pretty lightly, all things considered. She hadn't thought she could dislike her and Rich more, but, hey, it turned out she hadn't been trying hard enough.

'I found something.'

She almost gasped. 'You . . .?'

He rubbed a hand over his forehead. 'Sian told me she looked at Rich's credit card statement and she couldn't spot anything. They must be paying somehow, right? For the hotels and stuff. I looked at Lottie's but there was nothing. So, I checked the shop's accounts. There was a payment at the bar at the Marylebone last Monday. Lotts was supposed to be out with a friend –'

'Maybe that's where they went,' Kitty interrupted.

He shook his head. 'They were at the cinema in East Finchley. That's what she told me. And when I told Sian, she said Rich was playing padel with a bloke from work. She said he'd had a shower by the time he got home.'

'Fuck. So you think they had a room too?'

Andrew gave her a faint smile. 'Honestly, I just can't wait to bring it all to a head now. It's really bothering me that they think they're getting away with it. Is that petty?'

'Not at all. And besides, they're not, remember. You and Sian hold all the cards.'

He scuffed at the ground with the toe of his boot. 'Yeah.'

'It's good that you know for certain.'

'That's what I keep telling myself.'

It was out before Kitty could stop herself. 'Do you want a drink or anything? Before you leave? I . . .'

'Oh, *you're* here!'

Kitty jumped. She hadn't even seen Lottie pull up behind the van on a pink sit-up-and-beg pushbike. She smiled at Andrew. 'I'm just dropping off a bag for Sian. Is she in? Hi, Kitty.' She was looking cute in the pedal pushers and a rose-coloured cap-sleeve blouse, her hair pulled back into a tiny high ponytail.

Kitty tried to control her blush, but thinking about it made it even worse. She had basically been propositioning the woman's husband right as she appeared.

Lottie leaned over and planted a kiss on Andrew's cheek, leaving a coral lipstick mark. Kitty noticed him tense up.

'No one's in,' Andrew said. 'She's taken Dante to the park. She'll probably be back soon, though.'

'I can't hang round. I could post it through the door if it'll fit. Oh. Or could I leave it with you, Kitty? For Sian? No urgency?'

'Sure,' Kitty said, reaching her hand out for the bag, which was a boho-looking pale blue denim with a shoulder strap and a colourful peace sign embroidered on the side. 'Sixties?'

'Seventies, I would guess. Cool, right?'

'Very Sian. I'll give it to her.'

'You're a star. I'm on my way back. To the shop. Kira needs to leave early. I'll be home to eat. Sevenish.'

She was gone in a second, but the moment was broken. They watched in silence as she cycled off.

'You've got . . .' Kitty indicated her cheek.

Andrew wiped his own with his hand. 'I should go too. Another time, though.'

Kitty nodded breezily. No big deal. 'Sure. You know where I live.'

'Remind me again,' he said, and she couldn't help but laugh.

'Seriously, if you want anyone to talk to. I mean, you have Sian, but, you know. If Rich is around . . .'

'I might well take you up on that,' he said, and her traitorous heart stuttered a little bit.

She was washing up, idly watching Betty aggressively sweeping the section of pavement in front of her drive with a stiff broom, when she spotted Sian walking Dante towards home and grabbed her keys and ran out after her.

'I bumped into Andrew out here earlier,' she said breathlessly.

'Did he tell you?' Sian half whispered. 'About the bank statement?'

Kitty nodded. 'He believes you now.'

'Thank Christ,' Sian said, pulling the dog away from a sandwich wrapper he was sniffing hungrily. 'Let's do another loop. I don't think he wants to go home yet.' Kitty followed her back towards the park. She waved a hello at Betty and was greeted with a curt 'Good afternoon'.

'I hope you pick up after your dog,' Betty called after them. Sian pulled a roll of poo bags from her pockets and held them up, not looking back.

'Nosy old Karen,' she muttered.

'Did they have a room payment on there as well? Andrew said you didn't find anything on Rich's.'

'You know what I think? Rich must have a secret card. Or *she* does, but then why risk putting the drinks bill on the shop one? Unless she was more worried about writing it off against tax than getting caught out. Because I can't imagine they were just meeting up for cocktails.'

Kitty pondered that for a second. 'I think you must be right. That makes it all seem much worse somehow, if that's possible. The planning . . .'

Sian put an arm out to stop Kitty stepping into the road as a bike whizzed by. 'He'd better be robbing fucking banks in his spare time to pay it off.'

'God, I hadn't even thought about that.'

'You know where we stayed the last time we went for a night away? A DoubleTree. Which is fine. It was quite nice, actually. But it was not the fucking Marylebone. Because we can't afford to stay in hotels like the fucking Marylebone.'

'They'll get theirs,' Kitty said, putting a hand on Sian's arm. 'Just hang in there.'

Now she splashes water on her face, wrecking her mascara, and stares at herself in the bathroom mirror wondering how her Saturday turned out so different to the thrilling day of admin that she'd had planned. She did her big shop this morning, lugging Sainsbury's bags for life home in an Uber. She cleaned the kitchen and cooked a batch of quinoa. Not that she'd admit it in public, but Kitty loves chores. She finds them therapeutic. Both mindless and mindful at the same time. Only her own, just to be clear. Washing Geth's underwear did not give her the same thrill.

She was slumped on the sofa with a post-lunch coffee, weighing up the pros and cons of cleaning the bathroom versus changing the bed, when the doorbell rang. She knew Sian and Rich had driven down to Brighton to spend the weekend with Rhys. And since their bonding evening at their house a few weeks ago, all the neighbours had sealed themselves back in their own bubbles, although Vernie occasionally popped over with a Tupperware of homemade brownies or, on one occasion, a whole Victoria sponge, which Kitty had consumed in the space of a few blissful hours in front of reruns of *Fleabag*. So, it was almost certainly an Amazon delivery, although she couldn't even remember what, if anything, she'd ordered. She peered through the spy hole. Andrew was standing on the doorstep.

Instinctively she looked down at what she was wearing – a fetching combination of khaki mid-calf joggers and a baby-pink T-shirt with Boss Bitch emblazoned across the front, which her team had given her as an ironic Christmas present and which she never wore outside the privacy of her own four walls. She kicked off her fluffy sliders and edged them into the corner.

'One second,' she shouted. She needed to do a quick upgrade, but the truth was, she didn't want him giving up and leaving. She undid her top knot and dragged her fingers through her hair. Pulled a grey jumper, fresh back from the dry-cleaner's, from the coat rack and over her head and the offending T-shirt. Short of getting him to wait while she redid her make-up and brushed her teeth there was nothing else she could realistically do. And it wasn't as if Andrew would be checking her out anyway. He'd come looking for a shoulder to cry on and Kitty was happy to provide that.

'This is a surprise,' she said as she opened the door, and then she worried he'd think she meant it not in a good way, so she added, 'A nice one. Come in.'

'Are you sure?' he said. 'Just say if you're busy.'

She stepped back so there was room for him to follow. 'So not busy I was almost comatose.'

'I just . . . well, you said it was OK to come over . . .'

She turned and looked at him. He still looked tired, but maybe not completely destroyed. Not as bad as she'd imagined he might. It was amazing how quickly you could come to accept the new status quo. 'Do you want to sit in the garden? They're away next door.'

'Lovely. I can survey my work from the other side.'

She unlocked the patio door. 'Are you just avoiding him, though, Rich? Won't he suspect? Do you want a drink?'

"Pretty much. Hopefully not. And yes, please. I'm claiming a big job is keeping me busy. I can keep that up for a while. I'm still turning up for football, stuff like that.'

'And Lottie?'

'I'm spinning her the big-job thing too and telling her I'm too knackered to go out in the evenings. Which in itself is knackering. I'm not a good liar.'

'Tea, coffee?' She looked at the clock. 'Or it's half three, that's probably an acceptable time for a beer somewhere.'

'I will if you will.'

She was feeling nervous. A beer would definitely take the edge off. 'Oh god, definitely. You go on out. I'll get them.'

The beer was probably the first mistake.

20

Technically, is kissing a married man still a crime if his wife is already cheating on him?

Because she kissed him.

She did.

And she liked it.

A lot.

Not right away. Obviously. And it didn't go any further than that. Kitty thought they were both as surprised and shocked as each other. But they both leaned into it; there's no doubt about that. Just for a moment, but there was definite leanage.

They sat in the sun and chatted until they finished their beers, and the dark clouds that had plagued the whole week thus far came over, which wasn't as long as you might imagine. Twenty minutes maybe. She can't even remember exactly what they talked about, but she knows they kept it light, avoiding the topic of Lottie and Rich as if by prior agreement. Kitty decided that if he wanted to offload he would, but otherwise she wouldn't bring the subject up. Maybe he just wanted an afternoon away from any reminders of what was happening in his life. When she started shivering and her bottle was empty, she asked if he fancied another, and if he wanted to go in the house to drink it or take responsibility for her impending hypothermia.

Inside, the atmosphere felt more loaded. Maybe because there was no fresh air to dissipate the pheromones, so they just filled the space, like being inside an over-blown-up balloon. It was all in Kitty's head, she was sure. That adolescent awkwardness that threatens to derail even the most banal conversation. They chatted about Harry's exams, how Archie was struggling to fit in at Durham, about work, both his and hers, about Kitty's worry that looking after her mum was too much for her dad. The conversation was easy. It was the pauses in between that she was starting to find troublesome.

Eventually the topic turned to Lottie. He'd reached acceptance, he told her, on the official table of post break-up grief.

'What are the others again?'

'Devastation, breaking things, more devastation, crying a lot, swearing uncontrollably, acceptance, indifference and wondering if it actually might be a good thing once the dust settles.'

'You're getting through them quickly. Is there a prize at the end?' She crossed her fingers he didn't mind her joking, but he'd started it.

'It's like an Argos voucher, I think.'

Kitty laughed. 'Seriously, though, do you really think you could ever get to the thinking-it-might-be-for-the-best stage? Even if that was really a thing?'

'She's not the person I thought she was, that's the way I have to look at it. The amount of soul-searching we did after the last time. The promises she made . . . I actually said to her that if she didn't think she could stick to them, we should cut our losses then and split up as amicably as we could. That I wouldn't make it hard for her if that was what she wanted. But she swore it was a mistake, one terrible decision, whatever. I had absolutely no reason not to believe her. And I wanted to believe her, obviously. We've been happy since. Really happy. Or so I thought. I didn't even spot it happening. Even now I know about it there are no clues. For all I know, Rich is the latest in a long line, that's how good she is at covering it up. God, you must think I'm stupid.'

'Not even slightly. You have to give people the benefit of the doubt. You have to give them the chance to prove you wrong.'

He reached for his beer. 'Anyway, the answer to your question is yes. I mean, not immediately, but one day. Does that sound harsh?'

'Absolutely not. It sounds like a plan.'

'I know it's what everyone says, but I just need to make sure this is as gentle on the kids as it can be.'

'Stay focused on what's important. It'll help.'

He gave her a smile that almost reached his eyes. 'We should put this out as a podcast. It's as if we both know what we're talking about.'

Kitty drained the last of her drink, wondering if she should suggest another. 'We could call it "Clichéd advice for the Clueless".'

'Catchy.' His phone pinged and he picked it up and checked it. 'I should probably go. I didn't realise how late it had got. Lottie's home and wondering what time I'll be back.'

'Business as usual,' Kitty said. She checked her own phone and saw that it was gone six already. 'Any time, you know that.'

She followed him to the front door, pausing while he dropped his empty bottle off in the kitchen. She had her hand on the catch. She was almost home and dry.

'You're easy to talk to,' he said.

'I do my best,' she said, trying to be flip. 'Do you need me to call you a cab? You're not driving, are you?'

He shook his head. 'I'll find one on the main road. I'll see you soon, yeah? Thanks again.'

She should have just opened the door. She doesn't know why she hesitated. He leaned over to kiss her on the cheek and then he didn't quite pull back all the way. She looked up, straight into his eyes, her hand still on his arm. He gave a tiny groan and she practically melted on the floor. She felt his fingers on her chin, tipping her head back so her lips could meet his.

Jesus Christ, it was good.

21

She calls Grace. It's five minutes since Andrew left, them both having decided that they needed to put some physical distance between them or who knew what might happen. The temptation to ask him to stay had been almost suffocating. They went in one last time, his thumb tracing the softest touch down her neck and resting on her collarbone while she willed it to keep moving. Then she forced herself to open the front door and waved him off breezily like a polite acquaintance, while her heart pounded and her legs felt so weak they would barely support her. What just happened?

'Oh,' Grace says. 'I was wondering where you'd got to.'

'Sorry, I was busy. I need you.'

There's a long pause. 'Right.' Great, just when Kitty needs her, Grace has decided to punish her for not being a better, more present friend.

'Can you come over? No, wait, I'll meet you somewhere.' She suddenly doesn't want to be in her house any more. She feels as if Grace would be able to smell the sexual tension in the air the minute she walked in.

'I don't feel like going out, Kitty. I'm tired.'

'I know, I'll come to you.' Kitty has never set foot in Grace's place, just as Grace hadn't in hers until recently. That's one of the weird things about living in a city as vast as London – rarely does it ever seem like a good idea to travel an hour and a half to hang out in someone else's home. Kitty knows Grace lives in Barnes and that that's a long way from here, but that's as far as it goes.

'Are you OK?' There's suddenly concern in her voice, and Kitty realises Grace isn't used to her offering to make an effort.

'Kind of. I don't know. Please can I come over? I'll bring wine.'

Ten minutes later Kitty is in an Uber clutching two bottles of red. She'd thought about negotiating public transport but the multiple changes between buses, tubes and even British Rail had seemed too much to negotiate in her current state of discombobulation. She just wants to get there. She wants to share this secret as soon as she possibly can to make it real, to cement the memory in her brain.

'Can we do this again?' Andrew had said as he left, his hand entwined in her hair. 'You don't have to say yes, just a maybe is good.'

'Definitely.' She sounds, she realises ironically, like Lottie eating food. Maybe that's his thing. Women breathing heavily. She can't help herself, though. She doesn't think a kiss has ever made her feel like this. That is, she's had some good ones, just for the record, but, even in the early days Geth's were more about wooing than lust. Romance rather than sex. Very overrated in her humble opinion. Her rare post-Geth encounters have either been short-term relationships with people she was never very sure about in the first place, and consequently didn't melt like a puddle on the floor when they made a move, or even shorter itch-scratching one-nighters that generally passed by in a fug of alcohol and regret. And, if she were being completely honest, absolutely non-existent for the past two years.

Grace's flat is in a smart, new – if utterly soulless – block with an oblique view of the Thames that the property agents doubtless all make a huge song and dance about as part of their sales pitches. Grace buzzes her in, and she walks up to the first floor to a door on the non-tiny-view-of-the-river side. Grace opens it before Kitty even hits the top step and stands there looking at her wide-eyed. Of course she's worried. She probably thinks Kitty is about to tell her she only has weeks to live.

'This is nice,' Kitty says, but Grace isn't buying it.

'What's up? Are you OK?'

She's dressed in Grace's idea of casual slobbing-about-at-home wear: a pair of blue trousers, a cashmere V-neck sweater and brown loafers. It makes Kitty feel exhausted just looking at her.

'Yes. I'm fine. I just . . . something happened, but nothing bad. I don't think, anyway. I need to talk to you.'

'You're worrying me now. Come inside.'

'I just need advice. Or to offload, I don't know. And you're the only person I can talk to.'

'Was Sian not in?' Grace says with a snippy note of bitterness that she clearly can't help. Kitty has to stop herself from saying *What are we, twelve?*

'Actually, no, they're away. But I don't know if I would be telling her anyway. It's complicated.'

She sees Grace let her defences down a little. She follows her into a small buttercup-yellow hallway and through to a living room. There's a pale pink sofa with chrome arms that must have been transported straight from the 1990s. Two matching armchairs. Black-wood shelving. Like her own place, it's overly tidy, not an item out of place, as if Grace has way too much time on her hands and nothing else to do with it. But, unlike Kitty's, there are little knick-knacks everywhere. Groups of frogs: carousing, sad-looking, even menacing. Grace catches Kitty looking and laughs nervously. 'Oh yes, the frogs.'

'You kept that quiet.'

She looks a bit embarrassed. 'It's got a bit out of hand.'

God, Kitty thinks, the pair of them are sad.

'Hal hated them, and I think that just made me want them even more.'

'Whatever makes you happy.'

'I'll make tea,' Grace says and goes off to, Kitty assumes, the kitchen. Kitty perches on the edge of the sofa, trying to ignore her little green friends. This is not a room that invites relaxation. Her sweaty excitement of earlier has already been dampened down by the slightly depressing air in Grace's flat. By the time Grace comes back carrying a tray with a pot, a milk jug and two cups, like a 1950s housewife entertaining her husband's work colleagues, Kitty is wondering what she's doing here. What felt thrilling and daring now feels like it might be a bit embarrassing to share. They're two middle-aged women, not a pair of giggly schoolgirls. Grace's home has firmly reminded Kitty of that.

'What, then?' Grace says. 'What's going on that was so urgent?'

'Nothing. I mean, it feels stupid now.'

Grace frowns. 'You've come all the way over here not to tell me what you needed so urgently to tell me?'

'Something like that.'

Grace fusses around with the tea things. 'What's going on, Kitty?'

Kitty looks out of the window for a moment. She can't keep a smile from creeping over her face. 'Andrew and I kissed.'

Grace clatters the milk jug down. 'What? Wait, this is huge. I need the details. Start at the beginning.'

Kitty gives her the basics. She's thoroughly uncomfortable with describing a sexual encounter (which it most certainly was, even if it didn't go beyond the lips) with anyone, but Grace and the frog chorus more than most. Despite her apparent evidence that she's sex on legs, Grace can be a bit of a prude. She's looking a bit giddy, though, as Kitty fills in as many of the details as she can bear to share.

'Oh, My. God,' she says eventually. 'Do you really like him?'

Kitty considers for a second. 'I think I do. I mean, it's a bit messed up, though, don't you think?'

Grace shakes her head vigorously. Her stiff hair barely moves. 'Lottie's made her choice.'

'I suppose I just worry that Sian might think it's a bit off, me moving in on her friend. Like I'm taking advantage or something. Or that if it all goes wrong, it might end up being really awkward.'

'You might be right. People can be weird about stuff like that. So, what was it like?'

Kitty deflects by taking a sip of her too-hot tea. 'What was what like?'

Grace rolls her eyes. 'The kiss. Or kisses plural, should I say?'

'Pretty fucking spectacular. That's as much as you're getting.'

'Well, they sent you running halfway across London, so I'm guessing they were impactful.'

'I really, really, want to do it again,' Kitty says decisively.

Grace beams. 'Well, well, well. Kitty Harbinson is smitten. That's a first.'

'As if,' Kitty says, because she knows she can't try and defend herself without looking guilty.

'Good for you,' Grace says. 'You deserve a bit of fun.'

'There's something else . . .'

Grace's eyes almost pop out of her head in anticipation.

'Andrew found a charge for drinks at the Marylebone on Lottie's bank statement. Well, the shop's, actually. And, according to Sian, Rich was out that evening too.'

Grace actually gasps. 'She must be very confident that he trusts her and he's not snooping around.'

'That's what I said. It makes me dislike her even more.'

'Pfft,' Grace huffs dismissively.

'Anyway, he's stopped questioning if it's true.'

'Hence . . .' Grace says. She makes an over-the-top kissy face.

'Indeed. So, I think I'm probably the knee-jerk rebound.'

'Do you mind?'

'There are definitely worse things to be.'

They move on from tea to gin and tonics. Kitty follows Grace into the kitchen when she goes to make them and comes face-to-face with William and Kate smiling out from a picture on the cork noticeboard.

'No, Grace. No.'

Grace looks round, confused. 'Oh, are you Team Harry?'

'I'm not team anyone. Why are they on your wall?'

Grace opens the freezer. 'I think I have ice somewhere.'

Kitty knows she's fighting a losing battle. 'This is a nice kitchen.' It is. It could be. With a bit of pruning.

Back in the living room, drinks in hand, Grace relaxes a bit and kicks the loafers off under the coffee table. Every time they talk about other things, the conversation ends up circling back to what just happened, because Kitty can't keep Andrew's name out of her mouth. Before long they're a bit giggly. Kitty knows it's as much a release of the tension that's been building up between them lately as anything.

'It can't go anywhere,' Kitty says, once they've calmed down.

'You don't know that,' Grace says. 'But either way, enjoy it while it lasts.'

'I'll try,' Kitty says. And she means it. Maybe it's time for something good to happen for her at last. Maybe she's finally going to get her shiny new life after all.

22

Forest Streets Residents' WhatsApp Group:

E.W. Millman BSc (Hons): Suspicious-looking chap walking up and down the Close peering in all the gates. Be vigilant.

Linz G: That was Sam, lol! Looking for our Amazon parcel. He does look a bit suspect tbf.

Fourteen fights over seats (eleven of them because some-one who had paid for a window or aisle seat refused to swap with a parent who had decided it was worth risking their toddler sitting next to a random weirdo for several hours rather than pay the extra £9 to secure seats together), eight disputes concerning overhead locker space, seven food issues ranging from lack of choice to unexpected items in the sandwich area (*an acrylic nail painted in what looked like Bold AF from the 2AM range; it was a nice colour, actually*), four com-plaints about rude staff (a record low), one person upset about the meal choice or lack of it in the laughably named business class and one reporting the *revolting fishy smell in the cabin*. 'I asked him them what they had for lunch onboard,' Jacob had added. 'And they said fish finger wrap.' Kitty's brain replays her kiss with Andrew on repeat.

'What's up with you?' Ross says when he catches her staring off into space with, probably, a lascivious smirk on her face.

'Nothing,' she snaps. 'Absolutely nothing.'

'Yeah, right,' he says with a smile.

She smiles back. 'Well, nothing I'm going to tell you about anyway.'

'NSFW?'

'Definitely.'

'Eeew,' he says, as if he wasn't the one who brought it up in the first place. Now he's confronted with the possible realities of over-forties sex he's not so keen to hear the details. Kitty is tempted to spell it out anyway, suitably embellished for shock value, but she would probably end up being hauled up to some kind of disciplinary tribunal and asked to explain herself, so she just tells him he can finish half an hour early as it's a quiet day. She knows how to inspire loyalty in her team. 'Tell Evie she can too. It's so quiet today.' Boss of the year.

It's not even forty-eight hours since Andrew and Kitty kissed, and she keeps getting sideswiped by images. Sensations. Concentrating on work has been impossible because she'll be halfway through a conversation with one of the team about, for example, the new health and safety directive that means they all have to complete a largely pointless one-day computer-based course in the next ten weeks (*A colleague falls down a flight of stairs and injures themselves. Do you a) pick them up and take them to A and E, b) cover them with a blanket without disturbing them and call an ambulance or c) put a hat on them and pose them for a photo to put on Instagram?* You'd have to be some kind of a sociopath not to pass. Jacob once ticked every most obviously wrong answer and no one even called him in to ask if he was OK; they just rescheduled a repeat of the test a week later. Still, it keeps management happy), when she'll suddenly feel a phantom whisper of a finger tracking her collarbone, or a shiver of a breath on her neck. She's a walking erogenous zone, like someone being thawed out after years in deep freezer storage, being assailed with inappropriate sensations in random places as the ice melts and long-dead nerve endings judder back to life. She's a liability. In the end she holes herself away in the little space that passes for an office and pretends to be busy, but, really, she's watching old episodes of *Call the Midwife* on her phone. The ultimate cold shower.

Sian and Rich arrived home late last night, unpacking the car quietly so as not to disturb the neighbours, just as Kitty was rereading the text exchange she and Andrew had had earlier in the day.

Well, that was a surprise! he'd sent at about nine in the morning. Kitty had been awake all night, post her visit to Grace. She'd rebuffed Grace's offers for Kitty to sleep in her spare room, knowing she'd feel better if she woke up in her own space. *A nice one, I mean. Do you have buyer's remorse?*

She liked that he was nervous. That he was echoing her anxieties when he'd turned up on her doorstep. Or maybe he was looking for a get-out clause. *I actually don't. Do you?*

She stared at the three little dots, as if she might be able to telepathically influence what he was writing. She still jumped when it beeped. *Definitely not. I was just thinking about how much I'd like to do it again.* She felt a smile creep across her face. *Me too*, she replied. For a moment she actually thought about inviting him over right then, but she didn't want to frighten him off by looking too keen, and besides, he would almost certainly be spending a family Sunday with Lottie and Harry.

She wandered back to the window. Rich was softly clicking the boot shut, a large cold bag in his hand. He glanced up at her window and she stepped back.

Would you like to meet up after work tomorrow? Andrew sent. *I mean, only if you fancy it.*

Kitty made herself count to thirty before she answered, as if she was pondering what her response should be.

I'd love to. You can come here if you want.

She waited.

Rich might be home. Not sure how I'd explain it to him if he saw me. He added a smiley face, which should have been a passion killer right there, but somehow wasn't.

Of course! Kitty hadn't even thought it through. Rich had no reason to think anyone was on to him and Lottie, and so she and Andrew would look like the bad guys if he found out something was going on between them. (Is that what this was? 'Something'? She blushed at the idea.)

God, well remembered. I'm not thinking straight. She pictured him smiling when he read that.

Me neither. How about a walk on Hampstead Heath? We could meet at Kenwood? I can get away as early as you like.

That sounds perfect, Kitty replied. Because it did.

They messaged back and forth a bit more with details of times (four forty-five, so Kitty could go straight from work), a meeting place (the gate by the car park) and an agreement they'd text if it unexpectedly rained and make an alternative plan. Later, Andrew sent her a photo of a portly French bulldog wearing some kind of frilly white tutu. *Meet Fifi. She's been following me round the garden I'm working on all afternoon.* Ah, so he was working. No happy families for him today. *Owners furious because I threw a ball for her and she got mud on her dress.*

Throw it again, Kitty sent. *Show Fifi a good time. I bet no one ever plays with her. They just dress her up and post pictures for likes.*

They push her round in a pram. I'm not even joking.

Is she old?

Not even slightly.

She's incensed on the dog's behalf. *Fifi needs an intervention. Poor little thing.*

I'm here for a couple of weeks. She'll be a different dog by the time I've finished.

She wonders what Lottie would think if she saw them chatting so easily. She has no idea they have any kind of relationship independent of Sian and Rich. Kitty wonders if Andrew worries that she'll look at his phone and ask questions. She's assuming he knows that she wouldn't. She's the one with real secrets to hide, after all.

It's a gorgeous day, thankfully. Kitty changes into her vintage jeans. (She doesn't think she'll mention they came from Lottie's shop. She doesn't want Lottie's ghost haunting their date. Is it a date? Or just a 'thing'? Is a thing less serious than a date? Or are they just two friends who are going for a stroll together? Maybe Andrew's plan is to tell her it can never happen again, that he made a terrible mistake in the throes of grief at his marriage breaking down. Kitty was a band-aid, a painkiller. Effective but temporary.)

She adds a fitted T-shirt in pale yellow with a white abstract figure on the front and changes her low heels for

Adidas flats. She hangs her uncomfortable work clothes in her office. She can deal with them tomorrow. She brushes her teeth in the toilets. Hair down. She's ready.

Of course her Uber gets lost and even though she arrives only minutes late she's as frazzled as if she'd got on the tube and walked the twenty minutes from Hampstead station. Andrew is leaning against a sandy-coloured brick pillar in front of the gates, hands in his pockets. Scruffy jeans and a faded blue T-shirt. Kitty assumes he's come straight from work. A smile lights up his face when he sees her. He peels himself away from the wall.

'I'm late,' she says as she clambers out of the car. 'I hate being late.'

'Barely.'

They give each other an awkward hug that wouldn't look out of place at a family reunion. He smells of citrus and earth and toothpaste. The fact that, like her, he's found somewhere to brush his teeth in anticipation of their meeting makes her feel light-headed.

'You OK?'

She nods. Suddenly she's tongue-tied. 'Yep. You?'

He laughs. 'Nervous wreck. Shall we walk? You're looking gorgeous, by the way.'

Kitty grunts something that might be 'So are you' or could equally be her coughing up a hairball. What do people say to each other?

They head down the path, close but not too close. It's beautiful. Ancient-looking gnarly trees close in on them. People are walking their ecstatic-looking dogs to and from the car park.

'I don't . . .' she starts to say just as he says 'Did you . . .'

'You first,' she says.

'No. You.'

'God, I was going to say something really boring about not knowing this bit of the heath.'

He smiles his lopsided smile. 'Mine was even worse. I was going to ask about your day at work.'

'Are we literally the two dullest people on earth?' Kitty says, and he laughs.

'I have a solution.' He takes her hand. She automatically looks round as if someone she knows might see them.

He leads her off the path towards a clump of vibrant pink rhododendrons. Actually, right into the middle of a particularly large bush where they can't be seen from the path. 'Is this OK?'

It's so OK she can hardly speak, so she just gives another grunt. Her heart is racing. Andrew turns her to face him and slides his fingers onto her waist. 'I figure maybe if we get this out of our systems now then we might be able to act normally.'

'Good plan,' she manages. She literally feels weak with anticipation. He looks straight into her eyes and traces her mouth with his thumb, his hand cupping her chin. Kitty thinks she's had quite a lot of sex, although she's not sure what she's basing that on. No more than the average single woman, she's guessing, but a decent amount of bad, fair, middling, and the occasional good, encounters. But she honestly thinks she has never experienced anything more erotic than this simple gesture. She catches her breath. His hand snakes round the back of her neck and he hesitates for a second as if waiting for her to move in first. She does.

They make out like they're two fourteen-year-olds with one chance at seven minutes in a locked cupboard. They stay hidden by that rhododendron bush for at least fifteen, and then, Kitty thinks, they both know that if they don't try and take a pause, it might never happen. And no one wants to consummate their new relationship leaning up against a shrub with leaves scratching their back and curious dogs wandering over to take a look, although in the moment she was tempted to just go for it, ants and all. So, then they walk and talk, occasionally holding hands when no one else is around. She feels as if Andrew was right. With some of the pent-up lust out of their systems they find words again; they remember how to form sentences. She couldn't even say what they talk about, but before she knows it they're on Parliament Hill, gazing out over the London landmarks like the heroes of their own 1990s romcom. She can't quite believe how well they get on, how much they have in common. How much she likes him. This is way too good to be true.

She has to stop herself making snarky remarks about Lottie. *The little girl voice she puts on! The performance when she's eating!* She doesn't want to be that woman. And besides, Andrew is in love with her. Or was – it feels as if that has been firmly extinguished now, the embers of mistrust from years ago fanned back to life. All the things about her that irritate Kitty must have appealed to him at some point, though. They are not the reason his marriage is over.

They sit on a bench, shoulders touching. 'We might have to stop off in that rhododendron again on the way back,' Kitty says after a few moments when the sensation of his skin warm on hers becomes too much. She can't quite believe she said it out loud. His face curls into a smile. 'There are others on the way. We can do a whole horticultural tour.'

She's finally catching up with Sian. It feels as if the world has changed irrevocably since she saw her last. Kitty's own corner of it, at least. Sian's had already been shattered.

Andrew had dropped her off round the corner on the main road, and she'd sneaked home trying to avoid anyone seeing what she thought would be her giveaway smudged make-up and flushed cheeks. When she'd spotted herself in the hallway mirror she was surprised to see she didn't look any different to normal. Just to be on the safe side she'd texted Sian: *Are you back? Do you want to come over tomorrow evening?* Kitty was dying to see her, but she didn't want to risk her popping over now. She didn't think she could keep what had happened to herself and her instinct was that she needed to ease Sian into the idea gently, with a bit of distance from the shock of Rich and Lottie.

Too right I do!!! Sian had texted back almost immediately. *I'll be banging your door down at 5. So much to tell you xxx*

She arrives at five to, brandishing a box of doughnuts with unlikely flavours like Rose and Pistachio and Chipotle Chocolate that she bought from god knows where, but it certainly wasn't around Ashdown Close. There the choice would be jam or no jam.

'Crouch End,' she says when she sees Kitty looking at the box. 'Lottie brought them over yesterday.'

Kitty feels her eyes grow wide. 'She came over?'

Sian nods, mirroring her expression. 'I've really missed you,' she says in a squeaky voice. An impersonation of Lottie.

'Did she eat one of these and basically have sex with it at the same time?'

'Pretty much. Rich was there, so . . .'

'Shit.' Kitty is stunned by how brazen Lottie is. Rich too, but Lottie is the one showing up at his house like nothing was amiss. 'And how did they seem?'

Sian screws up her face. 'Now I know, I can't believe I didn't see it before.'

'That obvious?'

She nods.

Now is the time to tell her about Andrew. Not the details. To be honest, no one wants to hear those, except Grace who prised most of them out of Kitty on the phone last night. But she could casually mention that they'd seen each other again. She doesn't know why, but it feels as if Sian might take it the wrong way, though. He was her friend first; Kitty doesn't want her to feel she's muscling in. So, she stays quiet.

23

This could not be more uncomfortable.

But also, if Kitty were being honest, slightly thrilling.

Sian, Rich, Andrew, Lottie, Grace and Kitty are sitting in Sian and Rich's back garden with four of Sian and Rich's other friends that Kitty and Grace met at the house-warming. Kitty remembers them, the men with the mos. Felix and Bertie, and the two tall, thin, serious-looking women, Vita with her severe black fringe and sulky-faced Seraphine. They all look to Kitty as if they're doing post First World War cosplay and she'd be prepared to bet at least two of them were actually christened something like Dave or Sue. It's one of Felix and Seraphine's children's birthday next week, and tradition apparently has it that the four families all get together the weekend before any of the offspring has a big day. Only this time they've invited Kitty and Grace too. It was Sian's idea. 'We need ballast,' she'd said with an apologetic grimace. Even without the latest developments, the tradition had been dead on its feet for a couple of years, she told Kitty, ever since Harry had a relationship with the birthday boy, Jerome, before she realised she wasn't sure boys were her thing ('Felix and Seraphine were literally booking the church and buying hats') and Bertie and Vita's daughter Riley declared Rhys and Archie to be 'basic' while they thought she was an entitled nepo baby. ('Which she is. She's got a plum job at

Vivienne Westwood off the back of Vita's being a bit of a muse.')

Kitty hadn't been able to take her eyes off Archie and Harry – currently inside with Rhys and the other kids – when she was introduced to them for the first time. Archie with Andrew's smiley eyes and Lottie's peaches and cream colouring, Harry with Andrew's dark hair but Lottie's rosebud lips. Her wiry like her dad, him softer like his mum. She'd coloured red when she'd spoken to them, as if they'd be able to read what was going on just by looking at her.

Now she's struggling to act normally, not just with Rich and Lottie, but with Andrew in front of the others, too. And, actually, the whole vibe *is* weirdly normal. They loll in deck chairs. There are ice buckets with small brewery beers and fancy soft drinks. Two large umbrellas shield those of them who want it from the sun. (Seraphine also has a large-brimmed black hat protecting her ghostly pale skin and, every few minutes, sighs and shuffles her chair around to find the shade.) But every now and then her eye catches Andrew's and she flushes a deep red and loses her train of thought.

Because, after nearly two weeks of meeting in random places for al fresco make-out sessions – Kitty is becoming very familiar with the early-summer flora of public London spaces – last night they finally moved it inside. Into her house, onto her bed, under her duvet, while they knew Sian and Rich were out for the evening and Lottie was (genuinely, for once, it seemed) working late to patch up and press the 1920s flapper dresses she'd sourced for a costume designer friend. They'd had sex and it was every bit as mind-blowingly good as the many ways in which Kitty has imagined it. Geth could never get it into his head that mixing romance with sex gave her the ick. He'd read somewhere that women needed gestures of love to get in the mood, and no amount of Kitty trying to tell him otherwise would stop him from whispering cloying protestations of his undying affection and respect for her in her ear. At a crucial moment he would pull back and stare lovingly into her eyes. He'd use his tenderest voice. *Hello, kitten.* She'd freeze. Hello, ick more like. Goodbye, orgasm. There would be no chance of getting it back. Thankfully Andrew had never got that memo. Or if he had, experience had made him tear it up and throw it away.

Andrew finally dragged himself away at about nine o' clock – no staying the night yet, obviously, but that suited her. She likes her own space. Although she wouldn't have said no to a repeat performance this morning. She looks over now as he laughs at something Bertie says, tipping his head back, and she gets hit with a flashback of the way he looked up at her last night, tongue travelling slowly – agonisingly slowly – up her thigh. She actually gulps.

She hears a snort and looks over at Grace. 'Remembering something nice?' Grace says with a smirk. She knows, of course. She's like Kitty's priest at this point, hearing her confession on a regular basis. Kitty is certain she'd never betray her confidence, but Grace does love to tease her about it. Grace is pleased for her in a way that Kitty knows must be hard for her, given her own situation. She has a new match, by the way. Alasdair. Forty-seven. First date on Tuesday. Grace's choice: she's taking him to see a stand-up she has never found remotely funny, to see if he laughs. Huge black mark if he does.

'Very nice,' Kitty says.

Afterwards (strictly speaking, between), they talked about what might happen. How the future might look. *Look at me*, Kitty remembers thinking. *I'm talking about the future with a man I really like.* Mostly that they wanted to carry on seeing each other. Everything else – the end of his marriage, telling his children, life without his best friend – seemed too traumatic to bring into their lovely little safe space in her bed.

'I didn't think this would happen so soon,' he said, meaning them.

'I know. We don't have to, you know, make it a thing. We can just take our time and see how it progresses.'

'It feels really good, though, don't you think?'

It weirdly does. It's too soon, it's too messy, he's too on the rebound, but what do you do if you meet the right person at slightly the wrong time? You just wait it out, don't you? You don't give up on it because the circumstances aren't perfect, because when are they ever? Kitty's pessimistic head is telling her that it will all fall apart one of these days anyway, so they should just enjoy it while they can, but her gut is screaming that this is something special. Which scares the shit out of her, when she allows herself to think about it.

'I'm going to get the kids' pizza orders,' Rich announces, standing up. 'Start thinking about what you want.'

Sian wanders over to Seraphine, who is fiddling with a corkscrew, and, before Kitty can even register it, Lottie is flopping down in her vacated chair. Kitty shoots Grace a panicked look.

'Hi, ladies. I feel as if I haven't seen you for ages.'

She's wearing the yellow and green-sprigged tea dress, bare feet with navy-blue toenails. A gold ring twinkles on her second toe and a delicate chain on her ankle. She curls her feet up under her. If you asked AI what feminine was, it would probably show you a picture of Lottie.

Kitty forces a smile. She daren't look in Andrew's direction.

'What have you been up to?' Grace says lightly. Now Kitty daren't look at her either.

Lottie opens her eyes wide. 'Work. So much work. Which is good. Obviously.'

Grace asks her about exactly what she's been doing, and Kitty is grateful for the distraction. Lottie chatters on about the difficulties of sourcing original inter-war beading and Kitty half listens while she looks around the garden. Bertie and Vita's six-year-old son Wilf digs in the earth with a stick, bored out of his mind with the grown-ups' talk and the lack of other smaller children to play with. Kitty sees Andrew engage him with some kind of garden chat and show him how to upend weeds from the borders. Wilf smiles for the first time all afternoon. A weird random thought pops into Kitty's head. *I wonder what it would be like to have a kid with Andrew. Stop it, Kitty,* she tells herself sternly. You have never wanted children. Don't start now. As she watches, Sian drifts over and joins them. She's wearing a soft pale khaki parachute-silk jump-suit, with the sleeves and hems rolled up. She looks tough and wiry and beautiful. A warrior.

'Sian really is gorgeous, isn't she?' Kitty says. 'I mean, sorry, Lottie, I didn't mean to interrupt . . .'

'God, no. She is. Goddess.'

They all watch Sian and Andrew, who have turned their attention away from Wilf (now happily scrabbling in the flower bed) and are having a quiet, slightly intense conversation. Kitty suddenly realises it might not have been a good idea to alert Lottie to this.

'Poor old Wilf,' she says, in an attempt to change the subject. 'Will the older ones not play with him?'

'No chance,' Lottie says. 'Harry actually said "Remember I'm not a babysitter" when we arrived and she saw him.'

That actually makes Kitty laugh.

'Riley was the same,' Vita calls across. 'She said she has enough of him at home.'

Thankfully Wilf seems oblivious. He holds up a worm triumphantly and then puts it back down gently. Kitty steals a glance at Sian and Andrew. They're still locked in conversation out of earshot of everyone. Caught off guard, Sian looks wretched. Tired. Sad. Broken. Kitty's heart goes out to her. To them both, although she'd like to think Andrew looks fairly perky, considering. He reaches a hand out and lightly squeezes Sian's arm, a gesture of solidarity.

'OK. Who wants what?' Rich emerges from the house, his list and a pen in hand. Everyone scrabbles for the menus he handed them earlier.

'Quattro formaggio,' Lottie calls out. 'With extra everything.'

Rich chuckles. 'So four cheeses with extra cheese, basically?'

'Mmmm . . . and mushrooms.'

'How are you not the size of a house, Lotts?' Vita calls over.

'Oh, it'll all catch up with me one day,' Lottie says with a tinkly laugh. 'I fully intend to spend my dotage wearing a tent.' Behind her back, Kitty rolls her eyes at Grace.

They all put their orders in, Rich getting confused over numbers and having to go round and double-check. He reads through his list out loud one last time and goes inside to phone Deliveroo.

'Get dessert,' Felix shouts after him, and Rich raises a hand in acknowledgement. Sian watches him go, her smile slipping when he's out of sight.

'You OK?' Kitty mouths to her, and she responds with a slight shake of her head. Andrew follows her line of sight to see who she's looking at and he and Kitty lock eyes for a split second before they both look away as if they've been burned. It hits Kitty how bizarre this all is that she's sitting next to his oblivious wife feeling absolutely no guilt about what they did last night because it would never have happened if Lottie hadn't betrayed him first.

She listens as Grace fills Lottie in on the Julian fiasco. Bertie and Vita and Felix and Seraphine are talking loudly about an artist she has never heard of, Bertie and Vita braying like two agitated donkeys while Felix and Seraphine pontificate in their Addams Family monotones. Kitty struggles to see how the four of them fit in with the jokey (on the surface) familiarity of Sian, Rich, Andrew and Lottie. She knows Sian and Vita were thrown together in a shared room in halls their first year of uni and Felix and Rich went to school together, and sometimes, Kitty thinks, history trumps everything. It's irreplaceable. Impossible to fabricate or replicate. She and Grace would have to stay friends till their seventies to rival what Rich and Felix have. She lets all the chatter wash over her and closes her eyes to the sun until the pizzas arrive in two batches seconds apart.

Organising the food gives them all a chance to shift position and Kitty's glad, because she has no desire to chat to Lottie for longer than she has to. They file into the kitchen and aimlessly open and shut boxes, looking for the pizza they each ordered, even though half of them can't really remember what that was. Kitty hangs around the edges waiting for everyone else to argue about whether their selection had olives or capers or onions or all three. From the reactions, she gathers this is all part of the tradition and the only reason why this artisanal-loving, organic-only, e-number-avoiding bunch order lukewarm Pizza Express delivered by a fume-spewing motorbike in the first place. Eventually she gives up and wanders off to the downstairs toilet. She'll just have whatever doesn't get claimed.

When she comes out, Grace is hovering by the door. 'Jesus,' Kitty says. 'You made me jump.'

Grace grabs her arm and wrestles her back into the bathroom. Shoves a piece of paper into her hand. 'Look.'

Kitty does as she's told. *American Hot x 2 Bert/Archie.* 'It's the pizza list. So what?'

'Rich's pizza list. You saw him writing it.'

She doesn't cotton on. Confused, she reads it again.

'Do you see?' Grace says.

Kitty turns the paper over as if it might give an answer.

She'd love to say yes, but she has no idea what this means. She looks at Grace for a hint.

Grace digs a hand into her pocket and brings out her phone. She starts scrolling through her photos. Something starts to crystallise in Kitty's brain. Grace holds a picture up for her to see. 'Look.'

Kitty exhales. 'It's not the same handwriting.'

'Bingo,' Grace says triumphantly. 'I think . . . it looks as if Rich didn't write the note we found in Lottie's bag.'

Kitty looks at her, peering closer. 'But Sian said he did. We even asked her if she was sure, and she made that comment about him always joining up the Os.'

'Exactly.' She points to Lottie's selection. 'Look. *Extra mushrooms*. Double O. Not joined up.'

Kitty sits down on the closed toilet lid.

'I don't get it.'

Grace frowns. 'Me neither.'

Kitty looks up at her.

'Shit. What the fuck does this mean?'

PART TWO

24

They left the party almost immediately.

'So sorry, guys, she's sick,' Grace said over and over as she ushered Kitty through, holding her by the elbow. Kitty clocked Andrew flicking her a concerned look. She imagined she did look queasy at best. 'I think it must be the mussels we had at lunch.'

Everyone made sympathetic noises while taking a step back just in case she had the actual plague.

'I'm taking her home.' Grace propelled her towards the front door. Kitty almost reached out and grabbed a pizza on the way. Despite everything, she was starving. Contrary to rumour, she hadn't actually had any lunch beyond a bag of crisps and a lump of Cheddar. 'Thank you all for such a lovely evening.'

'Sorry,' she managed to mutter to Sian as she passed her. Sian reached out a hand and rubbed her back.

'Do you want me to come with you?'

'No!' Kitty said, too hastily. 'I'm just going to go to bed. Grace'll look after me. I don't want to ruin everyone's evening.'

'Grace, take a pizza,' someone said. Lottie. 'You might as well.'

'No, it's . . .' Grace started to say. Kitty nudged her in the ribs. 'I mean, yes, if you're sure . . .'

Kitty picked up the nearest box and handed it to her. She could not get out of there quickly enough.

Now they're each stuffing in a wedge (chicken and spinach, god knows which masochist ordered that), huddled over Exhibit A – the note found in Lottie's bag – on Grace's phone, which she has laid out ceremonially on the coffee table.

'The Os are definitely joined.' She traces them with her finger. 'Booooked.'

'So, someone's trying to make Sian think it's Rich?' Kitty wonders aloud.

Grace pulls a face. 'But how would they know she'd see it? And, anyway, no, because he doesn't join his Os; we know that now.'

Kitty rubs at her eyes. 'I thought Sian said he did. I'm so confused.'

'Me too.'

They sit there in silence for a moment.

'It can only be one person, you know that, don't you?' Grace says, putting down her neatly nibbled slice. Kitty's resembles a scene from a road accident.

Kitty closes her eyes briefly. It's too much to take on board. Too mind-blowing. 'It can't be. It makes no sense.'

'Sian pointed us there. Didn't she even say *go through her bag, she leaves it out the back*?'

Kitty is still struggling. 'Shit. So, the person Lottie's seeing isn't Rich, but Sian wants us to think it is? I don't understand.'

Grace puts her hands on Kitty's shoulders. 'Kit, I think Lottie might not be seeing anyone. Or Rich, for that matter. I think Sian might have made this whole thing up. I just don't know why.'

Kitty hears the words, but they don't go in. She can't make a coherent sentence of them in her head.

'She must really believe it. She wouldn't just . . .' She tails off. How can she be so certain? None of them have seen the incriminating text message Sian said she found, except Sian. 'You think she planted the note for us to find?'

Grace dabs at her mouth daintily with a bit of kitchen roll. 'That's what I think. She knew what day we were going down there; she could have done it any time. And that bag of Lottie's is basically like a mobile jumble sale; she never would have spotted it. Or known what it was if she did. Worst-case scenario she found a random scrawl on a piece of paper and threw it away.'

'You think Sian set me up? Us?'

'I think it's looking that way.'

Kitty closes her eyes for a second. Is this just Grace's skewed perspective, taking a swipe at the person she feels is edging her out? 'Shit. I don't know. What about Lottie sneaking out of their house, trying to avoid being seen? You can't tell me that was normal.'

Grace shrugs. 'It's like the big bang. You know there's an explanation, you just don't know what it is yet.'

'But you saw them together . . .'

Grace has the decency to look guilty. 'Maybe I misinterpreted something. Maybe it was just a, you know, platonic hug. Maybe the thing at the party was too. They're just old friends who are affectionate with each other.'

Kitty opens her mouth to say something. Closes it again. 'No. Wait. Andrew saw the transaction on Lottie's bank statement. The drinks at the Marylebone. Why would he make that up?'

'He wouldn't. There must be an innocent explanation.'

'She told him she was in East Finchley, though. At the cinema.'

'Kit! I don't know. She lied for some other reason. Maybe she was at a support group for people who fake orgasm when they eat.'

Kitty almost laughs but then she's struck by a lightning bolt. 'Fuck. No.'

Grace freezes. 'What?'

'Andrew. Fuck, Grace. I slept with him. If Lottie isn't having an affair with Rich . . . Fuck.'

'Oh.' Grace says. 'Yes. That's not good. We're going to have to tell Andrew. Like right now. You can't see him again. Obviously. And Lottie, someone's going to have to tell Lottie.'

Kitty catches her breath. She knows Grace is right, but it's not fair. Nothing about it is fair. She finally meets someone she likes – really likes – and who seemingly likes her back and it turns out the whole thing is based on false pretences. She was actually starting to feel as if there might be something there. She would never have allowed that possibility in, have opened herself up to that vulnerability, if she'd thought it could never have a chance.

If she'd thought that the wife of the man she was sleeping with still believed they were happily married.

25

'Come here.' Grace grabs her in an awkward hug. It's two days later – two long, tortuous, soul-searching days – and they're at a spa in Pimlico, Grace's treat to attempt to cheer Kitty up. They're each having a massage and a facial and Kitty has already changed into her fluffy robe by the time Grace arrives, so she feels like an invalid aunt being paid a duty visit. 'How are you feeling?'

'Miserable.'

Grace squeezes her tighter, Kitty's face pressed up against her stiff helmet of hairsprayed hair. 'Poor you.' She steps back, hands on Kitty's shoulders, and gives her a sympathetic look. 'How did he take it?'

Kitty shrugs. Lets out a sigh. 'I can't talk about it . . . I just . . .' She puts her hands over her eyes and feels Grace wrap her arms round her again.

'I know you really like him. I know it's hard.'

Kitty gulps loudly in her ear. 'I never meet anyone I like. Never. You know that.'

'There'll be someone.'

'I didn't even care about meeting anybody for fuckssake. I was fine on my own before.'

'It'll get better. Give it time.' Grace might sound like she's swallowed a dictionary of clichés, but she's being so sweet Kitty almost loses it altogether. She's never been able to deal with people showing her sympathy. It's as if she can hold herself together so long as no one else acknowledges there's anything wrong.

'Is he going to tell Lottie?' Grace says in a half-whisper.

Kitty nods. 'She's going to hate me. I mean, of course she is.'

'It's Sian she should blame. I don't . . .' Grace starts to say, just as a young woman with a perfectly neat, unfeasibly shiny ponytail calls Kitty's name and tells her it's time for her massage. 'What exactly is Sian up to, that's the big question . . .'

'Search me,' Kitty says as she stands up. 'I don't think I even want to know.' She realises as she's saying it, it's not true. She wants to know everything.

Sixty minutes of heaven later she reconnects with Grace beside the pool. Grace's face is glowing like she's radioactive. Kitty's not sure she's ever seen her without a full face of make-up, and she looks ten years younger and almost heartbreakingly vulnerable. Her stiff hair is held back with a band.

'You should wear your hair back more often,' Kitty says when she sees her. 'It really suits you.'

Grace huffs and plonks herself down on the lounger next to her.

'So, are you going to confront her?' she says as if they're still in the middle of the conversation about Sian.

'No! What? I'm keeping out of it.' Kitty feels all the benefits of the past hour start to slide away. Her shoulders tense. The reality is, curiosity is eating her up. She thought she knew Sian. She thought they were friends. She keeps picking up her phone to text her some random funny thought, or to see if she's up for a walk or a coffee, and then remembering Sian has been deceiving her all along. Kitty can't get her head around it. Sian wanted to destroy Lottie and Andrew. She didn't care that Andrew's friendship with Rich was collateral damage. But why?

'Good. Just keep out of their way. All of them.'

Kitty looks at her. 'I thought you'd be telling me to storm in there and have it out with her.'

Grace shakes her head. 'She's never going to tell you the truth anyway. We'll have to find out some other way. Do you want to eat? We just have time before our next treatment.'

'Sure.'

'That's it for Lottie and Sian, right? They can't be friends after this.'

Kitty ties her robe a bit tighter, desperate not to lose the massage warmth. 'None of them can.' She's hit with another wave of sadness at the loss of Sian's friendship. Can it really be true? Could they have missed something and it's all a misunderstanding? It seems unlikely.

'I'm going to have to move house.'

'Don't be daft. Anyway, you were there first. Let them move if they've made everything uncomfortable. Or yes! You move. You hate where you live anyway. Come to Barnes.'

It's actually tempting. Not Barnes. Not on Grace's doorstep. And she almost certainly couldn't afford it anyway. But maybe Kitty should use this as the impetus she needs. Sell up and buy a tiny one-bedroom flat somewhere with a bit more life. Buy with her heart and not just her head.

'Anyway, let's talk about something else.' She reaches for the laminated menu on the side table. She has absolutely no appetite, but it's a distraction. A way to get Grace off the subject.

They order food. An avocado and mango salad for Grace and a brie and chutney ciabatta sandwich for Kitty. Pungent green juices. Grace is like a dog with a bone, though. She keeps circling back around: who's going to tell Rich what his wife has been up to? What are the chances Lottie can forgive Andrew once she knows the full story? Can Andrew and Rich maintain their friendship if Rich doesn't give Sian the boot? They're all valid questions.

Sort of.

Kitty cuts the day short as soon as she can without looking ungrateful. Grace gives her another of her sympathetic bear hugs and Kitty promises to call her in the morning.

'What are you doing tonight?' Grace says, pulling a sad expression.

'Deliveroo and an early night,' Kitty says. 'Get my head straight.'

If only Grace knew.

She hasn't checked her phone all day. She stashed it in her locker, telling Grace it would be good not to have any distractions. The truth is, she knows she's not a good enough actress. She digs it out now. Two messages: *Have fun. Don't fall asleep on the massage table!* and *6.30? Or is that too early?*

6.30 is perfect, she sends.

She's going to hell.

26

The Premier Inn in Archway isn't exactly the Marylebone, but it's clean and comfortable and they don't give you filthy looks if you order food in from outside. Kitty wasn't completely lying to Grace about Deliveroo and an early night.

She smiles at the receptionist and asks her to call up to Mr Hart's room. No fake names here. They're not sneaking around trying to cover their tracks. They're just trying to ensure they keep things private until it's time to tell Andrew and Lottie's kids. At least that's the official line.

She was going to come clean with Andrew. She truly, honestly, genuinely was. She actually drew breath, opened her mouth and willed herself to say it: *I've found something out. I need to tell you* . . . But, when it came to it, she just couldn't do it. Their relationship would end the second he found out Lottie hadn't been cheating on him. He was a good, honourable man. He would do the right thing. Whatever he felt about Kitty, however his feelings for Lottie might have changed recently, it would make no odds. And Kitty wasn't prepared to give it up yet. So, she stifled the words before they came out. *Just one more day*, she told herself. She would tell him tomorrow. The damage had already been done; what difference would it make?

And then the next day came, and she couldn't find the words to tell him then either.

Only she and Grace knew the truth about Sian's lie. If Grace believed Kitty had put things right, she would have no reason to get involved. As far as she was concerned, Kitty's days of socialising with Sian and co. were over. She wouldn't be expecting any invitations any time soon. If Kitty kept up the front – pretending to Sian that all was fine, pretending to Andrew that she still thought Rich and Lottie were the devil's spawn and Sian was a tragic victim like him – then, when it all came out, as, inevitably, it would one way or the other, none of them would ever realise that she'd already found out the truth (most of it – Sian's motives were still a mystery to her) and kept it to herself. She'd be viewed as as much of a casualty as the rest of them.

She knows how wrong this is.

She knows what she's doing to Lottie.

She knows it will end in tears.

But she can't break it off now.

Because maybe, by the time Andrew finds out that Lottie was never cheating, he'll have fallen so hard for Kitty that he won't even look back. She can't even think about the morality of that one.

Andrew opens the door before she has the chance to knock twice.

'Finally,' he says, slipping his hands round her waist and pulling her closer.

She looks at her phone. 'I'm two minutes early.'

'Exactly.' He leans in and kisses her. The whole thing, Lottie, Grace, Sian, fades into the back of her brain. This is all that matters. 'I missed you.'

'Me too,' she breathes into his ear.

'Are you hungry? Do you need to eat?'

'Later,' she says.

He slides a hand under the hem of her top. 'I was hoping you'd say that.'

'I have some hellebores I want to drop round. But I only want to do it when you're there, so I can see you.' They're lying on their sides facing each other, a half-eaten cup of Five Guys fries between them.

'God, you really do know how to get a girl going.'

He laughs. 'The burger didn't do it?'

'Foreplay. The free plants have clinched the deal.'

'Can you sneak off for an afternoon? Not Wednesday, or Sian'll be there.'

Kitty digs around the scratchy, salty dregs. 'That's the beauty of being the boss of a department. Tuesday, maybe? Sian does detention duty till five. I could probably leave at two-ish.'

He hooks a bit of hair behind her ear. 'Perfect. I'll get to yours for three. We'll have mind-blowing sex till quarter to five and then I'll plant some perennials.'

She has somehow managed to forget about Sian for the past couple of hours. Now it all comes crashing back. How all this – her and Andrew – is on borrowed time. How it can never end well, however much she hides her head in the sand. How she's storing up pain not just for everyone else but for herself too, the longer she lets things slide. She forces herself to make eye contact, needing validation. 'She couldn't be wrong, could she? Sian? About Rich and Lottie, I mean.'

He frowns. 'Where's that come from?'

'I just want to be sure. That what we're doing is OK.'

Outside a car alarm blares. He shakes his head. 'Don't worry. It's all the sneaking around, it's making it feel as if we're doing something wrong. We're not.'

'No,' Kitty says quietly.

'Hey,' he says. 'Lottie's made her choice. And that's made me realise that it was over anyway. It had run its course and I was in denial. What's happened has just made me see things clearly, that's all. I'm not . . . we're not . . . compatible any more. We probably weren't even before all this . . .'

Kitty actually feels her heart speed up. 'You're not tempted to give her another chance? For the kids, or whatever?' She hates that she sounds so needy, so pathetic, but she needs to know that in Andrew's head his relationship with Lottie is dead and buried. If he's convinced of that now, it'll be harder for him to tell himself otherwise later.

'She's done me a favour,' he says, with the first hint of bitterness Kitty has seen. It makes her feel better, she's not going to lie.

At work the next day (still smelling of musky hotel soap – she had stayed the night after Andrew had left because why waste the room and she had nothing to get home for) she has a bad case of mentionitis. Andrew says this. Andrew thinks that. After a couple of hours Evie finally says, 'Are you seeing someone called Andrew?'

Kitty blushes a furious red and then thinks, *Why not tell them*? It's not as if her two lives coincide here.

She raises her eyebrows theatrically. 'Whatever makes you think that?'

Evie laughs loudly. 'I knew it! Tell us everything!'

So, Kitty tells them about her new landscape gardener boyfriend. Funnily enough, she doesn't mention his wife.

When she gets home, Sian is on her doorstep within minutes, tapping on the door. Kitty thinks about pretending she's out, but she knows Sian will have seen her arrive, and besides, she doesn't want her to realise anything's wrong. Kitty needs to look as if she's still buying into Sian's drama. Not to mention that she needs to stay one step ahead of her. She has to find out what Sian is up to, because if she's planning a big 'gotcha' reveal that it was all some kind of hilarious practical joke, then Kitty has to be primed to derail that. Not that she thinks that's going to happen. Sian has planted a bomb under Andrew and Lottie's lives; no way could she think that was funny.

'Where have you been?' Sian says, pretend-outraged, when Kitty opens the door. It's true Kitty has been avoiding her texts. Sian looks just like her usual self: hair in a messy topknot. Lean arms white against her smoky-blue vest top. 'Are you OK? I thought maybe your food poisoning had turned out to be something else.'

'Oh god, sorry. Yes. I mean, no. Grace had a crisis. She's fine,' Kitty adds hastily in case Sian decides to check that Grace is OK. 'Just typical Grace stuff.'

Sian wanders in, so at home she doesn't think to wait for an invitation. A few days ago, Kitty would have loved this. The ease they'd developed and the way it didn't feel oppressive. She follows Sian into the kitchen where she is already filling the kettle at the sink. 'She's OK, though?'

'What? Yes. Fine. You know what she's like. How have you been?'

Sian does the so-so hand thing. 'Up and down. I keep thinking I don't want to lose Barbara and Ray.'

Kitty gets two mugs from the draining board. 'You won't. They'll still be Rhys's grandparents.'

Sian leans on the unit, head down. 'It won't be the same.'

Kitty summons all of her acting skills. Walks up behind her and puts an arm round her shoulder, pulling her in. 'It won't. But it'll be fine. It's not as if anyone's going to blame you for anything.'

The kettle clicks off and she leans past Sian and picks it up, putting teabags in both mugs with the other hand.

'How long till you can come clean now?'

Sian counts on her fingers. 'Still about nine weeks.'

It's not really that long, Kitty thinks, and a wave of panic hits her. She's been avoiding thinking about what will happen next. 'Can you keep it up? The pretence?' She daren't look at Sian as she trails her over to the table and sits down.

'I think so. I mean, I fucking hate him. Both of them. But yes.'

Kitty puts a hand on top of hers and squeezes it. Composes herself. 'How's Andrew bearing up, do you think?'

'Weirdly well. Better than me.'

Because he has me, Kitty thinks. *Because he's falling for me.* 'Really? He's not upset about Lottie?'

Sian sips her tea, scowling because it's too hot. 'He is,

but more because he's angry than he's devastated, I think. Don't let on I told you this, but she's done it before.'

Kitty feigns surprise. 'Lottie? No! I can't imagine it . . .'

'I'm not meant to know, but Rich told me, even though he wasn't supposed to. I mean, it was a few years ago . . .'

Kitty has thought about this often. She wants to convince herself that Lottie isn't a totally innocent victim, that in some way she deserves what has happened to her. It makes what she's going to do easier. 'She had an affair? Who with?'

Sian shrugs. 'Some bloke she met in a café where she worked before she had the shop. Not an affair, really. A "fling".' She makes air quotes. 'Like that makes it better.'

'I mean, it does a bit, doesn't it? Just physical, not emotional.' She doesn't know why she feels the need to defend Lottie. That is, she does; it's her own guilt talking.

Sian scoffs. 'I'm sure Andrew thought that made it all OK.'

Kitty doesn't want to fall out with her, so she nods. 'I'm just playing devil's advocate. It's horrible either way, obviously.'

'I don't know why he stuck with her to be honest. And this is how she repays him.'

'It's impossible to fathom the dynamics of anyone else's relationship.'

'It's kids.' Sian rubs at a spot on the table with her fingertip. 'Kids change everything. You can't just walk out.'

'Do you think he will now? Once the holiday is over?'

'He has to. There's no "it was just a fling" this time. It's his best mate. Honestly, if he doesn't, I'll drag him away kicking and screaming.'

Kitty leans back in her chair, her heart pounding. 'And how about you? Do you have a plan for when it all blows up? I assume you'll stay put and Rich'll have to find himself somewhere else to live?'

Sian rubs at her eyes. 'That's fair, right?'

Kitty nods, trying to process what this actually means for Rich. Is Sian going to go through with it? She's going to kick him out of his home? Despite his – genuine – protestations of innocence. The woman's a monster. Riding roughshod over everyone she supposedly cares about to achieve ... what? *Maybe she's just unhinged*, Kitty thinks. Maybe she should sneakily text Grace to say *If I'm found with a meat cleaver in my head, it was Sian*.

'What are you going to do if he won't admit to it? If he, like, digs his heels in?'

'How can he? Do you think he'd risk me showing Rhys the things I've found?'

'You wouldn't?' For a second she forgets that these things don't actually exist, she's so sideswiped by the idea Sian would even think about involving their son in this mess. Although the payment Andrew uncovered in Lottie's accounts is burning a hole in her brain. That existed.

Sian sighs. 'Probably not. No. I wouldn't. But Rich would never want to take that risk.'

'And do you think Andrew will do the same? Kick Lottie out?'

Sian laughs. 'No way. He thinks she needs to stay in the family home with Harry. Even though Harry will be moving to York in September.'

Kitty knows this, obviously. And even if the whole story were true, she'd approve. Andrew thinks Harry will need her mum to come home to, whatever her mum may have done, and he's not vindictive enough to want to disrupt that. 'That's tough on him, but it makes sense. Is he looking for somewhere else already?'

'I think so . . .'

(He is. Kitty knows this. He went to look at a rental in Muswell Hill yesterday)

'. . . I'm going to ask him if he wants to stay here for a bit, though. It's crazy to have to shell out on a second place when he's done nothing wrong. And I've got room . . .'

Kitty thinks about Andrew sleeping twenty feet away every night. About how easy it would be for him to sneak over when the coast was clear. She nods emphatically.

'I think that's a great idea. It might be good for both of you to have the company while you work things out. Do you think he'll say yes?'

Sian gives her a smile. 'We'll see, won't we?'

27

It's hard keeping secrets. Lottie is just not constitutionally cut out for it. She's a sharer. A soul barer. Not to mention a people pleaser. It's why she loves what she does so much – making things not just for her customers, but her friends too, or finding them some trinket they'll treasure. It's her way of saying, *Look how hard I worked on this for you, look how nice I am. Like me. Please.* Her desperation to be liked is one of the things she most despises about herself. If only she didn't give a shit, like Sian. That was a superpower right there. Something to be envied. There was a lot, if she were being honest, that she envied about Sian.

She had watched in awe when she first witnessed the skinny woman with the rows of silver rings in her ears and the perfect neat bump, arguing with the midwife that if she was made to look at pictures of a baby ripping its way out of a vagina again she was going to go straight and book an elective caesarean. ('I know what's going to happen,' she'd said. 'I just don't need to see it. Surprise me. It'll be like Christmas.') Lottie never caused a fuss, never got into arguments. They had ended up sitting at the back of the class muttering comments to make each other laugh, and they'd been friends ever since. A few weeks in and they'd introduced their partners, and that was it. It had been the four of them from then on. Dinners. Drinks. Eventually holidays once they emerged from the intensity of the tiny baby years, at first a long weekend in the Lake District to try the idea on for size, and then, when that was an unqualified success, weeks in the Med or Prague or New York.

Motherhood had hit Lottie hard. She adored her kids, adored Andrew – easy, laid-back, funny, reliable Andrew who loved them all back, and who helped out as much as he could, but who was also the one with the proper career who worked all hours to maintain the business's five-star reputation – but she'd lost herself. Sian had fully known who she was before she became a parent, but Lottie had felt half formed. A work in progress. And then, once they had Archie, it made sense to give him a sibling while she was still on what she euphemistically referred to as a break from the job she'd always hated and had no intention of ever going back to. She just needed to find her 'thing'. Her identity. Herself.

As the kids got older she'd dedicated her afternoons to her eBay shop selling vintage clothes that she picked up in charity shops, repaired and sourced buttons for and sold on at a tiny profit. She loved old clothes. Loved the care that had gone into making them and the portal they created into another, seemingly much more glamorous world. But it was a hobby rather than a career. Pin money, her mum would have called it. So, she worked in a café in the park four mornings a week to at least feel she was contributing, and buried the idea that her life was drifting.

She knew that was why she'd had the affair. Not affair, no. She wouldn't dignify it with that name. Twice, that was all it was. It was barely even sex, almost as if they felt that that was what they'd signed up for but neither of their hearts was really in it. It was affirmation. To remind herself that she was alive.

Damian, his name was. Damo. She didn't even notice him at first, but what she did soon start to notice was the attention he paid her. She started to look forward to him coming in. The few minutes of chat while she made his oat flat white. He remembered every little thing she told him about herself. He'd ask questions about the clothes. Had she had any good finds? Any exciting auctions? The whole thing was ridiculous, she could see that now. Could see that immediately after occasion two, in his post-divorce sterile, grey and black flat, when she came abruptly to her senses and realised with horror what she'd done, what she could have lost. She adored Andrew. She always had. Him, the kids. They were her world. She was risking losing all of them for a man she knew with absolute certainty that she had no long-term interest in. What had attracted her was being noticed, the idea of something different, something that was just her own. It wasn't about Damo; it was all about her. She was pathetic.

She gave in her notice at the café and then cried off working it. She couldn't face going back.

And then, one evening when both kids were off with their friends, she'd told Andrew. She'd thought about burying her secret. She knew there was no chance he would ever find out. Damo had been relaxed when she'd let him know she couldn't see him again. He'd sympathised with her feelings of self-loathing. He was a nice guy, no threat. But she knew she couldn't live with that version of herself. That the guilt would eat her up. It was lose/lose. She'd ruined her relationship either way. But at least if she were honest she could hold her head a tiny bit higher.

She'd felt sick. Certain that Andrew would up and leave. She knew it would blow every perception he'd ever had of her, that was the worst thing. That his absolute trust would be gone forever. If he gave her the chance, she would spend the rest of her life proving to him that she was worth it.

28

Kitty watches Andrew sleep, feeling the light exhale of his breath on her cheek. His mouth is turned up at the corners as if something in his dream is making him smile. She hopes it's her. He's staying the night. Kitty knows they've taken stupid risks – getting carried away with the novelty of the idea once Andrew knew Lottie and Harry were planning a night away, a break from Harry's revision, and Kitty remembered the party that Rich and Sian were dreading but felt obliged to go to. He had waited for her call when she saw them leave and then appeared half an hour later, phoning from the main road to check the coast was clear of nosy neighbours after the taxi dropped him off. Kitty had kept watch as she waited for him, just in case. They'd both got a bit giggly, whether from anticipation or from the fear of getting caught she wasn't sure. It felt like a milestone.

Spending a night with someone is make or break, she's always thought. It isn't just the obvious red flags like snoring or leaving crusts of toothpaste round the sink. How someone shares the bed gives away volumes about what they would be like to have a relationship with. Geth had always crowded her. Arms draped over her from behind, clamped on like a baby panda on a zookeeper's leg, while she sweated through the urge to shove him away and waited for him to fall asleep so she could extricate herself.

Now she wonders why she hadn't just told him she hated it, not caring if it hurt his feelings. She wasted hours of her life lying there fuming. So, she waits in the half-light for Andrew to suggest spooning, telling herself to be firm and put her foot down, not to censor herself for fear of putting him off.

'How do you like to sleep?' he says as she lies with her head on his chest, his heart beating in her ear.

She pushes herself up on one elbow and looks at him. 'I get way too hot. I can't stand feeling trapped by the covers or under someone's arm or whatever. I like my space. Not to say don't touch me. Definitely. Just, you know . . .'

'Great,' he says, laughing. 'I actually only meant on your side or your back, or whatever. I was curious. But I'll absolutely take all that on board.'

She's glad he can't see her blushes.

'And, for the record,' he adds, kissing the top of her head, 'I'm exactly the same. Get over your side of the bed and stay there. Keep your sweaty extremities away from me.'

At two they hear Sian and Rich trying to shut their taxi doors quietly, clumsy with alcohol, and both instinctively hold their breath as if they might give themselves away otherwise.

'We haven't worked out how you're going to get out in the morning,' she whispers. 'You might end up trapped here forever.'

'Worse things have happened.'

They end up talking until gone four, still facing each other when the dawn begins to tear the sky.

She feels cracked open. Dizzy with the thrill of it all.

*

Kitty meets Grace for a drink and listens to her ramble on about Alasdair. ('Quite nice, quite good-looking, quite funny. Just 'quite' everything really. Bad shoes.') It should be entertaining, but all Kitty's brain can do is try to process what she can and cannot tell her. She needs to talk to someone, and Grace is currently her only option. But she can only give her half the truth. And, even then, it's dangerous. What if Grace decides to get involved? What if Magda rises from the dead and starts sending vengeful messages again?

She can't help herself, though.

'Sian's going to ask Andrew if he wants to stay at hers,' she says, in an effort to stop herself talking about anything deeper, after Grace has described the meal at Hutong in agonising detail.

'Who paid?' Kitty had butted in, in an effort to speed towards a conclusion.

'We split it. That's a rule with the Marriage Brokers. All costs split on the three compulsory dates.'

'That's good, I think,' Kitty had said, fingers in a bowl of peanuts. 'I hate that crap that men are expected to pay for everything even if you both have decent jobs. So patronising.'

Grace had shrugged. 'Alasdair said it felt a bit wrong to him.'

'Easy once you know you're off the hook,' Kitty said, and Grace had laughed.

'He's quite old-fashioned, I think, but there's nothing wrong with that.'

'He'll be asking you to darn his socks next.'

Grace had pulled an eew face. 'Not if they've been in those shoes.'

'Not at all, Grace! Whatever shoes they've been in,' Kitty said. Honestly, Grace was a lost cause.

'She's throwing Rich out?' Grace asks now as she sloshes more Merlot into their glasses. Kitty dabs at a spill with a small white napkin. 'That's the plan, apparently.'

Grace sits up straighter. 'Tell me everything.'

This is a mistake. Grace is way too eager for the gossip.

Kitty shifts uncomfortably in her seat. She can hardly say Sian came round for a cup of tea. 'I bumped into her . . .'

'Oh god,' Grace says.

'I mean, it was always going to happen. I'm hardly going to be able to avoid her for the rest of my life. I've backed right off, but it's going to take a while for her to get the message. It's not like primary school where you can just say "I don't want to be friends with you any more" . . .'

'No. Right. Anyway . . .'

'And she just said that. That she's going to ask if he wants to move in with her . . .'

She jumps as Grace slams a hand on the table. 'That's it!'

'What? Shit. Don't do that again.'

'That's what all this is about. Her motive.'

'Grace, I have no idea what you're on about.'

Grace moves to tuck her hair behind her ear, but it's stiff with hairspray and doesn't comply. 'I'm beginning to think Gritty's powers of observation aren't as good as we thought they were. How did we miss this?'

Kitty fixes her with a frown. 'Stop talking in riddles. Just tell me.'

Grace sits up taller, ready for her big moment. She always sits with her ankles daintily crossed while Kitty sprawls. 'Varicose veins,' Grace had said once, nodding towards Kitty's pretzelled legs. 'You're cutting off the blood flow.'

'It's one of my few pleasures in life,' Kitty had said, drily. 'Please don't make me give up my bad posture.'

Grace had rolled her eyes. 'You'll regret it one day when your calves are all lumpy.'

'Trust me,' Kitty had said. 'If slouching is my biggest regret, I'll have got off lightly.'

Now she tries to keep a lid on her irritation and waits to be enlightened.

'If Sian just wanted to split up with Rich, she'd tell him, right? She wouldn't go to all these convoluted lengths and involve us. So, there's something else. She likes him. Andrew. She's hoping she can break up Lottie and Andrew and have Andrew for herself, that's what this is all about. She knows he'd never leave Lottie for her unless she can give him a motive. She needs him to believe Lottie is cheating on him so he'll fall out of love with her.'

Kitty lets out a dismissive laugh. 'Don't be ridiculous.' But she can't help a sneaking suspicion that Grace might be on to something.

And then another thought strikes her. Isn't that exactly what she's doing too?

Shit.

'And she knows he would never make a move on his best friend's wife unless he thought that best friend had mortally wronged him. So, she has to vilify them both.'

'That's crazy,' Kitty says, doubling down, but even as she says it she can see the logic.

'Can you think of another reason?'

'They're old friends and she doesn't want him to have to shell out for somewhere to live just because his wife is shagging around?'

Grace winces at the language. 'She's not, remember. It's all a lie. Sian's lie.'

Kitty closes her eyes for a moment, trying to get her thoughts straight in her head. She should have known confiding in Grace, with her stupid theories, was a mistake. 'They must have done something to her. Rich and Lottie. It's payback, it has to be. Something's happened between them all that we don't know about.'

'Or I'm right.'

She can't be. Sian and Andrew? It doesn't bear thinking about, although, weirdly, she can see them together. Their energies match. She feels a crushing wave of insecurity. What if he realises that for himself once Sian propositions him? 'No. That's insane.'

'What does Andrew think?'

See, this is why she should have kept her mouth shut. Grace is never going to understand why she hasn't shared her suspicions with him. She can hardly tell her it's because he doesn't know the half of it. That he has no idea Sian's whole Rich and Lottie story is made up.

'I haven't asked him. It's all a bit . . . weird. I think it's better if he and I aren't in touch, you know.'

Thankfully Grace totally buys it. 'No, god, of course. I wasn't thinking. He needs to steer well clear of you if he wants to work it out with Lottie. So, you have no idea if he's told her yet? About you and him?'

Fuck. She's opened a box she can't close. 'No. None. Honestly, Grace, I'm just keeping out of it.'

'What if they're actually the ones who've been having the affair? Sian and Andrew? What if he was sleeping with her and you at the same time?'

Kitty pushes her chair back and it squeaks loudly, making her jump. 'I'm going to the loo. I'll get another bottle on the way back, but then any more talk about Sian and co. is banned. They're taking up way too much space in my head. I want to hear more about Alasdair. Did he pass the no-laughing test?'

Grace pulls a face that tells Kitty Alasdair made the fatal mistake of looking as if he was enjoying himself.

'Oh good,' Kitty says, forcing a smile. 'Can't wait. I'll get snacks.'

29

Could it be true? Could Grace have got it right? Kitty paces round her kitchen, too wired to go to bed. She got through the evening somehow, mainly by just letting Grace talk uninterrupted, nodding and pulling what she hoped were appropriate facial expressions from time to time. But her brain had gone into overdrive. It made sense, that was the problem. It explained everything.

Her impulse is to warn Andrew: *Don't let Sian get into your head.*

She realises that what she is actually scared of is that Sian will succeed. That all this will be for nothing if Sian and Andrew ride off into the sunset together. She's forty-three and putting herself in competition with another woman over a man. It's tragic.

And not a little weird, when that man already has a wife.

But she can't bear not to give what she has with him a fair chance. Just in case. What if he's the only man she ever feels this way about and she doesn't try to pursue it? What if she walks away and it turns out he doesn't want Lottie any more anyway? Or Sian either for that matter.

She feels as if she's had a taste of how good a relationship could be and suddenly all her bravado about being happily single has crumbled round her ears. She's sick and tired of being on her own, of never being able to wake up in the morning next to her soulmate and say, 'What shall we do today?' Of ready meals for one and tedious TV shows to fill the silence. Of not being anyone's number one. She wants to be loved. She barely recognises herself.

Her phone beeps, interrupting her pity party. Andrew.

Hey, gorgeous. How was your evening?

Despite everything she smiles at her phone. *I had fun with Grace. She's torturing another potential husband. She's written him off already.*

Haha! Poor bloke.

She tells him about Alasdair and his unfortunate shoes and the black mark chalked against his name for the crime of laughing.

I've got to go and pick Harry up from her friend's. Call you tomorrow?

She smiles to herself. *While I'm at work. I'll be dying of boredom.*

Deffo.

She's falling in love with a man who says 'deffo'– how did that happen?

In bed, later, she tries to remember any conversations she's had with Sian about him. Sian has always spoken of him fondly, but why wouldn't she? They've been friends for years. There was a curl of a smile when she'd said, 'We'll see, won't we?', after Kitty had asked her if she thought Andrew would take her up on her offer to move in. Was there something behind it? In Kitty's memory now, Sian smirks knowingly like an overacting *Hollyoaks* star, but obviously that didn't happen. She can't have asked him yet because he would have mentioned it. Wouldn't he? She has to stop herself from phoning him back to grill him. Or maybe she should. Just casually throw it into the conversation. *Sian mentioned she's thinking of asking if you want to move in with her for a while.* But what if that made him think it might be a good idea? What if she pushed him right into Sian's waiting arms?

30

Of course she forgot about the Salon. Of course she did. But now Sian has sent her a text reminding her that it's tomorrow and that Sian has got the OK to bring a newcomer from Brown Owl or whoever the fuck is in charge, as if that's some kind of a majorly big deal. Kitty stares at her phone. She could feign some kind of emergency. Arrange to meet Andrew knowing that Sian and Lottie are safely out of the way. She hasn't seen any of them since Grace dropped her bombshell that Sian could be doing all this because she wants Andrew for herself.

She asks herself what Grace would do, and she knows without a doubt that Grace one hundred per cent would relish the chance to go along and use it as a fact-finding mission. Study the interaction between Sian and Lottie and look for clues as to Sian's motivation. Kitty is definitely not Grace. But she can see the potential in the evening.

Grace, of course, is expecting dinner at Gymkhana. She's been talking about what she might wear for days.

Great, Kitty sends back. *Can't wait.*

She'll message Grace to say that she's ill in the morning. She tries not to think about how bad a friend she is.

She doesn't know how to feel about seeing Lottie. That is, she knows how she *should* feel: guilty, remorseful, horrible. Kitty is sleeping with her husband. But she can't allow herself to think about it too much. It's not the kind of person she is. Except apparently it is.

Despite everything, she's excited. Saddo that she knows she is, she's been making notes about plays that she's seen and books that she's read lately. None of them feel highbrow or edgy enough, so she reads up on an avant-garde mixed media art exhibition in Walthamstow ('psychologically involves the viewer in the existential essence of both being and non-being through audacious use of human excrement and semen') and the latest immersive theatre production ('selected audience members become the set, thus experiencing the full breadth of the piece's emotional tumult from the viewpoint of everyday objects. My wife and I were table lamps thrillingly placed in the thick of the action') and hopes that she can blag a conversation (both sound awful. Is she allowed to say that? What if they've all been and loved them? Or worse, ask questions she can't answer?). She's suddenly overwhelmed with anxiety that she's going to make an idiot of herself, and she has to sit down to try to catch her breath. This is what you wanted, she reminds herself. New friends. Intelligent conversation. Life. As if on cue, her phone beeps with a message. She picks it up, sees Lottie's name and almost drops it again.

Just remember they'll be more scared of you than you are of them! Glad you're coming. It'll be fun xx.

It makes her feel better before she immediately crashes back down and feels much worse.

She's decided not to go home first and then have to trail back into the West End. Mostly to avoid the journey in with Sian if she's being honest. Lottie is meeting them at the venue – a private members' arts club in Frith Street. Because she has no idea what to wear, Kitty has taken three whole outfits into the office that are currently hanging on a cupboard door. She's swapped shifts with Jade so she can finish at six, spend forty-five minutes in the toilets panicking about the image she's giving off and get to the venue for seven fifteen. She sends Andrew a message while she's getting ready. They've already bemoaned the fact that they could have had a rare evening together, so she snaps a photo of herself in her chosen outfit: the vintage jeans, her favourite gold thong sandals and a sheer, wide-sleeved top in pale blue, her hair centre parted, in loose waves. She's hoping for 'Laurel Canyon in the early 1970s', but she's probably giving off 'just got off a cruise ship in Lanzarote and buying tat in a tourist shop'.

Very cute, he sends back. *Very Joni Mitchell.*

She breaks into a grin. He gets it.

She finds the unassuming wooden door with its peeling red paintwork on her third recon of the street. A tiny brass sign on the stone architrave reads *The Parker*, a nod to Dorothy, the inspiration behind this self-styled forum of ideas. She rings the bell and explains that she's come for the Salon before being buzzed in. She expects to be grilled, or at least asked for her name, but the young man on the reception desk at the end of the creaky hall just points her up the even creakier stairs to the first floor.

'Have fun,' he calls after her as she makes her way up.

She can hear a hum of chatter and laughter as she gets closer. She stops four steps before the top, rests a hand against the wall and takes a deep breath. Why didn't she arrange to meet Sian somewhere first? She's never been good at boldly entering rooms full of people on her own, especially people she doesn't know.

'Oh no, you are not chickening out.' Kitty jumps when she hears Sian's voice behind her. 'Up those stairs now.'

Kitty tries to style it out. 'I was just going to adjust my shoe, it's rubbing.' She lifts a foot and rubs at her toes where the thong genuinely is cutting in.

'Yeah, right,' Sian says. She loops a hand under Kitty's elbow and propels her forward. 'You'll have fun. And if you don't, we can sneak out and go to the pub. Deal?'

That decides her. Better a room full of strangers than Sian on her own.

There are about twenty women milling round a large oak table laden with bottles of wine and bowls of nuts. Kitty is not sure what she's expecting, but this looks pretty much like the set-up of every works do she's ever been to. The people, though, are a cut above the work force of JetBetter in the glamour stakes. Kitty's boho chic feels suddenly drab and suburban next to the asymmetric bobs and black tailored suits. Two of the women are wearing some kind of mesh veils a bit like in the photos she's seen of the New Romantic scene in the 1980s. Three sport jaunty angled berets. Even here there's a uniform, she realises. They're trying so hard to be outré they've ended up conforming. She spots a blur of colour that is Lottie flying over from the other side of the room in a lilac and blue tea dress and shocking red lipstick.

'You're here! Come and meet everyone. Hi, Siany!' She hugs them both and Kitty wills herself to relax into it. To her utter horror, Lottie picks up a cheese knife and raps on the side of her glass. There's immediate silence and all eyes turn their way.

'Everyone, this is Kitty. A friend of Sian's. And mine . . .' Kitty dies a small death. 'We thought she'd be a perfect addition. So best behaviour, please.' There's a chorus of hellos and welcomes. Kitty smiles and nods and blushes and sweats. Lottie rattles off everyone's names and Kitty forgets them immediately. 'Oh, and look, she's wearing a pair of jeans from my shop – doesn't she look fab in them? If I had that arse, I'd never take them off.'

Thankfully, Kitty is saved by the door opening and two women carrying platters of cheese and sliced meats and large baguettes momentarily steal everyone's attention. 'Lottsie, food,' one of the women says like she's talking to her pet spaniel.

'Amazing. I'm starved,' Lottie says, thankfully distracted. She starts loading up a plate.

'Who pays for it all?' Kitty says quietly to Sian. 'The wine and stuff.'

'Edith's mum owns the club,' Sian says, indicating one of the berets. 'Freebie.'

'So, Kitty, what do you do?' a woman holding a vape shaped like an old-fashioned cigarette in a holder says. *Kill me*, Kitty thinks. *Shoot me now.* She thinks about making up something exotic. Burlesque performer or Arctic explorer. Nobel prize-winning physicist. And then she thinks, *Fuck it*, and says, 'I work in Customer Service for an airline. Not every exciting, I'm afraid.'

There's a lot of nodding and smiling, but clearly no one can think of anything to say.

'She has some great stories,' Sian says, and Kitty panics and tries to remember one, just in case they ask, but no one does. She can't decide if she's relieved or offended.

'Oh, yum.' Lottie is diving into her food. 'God, Camembert. Mmmm. Oh!'

Kitty is just happy the focus is off her for a moment.

In fact, it's off her for most of the rest of the evening. Not that anyone is rude or dismissive; they're just not that interested in her. Which is fine. Why should they be? They're a bunch of old friends and she's a newbie. She listens while they discuss a book on surrealism that a couple of them have read, in terms that feel learnt. She doesn't join in.

In the end she actually has a pleasant evening. The chat loosens up after the half-hearted attempt at cultured discussion and a few glasses of wine. The other women are friendly enough in a vague way. One even confesses to Kitty that she used to work in the finance department for Ryanair. Kitty asks every person who speaks to her about how they know Sian, hoping to get some insight. She knows it's the most suburban of questions. Cocktail party talk for those with nothing to say. But she doesn't really care if they think she's dull now. These people, she realises, these cool, plugged-in, sophisticated fashionistas, are actually entirely ordinary behind the façades.

Pleasant enough but definitely not the answer to all her problems. She won't be rushing to attend the Salon again unless she feels in dire need of free cheese.

There's nothing much interesting in the answers. Mostly it seems to be a chain reaction of meeting a friend of a friend of a friend. She eventually finds Patient Zero, a woman called Xanthe who went to art classes with Sian 'but a billion years ago'. None of them really seem to know Rich apart from in passing, or Andrew for that matter. They're all fond of Sian, Kitty can see that, but without exception they gush with affection about Lottie. 'Such a sweetheart,' Xanthe says, in an echo of several before her. 'Would literally do anything for anyone.'

Kitty's self-loathing ratchets up a notch.

'OK. Time to go.' She jumps as she feels an arm drape round her waist. Lottie. 'I'll get a cab. Yours?' Kitty looks at Sian, who nods with a tight smile. Lottie digs her phone out of her pocket and jabs at an app.

'Of course. We always go back to mine for a nightcap,' Sian says to Kitty. 'And now you have to come too.' She pulls an apologetic face behind Lottie's back and Kitty feels obliged to reciprocate. She hadn't even got as far as thinking she'd be expected to travel home with Sian and that Sian – oblivious to the way Kitty now feels about her – would almost certainly invite her in.

'We won't be disturbing Rich?' she says, somewhat desperately.

'He's used to it. Or we can always go to yours?'

'Sure,' Kitty says, wishing she hadn't opened her mouth. She wonders how soon she can claim tiredness and throw them out.

'Good call,' Sian mutters as they follow Lottie down the stairs after an extended goodbye with much air kissing. 'I don't think I could stomach the two of them fawning over each other.'

'How was that?' Lottie asks once they're in a taxi heading through Soho Square.

'Um. Great. I thought it would be a bit more formal . . .'

'It's just an excuse for the girls to get together, really. Five minutes of culture and then gossip.'

Kitty ignores the unlikely classification of the group of slightly stern women as girls. 'Yeah, it wasn't a criticism. Bit of a relief, actually.'

Lottie yawns. 'I've literally never seen any of the exhibitions they talk about. No time.'

Despite everything, Kitty laughs. 'I wish one of you had told me. I was panicking.'

'Shit, sorry,' Sian says. 'I did that the first time I went. I should have remembered.'

'Anyway, they all loved you,' Lottie says sleepily. Kitty knows this is categorically not true. Liked her maybe. Most of them. It strikes her that she has never heard Lottie be mean about anybody.

Don't think about it.

31

They don't stay long. Kitty makes gin and tonics, because opening a bottle of wine feels like she would be suggesting the whole thing be drunk and she wants to keep this short. Lottie fights sleep like a toddler after a play date, and eventually gives in after two sips, curling up in the armchair, a cushion hugged into her chest like a much-loved teddy. Kitty struggles to think of things to say to Sian and settles on asking her questions about each of the women she spoke to at the Salon, the answers to which she has no interest in knowing. Sian, she realises, is a bit in awe of them herself. Kitty wonders if they're all like that: anxious about how they measure up, exactly how cutting edge they're perceived as being, whether they are owning up to liking the right things. She's tempted to go again just so she can walk in and say, '*Mrs. Brown's Boys* — isn't it great?' and watch them all spontaneously combust. Alarmingly, she thinks she'd rather spend an evening drinking warm Sauvignon Blanc and eating pub chips with Grace. A sentence she never thought she'd hear herself say.

It's getting late and she has work tomorrow. She nods over at Lottie. 'I should get her an Uber.'

Sian pulls a face. 'Stick her in the garden to sleep for all I care.'

Kitty pretends a laugh. 'Do you have her address?' *Andrew's address*, she thinks. It feels dangerous to know it, as if she might suddenly find herself outside looking in. Sian rattles it off and Kitty searches for the app on her phone.

'Did you ask him yet?' she asks in a whisper, looking at Lottie all the time to check she's not stirring.

Sian shakes her head. 'Haven't had a chance.' She yawns.

'You can leave me to it, it's OK,' Kitty says. Not that she really wants to be alone with Lottie, but at least she won't have to chat to her. She glances at her phone. No takers yet.

'Are you sure? I'm just worried I might fall asleep too, then you'll have to deal with two of us.'

A notification pops up. Kitty holds her mobile up for Sian to see. 'Nine minutes. I'll be fine. I'm just going to go to the loo before you go, otherwise I'm worried Lottie might wake up and not know where she is.'

Sian laughs. 'I think she's out for the count.'

In the little toilet under the stairs, Kitty sits on the closed lid. She can waste a couple of minutes in here, leaving Sian to babysit Lottie, before she goes back out to make sure the Uber is definitely still coming (don't get her started on the time a rogue driver decided to take another job after he'd already accepted hers and turned up with a complete stranger in the back of the car who was just as shocked as she was) and then count down the seconds till the evening will be over and she can be on her own.

When she forces herself to return to the living room, flushing first for authenticity, Sian hauls herself to her feet. 'Can we do something soon, just the two of us?'

'Definitely. I'll ring you.' She needs to line up some excuses. She picks up her phone and checks the car just as six minutes somehow flashes back to seven. She briefly panics that the whole evening is going to play out in reverse.

'Do you want some help waking her up?' Sian says. 'Maybe wave a bit of cheese under her nose.'

Kitty makes herself lean in for a hug. 'Go to bed.'

She waits until she hears the front door click shut and then gently shakes Lottie's shoulder. 'Time to go.' Lottie sighs like a contented cat. Kitty shakes her again. 'Lottie. Wake up. Time to go.'

'Oh! Sorry. Was I asleep? Shit. God. Sorry.'

'It's OK. An Uber is going to be here any minute.'

'Is it here now?' She sits up abruptly, rubbing her eyes, leaving a trail of deep black liner.

'No. You've got about six or seven minutes. Do you want some water?'

'No. I'm OK. You called me an Uber? That's so nice of you. Tell me what I owe you. God, I could have slept all night. Your sofa is comfy.'

Kitty realises Lottie is more than a little bit drunk. To be fair, so is she. She's such a lightweight these days. She stands up. 'I think *I* need water. I'll get us both some.'

Lottie follows her through the hall and into the kitchen. 'This is so kind of you. To get me a car. Sorry to be a pain. Where did Sian go?'

'Home. She said to say goodnight.'

'I'm glad she moved in next to you. I think she was a bit worried about living out here, although I was thrilled because we're so much closer to each other now. And then she met you, so *I* met you and I never would have met you otherwise . . .'

Kitty fills two tumblers with water and hands her one.

'You can never have enough friends, that's what I think. How's Grace?'

Kitty is relieved at the change of subject, so she fills Lottie in about Alasdair. She sneaks a look at her phone as she talks. Five minutes.

'She deserves to find someone lovely,' Lottie says. 'And you. I mean, you do too. If that's what you want.'

'I'm not bothered,' Kitty says with a strained smile. Why does Lottie have to be so goddamn nice all the time? No one's that nice.

'Good for you. I never understand those people who settle rather than be on their own. If you're going for the long haul, it needs to be right, right?'

Four minutes. 'Right.'

'I mean, look at all the couples you know who have been together for a long time. Look at Sian and Rich. Oooh,' she says, stumbling a little as she leans over to refill her water glass. 'I have a secret about them.'

Kitty freezes. She has no idea what Lottie is about to tell her. She's not even sure if she wants to know. Except that, of course, now she knows there's something, she needs to hear it. And then she thinks, *Can those four even have any more secrets? This is getting ridiculous now.*

'You have to promise not to tell.'

Marek is going to arrive any minute in his Toyota Corolla, but Kitty now crosses her fingers he'll be held up long enough for her to get to the bottom of whatever it is Lottie is about to confide in her. Does she know Sian is unhappy? That she's about to blow her marriage up? And not just her own.

'Promise,' Lottie says.

'Of course,' Kitty says impatiently. She needs Lottie to say whatever she has to say before she thinks better of it.

It all comes out in a tumble. 'Rich has arranged for them to renew their vows when we're away in Santorini and Sian has no idea. I've been helping him plan things. I'm altering their wedding outfits so they can wear what they wore originally, but trying to do Sian's without her knowing is almost impossible. I have to keep sneaking round there and measuring her clothes when she's not there.' She grabs hold of Kitty's arm. 'Isn't that lovely? Isn't that, like, the most romantic thing ever?'

32

So that was why Lottie had been sneaking out of the back gate when Sian arrived home from work early that day. The explanation is so innocent, so wholesome, that Kitty almost confesses everything to Lottie right here, right now: how she'd thought there must be something going on between Lottie and Rich, how Sian had confirmed it, how she and Grace had searched Lottie's bag.

How she had allowed herself to believe it all.

She blushes purple at the thought of it.

'We're doing it too,' Lottie says in a stage whisper. 'Me and Andrew. But he doesn't know yet either.'

Kitty steadies herself with a hand on the back of a chair. 'You're renewing your vows? You're surprising them both? You and Rich?'

'Yep. Imagine if they both turn round and say, "No way do I want to marry you again!" She gives a little laugh. There's definitely no chance it has ever crossed her mind that this could happen.

It's too much of a coincidence that Sian confided in her about Lottie's supposed affair with Rich, Kitty thinks. She had thought that Sian must really value her as a friend, must trust her with her secrets, but in reality she barely knew her. She must have known that Kitty would buy into her story, that she'd back it up with Andrew, fuelling the fire that Sian had lit. She must have spotted her that day, watching Lottie creep out trying not to be seen, and Rich acting flustered like a guilty man, that's the only explanation.

She feels sick.

She feels used.

She feels utterly fucking ashamed of herself.

'That's lovely,' she says, conscious that Lottie is waiting for an answer. 'What an amazing thing to do.'

'She's going to kill me when she finds out I've been sneaking around –'

Kitty's phone beeps and she audibly gasps. 'Your car's here,' she interrupts.

'Brilliant. I wish you were coming. On the holiday. Why don't you? I bet there's room . . .'

'Have you got everything? Your bag?' Kitty ushers her towards the front door. Lottie wraps her arms round her, planting a kiss on her cheek.

'Night night.'

'Text me so I know you're home safely,' Kitty says, her autopilot kicking in.

She watches until the car pulls away and then leans up against the inside of the front door, eyes closed.

Sleep is impossible. She'd worked out, of course, that Lottie and Rich were innocent of the deception they were being accused of, but, if she were being honest, she'd assumed there must be something wrong at the heart of Sian and Rich's marriage to have caused Sian to go to such lengths. That Rich must want out too, whether he was ready to admit to it or not. She's dismissed him in all of this, she realises. She's been so caught up in the drama between Sian and Lottie, in her own role in it, that she hadn't even considered how devastating it will be for him. Is Sian intending to go through with the façade of renewing their vows only to shatter her marriage a few days later? Because she obviously knows about the vow renewal, whatever Lottie believes. (Kitty's pretty sure Sian knows why Lottie has been sneaking in and out of her house too – she just doesn't know how yet.) It's too cruel.

She thinks about Lottie excitedly altering her best friend's wedding dress as a surprise, not knowing that friend is about to try and break up her own marriage.

And what are you doing, Kitty? She actually hears those words in her head as if someone has spoken them aloud.

At 3 a.m. she sits bolt upright, her heart pounding. This is not who she is. Yes, she only got together with Andrew when she thought he was effectively single, but she can't pretend she doesn't know the truth now. That she hasn't for a while.

She's deliberately ruining someone's life.

She has to stop.

She thinks about Andrew, how compatible they are, the future they've been edging towards planning, the sex, the conversation, the way her heart stutters when she sees him, the end of the loneliness she didn't even realise she was mired in. But none of that matters. She has to tell him the truth.

She has to do the right thing.

A version of the truth. The timings will have to be fudged. Honest as she wants to be, she can't admit to having deceived him too.

Their relationship will be over, she has no doubt about

that, but maybe Andrew can salvage his marriage. If he still wants to. She knows she's poisoned his mind against Lottie. She feels sick at the thought of having to convince him that he should be with his wife and not her, but she knows she has to try. Lottie might be a bit annoying sometimes but she's a fundamentally good, kind person. In fact, Kitty wonders if she actually would have found Lottie so irritating if she hadn't already formed an opinion of her before they met. Cast her as the baddy. She'd have thought she was eccentric, maybe. Quirky. But she wouldn't have felt the visceral dislike that washed over her in that first encounter. Whether Andrew tells Lottie the whole truth about their affair – their relationship – or not, Kitty will have to leave up to him and then respect his decision, but, god, she hopes he doesn't. It's going to be bad enough to lose him without suddenly becoming enemy number one.

She'll tell him when she sees him next. It's not something she can do over the phone.

Two days.

Mind made up, she turns on her side and cries herself to sleep.

When he texts her in the morning – as he does every morning; she's become addicted to those little exchanges, to the idea that he wakes up thinking about her as she does about him – she doesn't respond. Now she's promised herself she'll do right by Lottie, she needs to honour that promise. She and Andrew have a plan to meet on Saturday afternoon and she fully intends to try to avoid him till then. The sky is black with clouds and she's tempted to huddle back under the covers and call in sick, but she knows she needs the distraction of work. That without it she will spend way too much time in her own head and almost certainly talk herself out of her resolve. She drags herself out of bed, throws on the holey old hoody that serves as a dressing gown, and shuffles downstairs to flick on the kettle.

She has fucked everything up.

Again.

She dresses like it's November, not June, and forces herself out into the rain.

She doesn't have her own office, but she has a kind of cubbyhole that separates her from her team visually if not aurally. This is considered a huge perk in the world of open-plan working, and today more than any other day she appreciates it. They're busy due to a weather event the day before that caused severe delays to transatlantic flights, so she opts to put her headset on and answer calls, something she does occasionally when the phone traffic is high, so she hopes it won't draw attention to the fact that she's being anti-social.

At five past twelve she looks up and sees a deposition. Evie, Mark, Ross, Jacob and Jade, her whole team, huddle round the gap in the cubbyhole's temporary walls.

'You're coming for lunch,' Jacob says. 'No excuses.'

'Didn't you only start work five minutes ago?' she says grumpily, but she feels touched.

'Yes, and the first thing they said –' he indicates Evie, Ross and Jade – 'is how you've been moping round all morning with Resting Sad Bitch Face and you're bringing down the whole tone, so we need to do something about that before you drag the rest of us into the self-pity sewer with you.'

Kitty can't help but laugh. 'Who'll answer the phones?'

Jade shrugs. 'They can leave a message. They're angry already, so what's the difference?'

'Nice attitude,' Kitty says. 'I've taught you well.'

'You don't have to tell us what's wrong,' Evie says with a grimace.

'Oh no,' Kitty smiles. 'If I come I'm telling you every last anatomical detail. No erogenous zone left unturned.' She wishes she had a camera to capture the sheer look of horror that passes over their faces like a Mexican wave. 'Actually, I'm splitting up with my boyfriend and I'm really sad about it. That's all you're getting. No questions. Now, where are we going?'

It's the right decision. They all get a bit tipsy and they're late back and a bit offhand with the clientele, but she couldn't care less at this point, and it gets her through the day without a major meltdown.

On the way home from the bus stop she spots Rich, bag for life in hand, walking out of the mini-mart. Her first instinct is to hide before he sees her, but she knows she owes it to him to make an effort. From his startled reaction when she catches his eye and smiles as if she's delighted to see him, she knows he has picked up on her recent frostiness.

'Don't tell me you actually found something edible in there?' she says as she reaches him.

He returns her smile. 'You can't really go wrong with a packet of dried spaghetti and a bottle of red wine,'

'They could find a way. I once bought a jar of instant coffee from them. Still sealed. When I opened it, it was one solid fused lump. I couldn't even chip a bit off.'

They fall into step beside each other. 'Did you take it back?'

She shakes her head. 'Too desperate for caffeine. I poured boiling water on top of it and sort of tipped it into a mug.'

'Nice.'

She shrugs. 'I have skills.'

They walk in silence for a moment, Kitty willing the time to pass.

'We haven't seen much of you lately,' Rich says, as she trips over a bump in the pavement.

'I know! I've been stupidly busy. I don't know what with, honestly, but, I just, you know . . .' *Stop talking, Kitty. Don't edge yourself into a corner. Quit while you're ahead.*

'How's Rhys?' she says with a – hopefully – subtle swerve. 'Didn't Sian say you were going down to see him soon?' She knows this. Knows that she and Andrew are safe to meet without prying eyes tomorrow.

'In the morning. Just for one night. I can't help thinking it must cramp his style having his mum and dad keep showing up, but it was his idea . . .'

'His style is uncrampable. It's nice that he wants to spend time with the two of you.' *While he can*, she thinks. 'He seems like a lovely boy.'

Rich grins. 'I have no idea what it was, but we did something right. You should come over tonight. We've not got anything going on, and Sian would love it.'

Shit.

She pulls a face. 'I'm out later, annoyingly.' This time she manages not to elaborate. Great. Another night hiding in her bedroom with the lights off. Maybe she really should go out. She could ring Grace and see if she fancies a meal. Except that Grace would spot there was something majorly wrong immediately, and Kitty would trip herself up trying to remember her own lies.

Thankfully Rich doesn't seem to realise he's being snubbed. 'Next week maybe, then. If you fancy it.'

Kitty makes non-committal noises as they turn into Ashdown Close. She spots, even from here, that Lottie is standing on her doorstep. She almost whoops, she's so thankful for the distraction. Any distraction.

'Is that Lotts?' Rich peers.

'It is. At mine, I think.' She waves. Weirdly, Lottie does not wave back, even though she's looking right at them. 'I wasn't expecting her.'

'Maybe she's been at ours and she just thought she'd drop in.'

'Maybe.' She's starting to feel a bit uneasy. Something about Lottie's body language is off. Kitty feels a sudden urge to turn and run.

Rich flaps an arm in Lottie's direction and she still doesn't wave back; she turns away and paces a few steps back and forth. 'She is a bit short-sighted to be fair,' he says. 'She probably doesn't even realise it's us.'

He's wrong, Kitty thinks. *She definitely does.*

Lottie comes at her like a Tasmanian devil. Rich hasn't even had time to open his front gate, and he stops abruptly, frozen to the spot.

'How could you?' she shouts, tiny fists pummelling at Kitty's chest. Kitty takes a step back, hands raised. 'How fucking could you? I thought you were my friend.'

'Lotts?' Kitty hears Rich say. She wants to turn and tell

him it's OK, go inside. Don't listen to what Lottie has to say. She sees a curtain twitch at number 7. Julie.

'Come in the house,' she says. 'I can explain.'

But Lottie is having none of it. 'Did you know?' she calls to Rich. 'About Kitty and Andrew? Did you know what your best mate was up to?'

'I don't . . .' he says, clearly wishing he'd kept walking up the path and right through the front door.

'Sian sent me a photo of some messages. Do you want to see?'

She digs around in her bag for her phone and then throws it across the drive in frustration when she doesn't find what she's looking for. She bursts into noisy tears. Kitty instinctively makes a move towards her and reaches a hand out to touch her arm. Lottie snaps it back like she's been stung. 'Don't touch me.'

Kitty looks at Rich, who is still standing open-mouthed. 'Can you leave us to it?' She thought he'd be grateful for the reprieve, but now he's seen Lottie break down it seems he's reluctant to abandon her. 'We'll be fine.'

'Lottsie?'

Lottie whips her head round to face him. 'It's OK.'

He makes a break for the door. Kitty somehow manages to get her own open and goes inside. Now Lottie has found out, Kitty knows she can't deny it. As Lottie grabs her bag and follows her, Kitty wonders if she's confronted Andrew already. If he knows that his wife has come to have it out with her. If he'll come riding in on a white charger and save her.

33

'You bitch. You absolute fucking bitch.' Lottie's face is flushed red. Kitty turns and leads her towards the kitchen and then decides the soft furnishings of the living room are a more sensible option. 'How long?'

'Six weeks. Almost. Bit less.' She sinks down onto the sofa. 'I'm sorry, Lottie,' she says, her voice barely above a whisper.

'*Six weeks?* No.' Lottie's face crumples, all the fight gone out of it. 'How could you?'

Kitty can't even begin to explain in a way that might sound believable. She scarcely believes it herself. 'Sit down. Please.'

Lottie almost falls into the armchair. Tears are streaming down her face. Kitty has to resist the urge to go over and comfort her, because she knows – she absolutely understands – that she wouldn't be welcome.

'I can explain. I don't mean make an excuse . . .' she adds as Lottie scoffs. She tries to think where to start, how to couch it so it doesn't sound ridiculous. She has no idea why Lottie should believe any of it, it sounds so far-fetched. She owes it to her to try, though.

'Sian told me you and Rich were having an affair. That's where it started.'

Lottie can't keep the surprise off her face. She wasn't expecting that. She clearly doesn't believe it, either.

'Grace'll back me up. And Andrew. She told Andrew that too.'

'Why would she do that?'

'I don't know . . . I have a theory . . .' Even as she says this, she realises how unlikely it sounds.

Lottie is having none of it. 'She's my best friend.'

'No. She's not . . .'

Lottie scowls at her. 'Even if, for some mad reason, she thought it was true, she would have talked to me. Or to Rich. Not to you.'

Here goes. 'She needed me to believe it . . .'

'Because you're the most important person in her life, clearly. She's known you, what? Three months?'

'She was using me. Setting me up.'

'So, she's some kind of con woman now?'

Kitty shakes her head. 'I know this sounds insane. But Grace can back up everything I'm telling you.'

'Grace knew too? That you were screwing my husband? And the two of you came to my shop and acted as if we were all friends . . .'

'It hadn't started then,' Kitty says quietly. 'In fact . . . I know this is going to sound mad, but please just hear me out. Then you can call Grace and she'll confirm it all . . .'

Lottie doesn't say anything. Just waits.

'Sian asked us to go to the shop. She told me she'd found out about you and Rich and she wanted us to go and have a poke round. See if we could find anything to confirm it.'

Lottie's face contorts into a sneer. 'You want me to believe that Sian sent you to spy on me? Are you on something?'

'Ask Grace. Ask Andrew for that matter.'

Lottie bristles at the mention of his name. 'Andrew would have come straight to me if he thought any of this was true. Even if he didn't, he would have told me if Sian had even hinted at it.'

'He wanted to wait until after the holiday. After Harry's exams. For her sake.'

'Don't you fucking talk about my family as if you know anything about them.'

'She told us your bag would be in the back room. Sian. And said we should have a look through it. Grace did and found a note . . .'

Lottie glares at her, face blotchy. 'What note?'

Kitty knows it by heart. '"Booked. My name. Tues. 2? R." With a kiss. On a piece of paper from the Marylebone Hotel. Grace took a photo of it, and we showed it to Sian and Sian said it was definitely Rich's writing. It's probably still in there. In the little pocket of the red bag. Except I expect Sian got rid of it. She couldn't risk you finding it.'

Lottie opens her mouth then shuts it again.

'I'm not making this up, Lottie.'

'So, even if I believe you about whatever this is – which I don't by the way. There must be some kind of logical explanation – what does that have to do with you sleeping with Andrew?'

'She told Andrew about it. What was he supposed to think?'

'And then he came round here and got straight into bed with you as, what? Revenge? You're delusional.'

'It wasn't like that,' Kitty says quietly.

266

'Oh, so please do tell me what it *was* like,' Lottie says sarcastically. 'I'm dying to know.'

'He was devastated.'

'So, you slept with him to cheer him up?'

Kitty bites her tongue. Nothing can be gained by snapping back. Lottie is the wounded party here; of course she's firing shots. 'It happened gradually. Once Sian convinced him what she was telling him was true, then it was over with you in his head. He never would have otherwise . . .'

'Well, good for him. How moral. How lucky for you that he believed it so readily.'

'He saw a payment to the hotel. On your statement. And that sort of confirmed it to him.'

Lottie scowls. 'What hotel?'

'The Marylebone.'

'I've never been to the Marylebone Hotel in my life. I don't even know where it is. So I know you're talking bullshit.'

'Just drinks, I think he said. But it was the same hotel, so . . . It must just have been a coincidence, I suppose.' As she says this, she realises it probably isn't true. There are no coincidences.

'Did you hear what I said? I've never been to the Marylebone for drinks or anything else. So, one of you is lying.'

Kitty gulps. 'Ask Andrew. He's the one who found it.'

'Well. He didn't because I've never been there.'

'I just know what I was told, Lottie.'

'Good for you. Great get-out clause.'

Kitty doesn't rise to it. She can't. Lottie is a cornered animal fighting for her family.

'Lottie, I feel awful. Genuinely, I do. But it's Sian who's your enemy here.'

Lottie stands up. Five foot nothing of raging fury. Kitty almost flinches. 'I'll decide who my enemies are.' She storms towards the front door. Kitty opens her mouth to say *Does Andrew know that you know?* but she stops herself. She can't. She can't even tell Lottie that she was about to do the right thing finally. Because what difference would that make to her? The damage has been done.

Instead, she waits until she hears the front door slam and sends him a text: *Sian has told Lottie about us.*

And then she turns off her phone, goes upstairs to her bedroom, crawls under the duvet and pulls it up over her head.

34

She stays there until the morning. She can't sleep, obviously. Her brain is a firework display of questions and regrets and panic about the future. After what feels like hours, she turns on her phone long enough to look at last night's texts from Andrew. She ignores the five new ones on her home screen. She can't deal with that now. She flicks back, catching the odd word: *devastated, don't understand, denying it, how did she know?????* She can't imagine how confused he must be.

Her memory is hazy. She thinks there were two messages from him after they got back to hers, after the Salon. Did she see them both as they arrived or could Sian have intercepted one when Kitty was occupied doing something else? She left her mobile in the living room while she skulked in the bathroom killing time after calling Lottie's Uber. She dredges her memory, trying to remember. She knows she kept the phone face down while they were having a drink, afraid that Sian or Lottie might see Andrew's name pop up. Was she that careful after she booked the car? Was there a new text after she came back from the toilet? When did she read it?

Either message could have given them away.

Call me as soon as they've left. It'll take Lottie twenty minutes at least. Easily time for a quickie! With the stupid laughing face he was so fond of.

And then the killer. *Can't stop thinking about you. What have you done to me???* (Two fucking laughing faces.) *Phone sex isn't going to cut it. When can we see each other?? Xxx*

Shit. Fragments are coming back to her. Her phone was on after she booked the Uber and then she left the room. She checked to see how far away the car was as soon as she came back in and there was definitely no message waiting on her lock screen. Could Sian have clicked on it when it arrived and accessed her and Andrew's whole conversation? It didn't bear thinking about.

35

In the silence that follows she realises that all she has is Grace, and that, actually, prudish, judgemental Grace is exactly who she needs right now. But Grace still doesn't know the whole story and Kitty can't face coming clean even to her. Not yet. Andrew leaves her messages: *Are you OK? Should we meet? Lotts is denying everything. I have no fucking idea what's going on. Kit, please. Let me know you're OK.* She bats him away, telling him he needs to sort things out with Lottie before they speak. *I honestly think Sian might have made the whole thing up*, she sends, the closest she can get to a confession, and then turns off her phone again. She cries off sick from work and ignores any ringing on the doorbell unless she's turned her phone on long enough to order Deliveroo, in which case she hovers in the hall-way ready to snatch the bag from the driver's hand and slam the door in his face before anyone else can see her. She pays no attention to the missed calls and messages mounting up like snowdrifts, knowing that if she looks at one she'll see them all and that will be her undoing.

She sees Sian and Rich coming and going, together, seemingly happy, Rich casting occasional venomous glances at her windows.

She phones home. Her mum would understand. About a year after Kitty moved to London her mum had called her one day and opened the conversation with 'I never thought he was right for you. He stifled the life out of you.'

'Why didn't you say anything?' Kitty had said, incredulous.

'Because you had to come to that conclusion yourself. I was relieved when you moved to London, even though I hate you not being up the road.'

Her mum always knows the right thing to say.

Her lovely mum who adores her unconditionally and always listens without judgement. Who would do anything to make her daughter feel safe and supported, to brush over her fuck-ups and tell her the only thing that mattered if you made a mistake was to put things right and learn from it. But today her mum is stuck in a loop of thinking she's talking to her schoolfriend, Wendy, twelve years old again. Kitty plays along, trying to smooth over the fictional argument between the two of them that is making her mother fret. Maggie wrings her hands over and over. 'I didn't mean to,' she says. 'You have to believe me, Wendy.'

'I do,' Kitty says, gently. 'Don't worry. Don't worry about anything.'

She's so lonely she feels it as a physical ache. An emptiness in the pit of her stomach. Hollowed out.

On the fourth night she opens the door to an American Hot pizza to find Grace trying to wrestle it from the unarmed cyclist who is clinging on valiantly.

'I knew you were here!' she exclaims, letting go. The pizza box goes flying and somehow, miraculously, lands unopen and the correct way up. Kitty almost smiles but then remembers her life is destroyed and checks herself. She tries to retreat inside without Grace noticing but Grace shoves a loafer-clad foot into the doorway and Kitty can't bring herself to slam the door shut on it.

'I'm going to have to tip him a fortune now you've basically assaulted him,' she says.

'OK. Enough,' Grace says, stomping into the kitchen and flicking on the kettle. 'What's going on? Are you ill? I spoke to someone in your office . . .'

She thinks about saying yes, she has a bug, sorry, been feeling terrible, blah blah blah, but suddenly she feels the walls she's built start to crumble. She can't do this. Not on her own.

'Sian told Lottie about me and Andrew.'

'What? Why? How did she even know.' Grace spots three empty identical pizza boxes stacked up amid the fetid pile of detritus on the kitchen counter. 'Wait.' She picks up the newly delivered American Hot. 'This is going straight in the fridge. I'm cooking you a proper meal.' She starts rootling through cupboards. 'Do you even have any food?'

'I think she saw messages on my phone. The other night.'

Grace stops what she's doing and looks at her. 'When? What messages?'

Kitty gulps. 'Thursday. I lied to you. It's still going on. Was. Not now, obviously.'

'I thought you were ill on Thursday.'

Shit. Kitty had forgotten that particular misdemeanour. 'Sorry,' she mutters.

'After you knew that Lottie wasn't cheating on him?'

Kitty feels her eyes fill up with tears. 'Don't hate me,

273

please. Don't lecture me. I know it's wrong, but it happened. I can't change that.'

'I'll make pasta,' Grace says, blithely. 'Do you have any tomatoes?'

'Grace . . .'

Grace puts down the tin she's holding. 'You can't expect me to think it's OK, Kit.'

'I don't. It's not.'

'Why didn't you confide in me? I'm your friend.'

'Because I knew what you'd think. I knew how fucking disappointed you'd have been in me, and you'd have been right.'

'OK. Tell me everything now. The whole truth this time, though. I won't judge. At least, I'll try not to.' She gets the pizza out of the fridge again, hands the box to Kitty. 'Eat this. It's better than nothing. We can start eating healthily tomorrow.'

She leaves nothing out. Every gruesome detail. It's almost as if she wants to shock Grace into having a reaction, but Grace's fixed expression doesn't change, she just nods occasionally or makes a kind of grunt of encouragement. Kitty closes her eyes when she gets to the part where she has to confess the worst crime: not telling Andrew when she found out Lottie wasn't cheating. She wills herself just to get through it. She has nothing more to lose now anyway.

When she gets to the end there's a resounding silence. She opens her eyes to find Grace staring right at her. She waits, a felon facing a firing squad. Grace stands up and moves towards her.

'Come here,' Grace says, arms out. She pulls Kitty to her feet and before Kitty knows what she's doing she's buried her head in Grace's shoulder, and she's sobbing uncontrollably. Grace puts an arm round her and rubs her back. 'It's OK,' she says. 'It'll be OK.'

Kitty tries to catch her breath, but she can't stop crying. Grace pulls her in closer and holds her there while Kitty floods the collar of her cream blouse with salty water and who knows what else.

Eventually – she doesn't know after how long – she cries herself out, her sobs turning into hiccupy gulps. Grace is still stroking her hair, making soothing noises and, awkward as it is, Kitty can't bring herself to move.

36

'Let's go for a walk,' Grace says decisively. 'Just up the road. You need to breathe some fresh air.' Kitty sits immobile, her face raw. Grace rattles round in the cupboard in the hall and comes back with a pair of trainers Kitty had forgotten she even owned.

'I don't want to.'

'Ten minutes. It'll make you feel better, I promise.'

Kitty allows herself to be wrestled into her shoes like a sulking toddler. She doesn't have the strength to argue with Grace when Grace is on a mission. She'll concede to being led round the block once and that's it.

'Let's get it over with,' she says.

Outside it's warm and sunny in a way that makes her feel as if the weather has betrayed her. It should be dull and colourless, a mirror to her life. People are out and about with smiles on their faces. An alternate universe. Sian's front door opens and a boy of about eight exits with his mother. Kitty keeps her eyes on the pavement. '*Adios,*' she hears Sian saying cheerily. '*Hasta la proxima.*' She must have found a private pupil on Nextdoor.

Grace takes her arm and propels her along, keeping up a running commentary: *I should have brought my sunglasses, ooh there's a cat, why do people leave stuff outside their houses that they know the binmen won't take?* Kitty doesn't even try to formulate a response. The fact that the world is going on uninterrupted around her seems unfathomable.

'Isn't that that couple who were at the party? Sam and Linda?'

Kitty looks up. 'Linz.' They're on the opposite side of the street, ambling back from the shops with a bag of groceries, chatting animatedly. Kitty readies herself for a hello. She doesn't want to look rude, however daunting the effort of being sociable might seem. Linz looks up as if about to cross the road. Kitty raises her hand in a wave. Linz looks away. Kitty shoots a look at Grace.

'She can't have seen you,' Grace says quickly. Protesting too much.

'She definitely did,' Kitty says, her voice cracking. 'She saw me and pretended she didn't. Sian must have told her. About me and Andrew. I'm going to be the street fucking pariah.'

'Or she's just got bad eyesight. Don't overthink it.'

Kitty turns abruptly. 'They're all going to think I'm about to try to steal their husbands. I'm going home. I can't . . .'

'You don't know that's it,' Grace says, but she doesn't really argue. And because of that, Kitty knows unequivocally that her suspicions are right.

'I don't know what I'm going to do.' It comes out as a wail.

'Look on the bright side,' Grace says. 'At least you won't ever have to have a "cheeky" drink with her now.'

Kitty can't do it. She tries, but she can't bring herself to laugh.

Grace looks at her. 'Fuck them.' She turns back to

where Sam and Linz's front door is closing behind them. 'Really, though. Just fuck them. All of them.'

'I appreciate the swearing,' Kitty says, an attempt at a joke. 'I know how hard that must have been.' She turns and walks in the opposite direction, up the path to number 3.

'Wait. Where are you going? No, Kit,' Grace says helplessly as Kitty marches up to Vernie and Malcolm's front door. 'Don't.'

Kitty rings the bell. She stands there caught up in the righteous fury of the drama, which dissipates with every slow, shuffling step she hears her neighbour take along the hall.

'Wait. Wait,' she hears Vernie call and her bravado crumbles. She could probably make it home before Vernie even reached the door if she ran. It's tempting. She turns and looks at Grace who is hovering by the gate, a concerned expression on her face. She turns back. She needs to know how bad it is.

Finally, she hears the scrape of the chain being slotted into place. She arranges her features into something less panicky. More friendly neighbour just popping round to say hello. The door eases open and Vernie's face looms into the widening gap.

'Hi!' Kitty says with a forced jolliness. 'I was just . . .'

'Oh. It's you,' Vernie says with a sigh. Kitty's fake smile drops. Vernie fiddles with the chain until the door opens. 'What can I do for you?'

'I wanted to check you were OK, you and Malcolm. If you needed anything . . .'

'We're just fine, thank you.'

They stand there for a second, the silence resounding.

'Right. Good. I'll leave you to it.'

Vernie exhales. 'Why would you do something like that, Kitty? All Sian ever did was welcome you into her house and her friendship group . . .'

So, she didn't imagine Sam and Linz's cold shoulder. Sian has been getting her version of the story out there, painting Kitty as the villain before she had the chance to defend herself.

'It's not like you think, Vernie,' she says, flatly. 'Nothing is like you think.'

She turns and walks away. She can't even look at Grace. She doesn't know if she's more angry or upset. Actually, she does; she's just plain devastated. She feels as if all the fight has been knocked out of her, a balloon deflated.

'Why don't I run you a bath when we get in?' Grace says, trotting along behind her, trying to catch up. 'It might help you feel better.'

Kitty nods, happy to let someone else take charge. 'Sure. Why not? Maybe I should just confront her. Sian,' she says. She hasn't spoken to either her or Rich since Sian exploded her bomb, torn between wanting answers and fear of what else Sian might throw at her. She's never been good at standing up for herself. 'Shouldn't I?'

'What would be the point?' Grace says breathlessly. 'Don't give her the satisfaction of letting her know she's rattled you. She's trying to provoke a response. Be the bigger person.'

'Did you swallow a self-help book?' Kitty snaps.

She lies there until the water goes cold and then tops the hot up again. She feels a bit more human after a soak and a change of clothes. *Time makes everything less painful,* her mum used to say whenever she was upset. Kitty knows that's true, even if she doesn't feel it at the moment, but presenting a clean, fragrant front also helps. When she comes downstairs Grace is wiping down the kitchen counter, a bulging black rubbish sack by her feet.

'I'll put this outside,' she says. 'The kettle just boiled if you want anything.'

'Thank you,' Kitty says. She's actually not sure her kitchen has ever been this sparkling. She finds two mugs in the cupboard and spoons coffee into them, wiping up a spill as she goes. She sees Grace cross the front window on her way to the bins, then hears something. Voices. Raised voices.

Grace lugs the stinking bag round the corner to where Kitty's bins sit lined up neatly on the little path to the back gardens. She's trying not to show it but she's furious on her friend's behalf. Yes, Kitty did wrong. Yes, Grace disapproves. But that doesn't outweigh the fact that Sian created this whole situation in the first place. She reeled them in with her stories about Lottie and Rich and her so-called evidence. She convinced Andrew that his wife was a villain. She . . . well, Grace doesn't even want to think about the other thing. What kind of person deliberately messes with other people's lives like this? Not caring what devastation she causes. *A fucking psychopath, that's who,* she thinks, enjoying the feel of the language in her head. She's never sworn so much in her life – even in her own thoughts – as she has the last few days. She slams open the wheelie bin and heaves the bag in, just as

Sian appears at her own back gate. She freezes when she sees Grace.

'What the fuck?' Grace says. She never loses her temper. Even when she found out about Hal's deception she had confronted him calmly. Reasonably. Fat lot of good it did her.

'Grace.'

'What the hell are you doing? Why did you tell Lottie?'

Sian gives a half-smile. 'You don't think she deserved to know that her husband was cheating on her?'

'You set the whole thing up in the first place. You made us believe Lottie was playing away. With Rich, for godssake.'

Sian's brow crinkles. 'You've lost me.' She opens the blue recycling bin on her side of the alley and starts tossing bottles in one by one.

Grace struggles to hear herself speak over the crash of glass. 'The text. The note we found. You asked us to go and poke about in Lottie's shop.'

Sian actually cackles. 'I literally have no idea what you're talking about. Have you had a few too many wines?'

'You even confirmed it was Rich's writing when I showed you the photo. You got me involved. Both of us.'

'You know this actually sounds insane.'

'That whole thing with . . .' Grace starts to say, but then she hears the gate open again and Rich pokes his head round.

'What's going on? Oh . . .' He stops as he spots her. 'You.'

'Kitty's little guard dog is in attack mode.'

Grace feels cornered. She's no good at fighting. But

she's so incensed on Kitty's behalf. She looks at Rich. 'This whole thing started when Sian told Kitty you and Lottie were having a thing.'

Rich scrunches up his face in confusion. Sian snorts. 'You know she barely tolerates you, don't you? You know she's only friends with you because she hasn't found anyone better. Clingy, that's what she described you as. You're a charity case. You both are.'

'Sian . . .' Rich says, with a slight warning note. Grace knows that Sian is firing arrows to prevent herself from being hit, but it still stings. Because she suspects there's an element of truth to what Sian is saying. She knows Kitty finds her irritating at times. That her constant chatter drives Kitty crazy. That they have next to nothing in common except that they can make each other laugh. But they have a bond somehow. One that means everything to Grace.

'I'm right,' Sian is saying. 'You didn't notice how she dropped you like a hot potato when I moved in next door? She didn't need you any more. You're basically like an aunt she has to duty-visit occasionally at this point.'

Grace stands there fighting tears. It's true that she's been anxious that she was losing Kitty since Sian appeared with her promise of boho glamour and the keys to a cooler, edgier city. She put it down to her own insecurities, her own lack of self-esteem. It's true that because of that she acted out of character. But she won't show Sian any weakness. She refuses to.

'Come on, let's go,' Rich says, taking Sian by the arm and edging her back towards the gate. 'They're not worth it.'

'You're a horrible person,' Grace says to Sian's back. 'I hope that keeps you awake at night.'

Kitty knows she should storm outside and defend her friend, but she's paralysed. She can't face the confrontation. She can only make out half the words over the percussion session that is Sian putting out the empties, but she knows how much Sian's comments will have hurt Grace. Of course Sian was denying everything, knowing that Rich was in earshot. It would be a thankless task to try to get her to own up. She heads back into the kitchen and puts the radio on loud when she realises Grace is returning. She tries to calm her brain. *You didn't hear anything.* She hopes that Grace will assume anything that comes out of Sian's mouth at this point is garbage. Kitty should never have confided in her. She should never have been so disloyal to Grace.

'I just saw Sian,' Grace says as she comes in through the front door. 'She's denying all knowledge of the text, the note, all of it. It's actually crazy.'

Kitty braces herself for her to add *and she said you told her you didn't even like me much*, but Grace busies herself with finding a new bin bag under the sink.

'Maybe Rich is home, and she thought he might hear,' Kitty says, feigning ignorance.

'He was! He came out. And she was totally convincing. She lied straight to his face and it was utterly believable.'

'So, that's how she's going to play it? Denial? It makes no sense.'

Grace thinks for a second. 'Maybe she'll just bluff it out. Who's going to believe anything you or Andrew say now? She's made you look like the bad guys.'

'Maybe.' There's something nudging at the edges of Kitty's brain. She struggles to bring it into focus. 'Wait, no. Not if she's doing all this because she wants him for herself. That makes no sense. The rest of it she could explain away somehow, but not the fact that she said she saw an explicit message from Lottie to Rich. Actually saw it. He'll know that bit was a lie.'

Grace exhales noisily. 'That's true.' She climbs onto a barstool and puts her elbows on the island.

Kitty opens a drawer and pulls out a ring-bound notebook, then scrabbles around to find something to write with and comes up with a black Sharpie. She puts them in front of Grace and sits on the second stool. 'OK. Let's unpick it. Step by step.'

Grace doesn't seem quite as excited about this idea as Kitty thought she might be. Sian must have really rattled her. 'So, what was the first thing that happened? Sian told me about the text she'd seen. Write it down.'

'Why me?'

'You have much nicer handwriting than me.'

Grace starts to write. A big number one, underlined. 'Wait. Was that before or after you saw Lottie sneaking out of the house?'

'Oh. After. I mean, I did wonder later if Sian saw me that day . . .'

Grace writes it down, numbering it A1. *Kitty sees Lottie leave R and S house. Did Sian spot her watching??*

'You need a deerstalker and a pipe.'

'I'd like to think I'm more Miss Marple,' Grace says. 'Then what? She tells you about the text?'

Kitty nods. 'Well, then it was the party and we both

thought we saw Rich and Lottie being a bit touchy-feely with each other, but we dismissed that pretty quickly. But then you thought you saw them copping off at the dinner –'

Grace interrupts. 'I've accepted I must have got it wrong. I won't add that to the list.'

'Except that did help to convince Andrew it was true.'

'Let's stick to the facts,' Grace says testily. 'Sian volunteers the info about the text.'

'Yep. In the park. I was kind of testing the water to see if she would want someone to tell her if they knew a secret about her, and she just came out with it.'

Grace writes a number two. *Sian tells K about text from L to R.* Then she adds *Explicit!!!* 'That was the term she used, wasn't it?'

'It was. And she said it had been deleted since.'

Grace writes *Supposedly deleted. Convenient!*

'That's opinion,' Kitty says. 'I thought we were sticking to the facts.'

Grace huffs and scores through the word 'convenient'. Kitty laughs and pulls her in for a hug with one arm. Grace squirms.

'OK. Next.'

'I think it was her asking us to go to the shop.'

3. Shop. 'And she specifically said to look in Lottie's bag, didn't she?'

'She did.'

'So, we found the note and reported back. Then what?'

'She told Andrew about it, I think. He came round.'

4. Sian tells Andrew it's true and she has proof.

5. Andrew confirms with Kitty.

285

'What else? What did Andrew know already when he came and asked you about the note?'

'Sian had told him she had suspicions something was going on. Then the note.'

'Not the text?'

Kitty shakes her head. 'I told him about that. She said she hadn't had a chance.'

Grace looks at her sceptically. 'And, just to confirm, you didn't see it?'

Kitty shakes her head. 'She said it had been deleted next time she looked.'

'You'd take a photo of it, wouldn't you? Just in case.'

'I know.' Kitty leans her head down on the counter. 'God, I'm so stupid.'

'Confirmation bias. You had your own suspicions and so you wanted to believe her.'

'I bet she couldn't believe her luck when someone as gullible as me showed up. No wonder she was so keen to be friends with me.'

'There was no reason for you not to believe it. We were both taken in by her. And I assume he asked her about it at some point. It just maybe added weight to it that you got there first.'

'I suppose. OK, but then the drinks at the hotel. The payment. Only Andrew saw that. Where the hell does that fit in?'

'That's a McGuffin.'

Kitty looks at her blankly.

'Like a false clue. A red herring. It's an admin error or he read it wrong. More confirmation bias.'

'Write it down anyway,' Kitty says. It bothers her.

'It'll just confuse us.'

'It was a big part of Andrew believing the whole thing in the first place. No coincidences, right? Indulge me.'

Grace sighs and writes a six. *Drinks payment. Seen by Andrew. Lottie was supposed to be in East Finchley. Lottie denies ever going there. Probably irrelevant.* She underlines the last word.

'I'm sorry you got caught up in all this,' she says.

Kitty can't help but smile.

Grace shrugs. 'Well, I am, so she can bring it on.'

Despite it all Kitty laughs out loud. 'You go, girl.'

Grace guffaws.

'I'm glad you're here,' Kitty says. 'You're the only person I can face seeing to be honest.' As she says it, she realises it's the truth. There's no one else.

Grace gives her an uncertain smile and flushes red. Kitty's guilt-o-meter ratches up a notch. 'Are you up to going through your messages yet?' Grace says. 'Just in case there's anything . . .'

'There's . . .' Kitty hesitates. Here goes. The point of no return. 'Gracie, I haven't told Andrew that I found out it was all made up but still carried on. I can't . . .' She waits for Grace to tell her she has to, that absolute truth and honesty is the only way to go.

Grace worries at a patch of skin on her forearm, something she does when she's anxious. 'Only we know, right?'

'Right.'

'Well, I'll never tell anyone. It won't make things any better for either Andrew or Lottie, so let's just forget about it.'

Kitty feels as if she's going to faint with relief. 'Can we have a drink now? What time is it?'

'Four o'clock. That'll do.'

Kitty unlocks her phone and hands it to Grace. 'Just tell me if there's anything urgent. About my mum or anything.' She peels the foil from the top of a bottle of Shiraz.

Grace scrolls. 'They're pretty much all from Andrew. Do you want me to read them?'

Kitty shakes her head. 'No. I'll do it later. I can't . . .'

'Your dad.' She holds up the screen so Kitty can read the message. Just telling her he took her mum for a day out to Wrest Park. *She knew she'd been there before. Do you remember we went when you were kids?* Kitty takes the phone from Grace to reply: *Sorry I didn't reply, Dad, been ill for a couple of days. Just a virus. Glad you had fun! Xx*

She spots Jade's name, Evie's, Mark's, and tells herself to remember to answer them later. They'll cope. She tries not to look at Andrew's latest message. *I'm worried about you . . .*

'I think you should come and stay with me for a few days,' Grace is saying. 'You don't want to be bumping into Sian or Rich every time you go out.'

'I'm not going out.'

'You know what I mean.' Grace puts the leftover pizza in the fridge. 'It's not healthy. Just for a couple of days.'

Kitty shrugs. She doesn't have the strength to argue.

'I can stay here tonight, if you like, and we'll get an Uber over tomorrow.'

'Don't you have anything else to do?' Kitty says. Thankfully it comes out less mean-sounding than it could have.

Now it's Grace's turn to shrug. 'Not really.'

'Sure,' Kitty says, realising she doesn't want to argue. 'Why not?'

*

They spend an age deciding which film to watch. Kitty doesn't even care so long as she doesn't have to sit through Grace's favourite – *Notting Hill* – or any of the other implausible saccharine romances Grace is so fond of. 'Can we watch people killing each other?' she says. 'Or something where evil demons burst out of people's stomachs?' They settle on the recent remake of *Rebecca*. Kitty can't concentrate anyway, but there's a comfort in vegging out in companionable silence. Grace makes tutting sounds every time Mrs Danvers appears as if she's in the audience of a panto.

They've just paused for a cup of tea break, the wine from earlier sitting heavily on both their stomachs, when the doorbell rings.

'Ignore it,' Kitty says. 'I'm not expecting anyone.'

'It's probably just the postman. I'll get it.'

She goes before Kitty can object again. Kitty hears the front door open and then voices, both of which she recognises immediately. Her heart starts pounding and her flight mode kicks in. Could she run out of the back door? Upstairs to hide?

Because Grace seems to be inviting them in.

Andrew and Lottie.

37

Grace hadn't even thought that it might be Andrew at the door. He was too busy, she imagined, consoling his distraught wife.

She certainly hadn't imagined he would bring that distraught wife with him.

'Oh,' Andrew had said when she'd thrown open the door, game face on in case it was Sian come for another fight. He looked thinner. Dark circles under his eyes. Behind him Lottie looked a shadow of her rosy self, her hair lank. 'We need to talk to Kitty. Is she here?'

She could have said no. That Kitty had gone away and she, Grace, had just come over to water the plants (there were no plants, but she hoped that might go unnoticed), but actually, she thought, things needed to be aired out. Lottie, she was sure, needed answers. Validation of whatever Andrew had told her, which, Grace was pretty certain, because he seemed like a fundamentally good guy, would have been his understanding of the truth. And besides, Kitty was never going to be able to move on until the air had been cleared. They could do this and then she and Kitty could relocate to hers where none of the parties involved would be able to find them.

'Um. Yes. I suppose . . . come on in.'

She hoped that Kitty would forgive her.

*

Kitty sits rigid, welded to the spot. It feels like a dream. A nightmare, to be more precise. A hallucination brought on by a fever. She checks her forehead just in case. Raging Covid would be preferable to this. It's traitorously cool.

She wonders if Andrew tried to warn her. If Lottie has dragged him over here kicking and screaming for a showdown, and he managed to send an alert by text so that she could pretend to be out, or pre-arm herself with a baseball bat just in case. Her phone sits face down, sound off, on the counter by the kettle. Too late now.

And then, there he is. Grace leads them in like the head pall-bearer down the aisle. She pulls an apologetic face. Kitty barely registers it because behind Grace Andrew is looking straight at her, face gaunt, a haunted expression. And behind him, looking anywhere but at Kitty, is Lottie.

'Um. Actually, you all go in the living room and I'll make some tea,' Grace says. She squeezes Kitty's arm as she passes.

'Don't be long,' Kitty mutters. She can't face them on her own.

She follows Andrew and Lottie, thankful at least for the bath and the clean T-shirt. Lottie wears a faceful of make-up like a suit of armour: black eye flicks, pink blusher and ruby-red lips. But she's lost her natural glow, her cheekbones look hollow, her eyes dull. She and Andrew sit on the sofa, one either end, not touching. Kitty takes the chair. So far none of them have said a word to each other. She looks up and accidentally catches Andrew's eye. Looks away.

Andrew clears his throat. 'We need to get everything

out in the open,' he says, and then coughs as if the effort of speaking is too much. 'For all our sakes.'

In the kitchen Grace is clanking crockery around. Kitty imagines her trying and failing to find a milk jug or even a teapot and almost laughs.

She closes her eyes. Here goes. 'I'm sorry, Lottie. I know you don't believe me, but I am.'

She waits for a response. Surely they came here to get something off their chests. They're the ones who invaded her safe retreat uninvited.

'I think . . .' Andrew says. She forces herself to look at him and he's staring right at her. All she wants to do is to throw herself into his arms and comfort him – he looks so dejected. 'I thought . . . maybe you could tell the whole thing from your perspective. It might help Lotts see that it's the truth . . .'

So, all of this is for Lottie's sake. Kitty gets it. Lottie is the only real victim here. But it still stings. Andrew didn't come because he couldn't bear to not see Kitty any longer. He came for his wife. And, of course, Kitty owes it to her too.

'Sure.' She swallows. She needs to lay the facts out without emotion. 'I've told you this already, but it all came from Sian. She told me you were sleeping with Rich. She was devastated, that's what she said. She thought Andrew deserved to know . . .'

Grace clatters in with four mugs, a half-litre of milk under her arm. 'I didn't know how anyone took it . . . Here's yours.' She plonks one down on the coffee table in front of Kitty.

'There's sugar if you . . .' she says as Lottie accepts a cup. No one responds. Grace looks at the fourth cup in her hand as if she's forgotten who it was for. 'Oh. I'll just take mine . . .' She waves towards the kitchen. 'Unless you want me to stay, Kit?'

Kitty forces herself to look at Lottie. 'Grace can back up what I say, but maybe you'd rather talk to us separately, so we can't . . . I don't know . . . collude.'

'I could hear you from the kitchen anyway,' Grace says. 'Tell you what. I'll walk round the block a couple of times and when I get back you can ask me anything you like.'

Kitty gives her a grateful smile. She waits for the front door to close. Exhales. 'Right.'

She tells the rest of the story to the floor, her tea going cold in front of her.

'Grace can show you the photo of the note,' she says. 'If you want.'

When she reaches the part about her affair with Andrew she hesitates.

'It's OK,' he says, when he realises why she's gone quiet. 'There's nothing I haven't told her.'

Kitty assumes he doesn't mean he's described the way he gasped when she first traced her tongue down his stomach, or the fact that he knows he can drive her wild by just breathing on her. That eventually she will grab hold of his head and push herself towards his mouth. She keeps it PG, but she tells Lottie the facts: the accidental first kiss, the outdoor meet-ups, the hotel, her bed.

'The one thing I don't understand is the payment you said you saw.' She risks a look at Andrew. 'Because Lottie told me she's never even been there.'

There's a pause and then Lottie finally speaks. 'And that's true. But it's on there. I've seen it.'

'On the shop card?'

Lottie exhales loudly. 'Yep.'

'Could it have been your part-timer? Does she ever use it?'

'No. She'd never have a reason to and it's not like I leave it lying round in the shop.'

'Could Sian have got hold of it?' Kitty says hesitantly.

'I mean, in theory . . .' Andrew says, looking at Lottie. 'I suppose it's possible.'

'That's just ridiculous,' Lottie snaps.

'Well, it got on there somehow,' Kitty says. 'What date was it? Maybe we can work out where Sian was.'

'The fifth of May,' Andrew says. 'At half seven in the evening.'

'I was at the cinema,' Lottie says. 'Miles away.'

'It was a Monday,' Andrew says, looking at his phone.

Kitty remembers. They got a cab to Hampstead and sat in the rickety old Holly Bush drinking red wine. 'Shit. She was out with me.'

'Well, there you go,' Lottie says. 'That's your whole stupid theory blown.'

'Lotts . . .' Andrew says placatingly.

'Don't "Lotts" me. You're just trying to make me feel stupid. Both of you.'

'We're missing something,' Kitty says.

They sit in silence for a moment. Lottie clears her throat. 'I don't understand why Sian would do it. If you're right.'

'We think . . . Grace and I . . . that she wants Andrew herself.' She looks at Andrew. 'That's why she's suggesting you move in with her. She wanted to make you fall for her while she convinced you Lottie was cheating.'

294

'No,' they both say at the same time.

'No way,' Andrew says again. 'I would know if she was interested in me. She's never given me any signs of that.'

'I don't think so either,' Lottie says quietly.

There's a bang as the front door shuts again. *Grace must have taken the keys*, Kitty thinks, *so she could let herself back in.* She must hear the silence because she peers round the door. 'Everything OK?'

'We were just talking about Sian. About why.' Kitty takes a sip of her tea and almost spits it back out it's so tepid.

'Because she fancies Andrew, right?'

'Apparently not. They don't think . . .'

'Oh. Well, I suppose it was stretching it a bit to think all three of you were lusting after him.'

'Gracie . . .'

'I don't mean . . . sorry, I'm nervous. I babble when I'm nervous. But you know what I mean. Too obvious. Too easy. That's all. No offence.'

'Grace, show Lottie the picture of the note.'

Kitty is amazed at how calm she's being, when inside all she wants to do is to beg Andrew to tell her things will work out somehow, that Lottie had announced she was happy he'd made the decision to end their marriage because she was about to do the same thing, and by the way wouldn't Kitty make a gorgeous step-mum to Harry and Archie? No one's body language is indicating that this might be the case. She also feels wretched for him. A thought hits her: *I must be in love with him, because I just want him to be happy, even if that means without me.* And for a moment she's almost derailed by the thought that she loves someone, that she's capable of that vulnerability.

She had told Geth she loved him, of course she had. You had to if you had a joint mortgage, a shared Netflix password and an assumption of a lifetime together ahead. It had never, for a moment, felt like this.

Grace eventually finds the photo and then tells Lottie the whole story from her perspective, embellishing here and there when she really doesn't need to. But the basic facts are the same. Sian set the whole thing in motion. Sian is public enemy number one. Lottie has to believe them now.

'Why did you tell her you saw us together? Did you just make that up?'

Grace gulps. 'Um. Because I thought I did. When Rich was showing you the jacket . . .' Kitty nods her encouragement. Grace gives her a weak smile. 'I realised later I must have been wrong. Misinterpreted something innocent. We were just all riled up thinking Rich was cheating . . . I'm really sorry.'

Lottie starts to speak and then clears her throat and tries again. 'What if it's to do with Andrew but it's not because she fancies him?'

Kitty looks at her and Lottie catches her eye for the first time. Lottie switches her gaze to Andrew.

'I told her about my new job.'

38

'I'm lost,' Kitty says.

Lottie hooks her hair behind her ear. She looks at her hands while she speaks, avoiding eye contact with them all.

'I've sometimes thought she resents me. A bit. For, you know. Having the shop. Not having to slog away at something I hate.'

'That's just ridiculous, though,' Grace pipes up. 'She's trying to ruin your life because you like your job more than she does hers?'

Kitty suddenly remembers a comment Sian made about Lottie's shop basically being a hobby. Was there something more to it? Something meaner?

'Because I can do what I love while Sian and Rich both slave away at jobs they hate and wish they could follow their passions for even a second, but they can't afford to. Moving out here, all of that, she felt like it was giving up. Having to take on more private tuition to make ends meet, so she has no time to paint.' Lottie pauses. 'And she hates that Rich is so passive. Her word. That he's OK to just coast along.'

Kitty picks at a bit of thread that's coming loose from her Orla Kiely cushion. 'That's hardly your fault, though.'

'Sorry, but I still don't get why she would try to ruin yours and Andrew's lives,' Grace says with a frown. 'Just because she's envious?'

'And her own,' Kitty says. 'She's blowing up her own too.'

'I think you're right about her wanting to take Andrew away from me. Just not because she's in love with him.'

'Are you rich or something?' Grace says, and for once Kitty is grateful for her bluntness.

Andrew's cheeks flush. 'No. I mean, a bit. Not rich. But I do OK. I inherited the business . . .'

'And he made it ten times better,' Lottie chips in, loyally. 'It's not as if everything got handed to him on a plate.'

'It did a bit,' Andrew says, and Kitty thinks now she understands. The guerrilla gardening, the favours of free plants and hours of labour. It's about offsetting his privilege. Soothing a prickly conscience. She loves that about him, that he feels guilty his life is a bit more comfortable than other people's. This makes no sense to her, though. Sian might not have everything she wants in life but who does? Most people wish they could give up their nine to five, and most people can't. She can't quite process it. It's too vague, too nebulous. There must be something else. Something they're missing.

'I mean, it's a bit drastic.'

Lottie sighs. 'I confided in her about something recently . . .' She puffs out her cheeks. Kitty turns to Andrew who gives Lottie an encouraging half-smile.

'It's OK,' he says quietly, and the tenderness, the years of history behind their connection, hits her like a punch in the stomach.

'My shop's a bit of a vanity project,' Lottie says, looking Kitty straight in the eye. 'It doesn't make money.'

'She's exaggerating,' Andrew says. 'It's just . . . it takes a while for businesses like hers to take off, that's all.'

'I told Sian a while ago that I felt bad that the shop was basically a folly and that I was only staying afloat because we were OK without me earning anything . . .'

'To be clear, it's not like I'm bankrolling it,' Andrew interrupts. 'I'm not exactly David Beckham. It basically breaks even . . .'

'But I get to do my passion. I thought, I don't know, as if it might make her feel a bit better hearing that. Like I'm not more successful than her or something. And then I got offered a contract to work on a new Netflix period thing. A series. I'm not the costume designer, obviously, because I wouldn't know where to start, but I'm working with them, like a kind of advisor. And I get to be on set the whole way through to oversee the details. It's Regency. It's my absolute dream . . .' She looks between Kitty and Grace, as if waiting to see if they understand. For a split-second Kitty feels irritated. Things really do seem to fall into Lottie's lap. But she checks herself. Lottie is clearly qualified for the position she's been offered. And it's not as if Andrew had any influence there. Lottie just needs help to make it work, like scores of women who've come to their careers late because they've given up half their lives to raising children.

'Congratulations,' she says, because she's not sure what else to say.

'That's amazing,' Grace adds.

'But obviously the shop can't run itself. And it can't afford the extra staff on its own . . .'

'So, Andrew is helping out?' Grace says.

Lottie colours. 'Yes. I mean, he was. I'm not sure what's going on now.'

'I am,' Andrew says firmly. 'I said I would, and I will. Whatever happens.'

Kitty looks anywhere but at him. 'And you told Sian this?'

'Yes. I mean, she asked me what would happen with the shop. The shoot is six months. I couldn't exactly lie about it.'

'And what did she say?'

'Nice things. I mean. Obviously. But I felt as if she was pissed off. I remember wishing I hadn't said anything.'

'When was this?' Kitty says. She blinks. She feels as if she's getting a headache behind her left eye.

Lottie looks at Andrew as if he might be able to help. One of those subconscious gestures couples make. He shrugs. 'You didn't mention it to me.'

'A while ago. I wasn't supposed to tell anyone, apart from Andrew obviously, not until the project was officially announced. They made me sign a confidentiality thing. Anyway, it was not long before their party, I think, because I remember being worried that night that she might be a bit pissed off with me.'

Grace has been opening and shutting her mouth like a baby bird hoping for a worm, waiting for a gap in the conversation. (*I think I talk too much*, she'd said to Kitty earlier. *I'm going to make a conscious effort to listen more.*) 'So, what? You think she wants to bag herself a rich man to keep her in the style she thinks she deserves? That's not very twenty-first century.'

'I'm not rich,' Andrew says. 'Just for the record.'

Lottie exhales. 'I mean, there might have been an element of that. Not in that kind of Victorian housewife way, but maybe she thinks it's her turn to be able to give her dream a shot and there's no other way she's ever going to be able to do it. Or she might just think it's unfair that I've got it so much easier.'

She sniffs. Pulls her sleeve over her hand and wipes her eyes.

'She must be loving this.' She looks at Kitty, red-eyed. 'You and him.'

39

The silence is resounding. Andrew reaches out a hand to console his wife and then snatches it back as if he's stepped out of line.

Kitty closes her eyes. 'We can't take it back,' she says. 'Trust me, I would if I could.' She can feel Andrew looking at her.

A fat tear drips from Lottie's nose, and she rubs her arm over her face again. 'I know.'

Kitty exhales loudly.

'I don't hate you,' Lottie says. 'I'm not trying to make you feel bad.'

'You should. I'd understand.'

Kitty's aware of Grace's head flicking between the two of them, an umpire at a tennis match. She lets out a little cough. 'Kitty's my best friend and I honestly believe she would never . . . not knowingly.'

Kitty feels a rush of affection, shame, guilt and more shame.

'I know,' Lottie says, her voice small.

'No one in this room is at fault,' Grace continues. 'None of you. It might not feel that way at the moment, but that's how it is.' Kitty reaches out a hand and squeezes the only bit of Grace she can reach, her sock-clad foot. She doesn't deserve such loyalty.

She wishes they'd leave, Andrew and Lottie. Off into

the sunset to rebuild their shattered lives. They'll do it, she thinks. They'll get through it. There will be a shadow in the background – way bigger than the one cast by Lottie previously, but it will fade. She wishes them luck, but she doesn't want to have to witness it. So, it doesn't feel as if there's anything more she can say. She gets up and gathers up their mugs, hoping that will signal that it's time to go. Andrew is clearly still in tune with her body language because he stands as she passes. He's so close she could reach out a hand to touch him.

'We'll leave you in peace. Lotts?'

Lottie nods. 'Sure.'

It's awkward. Kitty doesn't know how to say goodbye to them. Is this the last time she'll ever see Andrew? They obviously can't be in touch, she knows that, however much it pains her. She'll block his number as soon as they leave, just in case. And he's hardly likely to be popping to number 8 for a cup of tea any time soon. She thinks of her half-improved garden and wonders if she'll ever be able to sit out there again: the traces of Andrew, the threat of Sian next door. She'll call an estate agent tomorrow. She'll put the house on the market. Maybe she will move closer to Grace. Stranger things have happened. She'll leave all this behind and start again. Again.

'Wait.' Grace jumps to her feet. 'We're not just going to let her get away with it? Sian? She's ruined all of your lives, all three of you. She at least needs to know you've rumbled her.'

Kitty opens her mouth to say something sensible and grown-up like *Let's just all put it behind us*, or *At least we have the moral high ground*, but then she thinks: *Fuck it*. Why should she have to cower with the curtains closed just to avoid Sian? Why should Andrew have to lose his best mate just because his best mate's wife is a vindictive psycho? She's sick of meekly accepting that her life is compromised every way she turns. She's sick of it all.

'Grace is right,' she says, standing up as if to stop them leaving. 'She's right,' she says again with less certainty now they're all looking at her. 'Rich at least needs to know who he's married to.'

The problem is that they have no proof. Apart from a photo of a faked note, it's all hearsay.

'Maybe I should go and confront her after all. When he's not there. And secretly record it.' Kitty knows she's clutching at straws.

Grace shakes her head. 'She'd just deny it like she did with me.'

'Have you spoken to Rich?' Kitty says, risking a direct look at Andrew. She notices his hair is a whisker too long where he hasn't bothered with the clippers.

'I tried to call him, and he basically said, "Have you been sleeping with Kitty or not . . . ?"' He shoots a glance at Lottie. 'So, I kind of said, "Yes, but . . ." and he put the phone down. I texted him a couple of times, but he didn't reply, so I went to football and collared him there. I just wanted him to know it wasn't like she'd told him it was.'

'And?' Kitty says.

'He wouldn't have it. And, to be honest, I don't really blame him. When you spell it all out it sounds insane.'

'He's picked his side, and he can't let himself believe he's picked the wrong one,' Grace says. 'He'd need Sian to come clean to change his mind.'

'Just out of interest,' Kitty says, 'after I told you about the text, did you ever ask her about it? I've always wondered how she thought she could explain that away later.'

Andrew screws his face up, trying to remember. 'She played it down a bit. Said she'd told you she'd thought it was possible she might be overreacting to what she'd read, but that then you'd said about seeing Lotts sneaking out of the house, and Grace seeing them in the bedroom and obviously, later, the note you found sealed everything . . .'

'So, she basically implied it all came from me . . .' Kitty fumes. 'That I was the one pushing that whole narrative.'

Grace rubs at her arm, leaving pale red marks. 'She didn't mention the word "explicit"?'

He shakes his head. 'She was vague about what exactly was in it, if I'm being honest. I thought she just found it too painful to talk about. I did.'

'But she definitely said it was Rich's writing? The note?' Lottie says, and Kitty feels all eyes on her, as if they suddenly suspect she might have made the whole thing up.

'One hundred per cent,' Grace pipes up. 'She didn't even hesitate. I was there,' she adds.

'We all fell for her shit,' Kitty says quietly. 'Because we all trusted her.'

'Aren't you worried next door will see you?' Grace asks as Lottie reaches to open the front door.

'They'll think we've come to thrash it all out once and for all. Which, to be honest, *was* why we came. Although Sian keeps telling me I should just throw Andrew out.'

Kitty gulps. 'Sorry.'

'You can stop saying sorry. It's OK. I mean. It's not. But like I said, I'm not blaming you.'

Kitty opens her mouth to apologise again but manages to stop herself.

'So, that's it?' she says. 'She just gets on with her life?'

Lottie shoots a look at Andrew. 'I don't think we should stoop to her level. I think we just need to concentrate on us.'

That word. Kitty swallows hard. 'I get it.'

Grace tuts. 'It's not right.'

Kitty lays a calming hand on her arm. 'But's it's probably healthier, right? Be the bigger people and all that, remember. And besides, it would just be our word against hers.'

'Is it mad that I quite like her now?' Grace says once they're finally on their own.

'No. I do too, I suppose, which is just weird. More than I did, anyway. Or I think she's probably a nice person, which is not quite the same.'

'How did you feel seeing him?'

'Fine,' Kitty says curtly, effectively cutting off the conversation. 'He's trying to do the right thing, so that's good, isn't it?'

'But you must have felt . . .'

'Leave it, Grace,' Kitty snaps. 'Let's just all move on, OK?'

She just wishes it was that easy.

40. Sian

Honestly.

You couldn't make it up. Well, you could, but if you did, surely you would neaten up the plotting. Cut the whole thread where Andrew and Kitty fell for each other and fucked the whole thing up.

She hadn't meant it to get this messy. The truth is that she hadn't really thought it through at all. She'd been unhappy, she'd been frustrated, unfulfilled, irritated with Lottie, all of the above, and then she'd seen a way out and put a plan into motion that had spiralled. She'd had to double down and try to see it through, or risk being exposed and left with nothing.

The facts were these:

She was fond of Rich but his lack of ambition, his apparent satisfaction with his life as it was drove her crazy. She could see a future for him mapped out in commutes and performance reviews and the occasional promise of a sales bonus, and she couldn't understand why that didn't terrify him. Yes, he needed to earn money – they both did – but that didn't mean they had to forget who they were. And Rich, these days, was very much a domestic security consultant, not a sculptor. Not the artist with a job on the side to pay the rent she'd married.

And, to be fair, neither was she. She knew that part of what had fuelled her mid-life crisis – if that's what this was – was her disappointment in herself. Part-time Spanish teacher scrabbling around for private students to make ends meet. She hadn't picked up a paintbrush since they'd moved. Even if she could have taught art, it might have patched up her soul a little. Scratched the itch enough to keep her sane. Reinforced her view of who she really was just enough. But even though people kept telling her there was a shortage of art teachers, there didn't seem to be any urgency by the schools in the area to employ them either. She could do an after-school art club, her headmistress had suggested. There was no budget for it, obviously, no extra pay to compensate, but the kids would love it. Sian had declined. She was a teacher by default, not by vocation. Giving up her spare time for free to fulfil the kids' creative ambitions rather than her own was definitely not her priority.

And then Lottie had told her the truth about the shop. Somehow, bizarrely, she had imagined it might make Sian feel better about her own life to know just how easy she actually had it. How pampered and privileged she really was. And now there wasn't just the shop; there was the film consultancy job too. Again, barely paid. She was doing it 'for the experience' and 'for my CV'. And she could afford to do that, to indulge her creativity, her passion, because Andrew was happy to prop her the fuck up. Like she was some kind of spoilt nepo baby and not his actual fucking wife who surely had a duty to contribute something, or at least not waste the family's money on her hobbies.

The bottom line was that Sian was eaten up by jealousy. It wasn't that she expected Rich to support her because he was the man – if he'd been the one still with artistic ambition and she'd been earning enough, she would happily have done the same for him – it was just that time was running out and there was no other way she was ever going to make anything of her life.

Unless she could somehow find herself the same safety net that Lottie had.

And then she'd spotted Kitty at her window, watching Lottie sneak out of the house. It was almost too perfect.

A few weeks before she'd been looking for some info on the Santorini holiday – travel planning was Rich's domain. The exact address of the villa, she thinks it was. And she'd come across an email about the 'event', the 'vows', the 'celebration'. It asked how many years both couples had been married for. Rich, god love him, ever chatty, had mentioned somewhere in the thread that he and his wife were intending to wear the same clothes they'd worn to their wedding, *after a few alterations, haha!*, so could there be some red in the flowers to match her dress? Stunned, confused, irritated, she'd sleepwalked to the wardrobe where her wedding dress resided, hidden away at the back. The garment bag was empty. It could only be Lottie.

So, she knew without a doubt that her clandestine visit to the house was innocent.

But, more importantly, Kitty didn't.

As ideas went it was a seed, a germ, an atom.

She had no idea what it might grow into.

41

Forest Streets Residents' WhatsApp Group:

**Sez de Courcy : Does anyone know where Magda went? She
dropped this truth bomb and then fucked off. But, you know, there's
no smoke without fire. Or maybe there's smoke but it's coming from
a different bonfire altogether. And maybe someone unexpected lit
the match . . .**

Kitty stares at the screen. There's a photo. A screenshot
of Magda's comment about the party. About Rich being
very attentive to one guest in particular. She's tempted to
march straight into her spare room and ask Grace what
the hell she's playing at, but it's three in the morning and
she's only seen this because she couldn't sleep.

She scrolls back. Shirley Howard Martin's introduction
of Sez was immediately before the offending comment.
There hadn't even been time for anyone to respond.
Grace must have been sitting there, fingers on the keys,
waiting to be accepted into the group.

'Fuckssake,' she shouts, throwing her phone down on
the bed. In the end she can't leave it. She needs to get
Grace to delete the comment before another local insom-
niac spots it.

She stomps straight in without even knocking, flicking
on the overhead light, brandishing her phone. 'I literally

don't know what you're doing,' she says as a greeting. Grace sits bolt upright, a small scream dying on her lips, wide awake in ten seconds flat. She blinks rapidly, reaches for her glasses. She looks like a cartoon hedgehog, hair spiked up in all directions.

'What? What's happened?'

'Like you don't know.'

'I have no idea.'

'Sez de Courcy.'

There's a pause. 'No, you've lost me. Are you sleepwalking? What time is it? My dad used to have whole conversations in his sleep . . .'

'I know it's you. It must be you.'

'Kitty, what? You're scaring me.'

'WhatsApp,' Kitty says, but she suddenly doesn't feel as confident. Why wouldn't Grace just own up? She may be annoying sometimes but she's pretty honest about it.

'What about it? Did something happen?'

Kitty exhales. 'It isn't you?'

'Wait. What?' There's genuine surprise in Grace's voice. 'Shit. Who the fuck . . . ?'

'OK. You have to tell me what's going on now. Someone's put something on WhatsApp? About Rich and Lottie?'

'Kind of. About Magda's comment. With a photo of it.'

Grace makes a whistling sound. 'I don't get it. Magda's been gone for weeks. Tell me exactly what it says.'

Kitty reads the message aloud. Twice.

Grace says nothing for a moment. 'And has she posted before? What's her name? Sexy Corgi? You might be able to work out who she is.'

'Sez de Courcy.'

'Sezda?'

'Sez. De. Courcy.'

'What kind of a name is that?' Grace says. 'Is she French?'

'I have no idea. Are you really a Polish cleaner? She's only just joined . . .' There's another silence while Kitty scrolls back. 'Please all welcome Sez. Sez lives in Summerdown Court, blah blah blah . . . No clue on her profile.'

'That's where I said Magda lived,' Grace interrupts. 'It's those big flats on the main road where the bus stop is. Wait, I thought you couldn't see posts from before you joined, otherwise you'd see all the times everyone had been slagging you off for putting your bins out on the wrong day. Sez must have been on there when Magda made that post to be able to get that screenshot, isn't that how it works?'

'She wasn't, though. But you're right, so it's someone who had access.' Kitty sinks into a chair. 'This is a bit creepy. Hold on, I'll have a look at the members list. I won't know when any of them joined, though, I don't think.'

Grace fiddles with her phone. 'It hasn't had any responses yet.'

'There are so many people on here. And half of them are just numbers . . . I mean, I can see most of our street here, I think. And that's the woman I bought the house off, so she's never left the group. And the man from number nine who died about three years ago. This is hopeless,' Kitty grumbles. 'We know from personal experience that Shirley lets any old person join under any old fake name. I don't think we're going to just work it out.'

'Why would someone want to stir things up?' Grace says. 'And why now? And what does it even mean? Why be so cryptic?'

'Magda wasn't exactly crystal clear in what she was saying.'

Grace ignores that. 'What do you think she's really trying to say?'

'Is it about me and Andrew, do you think?' Kitty says, screwing up her face.

'Wouldn't they just come out and say it if it was? I mean, if Sian's going round telling everyone anyway. No, I think it's something new. Like they want to let people know but they're scared to just come out with it.'

'We need to try and find out who it is,' Kitty says. 'There's a reason they've just posted it now.'

Grace's spare room is pristine. Pale green walls. Dark wooden bed. Crisp white bedlinen. Thankfully frog-free. There's a smell of fresh paint. Grace opens the window.

'I just redecorated. I decided the whole flat needs updating and this room had the least clutter, so lucky for you I started in here last week.'

'It's gorgeous. I can help you while I'm here. I love a bit of painting.' Kitty is only intending to stay a couple of nights while she licks her wounds and regroups. But she'll still feel awkward unless she can do something to pay her way.

Grace beams. 'You can help me choose colours. Oh, no,' she says suddenly. 'I completely forgot I have date two with Alasdair.' She looks at her phone. 'Five minutes ago.'

'Shit. That's my fault. Call him quick and blame it on me.' They'd slept in late once they'd eventually gone back to bed confused and exhausted. The whole day had been out of kilter.

Grace huffs. 'I'll just send him a text cancelling.'

'Grace! You can't do that. He's got all ready and got on the tube just to see you. Where is it anyway?'

'His choice. A ping-pong bar in Farringdon, then lunch. There'll be other people he can play with.'

'I don't think that's the point. Poor bloke.'

'It's pointless anyway.' Grace pulls a face.

'You'll get a black mark against your name. Think of all the money you've paid.'

Grace's phone beeps. 'That's him.' She holds it out. *I'm here. Do you need help to find it?*

'Phone him,' Kitty says.

'I'm really sorry,' Grace says as soon as Alasdair answers. 'My friend had a crisis and I've been with her . . .' She shoots Kitty an apologetic look. 'And I, well, I forgot . . . Yes, she's fine. Ish. She's at mine now. Of course . . . Well, Kitty might still be here then, so I probably shouldn't . . .' Kitty touches her arm and gives her a glare that she hopes says 'Don't not go on a date because of me.' It apparently works because Grace holds the phone away from her ear. 'Tomorrow?' she says to Kitty, screwing up her face. Kitty nods encouragingly. 'Hold on . . . Actually, yes . . . OK. See you tomorrow. Text me the details. Sorry again.

'He was actually really nice about it,' she says as she ends the call.

'Wow, he got a "really". That's a big improvement on a "quite".'

Grace rolls her eyes theatrically. 'You unpack. I'll make some tea.'

Kitty has never been good at staying with other people. However much they insist she make herself at home, she can't relax. She loves her own space, her own company. Just not all the time. It's tempting to crawl between the cool sheets and try to sleep her life away, but Grace is doing her a big favour, and she needs to make an effort.

When she walks into the living room, Grace is sitting at one end of the sofa with two gin and tonics and a paint chart the size of a house brick on the coffee table in front of her. Kitty moves a fat plushy amphibian out of the way and sits down.

Later she helps Grace fill two boxes with frogs and other accumulated tat and they stick it into Grace's battered old Fiat and drive it to the nearest charity shop who decline to take it.

'We'd just never get rid of it,' the woman says with a sneer.

So, they line it all up on the low walls outside Grace's block with a sign saying 'Help Yourself' and watch from the window as passing kids grab whatever they can. When one sad-looking stuffed green abomination is left, Grace says, 'I can't leave him there on his own. I just can't,' and goes down to rescue him. They sit him on the sofa between them and veg out watching reruns of *Escape to the Continent*.

'We should go on holiday together,' Grace says out of nowhere. 'I mean, just a weekend or something. Sorry, that's a stupid idea, isn't it? Forget I said it.'

And Kitty, who has never had any desire to spend

more than an evening in Grace's company and then only because she doesn't have a better offer, surprises herself by saying, 'It's a great idea,' and meaning it.

When Grace leaves to meet Alasdair the following night – him having texted her the address of a Lebanese restaurant conveniently close by in Hammersmith earlier, along with a message saying she should feel free to bring her friend along with her if she was worried about leaving her on her own, to which Kitty had replied that despite the fact it was thoughtful of him she'd rather stick a fork in her eye – Kitty knuckles down to an evening spent lining up strips of masking tape around the sockets and windows, and trying not to think about Andrew. She finds an upbeat 1990s playlist on Spotify and turns it up loud.

She pours herself a glass of wine and picks at the end of the tape. It's raggedy and she tries to rip it so it's neater, but she only succeeds in making it worse. She decides she needs scissors to cut each edge precisely. She rifles through the drawers in Grace's kitchen, finding every-thing exactly where she would expect it to be, everything clean and tidy. In the third drawer down, under the kettle, there's a jumble of bits and pieces – a ball of elastic bands, a bag of plastic food clips, a pile of take-out menus from local restaurants (she knows that Grace likes to peruse an actual menu before logging in to Deliveroo). She shifts things around, certain that she's moments away from finding what she's after. She straightens up a small collec-tion of papers that she's disturbed. The top one catches her eye. It's a receipt. The name at the top: the Maryle-bone Hotel.

Kitty picks it up. Wouldn't Grace have mentioned that she'd been there? She looks at the date and her heart starts to race.

It's the same evening that Lottie and Rich supposedly had a drink in the bar. The same amount as the entry on Lottie's shop's bank statement.

The same payment she and Grace have discussed endlessly. But it looks as if Grace might have known the truth about it all along.

It looks as if Grace has been lying to her.

42

'Alasdair had a great idea,' Grace says, when she walks through the front door. She's actually beaming.

'You had a good time, then?' Kitty is pacing the living room, mind whirring. She's had to put her phone in a drawer to stop herself from calling Andrew.

'I told him the whole story because, you know, he doesn't know any of the people involved so I thought it might be interesting to get his opinion. It gave us something to talk about.'

Kitty fishes in her pocket, brandishes the receipt like a weapon. 'I found this.'

Grace's face falls and she crumples onto the sofa. *She doesn't even need to look at it*, Kitty thinks. *She knows exactly what it is.*

'I was going to tell you about that, I promise . . .'

'Of course you were.'

Grace's eyes flick to the corner of the room where Kitty's bag stands, packed and ready to go. 'No, Kit . . .'

'You've got about five minutes till my Uber comes.' In truth she hasn't actually booked a car yet because she had no idea what time Grace would get home. She can pick up a cab on the street when she leaves or book one from the corner. But she's four glasses of wine down and she wants to punish her.

Grace lifts her glasses and wipes her sleeve across her eyes.

Kitty crosses her arms. 'What are you? A kleptomaniac? You stole her card and then you couldn't admit it?'

'Don't be stupid,' Grace says.

'What, then? You found it in the street? Someone planted it here? I hope so, because any other explanation would be fucking insane.'

There's a heavy silence for a moment and then Grace closes her eyes. 'It was Sian. Now I realise she asked me because I said I saw Lottie and Rich snogging and she knew that couldn't be true. That I was making it up. That she could use me, and I'd go along with it. Because I did. I didn't misinterpret what was going on. I made it up. I didn't even go up there because I was scared they'd see me. I just used the downstairs loo and then told you what I'd supposedly seen. Because I thought it might help to persuade you to tell Sian about your suspicions. I didn't want Rich to get away with it.'

'So, you made something up? Have you got any idea how unhinged that sounds?'

'I just knew that if I were Sian, I would have wanted to know my best friend was sneaking out of my house trying to make sure I didn't see she was in there with my husband. And you weren't going to tell her.'

Kitty throws herself down into a chair. 'Because I didn't want to blow up everyone's life just on a suspicion. Fuckssake.'

'Anyway, then Sian told you she'd seen the text, so I felt what I'd done didn't matter any more. She'd seen proof for herself. It was definitely true.'

'Unbelievable,' Kitty says. 'So, what's the receipt got to do with anything?'

Grace closes her eyes as if she can't look at Kitty while she tells her. 'Sian called me. She said Andrew was struggling to believe it and she needed something just to tip him over the edge. There was so much evidence by then, Kit . . .'

'Except there wasn't! There was me seeing a woman leave a man's house, you making up something about them kissing and Sian fabricating a text . . .'

'You started it! The whole thing stemmed from you making a big deal of seeing Lottie sneak out!'

Kitty is momentarily silenced. She's never heard Grace raise her voice like this before. Grace's face is blotchy and mascara-streaked. She takes off her glasses and rubs at her eyes more violently.

'I didn't make a big deal of it. I just told you what I saw.'

'And we both came to the conclusion that something was going on between them. Anyway, Sian asked me to go to the Marylebone bar and buy a couple of drinks. She told me exactly when to go because she knew Lottie would be out without Andrew. She pinched the card out of Lottie's bag and told me to make sure I didn't spend so much I couldn't pay contactless. Then she would convince Andrew he should look at Lottie's accounts and he'd see it . . . She just wanted to put Andrew out of his misery once and for all, that's what she said.'

Kitty brandishes the receipt. 'And what? You kept this as some kind of trophy? Like a serial killer?'

'I thought it might be useful,' Grace says so quietly Kitty can hardly hear. 'Later. I don't know. Because it says two drinks . . .'

'And Sian told you not to tell me, obviously . . .'

Grace nods reluctantly. 'She asked me not to, yes. She said you would worry about it, but it was OK because she and I had both seen proof for ourselves, so we one hundred per cent knew it was true, and we were just doing Andrew a favour.'

'The kiss.'

'Yep.'

'And she knew you couldn't admit you hadn't actually seen them kiss because that would surely make you psychotic.'

Grace ignores the sarcasm. 'I didn't think I was doing anything wrong. Neither of us thought in a million years she could be making the whole thing up.'

'You must have thought you were, otherwise you would have told me about it, whatever Sian said.'

'I promised her . . .'

'Since when did you care so much about Sian? I didn't think you even liked her that much.'

'Andrew deserved to know the truth.'

Kitty squeaks, exasperated. 'You barely know Andrew. But you went on some weird vigilante mission all the same.' She suddenly remembers a story Grace once told her: she was at a Robbie Williams concert with a couple of women from the hospital a few years ago – a last-minute opportunity posted on the staff notice board when their friend dropped out – and she'd noticed that the bloke in front was sexting someone while sitting next to his oblivious partner. Nude photos, everything, were popping up on his carefully angled phone. When he went to get more drinks, Grace proudly told Kitty, she had actually tapped the woman on the shoulder and told her. As the boyfriend handed over the plastic glass of wine the wife had relieved him of his mobile too and clicked on his WhatsApp before he could stop her. Then she'd stormed out, taking his phone with her, and shouting 'You fucking pig' just as Robbie hit the chorus of 'Angels'. Grace had considered this a great victory. Kitty had always assumed it was one of Grace's tall tales, but now she's not so sure.

'How would you feel if it was you? And no one told you?'

'Grace, not everything is about you and Hal. You can't make decisions for the rest of the world based on a set of rules you made up!'

A single tear edges its way down Grace's cheek. 'I'm sorry.' Kitty looks away.

There's a heavy silence. Kitty looks at her phone as if checking on her Uber. She needs to get out of here before she says something she regrets.

Grace sighs. 'And I was worried I was losing you too.'

She says it so quietly Kitty isn't even sure she's heard correctly. 'What?'

'I thought if I could do that for Sian, she'd be so appreciative . . . she'd want me around, not just you . . .'

Kitty stares at her. She looks so pitiful sitting there like a small child after a dressing-down from a teacher.

'God, you really are pathetic,' Kitty says angrily. 'You couldn't even let me have that. Sian was right. I've always thought you were unbearably fucking clingy.'

Then she reaches for her bag and walks out.

43. Sian

Grace had been a gift.

Sian had been genuinely happy to run into Kitty. Someone her own age who seemed to be pretty cool and wasn't a member of a local darts team or chasing a horde of small, out-of-control children around, screaming at them all day. Some of the teachers at the school were OK, but their conversation mainly revolved around the kids, the curriculum, the cutbacks, the parents. She just wasn't interested beyond the odd bit of entertaining gossip. She was only there to cover maternity leave. She had no expectation of her position being made permanent. Which in itself gave her cause for anxiety, because what was she going to do then? Lottie, of course, was fairly nearby. But sometimes Sian couldn't face Lottie's cheery positivity. It must be easy to be happy if you were Lottie. It almost didn't count.

So, here's the way it had been going to play out in her head: confide her suspicions to Kitty (that is, unless Kitty came to her first to tell her she had suspicions of her own, but she couldn't rely on that). Feed her evidence that she could then relay to Andrew, thus leaving Sian with no blood on her hands if it all blew up. Andrew leaves Lottie. Sian comforts him. Andrew realises that he and Sian should have been together all along. Bingo. Rich and Lottie could protest all they liked, but hopefully, by then, too much water would have passed under the bridge, too many hurtful things would have been said, love would have been irretrievably lost. And there would always be a fug of rumour swirling about them however much they proclaimed their innocence.

Sian would have deniability insofar as Andrew, Rich and Lottie were concerned. Did she tell Kitty she'd seen an explicit text? Of course she didn't! She may have mentioned once seeing a message from Lottie to Rich that could have been up for misinterpretation. She can't even remember what it said now. It had just been a passing comment. It wasn't her fault that Kitty had run with it.

It would be Kitty's word against Sian's. Sorry, Kitty.

Sian liked her, it was true. But not as much as she liked the prospect of a brighter future for herself.

It would have to be a long game.

Or it would have been if it hadn't been for Grace.

Grace with her overblown sense of justice and decency and revenge on faithless men. With her desperation to ingratiate herself with the rival she thought might magic her best friend away. By the time Sian confided in Kitty, Grace had done some of the groundwork for her. And from there it was only a half-step further to convince her to provide another fake clue to lure Andrew in.

It had been almost too easy.

Well, at least Grace could have Kitty all to herself again now. At least one of them would be happy.

44

Kitty actually falls asleep easily, worn out by anger and righteousness. But she wakes with a start at three, in a pool of sweat, her last words to Grace resounding in her ears. An image of Grace's devastated face, as Kitty stomped off slamming the door behind her, lodged in her brain.

You really are pathetic.

Unbearably fucking clingy.

She deserved it, Kitty tells herself. She was the butterfly flap that had caused this whole tsunami.

Kitty had aired her suspicions, but it was Grace saying she'd witnessed Rich and Lottie together in the bathroom that had turned those suspicions into fact.

That and Sian claiming to have seen an incriminating text.

But Grace had lied because she had genuinely wanted to help Sian and Andrew. Misguidedly, admittedly.

Sian had lied because she'd wanted to destroy Lottie. And if that destroyed Rich too, then that was too bad.

When Sian told Kitty about the text, she hadn't even known about what Grace had supposedly seen. All she could have had to latch on to was seeing Kitty watch Lottie sneak out of the house. And Kitty's obvious desperation to be her new best friend.

How was Kitty's campaign for Sian's friendship any more pitiful than Grace's bid to keep hers?

Jesus. They're as bad as each other.

Eventually she gives in and goes downstairs to make tea. Ashdown Close is quiet, only the tiniest crack in the black sky hinting that it's almost morning. At number 8 a light is on. Kitty steps back from the window and watches from the dark of her kitchen as Sian puts the kettle on in hers. So, she can't sleep either. Kitty freezes as Sian looks over, looks right at her. She knows she can't be seen in the dark, but she doesn't want to take any chances. She tries to remember why she'd thought this woman was the answer to all her problems, but she can't. She feels nothing towards her.

Nothing positive, anyway.

Back in bed she reaches for her mobile. Usually she wakes to a download of Grace's brain on her phone. Every random thought she's had through the night. This morning there's just silence. Admittedly it's still early, but Kitty knows she won't hear from her. She's pushed her over the tipping point.

Despite the hour, she can't bear just waiting for the inevitable tumbleweed. She writes a message to Grace. *I'm sorry for what I said. I can't condone what you did, but I should never have spoken like that. It was the heat of the moment.* She sends it and then wishes she hadn't mentioned her disapproval of Grace's actions – now is not the time – so she deletes it (thank god for WhatsApp) and then sends just the apology.

She lies there staring at the ticks, but they stay resolutely grey.

She goes back to work. She can't stay home forever moping about for a life that's never going to happen. Everyone tiptoes around her a bit at first, but by

326

lunchtime it's as if she's never been off. She calls Grace over and over, but it either goes to voicemail or, on a couple of occasions, is cut off as soon as it rings. She leaves messages that she has no idea if Grace will listen to. She sends texts, getting more and more apologetic as the day goes on. She tells herself Grace is just making a point, but after a couple of days she starts to wonder if she's just going to have to accept that Grace is never going to forgive her. Kitty is definitely not going to give up yet, but she leaves longer between calls, fewer messages. Apart from work, she only leaves the house once she sees both Sian and Rich go off somewhere in the car and then, head down, she makes a dash for the shops or the bus stop. She's speaking to an estate agent on the phone on Saturday afternoon, tentatively making enquiries as to what her house might be worth, half watching out of the window as Sam chases the screaming children and the barking dog round the garden with a Nerf gun, when her phone lets her know she has another call coming through.

Grace.

'I have to go. Sorry. Bye.' She cuts him off without saying she'll call him back, but she can't worry about seeming rude now. 'Gracie!' she says. 'Did you get all my messages? I'm so sorry.' She can hear chatter in the background. She waits for Grace's flow of consciousness. She's prepared to be told off and she's OK with it.

'Um. Kitty?' It's a man's voice, and not one she recognises. Her heart starts racing as her brain reaches for the worst-case scenario.

'Where's Grace? Is she OK? Who is this?'

'My name's Alasdair. I'm a friend of Grace's. I don't have long . . .'

'What's happened to her?'

'Nothing! She's fine. Sorry, I should have started with that. She's just getting changed and I'm looking after her stuff, and her phone was open and that made me think I could look up your number. I wasn't snooping . . . anyway . . . all I want to say is please don't give up on her. She's so unhappy, and I think she's going to crack any second and pick up one of your calls, because she misses you so much. I just . . . She said you hadn't tried her today and I think she was a bit sad about that, so . . . sorry, this was stupid of me . . .'

'No!' Kitty feels as if she could cry she's so relieved. 'Thank you. I didn't know what to do. I thought maybe I should leave her alone.'

'She knows what she did was wrong. But you know Grace much better than me. She was trying to do a good thing . . . I should go before she catches me.'

Kitty gulps back a sob and smiles at the same time. 'I'll keep trying. Thank you for looking out for her. And me. I appreciate it. Really.' Loud music starts up in the background. 'Where are you?'

Alasdair chuckles. 'Pole dancing class. Worst thing I've ever done. We're having fun.'

She laughs. 'Be nice to her, or else.'

'You too,' he says lightly. 'Got to go.'

As soon as he ends the call, Kitty thinks of all the things she should have asked – which one of them booked a pole dancing class, what Grace is wearing for it, whether

Alasdair has sourced any better shoes, when Grace might be home alone. She misses knowing the minutiae of Grace's life with an intensity she never imagined possible. She's desperate to hear what she thinks of Alasdair. God, she hopes Grace is giving him a chance, because he clearly cares about her. That phone call has to go down as one of the sweetest gestures ever. She suddenly thinks she can't wait any longer. She throws on a jacket and leaves the house, not even caring that she might bump into Sian or Rich. For all she knows, Grace might be gone for the evening or be about to bring Alasdair home for their first night of passion, but she feels as if she needs to try.

45

There's no response when she rings the doorbell, so she takes up residence on the low wall and waits.

At twenty-five to nine she finally spots Grace, feet scuffing on the pavement, looking like she has the weight of the world on her shoulders. She's carrying a large tote bag and, apart from the air of despondency, she looks as if she made an effort to look nice for her date. Fitted black trousers and a pale green floaty top that should dwarf her tiny frame but actually looks cute. Kitty stands. Grace sees the movement and looks up. She speeds up and walks straight past Kitty without even acknowledging her, heading for the front door.

'Gracie,' Kitty says. 'Hold on.'

Grace fumbles her key in the lock. It slips from her fingers and clatters on the step. Kitty goes to pick it up, but Grace snatches it first.

'Go away,' she says. Tears start pouring down her cheeks. 'I don't want to talk to you.' Kitty notices she's wearing a necklace with a silver frog dangling from it. For some reason it makes her want to cry too.

'Gracie, I'm sorry. Really, really sorry. I didn't mean any of that stuff I said. I was just shocked and . . .'

Grace pushes her way through the door and slams it behind her. Kitty catches it and follows her in and up the stairs. 'Please just let me say my piece and then I'll go.'

Grace says nothing but, when she goes into the flat, she leaves the door open, which Kitty decides to take as an invitation.

'I just came out with the thing I thought would hurt you the most.'

'You thought it, though. You must have done.' She thumps her bag down on the hall table.

'No. I heard Sian say it to you outside when you were putting the rubbish out that time. I just . . . it was in my head, and I wanted to hurt you.'

'So, you didn't say it to her in the first place?'

'Of course not!' She sighs. Lying to Grace is not going to help anything. 'I mean, maybe something a bit like it. I'm not proud of it. And it wasn't anywhere near as bad as she probably made out, I swear. I've been a shit friend, I know that.'

Grace walks into the kitchen and reaches for a bottle of red and clatters it onto the counter. 'I'm sorry about the hotel thing. I shouldn't have got involved.'

'It's OK. I get it. Sian can be very convincing.'

'If I'd thought there was any doubt . . .' Grace suddenly screws her face up and dissolves into ugly sobs.

Kitty reaches out a hand and rubs her arm. 'I know. Shit. I didn't mean to make you feel like this.'

'I thought Andrew would confront Lottie about the whole thing and she'd come clean and then what I'd done would be irrelevant.'

'Let's just agree there are things we both could have handled better.'

Grace nods enthusiastically and rubs at her face with the back of her hands.

'I missed you,' Kitty says, pulling her in for a hug. 'Please let's never fall out again.'

'Now who's the clingy one?' Grace says. Kitty starts to laugh. Within seconds they're both more or less inconsolable.

'In the interests of complete transparency and honesty with one another . . .' Kitty says once they're sitting on the sofa side by side with a glass each. 'Please don't take this the wrong way. But Alasdair called me . . .'

Grace frowns. 'What? How did he even have your number?'

'It was nothing . . . don't get the wrong idea.' She knew that Grace would overreact. Her default position is to distrust any man who shows an interest in her. But Kitty doesn't think it's right to have this secret between them. She just needs to mitigate Grace's paranoia before it spirals. 'He used your phone while you were at pole dancing. He told me not to give up on you. It was really sweet. Honestly, I never would have dared to come down here tonight if he hadn't.'

'What was he doing going into my phone?' Grace says tetchily.

'Trying to do a nice thing. I think he was genuinely worried about you.'

'I don't need him to worry about me.'

Kitty reaches out a hand and puts it on Grace's thigh. 'We all need people to worry about us.'

Grace tuts.

'Well, I thought it was kind. I mean, it could have seemed weird and a bit controlling but I didn't get that vibe at all. I like him.'

'Mmm.'

'Do you?'

'He shouldn't be looking in my phone.'

'Grace! Stop finding reasons to reject perfectly nice people. Is he kind? Yes. Does he give you the ick? No. Was your ridiculous pole dancing class fun? Yes. What else?'

Grace pushes her glasses up her nose. 'OK. Yes. I like him.'

'Halle-fucking-lujah. When can I meet him?'

46

'He had a good idea. Alasdair.'

They're still lounging on Grace's sofa in her newly dusty pale blue and white living room. Kitty feels lighter than she has in days. If she ignores the ache in her heart where her feelings for Andrew lie, she actually thinks she's happy. Grace has filled her in on date three. (*I just thought the horse riding showed Julian's true colours, so this might be the same. And you keep your clothes on.*) Kitty now knows all about Alasdair's hyperextending knees (*I think he pulled something, but he was too nice to say*), the instructor's halitosis (*You know when a mouse dies under the floorboards and you come home after a week . . .*) and the underwear Grace wore (*Big! I was terrified I'd wee myself if they made me do an aerial invert*). She and Alasdair have an unprecedented date four planned.

'How were his shoes?'

'Awful. Same ones. But they're starting not to annoy me so much.'

Kitty feigned a shocked look. 'Grace Jackson! Are you thawing?'

Grace turned away but Kitty could see the edge of a smile on her face. 'As if. He's just not as bad as I thought.'

'Honestly, that might as well be you saying you think you love him and want to marry him. How does he feel about babies?'

Grace went full beam. 'He wants them. I told him I

couldn't wait that long, because what if there was a problem and I'm not getting any younger and I have no idea what his sperm count is like, and we might need to get help or try . . .' She laughed as she saw Kitty's horrified expression. 'Anyway, he didn't run away.'

'Huge tick for Alasdair.'

'Remember Sez? The residents' group thing,' Grace says now.

'Of course.'

'He said why don't we call her. Them. It might not be a woman. The number will be on their contact page or whatever you call it. On WhatsApp.'

Kitty props herself into a sitting position.

'Call and find out who they are and what made them post that comment. There might be something. Maybe they know Sian and she told them the same lies she told us.'

'That's actually a good idea.' Kitty grabs for her phone.

'I'm making a tea, do you want one?'

'Sure. Thanks.' She finds the residents' group and scrolls through.

Grace is still hovering. 'Are they still on there?'

'Wait a sec . . . There she is.' She hits the icon by Sez's one and only message. A photo of a sunset. 'And there's the number. Shit. Why didn't we think of that?'

Grace shrugs. 'Shall we try it now?'

Kitty stares at her mobile, trying to get her courage up. 'What am I going to say?'

'Would you rather I did it?'

'No. It's OK. I'm just going to ask them who they are, right? And play it from there.'

'Exactly. Easy.'

'Shall I say I'm me, or pretend to be something official?'

Grace grabs the phone out of her hand. 'Don't say it's you until you know who they are. We don't know what their motive is.'

'This isn't a murder mystery,' Kitty says, snatching the phone back. 'OK. Here goes. Don't put me off. Fingers crossed it goes straight to voicemail and they say their name.'

She inputs the number and hits speaker. The ring tone fuzzes with the static of a bad connection.

'Hello?' Kitty jumps and almost drops the phone. It sounds like a woman, distracted as if she was in the middle of something important when the call interrupted her.

'Oh. Hi. Who is this?' Kitty pulls a face at Grace who crosses her fingers.

There's a second's pause. 'You called me. What do you mean, who is this? Who are you?' The voice is distorted, Dalek-like.

Fuck. 'Um. I found your number and I just wondered who it belonged to.'

'Of course you did,' the woman says, her voice crackly. 'Are you going to ask me for my bank details next?'

Kitty grimaces. This isn't how it was supposed to go. 'No . . . I . . .'

There's a silence as the call goes dead. Whoever Sez is, she's ended the conversation. Kitty holds the phone up as if to show Grace. 'Shit.'

'Did you recognise the voice? I don't think I did.'

Kitty narrows her eyes, trying to recall it. 'There's

something familiar. But the line was so bad. Fuck. I should have eased her into it more slowly.'

Grace picks at a paint fleck on her thumb. 'Maybe we're clutching at straws. Maybe Lottie's right and we should just forget about the whole thing.'

'No. You were spot on all along. Rich has to know the truth. If Sian gets away with it, he's basically been duped into staying with her when she was happy to throw him under the bus and leave him there.'

The smell of paint is making her feel light-headed. She gets up and pushes open the window. 'We have to find a bit of evidence, and this Sez person is all we've got at the moment.'

'We'll think of something,' Grace says, but she doesn't sound convincing, even to herself. 'Do you want to stay the night?'

On Tuesday, after work, Kitty sneaks back to her house, knowing that Sian will be occupied at detention duty and so there's no danger of bumping into her on her way from the tube. Even though she's pretty sure she's safe, she walks the long way home to avoid going past next door.

The house feels unloved. *Because it is*, she thinks. Because she's never been happy here. *I'm putting my house on the market*, she texts Grace. *Help me decide where to live. Obviously I can afford almost nothing anywhere decent.* She'll find a little flat somewhere more lively. She doesn't need a second bedroom. She doesn't need a garden. She needs a life.

Twenty minutes after she arrives home, she sees Sian walking past. She's talking on the phone. Laughing. Smiling.

She looks as if she doesn't have a care in the world. Kitty feels a jolt of dislike so visceral she has to reach out a hand and steady herself on the kitchen counter. This was her friend. Her ally. She hates her, she thinks, identifying the unfamiliar emotion. She cannot wait for karma to catch up with her.

Brilliant. I'll make a list. Hold on, I'm calling you . . .

Kitty has no idea why Grace didn't just call rather than send the warm-up text, but she waits for her phone to ring.

'Alasdair had a brilliant idea,' Grace says as soon as Kitty answers.

'Another one?' Kitty says, wryly. 'Are you chatting between dates now?'

'I called him to tell him how the phone call went. I promised him I would. Anyway, it's Magda. Magda is the key.'

'You do know you're Magda? You know Magda doesn't actually exist?'

Grace tuts. 'Magda rejoins the WhatsApp group. She messages Sez. They compare notes.'

Kitty opens the fridge and sniffs. Nothing smells off but she hasn't actually shopped for groceries for over a week. 'That's actually genius. And so obvious. Can you just rejoin?'

'I'll send Shirley a message saying I had a bereavement and that I went off grid for a while. What's she going to do? Say no?'

'She can be a bit funny.'

'No one can argue with death. Or mental health. She'll welcome me back with open arms.'

'Magda, not you.'

Grace tuts again. 'You know what I mean.'

'Good work. Say thanks to Alasdair if you ring him again. Are you thinking of ringing him again?'

'I probably should if anything happens, you know. If she replies.'

'Right.' She puts on a sing-song voice. 'Gracie and Alasdair sitting in a tree. K. I. S. S. I –'

'Bye, Kit,' Grace interrupts. She ends the call before Kitty can respond.

Kitty smiles. Maybe Grace will get her happy ending after all.

47. Sian

In the end it had been Kitty who had ruined everything, Kitty who had somehow worn down Andrew's defences when he was at his lowest point. (At least she had been going to move slowly, invite him to stay with her, work on making him see her as someone other than his good friend. Offer a shoulder to cry on and eventually more.)

Fucking Kitty had been a dark horse.

If Kitty hadn't called an Uber for Lottie. If she hadn't checked how long it was going to be and then put the phone down screen up and left the room immediately. If Andrew hadn't texted right at that moment and Sian hadn't been sitting close enough to see his name pop up and allowed curiosity to get the better of her . . . well, who knows where they'd be, but if she hadn't believed in fate before, sign her up now.

Thank fuck she'd had the presence of mind to photograph their messages with her own phone before Kitty came back.

She'd been gobsmacked.

Devastated.

Furious.

And just a little impressed.

She'd known her plan was blown. Over. And she couldn't afford to throw Rich under the bus without a Rolls-Royce waiting to pick her up.

There had been only one thing to do and that was to detonate the whole thing and start again.

She wasn't going to lie, she'd still got more than a little satisfaction from watching Lottie's perfect life implode. But she'd had to do damage limitation. Get her side of the story out there first, regroup with Rich, and to hell with everyone else.

48

Kitty has to give it to Grace: she gets into character. Although Kitty is pretty sure she has modelled Magda's accent on the Compare the Market Meerkats this time round. Her grasp of English seems to have got worse. She has no idea if it makes sense that Magda's (non-existent) cleaning enquiries would have been terminally deleted along with her account or not, but she figures no one else will know either and it adds a kind of weird authenticity to the whole fiasco. She makes herself laugh thinking that Grace is going to somehow end up having to take a random cleaning job to keep up the lie, like the plot of a 1990s sitcom.

They have agreed that once Magda has established that she's back, Grace will send Sez a private message, bonding over their gossip about Sian and Rich, and then they'll just have to play it by ear. Grace has no intention of revealing who she is, so Sez probably won't either, but they can at least find out what she thinks she knows.

It's all they've got.

Kitty has to stop herself sending Grace a message telling her not to overdo it and give herself away. *You're not trying to win an Oscar. Just get in and get out.* She has to trust that Grace can handle it.

She distracts herself by FaceTiming her parents. Her dad looks exhausted, and she soon understands why. Her mum is in combative mode, trying to pick a fight with the man who is devoting his golden years to caring for her. She wanders around in the background picking things up and throwing them on the floor. From the lack of reaction by Kitty's father, it's obvious this is not the first time.

'Your mum's upset because I told her we can't go to the beach,' he says. The nearest beach being, probably, a two-hour drive.

'That man is keeping me prisoner,' her mum says, sounding genuinely distressed. She's wearing her dressing gown and big fluffy slippers that Dermot and his wife bought for her and which, to Kitty anyway, look like death traps on the shiny wood floor.

'She didn't want to get dressed today,' her dad says with a sad smile.

'He was trying to take my clothes off. That man.'

'That's Dad, Mum,' Kitty says. 'He was just trying to help.'

There's a crash as her mum swipes a decorative box that, for Kitty's whole life insofar as she can remember, has held a jumble of pens and pencils, off a side table.

'You really do need help, Dad,' Kitty says quietly.

He sighs. 'I think maybe we do.'

Call over, she fights tears and sends a text to her brother and sister telling them their father might be finally coming

343

round. *We need to find dad some proper support*, she adds. *And I need help. I can't do it on my own.* Sod it. Let them feel bad for once.

Her mobile beeps and she assumes it's an excuse-laden reply from one of them.

It's a WhatsApp. Someone called Paula has replied to Magda's post.

I'm so sorry for your loss. I'm looking for someone to do a couple of hours on a Tuesday or Wednesday morning if that suits? DM me with your rate if you're interested.

She stares at the screen. Grace must be on alert because there's a reply almost immediately: *Great! I DM.*

Fuckssake.

She goes to bed early. Through the windows she can see lights on next door and in the homes of Vernie and Malcolm and Julie and Pete; Sam and Linz are in their garden sharing a bottle of wine while – presumably – their kids sleep. These are fifty per cent of the people she knows in London to exchange more than a hello with, and they all want nothing more to do with her. Because of Sian. She lies under the duvet googling more local estate agents. She's just falling asleep, iPad on her lap, when her phone rings.

'She's replied,' Grace says, sounding hyper.

Kitty sits up. 'So, do you know who it is?'

'No, but you might be able to work it out. It's good. Honestly.'

There's an echo where Grace must have her on speaker. 'OK. Tell me.' She hears clattering. 'What are you doing?'

'Clearing out the kitchen. I'm going in with the

Raspberry Ripple tomorrow night. Then I'm going to get someone in to do the cupboard doors white. Do you want to hear what I've got to tell you or not?'

'Yes. Sorry.'

'So, Magda basically reiterated all the stuff about being away because her cousin died unexpectedly. Of sepsis. Tragic. She was only twenty-three.' She pauses for a reaction. Kitty refuses to oblige.

'Anyway,' Grace says. 'So, then Magda says . . . hold on, I'll read it to you.' She adopts an accent that could be Bucharest or Burkina Faso, it's hard to tell. *I interested what you say about truth bomb haha!'*

Kitty desperately wants to interrupt to ask Grace to just give her the gist, but she knows she has to allow her her big moment.

'*You talk about party, yes? But it turn out I was wrong. Rich not the one who playing around. Someone tell me is woman next door.*'

'You didn't?'

'I had to. I figured they'd have heard the rumours anyway, probably.'

Kitty groans and bangs her head back down on the pillow. 'Oh god. Then what?'

'Then . . .' Grace says, leaving a dramatic pause. 'Sez said this . . . *But Sian Selway Price started those rumours about her husband herself . . .*'

'What?' Kitty gasps. 'Did she say how she knows? Gracie, this is amazing.'

'Right? I asked why they thought that. Well, Magda did. And guess what they said . . .'

'I can't. Tell me quick. I'm going to have a heart attack.'

'They overheard Sian telling you about it. In the park.

They were coming over to speak to you about something, but then they saw that Sian was upset and they thought they shouldn't interrupt. But they were curious to check that she was OK, so they listened in for a minute. They heard her saying she'd seen an explicit message from someone on Rich's phone, they heard the name Lottie, and then they thought they should get out of there, so they did.'

'Shit. God. And why put that message up? Why now?'

'I asked that too. Because Sian told them the story about you and Andrew. About how it was all you, stealing her friend's husband, blah blah blah, and they felt bad for you because they knew there was much more to it, but they couldn't confront her about it because then they'd have to admit they'd been earwigging.'

'It's Julie,' Kitty says triumphantly. 'They were in the park that day. I didn't think they'd seen us, but they must have.'

'Bingo!' Grace crows.

'I should speak to them. But what if she doesn't want Pete to know she's involving herself?'

'Aren't they the ones who are joined at the hip?'

Kitty nods even though Grace can't see her. 'Even so.'

'Well, you have to say something. Be cryptic.'

'OK. Shit. I need to think about this. Can I come back to yours tomorrow? I can paint.' She hears a glass clink. She can picture Grace, gin and tonic in hand, surveying her handiwork.

'Of course. Long as you like. We'll make a plan.'

She tries to sleep after they say goodbye and then, when that fails, she tries to think through what she can say to

Julie and Pete to make one or both of them fess up. But her thoughts get crowded out by images of Andrew and Lottie. She hasn't heard anything since they came round. Hadn't expected to, despite the nagging hope in the pit of her stomach that she tries to ignore. She has no idea if they're working on their marriage. If they're – at this very moment – having make-up sex to try to reconnect. She throws the covers back and gets up. Goes downstairs and makes herself a cup of tea without turning the light on in case Sian or Rich look out of their window and spot her, then turns the TV on and searches for something mindless to watch.

49

They're saved by Deliveroo. The arrival of stuffed full boxes of sushi forces them to put down their paintbrushes and, Kitty knows, once they're slumped on the sofa to eat them there's no way they'll be getting up again except to refill their glasses. In fact, Kitty might not even do that. She might just hope Grace cracks first.

And they have decided what their next move is going to be. It's hardly a masterplan. They basically boiled it down to their only three options – have Magda try to gather more intel, call the number again or speak to Julie in person and try to wheedle the truth out of her. Her conscience is obviously pricked. How hard can it be? Julie and Pete like to go to the pub on Wednesdays, so Kitty and Grace are going to ambush them there. It's hardly the Hatton Garden heist but it's the best they can come up with, so it'll have to do.

There's no sign of either Julie or Pete when they get there, not that Kitty would ever expect to see one without the other. She's not even convinced they exist except as a couple. Buy one, get one free. She orders a bottle of white wine and two bags of cheese and onion crisps while Grace finds a table with a view of the door.

'What if Sian and Rich come in?' She doesn't know

why this didn't occur to her before, but now they're here it seems almost inevitable.

'We ignore them,' Grace says. 'What are they going to do?'

There's a rush of noise as four people come in at once, all chattering at the same time. Grace reaches out a hand and grabs Kitty's leg.

'It's them. Julie and Pete.'

They watch as they cross the room, the other couple leading the way.

'Shall I follow them?' Kitty hisses.

Grace shakes her head. 'Wait for them to sit down.'

'I feel sick.'

'There's no rush.' Grace tops up their glasses.

'I just want to get it over with and get out of here,' Kitty says. She means it. There are at least a thousand ways she'd rather be spending her Wednesday evening.

'You're going to feel so much better once you have proof that Sian lied through her teeth. She'll get what's coming to her and you can move on.'

'Why does she even care if Rich finds out, if she was leaving him anyway?'

Grace shrugs. 'Maybe she doesn't. But he deserves to know the truth either way.'

Kitty pushes herself into a standing position. 'OK. I'm going in. I'll just wing it.'

Grace holds up crossed fingers.

Julie and the two friends – a couple in their fifties, Kitty would guess – are listening agog as Pete gets to the end of a joke when Kitty arrives at the table, so she has to hover so as not to ruin the punchline (*It wasn't even her dog!*) and then for them to all fall around laughing.

Kitty coughs. Plasters a smile onto her face. 'Hi!'

They all look round. When Kitty thinks about the moment later, she imagines the whole pub falling silent, the piano player closing the lid. It's not much of an exaggeration. Julie's mouth arranges itself in a harsh line. 'Kitty.'

Kitty knows something's not right, but she can't really bail out now.

'Could I have a quick word?' she says, forcing the words out.

The other woman picks up her drink. 'We'll go for a game of pool. You can sit here, love.' The man follows. Never has a chair looked so unappealing, but Kitty drops into it. Julie and Pete just look at her, silent for once.

'Um. I don't know if you heard what Sian's been telling people about me, but it's not true. You know that, right?'

Pete sneers. 'Why would she make it up?'

So, Pete definitely doesn't know about Sez. Kitty looks at Julie. Is there a crack there? A tell-tale sign that Julie knows something? It suddenly occurs to Kitty that if Julie really had heard Sian tell her Rich was cheating on her, she would have gone straight back and told Pete. It would have been all round the Close by teatime. Of course it's not her.

As if to prove it, Julie scoffs. 'So, you didn't sleep with her best friend's husband, then?'

'Forget it,' Kitty says, standing abruptly. She stomps back over to Grace. 'Let's go.'

They don't even go via Kitty's house, even though Grace protests that there could be mail sticking out of the letterbox or, worse, a parcel on the doorstep. 'It's not as if any of your neighbours are going to take it in, is it?'

'I don't care,' Kitty says as they hover in the pub doorway waiting for their Uber.

Grace buries herself in her phone, clicking away at the keyboard. Kitty checks her own. 'Two minutes.'

'OK,' Grace says, looking up. 'I'm sending this.' She holds her mobile up for Kitty to see the screen.

Kitty peers at it myopically. '*You have tell neighbour what you hear. Otherwise not fair.*'

'Magda,' Grace says.

'No shit. I thought you'd had a stroke.'

'Can I send it? It might help.'

Kitty shrugs. 'Why not?' Because really, at this point, what harm can it do?

'Exactly. So now we just wait.'

50

She doesn't know why she's standing outside the house on North Hill, she just is, as if her feet took her there without her knowledge. She had tried to erase the address from her brain after arranging Lottie's Uber, but it clung on stubbornly, not helped by the fact that every time she looked at the app, there it was offering itself up as a potential destination. It's a smart three-storey semi, painted off white, with a – unsurprisingly, she supposes – verdant front garden. She hovers by a bus stop on the other side of the road, a few doors down. As if she might be able to claim she was just changing routes if put on the spot. It's almost true. Except that she got off the bus that was taking her towards home and walked out of her way for ten minutes to get here. It just happened.

In a top-floor window, a life-sized cardboard Daenerys Targaryen peers down – Harry's room, she assumes. She remembers Andrew saying his daughter had a huge *Game of Thrones* crush. Her birthday must be coming up soon, the holiday that was. Kitty wonders what she knows. If Harry thinks she's to blame for her mum and dad falling out with their oldest friends. For the problems in her parents' marriage. Or maybe there aren't any problems. Maybe all is bliss at the Hart mansion.

She can't think about that. How she might have been reduced to a footnote in their family history. Even though she knows that's as it should be. Even though she wants Lottie to be happy. Kitty just wishes she could be happy without her husband.

She stands there while three buses come and go. And then she turns round and walks off in the direction she came.

Her mobile pings. She gets it out warily, looking around for anyone who might snatch it out of her hand. Her heart almost stops when she reads the name: Lottie. Has she seen her? Is she sending a warning message? *Keep away from my family. I'm calling the police. I'm allowed to stand at a bus stop*, Kitty thinks defensively. She forces herself to look at what the text actually says. Stops in the middle of the pavement as she takes it in:

Sian and Rich are going ahead with the vow renewal. But here, in London. Seraphine told me.

Kitty feels a rush of nausea. So, Sian really is going to come out of this unscathed. Her marriage intact. Her reputation among their neighbours and friends unsullied. Rich has totally bought her shit.

She leans against a low wall and tries to think what to reply. She's not sure why Lottie is even telling her. It's not as if they're confidantes. They're hardly people who share titbits of gossip.

Wow, she sends. *So she's got away with everything . . .*

She makes it another hundred metres down the road before her phone beeps again.

You were right. We can't let her.

She resists sending back: *Are you all right? How's Andrew? Are you having sex? Are you going to stay married??? Can I have him if you decide you don't want him?*

Instead, she types *OK. Let's do it.*

51

Forest Streets Residents' WhatsApp Group:

Vernie at Number 3: Chipotle chilli and chocolate brownies anyone? Not sure Malcom's IBS is well suited.

She spots Sian as soon as she turns into Ashdown Close, waving off a twenty-something woman laden down with books. One of her private pupils, Kitty assumes. Kitty turns round and walks back the way she came, along the main road, down Sherwood Avenue and round. She's exhausted and she just wants to be home, her visit to Andrew and Lottie's house a fever dream, but she's not ready for a confrontation yet.

She's filling Grace in on Lottie's messages when the doorbell rings.

'Are you expecting anyone?' Grace says.

'No. Shit. What if it's Sian?'

'Look through the spy hole. Don't open if it's her.'

'I'll call you back.' She puts down her phone and creeps towards the front door. Betty is peering back at her. Kitty jumps back as if she's been seen and knocks an umbrella out of the little wicker stand. It clatters to the floor loudly. 'Jesus!' she says, before she can stop herself.

'Ms Harbinson, is that you? I saw you come in. Have you got a moment? It's Mrs Martin.'

Fuck.

'Um, sure. Hang on.' She tries to compose herself, takes a couple of deep breaths. What's the worst that can happen? Betty tells her she's an awful person and should be ashamed of herself. She's getting used to it.

She opens the door. Betty gives her the formal Margaret Thatcher smile that always seems more threatening than warm. 'May I come in?'

Kitty steps back. 'Sure.'

She stands in the hall, not wanting to give the impression she has all the time in the world for a social visit. Betty, it seems, doesn't pick up the signals, because she strides through to the living room. Kitty follows.

'Make yourself at home,' Kitty says, with more than a hint of sarcasm.

'Thank you.'

Kitty resolutely refuses to offer to make tea and waits out the awkward silence that follows. 'So, what can I do for you?' she says eventually.

Betty coughs politely into her hand. 'I understand Mrs Selway Price has a grievance with you —'

'It's not true, what she's saying,' Kitty interjects. Why does everyone feel they have to tell her how badly they think she's behaved? 'At least, it is in part, but I didn't think I was intruding on anyone's relationship.'

'I know,' Betty says. 'I overheard Mrs . . . Sian . . . telling you that she had caught her husband cheating with her best friend. The wife of the man you . . .'

'You're Sez?' Kitty interjects, incredulous. Betty was the last person she expected to try to come to her aid by creating a fake WhatsApp persona. Let alone one who used the kind of language Sez was using.

'Oh. Well, yes, actually. Don't tell me you're Magda?'

'No. It's complicated. So, you were there in the park the day she told me about Rich and Lottie? I didn't see you.'

'I was behind the two of you. I wanted to ask her about Spanish lessons for my great-grandson, but I saw she was upset and didn't want to intrude. I waited around for a moment to check she was all right and I heard what she told you.'

To listen in on the gossip, more like, Kitty thinks but doesn't say. She doesn't care why Betty overheard at this point, just that she did.

'So why say something now?'

'Sian told me her version of events. She's told most of the neighbours, I think. And I felt it was unfair that you were getting all the blame when clearly there was more to it than she was letting on. I remembered reading that odd comment that Magda made – I'd wondered what it was alluding to at the time, but no one else seemed to pick up on it – and I thought that maybe I could flush her out to say something less oblique and then I wouldn't have to. I didn't want to just come out with it and have the Selway Prices turn against me. It can make life difficult falling out with the neighbours. Who is Magda anyway?'

'My friend Grace. So, you believe me? That Andrew and I both thought his marriage was over – through no fault of his own – before anything ever happened between us?'

Betty nods. 'I do. And I'm sorry. I should have spoken up sooner.'

'You have no idea how grateful I am that you're speaking up now. Would you like a cup of tea?' Kitty says.

'That would be very kind.' She sits on the armchair nearest the French windows.

Kitty smiles to herself as the kettle boils. She texts Grace frantically: *It's Betty!*

Her phone beeps with a text immediately. She throws teabags into mugs before she looks. She knows it will be Grace.

What is?

Kitty frowns but then sees that her own text had autocorrected to *It's better!!*

Fuckssake. Betty. It's Betty. Sez.

The response is immediate. *Whaaaaaat??? I'm calling you!! No! She's here now! I'll ring as soon as she leaves.*

She turns her phone over just in case and shouts to ask Betty if she'd like milk or sugar.

'She probably told me because she thought I'd spread the gossip around,' Betty says, taking a mug from her. 'Thank you. And she usually would have been right, I'm afraid to say. It's made me realise I should check my facts more often.'

'I'm sure that's true for all of us,' Kitty says, perching on the edge of the sofa. 'But you didn't tell anyone at the time? What you overheard?'

Betty bites her bottom lip. She looks wary. Vulnerable. 'It seemed too serious. Even I have a filter. I thought you were good friends. You and Mrs Selway Price.'

'You and me both. I've realised now she was just setting me up to help ruin her actual best friend's life. Nice, huh?'

Betty tuts. 'I'm sorry you're in this position. What can I do to help?'

'Would you? I don't know what yet, but we don't want her to get away with it. Me and Grace. And Lottie. She wants the truth to come out too.'

'Is Grace the funny little thing who was at the party? The chatty one?'

Kitty laughs. 'That's her.'

'She seems lovely.'

'She is. She's getting me through it.'

Betty pushes herself out of her chair. 'Well, I should be off. Let me know when you decide on a plan of action. I'll say my piece.'

'Thank you.' Kitty takes the still half-full mug out of Betty's hand. 'I appreciate you coming round. Really.'

'You're welcome.'

'How's Mr Millman?' Kitty risks saying.

Betty actually blushes, then smiles. 'I have no idea what you're alluding to.'

Kitty laughs again. 'Good for you.'

She's straight on the phone to Grace as soon as Betty leaves. Grace peers at the screen myopically, a grey towel wrapped round her head.

'She basically told me she's Sez. Or, I asked her if she was and she said yes. She said she'll help us.'

'That miserable old bag?'

'She likes you. She called you a funny little thing.'

'That, Kit, is not a compliment. Anyway, whatever. It's great that she's come through. All because of Magda.'

'OK, I'll let you take the credit. You and Alasdair. What's his surname by the way?'

'Don't laugh.'

'Well, I will now, whatever, but go on.'

'Pace.'

Kitty snorts. 'Grace Pace. You absolutely can't.'

Grace ignores her. 'We still need a plan, though. What does Sian care about? What's she afraid of losing?'

'Rhys, obviously, But I'm not involving him. Rich, I guess. Now that she's made the decision to stay with him.'

'The vow renewal,' Grace says, eyebrows raised.

Kitty reaches out a hand and steadies herself on the kitchen counter. 'We need to find out exactly when it is.'

'You might need to call Lottie.' Grace pulls a face.

Kitty closes her eyes. 'I know.'

52. Sian

She struggles her way through another private class. A new student with only the basic holiday knowledge wanting to expand beyond 'Can I have two beers?' and 'Which way is the bar?' before a work trip later in the year.

'I don't want to look like the usual ignorant Brit,' he'd told her when he booked a course of twelve sessions, three a week for four weeks. She needed the extra cash, but she hated teaching beginners. Especially adults. There's something that feels so uncomfortable about asking them to repeat the most simplistic phrases over and over. Explaining the difference between *ser* and *estar* and steeling yourself for the never-ending corrections to come. God, she really isn't cut out to be a teacher. She just doesn't have the patience.

Her mind drifts as he – John, his name is – works at an exercise on a pre-printed sheet she has given him: *Circle the correct verb – 1.* Soy ingles *or* Estoy ingles. She's trying to get excited about the vow renewal, to at least think it will be a fun party, a chance to glam up (although no longer in her original dress, which is still missing in action, presumably at Lottie's being ripped into little pieces as we speak), to be the centre of attention. Rich needs it, she knows that, the validation, after everything that has happened. And she needs Rich. For now, at least.

Besides, weirdly, it's not as if there's anything wrong

with their relationship. They get on. They like each other. It's not forever; she knows that now. But she isn't ready to go it alone. There's no way she would be able to make ends meet. She just needs to buy herself time to decide what to do.

And it's not as if renewing your vows means anything beyond a bit of affirmation. She sighs.

'Are you OK?'

She'd forgotten about John. 'Sorry.' She forces a laugh. 'I was miles away.'

He smiles. Pushes the paper towards her. He's got all the answers right, that's something.

'Well done. Good. Let's do some oral exercises using those verbs. How about *I am* . . . what do you do for a living?'

'I'm an investment banker,' he says, pulling an apologetic face.

'Oh.' She looks at him properly for the first time. He's definitely more smartly dressed than the average person she teaches. Fancy watch. Quite dull and conventional, but still.

She smiles. 'OK, so, *banquero de inversiones*. I think that's the correct term. Which verb would you use . . .?'

'Kitty. Hi.'

Kitty had almost expected her not to answer. To sentence her to leaving a voicemail she would probably never even listen to. As it is, her greeting doesn't even sound unfriendly.

'Hi. Lottie. Um . . . how are you?'

She's not sure she really wants to know the answer. Not in too much detail anyway. She can't decide which response would be better – *Awful* would ratchet her guilt back up to stellar levels but *Great!* might almost be worse. *Fabulous! Never better! Exhausted from all the make-up sex!!!* She pushes the thought from her head.

'Yeah. OK. Thanks. You?'

Kitty decides to just cut to the chase. There are only so many pleasantries she and Lottie can exchange. 'I have something to tell you. It's important for me that you know to be honest.'

'Right.' Kitty can almost hear the nervousness in her voice. What now?

'Someone overheard Sian telling me that you and Rich were having an affair. Way back. Before . . . everything . . .' She tells her about Betty, about Magda, about Sez.

Lottie hears her out. 'Thank you. I believed you. Eventually. But that helps. I appreciate it.'

'Do you have any more details about their vow

ceremony thing? Me and Grace, we have an idea. Half an idea. For . . . you know . . .'

'Oh good,' Lottie says enthusiastically. 'Honestly, it's the only thing keeping me going at the moment thinking Rich might see her for who she really is.'

Kitty actually laughs. 'You and me both.'

'Middle of August. According to Seraphine. They're doing it at a pub in East Finchley. I'm not sure which one but I can find out. I never thought I'd say this about anyone, but it'd be good to ruin her day.'

54. Sian

Every now and then she sees Kitty edging towards her front door from the opposite direction. That woman must be getting some serious steps in, trekking round the long way whenever she goes anywhere. A tiny part of Sian misses the ease of having a mate next door – especially now there's no Lottie, and even Seraphine and Vita are being a little iffy with her. Not obviously, but she can tell that they're torn, a tad guilty maybe whenever they see her. She knows without doubt which way they'd go if they were held at gunpoint and told to take sides. But she keeps digging her heels in and claiming she's been misunderstood, and without any proof otherwise, what can they do? Felix and Bertie are happy to back up Rich's faith in her. God, it all feels so precarious.

She's hoping the vow renewal will be the end of it. A public declaration that she's Team Rich in front of their families, their friends and even their neighbours. She's invited the whole street – apart from Kitty obviously. Even the miserable old git from number 13 who growled at her when Dante ran up his path once. In all honesty she's hoping that Kitty will sell up and move soon. It would make life easier not to have to worry about whether she might bump into her.

In truth it would make life easier if she hadn't blown her whole life up so drastically, but what can you do?

She has three private pupils at the moment, all through

the Nextdoor app: little Oscar who would rather not be there, but his mum is insisting; Molly, a twenty-seven-year-old flight attendant; and John the investment banker.

John, she thinks, *is interesting.*

They've only had two sessions so far. But it's enough for her to realise that he's a little flirty with her. He's almost certainly one of those rich guys who feel like they're owed attention from women, especially ones they're paying, but he somehow doesn't read like that.

It's amazing what you can find out about a person when you're teaching them the absolute basics

I am an investment banker

I am forty-eight

I am divorced

She'd laughed and said, so should I teach you *I am single*? And he'd said, yes, he was, although he wasn't sure who he'd need to say that to at the symposium he was going to in Madrid.

'What's it about?' she'd asked, and he'd pulled the same face he had when he told her what he did for a living and said, 'If I told you, you might literally die of boredom.'

'You know we're not going to get anywhere close to technical language in twelve classes?' she'd said. 'You'll be able to pass a bit of polite chit-chat but not much more.'

'Really? I won't be up to discussing the merits of leveraged buyouts in mergers and acquisitions? I demand a refund.'

'Ha! The merits of a black cat over a brown dog, maybe. Although you won't know the word for "merits" yet.'

'I knew I should have done Duolingo.'

'Cheaper, too.'

He gave her a slightly lopsided smile, which, she'd decided, was his best feature. 'Not as much fun, though.'

Well, she thought, as she waved him off after overrunning by ten minutes. Maybe things wouldn't turn out to be so hopeless after all.

She wondered how soon she could teach him enough that she could ask him to describe his house, his car, his views on having a partner who wanted her own little studio to potter about in all day instead of going out to work.

Forest Streets Residents' WhatsApp Group:

Mrs B Martin: Whoever's dog has defiled my driveway needs to take it to the vet immediately. That is not healthy.

Julie and Pete Mortimer: Did it eat one of Vernie's scones? Haha!

Kitty's house is on the market. She's asked the agents not to put a sign up outside; she doesn't want to give Sian the satisfaction. If it hasn't had any interest by the time the vow renewal ceremony has been and gone, they can put it up then. It's only four and a bit weeks away.

Four long weeks. And a bit.

She just wants it to be over.

She wants to not bottle out.

She and Grace meet up with Lottie at the Bald Faced Stag in East Finchley – the venue for the party – to talk her through what they're intending to do. It seems important to get her approval somehow. She's already sitting at a table nursing a small dark beer when they get there, looking more like her old self, but a slightly jaded knock-off version.

She gives them a smile. 'Hi, ladies. They're bringing a bottle of red over. This –' she holds up her glass – 'was Dutch courage.'

Kitty smiles weakly. She doesn't think she'll ever feel

easy in Lottie's company again. Grace pulls out a chair and throws herself into it. 'How are you?'

'Fine. Yes.'

'Really, I mean.'

Kitty wills someone to bring the wine over. She really needs a drink.

Lottie gulps. 'Getting there.'

'And how's Andrew?'

'Gracie . . .' Kitty mutters.

'Um. He's OK,' Lottie says quietly.

'Right,' Kitty says loudly. 'So, this is the place?'

Lottie talks them through everything she has managed to glean from Seraphine and Vita about the evening. Fifty-odd people – friends, family and neighbours, Felix as DJ, a short, sweet, secular ceremony conducted by a Humanist friend.

'What's she wearing?' Grace says.

'What's that got to do with anything?' Kitty laughs.

'Because, you know, Lottie was doing her dress . . .'

'I thought about taking a pair of scissors to it for a while, but I couldn't bring myself. Then I was going to leave it on her doorstep, but I thought why should she have it? So it's in the Marie Curie shop. In Crouchie. She can buy it back if she wants it.'

'Brilliant,' Grace says.

'I'm going to get the wine. I don't think anyone's going to bring it over,' Kitty says, standing up. She thinks she's leaving them on a fairly safe topic. You never know with Grace. It takes her a moment to locate the member of the bar staff who knows anything about their order. As she approaches the table again, bottle and three glasses in hand, she notices Lottie wipe a tear from her cheek. Kitty stops in her tracks. Fuckssake.

Neither Grace nor Lottie notices her approach.

'. . . so quick to, you know. Give up on me. On us,' Lottie is saying in a hiccupy voice. Grace has a hand on her arm. 'Without even . . . not hearing my side.'

'I know, I know,' Grace says soothingly.

Kitty exhales loudly. Both women look at her. 'Everything OK?' she says with both eyebrows raised at Grace.

Lottie sniffs. 'Sorry. Stupid. I was just . . . Things just aren't the same. You know.'

Kitty's irritation with Grace gives way to an overwhelming feeling of sadness for Lottie. She puts down the things she's carrying and stretches her arms out. 'Come here.'

Lottie half stands and Kitty leans over and grabs her up in a hug. Lottie gives in to full-on noisy sobs and Kitty pulls her in closer, ignoring the stares from the other punters. 'It'll be OK,' she says, over and over again. Because it will. It has to be.

56. Sian

'I was thinking, we could get one of those summerhouse/ big shed things for the garden and you could have that as a studio,' Rich says over breakfast one morning. 'Get back into painting properly.' He beams at her, proud of himself and his idea. He's been anxious around her lately. Desperate for her to believe his innocence. It's irritating to be honest (after all, if anyone knows he's innocent it's her).

She bites her tongue so as not to say all the responses that flood her mind: *those things cost a fortune; I don't have time to paint what with school and my private lessons; inspiration doesn't come at specific times just because you suddenly find yourself with a free hour, you know that.* She wants to lose herself in her art again, not be having to keep checking her watch because Molly or Oscar or John are due to arrive any minute. She doesn't understand why he doesn't remember what it was like.

'Yeah, maybe,' she manages to say. 'I think you have to get approval, though. Kitty would probably report us to the council.'

Rich's face darkens as it always does when Kitty is mentioned. She has to give him credit; he's never once questioned if Sian's story is the true one. 'Let her fucking try,' he says, which doesn't mean anything because it would be easy; she'd just have to pick up the phone.

She exhales loudly. 'I just don't want to suddenly be old and be, like, I never gave it a proper shot. I mean, I know the chance of anyone ever having success with their art is pretty negligible . . . but, you know.'

'I do,' he says. 'Maybe in the summer holidays you'll have more time . . .'

'I have to get dressed,' she says, standing up abruptly. 'I want to drop something off at the dry-cleaner's on the way to work.'

Rich has strict instructions to get out of the way whenever she's teaching at home. Ever since she was running through directions with Molly (*My house is on the left. Where is the bank? Straight on. Next to the church*) when the sound of him rapping along to Will Smith, who was getting jiggy with it on the radio, burst through. The first few lines it had been funny, but after a while she'd had to go downstairs and tell him to shut the fuck up. It's getting complicated trying to accommodate five hours a week interruption-free, but she's agreed with Oscar's mum that she'll go to their flat from now on. Which adds twenty minutes on for her each way, travelling there and back. *Fuck my life*, she thinks. *Really, though.*

Fuck

My

Life.

She starts to look forward to the days she sees John: Saturday mornings when Rich plays football, Tuesday evenings when he and a friend have made a regular padel date, and Wednesday afternoons while he's at work. She knows she's flirting. She can't help herself. She feels anxious, as if her chances are running out – how many more wealthy, not totally repulsive single men are going to cross her path before it's too late for her to still be in good enough nick for them to notice her?

She starts taking a bit more care with how she looks before he shows up. She'd always imagined an investment banker's ideal woman would be four-inch heels, inflated lips, boobs the size and shape of footballs and an arse like a space hopper. Desperate as she is, there are some lengths to which she will not go. Besides, John doesn't seem that type. She can tell that he's interested in her. So, she just makes sure she doesn't have mascara flakes on her cheeks or spinach in her teeth, and puts on something cute and *her*, like her jumpsuit or her dungarees instead of whatever soul-destroying personality-less crap she wears to school.

Today she tells him she's had a rough day at work, and would it be completely unprofessional for them to share a glass of wine while they run through the colours? It's a risk, but she's already managed to ascertain that he's not teetotal or driving. He shows up every time in a cab – in a suit on Tuesdays and Wednesdays, straight from the office (thankfully no tie) – and jeans and a vintage Fred Perry top (which is a nice touch, she has to admit) on Saturdays. He has a son and a daughter (*Tengo un hijo! Una hija!*), the girl at uni, the boy at culinary school in Paris, and an ex-wife who has remarried a 'nice bloke' and with whom he has a very cordial relationship. There's a dog – a female goldendoodle named Delilah. Sian hopes to introduce her to Dante soon.

'I'd like that,' he says to the offer of a drink.

'*Me gustaría eso.* Although that's a bit advanced tense-wise.'

'God, let's not get ahead of ourselves,' he says, laughing. 'I think I can manage *vino tinto*, though.'

'Good. Which brings me neatly on to . . .' She indicates two of her paintings that she's dug out of the attic, apparently for this very purpose, and propped up against the sideboard under the vibrant red and yellow canvas that Kitty admired at the party. 'Colours.' It's lesson five already; she needs to step up a gear.

'Wow. These are fabulous. Are they . . .?'

She nods. She's made a passing mention of dabbling in art before. 'Not recent, though. I don't have the time these days.'

John peers more closely. 'They're incredible. I thought you meant you did the odd sketch. Do you sell them?'

'That's my dream. But I'd need to give it a proper shot. Get taken on by a gallery. Be more prolific. Maybe one day if we win the lottery and I can give up teaching . . .' She wonders for a moment if he's going to offer to buy one, if there's going to be an awkward, patronising moment where he makes a pity purchase.

'People would snap these up,' he says. 'I'm not just saying that.'

'You don't happen to have a cousin who's an art dealer, do you?' she says with a smile.

'*Un primo,*' he says excitedly. 'I have no idea why I know that.'

'OK. Big gold star for you. So, let's start with *Mi prima tiene una pintura roja.* What do you think?'

*

373

'What do you enjoy doing?' she says once their hour is up. 'I can tailor the classes round things that interest you. It definitely makes it easier to take stuff in.'

'Oh. Well . . .' His face is slightly flushed from the two glasses of wine. 'Let me think what's on my Hinge profile. I'm joking! Never online dated. Too weird.'

'Me neither. I mean, obviously, since I've been married forever.'

'I love travelling, food, history – mediaeval mostly. All the plagues and boils and hanging, drawing and quartering, you know, the fun stuff. Late seventies post punk.'

'You do not!'

'Totally. I went to see Dead Kennedys last year.'

Sian slaps his arm. 'Stop. You, Mr Wright, have hidden depths.'

'It was really sad to be honest. I like theatre, we could talk about that. I'm liking *this*. Doing these lessons with you . . .'

She doesn't imagine it. He looks her in the eye for a moment too long. Her heart flips. It's working.

'Me too,' she says quietly. She edges her hand from the stem of her glass onto the table, close to his. Is this it? Is it about to happen? She's gone over this scenario so many times in her head the past couple of weeks. Analysed how quickly she should move to keep him interested but not blow the sexual tension too soon. All she needed was for him to want to keep seeing her after his course was over. She knew he wasn't about to ask her to give it all up and move in with him overnight. But she could wait.

He moves his index finger to touch hers. She can feel

the loaded atmosphere. Wishes so deeply that this meant something. That it was anything other than a cynical transaction on her part. She allows her finger to rest on his.

The front door slams. Sian jumps. She looks at her phone. Shit, they've run over way more than she thought. She pulls her hand away.

'Hi.' Rich bursts through the door from the hall. Stops dead when he spots John. 'Oh, shit, sorry. I thought you would be finished. Am I early?'

'No! We overran, sorry. This is John. Rich, my husband . . .'

'*Ola!*' Rich says with a cheesy grin, and Sian cringes.

John gets up and holds out a hand. Standing next to Rich, it's all the more apparent who won the looks lottery but looks, as Sian knows all too well, definitely aren't everything. 'Good to meet you,' John says as they shake. 'I'll get out of your way.'

'No, stay if you want.' Rich eyes the bottle. It's obvious to Sian that he's had a couple already, post padel, with his friend Rufus. 'I'll join you.' She'd forgotten that this was one of the things she's always loved about Rich: his social ease, his friendliness.

'It might have to be another time, sadly,' John says. 'Rain check.' He looks at Sian. 'What's rain check in Spanish?'

'I have absolutely no idea. I mean, I could translate it literally but there's no guarantee that would make sense to anyone. I'll look it up. Let me see you out. You still on for tomorrow?'

'Looking forward to it.' He turns to Rich. 'Another time, definitely.'

Rich slaps him on the back matily as he passes.

Sian follows John to the door. 'Read through the colours again tonight and I'll test you.'

'Yes, ma'am.'

She opens the door for him. 'Night then.'

She's not sure who initiates it, but as he passes their fingers touch. It's so light she almost thinks she might have imagined it.

It's the big day.

Kitty feels like a proud parent about to meet her son-in-law. Not that Grace and Alasdair are that serious already. Or serious at all yet. But they've been on seven dates and announced to the Marriage Brokers that they're going to give it a go. At Grace's suggestion they have merely paused their memberships instead of cancelling, to avoid having to pay the joining fee again if it doesn't work out. She's been disappointed too many times not to be pragmatic.

'Also,' she told Kitty over a coffee by the river near her flat, 'if I ever get married again, I'm insisting on a prenup.'

Kitty had spluttered, spraying her drink. 'For what? Are you secretly stockpiling Bitcoin?'

'For my flat. I worked hard for it, and I've been paying extra off too. Hal refused to buy me out of our old one, and he refused to move either. Eventually I just stopped paying my share of the mortgage, but I never got my half of the deposit back, or anything for all those years I'd contributed.'

Geth, at least, had been fair. They'd sold their property and split the tiny profit.

'Shit. Fair enough. OK, so Alasdair has to sign a prenup. What else?'

Grace gives her a look that says 'very funny'. 'Me and Alasdair are not getting married.'

'OK, Gracie Pacey. If you say so.'

Now they're waiting on the towpath in Richmond for a walk along the river stroke lunch if it seems to be going well. It's quiet, because the sun's not out, but on the plus side it's not raining.

'Where does he live?'

'Near here. Shepperton.'

'Have you been to his place?'

Grace goes beetroot red. Nought to sixty in less than a second. 'Yep.'

'Grace! Tell me everything. Have you done the deed?'

'I'm not talking about it.'

'Oh my god. Was it good?'

'Yes. That's it. No more.'

Kitty grabs her. 'I love this! Did you . . . ?'

'Hi . . .'

They both whip round. Kitty's first instinct is to look at his shoes, but then she remembers to be polite and focuses on his face. He's kind-looking, that's how she would describe him best. Big and shambly. He looks like a vicar on a day off. In a good way.

'Alasdair?'

He gives her a huge grin and holds out his arms for a hug. She goes in. He smells comforting. Citrus and forests. 'Kitty! It's so lovely to meet you.'

'You too. Shall we form the Grace Jackson Appreciation Society?'

'Only if there are badges. Hey, Gracie . . .' He hugs her too, swamping her.

He called her "Gracie", Kitty thinks. *Like I do. He has a pet name for her!* Alasdair stands with his arm round Grace and the pair of them fit together so well, look so perfectly cute, that Kitty almost bursts into tears. *God*, she thinks, *I really hope I like him. What if I don't, but she marries him, and then I can never hang out with her without him being there?* For a moment she feels like, she imagines, Grace must have felt when Sian came on the scene. Terrified she might lose her best friend.

'Let's walk,' Grace says. They set off along the path, she and Alasdair holding hands (*They're holding hands!* Kitty thinks, ecstatically.)

'So, Alasdair. Was Grace your first match?'

'Kit, don't grill him,' Grace says.

'I have to.'

'It's fine. I don't mind. No, she was my third. Chloe, very nice but definitely not my soulmate, and Dani, also very nice, also not my soulmate. They felt the same, I think.'

'So, they're not going to turn up at the altar singing "It Should Have Been Me"?'

Grace stops dead. 'Kitty! Stop it. Oh my god.'

Alasdair guffaws. 'Oh, I hope they do. You need some drama at a wedding.'

'You have ten questions,' Grace says to Kitty. 'Proper ones.'

'Ten?' Alasdair says with mock horror. 'What if I get one wrong?'

Kitty thinks for a moment. Where to even start? 'OK. One. What do you do for a living? I mean, I know you work in tech, but I have no idea what that means, really.'

'Right, I know this one. Computers, obviously. I'm freelance and I go in and develop new software for companies who want to overhaul their systems.'

'And how is your job stability? Given that you're freelance?'

Grace sighs.

'Terrible. But I'm currently on a rolling contract to replace all Hounslow Council's systems from scratch, so that'll probably take me the next couple of years. More.'

'Blimey. Do you have people working for you? That's not one of my questions, by the way.'

'It totally is. And yes, as and when I need them, I bring people on board. Next.'

'Why don't you have children?'

'Oh god,' Grace mutters.

'Because my ex-wife wasn't able to. We tried.'

'Shit. Sorry. That was insensitive of me. Five . . .'

'Six,' Grace pipes up.

'Six . . . Do you like animals?'

Alasdair steps out of the way of a woman pushing a buggy. 'Love them. I had a dog when I was married and then we shared custody of him after. He died a few months ago and I'm desperate for another.'

'What was his name?'

'Hargreaves.'

'Aww. Why did your marriage end?'

'A man called Toby.'

'You or her?'

Alasdair laughs loudly, and even Grace cracks a smile.

'Eight . . .'

'This is nine.'

'You can't count the dog's name! Fine. Where do you see yourself in five years' time?'

'Married, kids hopefully, dogs, cats, house.'

'Good answer.'

'Last one,' Grace says.

'Um. OK, I can't think of anything else . . .'

'Thank god,' Alasdair says.

'. . . but I'm not wasting one. What's eighty-seven times fifty-three?'

Grace snorts.

He doesn't skip a beat. 'Four thousand, six hundred and eleven.'

Kitty laughs. 'Might as well be. I have no idea. Oh, shit. I thought of another proper question.'

She looks at Alasdair hopefully.

'Go on, then.'

'Why do you think they matched you with Grace?'

He thinks for a second. 'Because we want the same things. And we like the same things. And I said I wanted someone to have fun with. Oh, and I very specifically asked for someone with a frog fetish. That was a deal breaker.'

'He's great,' she says as she and Grace wave Alasdair off from their taxi. They'd had a long lunch in the end, at Bill's, and Kitty had basked in the evident affection between the couple. 'Are you sure you don't want to spend this evening with him?'

'I want to spend it with you,' Grace says. 'Just because I have a "boyfriend" now –' she does the finger gestures – 'doesn't mean I'm going to disappear. Do you really like him?'

'I do. He's funny. And nice. The big two.'

'Do you think he's genuine?'

'I mean, yes. Insofar as you can ever tell.'

'I can't ever know, though. Not until it's too late, anyway.'

'Grace, don't do this. Everyone gets one chance, right?'

Grace nods uncertainly. 'Right.'

'Don't push him away.'

Grace exhales.

'And I will personally kill him if he treats you badly. Does that help?'

'A bit.'

She reaches over and pats Grace's knee. 'Give him his chance.'

58. Sian

'Did something happen last night? Or did I imagine it?'

It's a beautiful day, so she has the patio doors open, with the two Parker Knolls just inside. She doesn't want the neighbours to witness the apparent frisson in the air between her and John. She was worried he wouldn't turn up this afternoon. That things would be awkward after their near miss.

'You didn't imagine it.'

They haven't even made a pretence of starting a lesson. He has brought his notebook, like a good student, but it sits unopened on the floor beside him.

'Should we talk about it?'

For a moment Sian thinks she's going to laugh in his face. *You think you really stand a chance with me?* Instead, she looks him dead in the eye. He can't hold her gaze for more than a second. He has none of the brash confidence that comes with money and success. Which is a definite plus in her book.

'I'm . . . it was probably horribly unprofessional of me . . .'

'Not at all. Did I overstep the mark?'

'God, no.'

'I don't want to ruin our lessons. Really. Genuinely. But I like you . . .'

She stages a gulp. Almost overdoes it and goes straight

to bullfrog. 'I like you too.' She sees the relief on his face. 'But obviously it's not straightforward.'

'You're married.'

'I'm married. I don't want to do the whole "we live separate lives" bit, but we kind of do. I think he would coast along forever for an easy life. But I don't know if I can do that.'

John exhales. 'I'm not the sort of person who would break up a marriage.'

'It's broken already,' she says, thinking this all sounds a bit like a script from a daytime soap. 'We're going through the motions. But I get that it makes you uncomfortable. Trust me, I'm not a cheater either. We can take it slowly and see what happens.'

'I'd like that. Do you think you'd ever leave him?'

'Yes. God. It's just the practicalities, you know. I'm only still here because I haven't worked out how to get by if I do.'

He nods. 'Interesting.'

They hold eye contact for a few painful seconds.

'*Me gustas*,' she says. 'I like you.'

'How do you say, "I like you too"?'

'*A mi tambien me gustas.*'

'*A mi tambien me gustas*,' he repeats.

Sian bestows a big smile on him. 'Good.'

She wonders if she can cancel the vow renewal. What seemed farcical but essentially benign, and necessary to protect herself from the (yes, justified, she knows) rumours that Kitty and co. would love everyone to believe, now seems like an act of cruelty. She knows Rich has done nothing to deserve the way she's treating him, besides be too happy with his lot. They're fundamentally incompatible. He's a nice, kind, caring man and she's a self-serving bitch. She's fully aware of this.

But it's still way too early with John to hope that it might all work out. She can't burn all her bridges this soon. The truth is that all the guests they've invited are going to hate her eventually anyway. Whether it's in a month or a year. Because she cannot – will not – live out the rest of her life in this dreary cycle of work, eat, sleep, see the in-laws, repeat. So, what's the difference?

When John leaves she reaches out and touches his fingers again. A reminder. He groans softly, and she knows she's got him.

She visits Celine in her studio, a collective of creative spaces on the fringes of Battersea. It's heaven on earth to her: the smell of paint, the sound of sewing machines whirring and theatre groups improvising. She would never complain again if she could spend the rest of her days in a place like this. Celine's parents are wealthy, and she's never had to work a day in her life, she just cosplays at being an artist. Bertie and Vita are the same. Propped up by family money, role-playing at glittering careers. Seraphine describes herself as an interior designer, based on the fact she occasionally recommends a nice lamp to friends and knows where the best shops are, while Felix self-styles as a DJ because he likes to take a turn on the turntables at parties. They're just killing time till one set of parents die – either one, it doesn't matter – and they inherit eye-watering riches. They'll claim they're still socialists while living in what might as well be a free stately home. In all honesty she won't be sorry to leave the lot of them behind. Ironically, Lottie's privileges had actually seemed timid in comparison. But they still would have changed Sian's life.

But who knows? Maybe John could change it even more. It's got to be worth a shot.

Betty has been invited to the party. 'Dress code: mid-twentieth century,' she tells Kitty with a sneer. 'What am I supposed to wear?'

'Just dress like you always do,' Kitty says and, as always with Betty, she waits anxiously to see if she's rewarded with a laugh. She is. Betty is gradually thawing around her. Mr Millman (Eric, apparently) has seemingly smooched some of her rough edges away.

They're in the café at Kenwood House, far enough away from home that they're hopeful no one they know will spot them. Waiting for Grace and Lottie.

'The only important thing is that Rich finally sees Sian for who she really is,' Kitty reminds them once they're all gathered round one of the outdoor tables by the café, coffees in front of them.

'And the rest of them do too,' Grace says. 'The friends and neighbours.'

The teenagers are having their own night – suggested to Seraphine by Lottie, who told her that her two were upset about missing out. Rhys has opted to join them, not wanting to be seen to diss his old friends (or to be the only young person at the do). They're gathering at Bertie and Vita's, overseen by the au pair who will also be supervising Wilf. 'No kids!' the invitation had screamed. Thankfully, because otherwise Kitty is not sure she could bring herself to go through with it. She feels bad about Rich's mum and dad, but she hopes that eventually, with hindsight, they'll realise Rich needed to know, even if they don't appreciate the way the news was delivered.

'Poor Barbara and Ray,' she says.

'Poor Rich,' Grace counters. 'He's going to be devastated. But he'll definitely be happier in the long run. We're doing the right thing.'

Betty passes the invitation around. It's the first time either Lottie or Grace have seen it. Dramatic gold letters on blood-red card.

Help us celebrate 20 years of Mr and Mrs Selway Price!!

Saturday August 16th 7 p.m. till midnight
(we're getting old!) at the Bald Faced Stag,
High Road, East Finchley

Please don't get us a present — you can contribute
to a communal bar fund here . . .

[There's a QR code underneath.]

RSVP. Sorry, no kids!

'I wonder how much is behind the bar so far,' Grace says. 'Loads, probably.'

'Do I need to add to it?' Betty says. 'I suppose I do, or it'll look rude.'

'They're going to think you're a lot ruder later,' Grace says, and Kitty guffaws.

Betty chuckles, then looks at Lottie. 'Are you all right, my dear? You're very quiet.'

It's true that Lottie has barely said a word since she arrived. She smiles weakly. 'Yep. Good. Thank you.'

'You'll feel better once we've done it,' Grace says gently. 'You'll be able to move on.'

Lottie nods, unconvinced. She gives a half-glance at Kitty. 'We might. Literally. Move on. Start again somewhere else.'

'What? Where? What about the shop?' Grace looks at her, horrified.

'We're trying to work it out. I can open one somewhere else. Bath, maybe. Somewhere like that, where Andrew can get enough business too.'

'Every other shop in Bath sells vintage clothes!' Grace says. 'There's too much competition.'

'Somewhere like that. Not Bath necessarily.'

Kitty sits with her eyes closed. Andrew is moving away. She'll never see him again. Lottie and Andrew need a clean break from her. From Sian.

She feels as if she's going to cry. And if she does, she might never stop.

'I'm moving away too,' Kitty says. What she means is *so you don't have to.*

'Are you?' Betty asks. 'That's a shame. Where to?'

'Not sure yet. South somewhere. Nearer Grace.' Grace beams. 'Wherever I can afford, really. I've put my house up. I'm looking at flats.'

'I think we all need a new start,' Lottie says quietly.

'Does Andrew know about what we're planning?' Grace blurts out.

Lottie stirs her spoon through her coffee. Clears her throat. 'He does. He thinks it's a good thing. Closure.'

'Do you think it's enough? Us all "speaking our truth"?' Grace says suddenly. 'What if everyone just thinks we're lying?'

'We have Betty. Our trump card,' Kitty says. 'No one will think she's making it up. Why would she?' But she's not going to lie; she's had the same anxiety herself. What if Sian just laughs it off and says Betty's a mad old meddler who has a grudge against her because she has a dog?

Kitty waves a wasp away. 'Let's just go over what she's going to say one more time.'

Grace shakes her head. 'We need more.'

'Fucking hell, Grace. Why are you doing this now?'

'She's right,' Lottie says. 'We need a deathblow.'

Kitty sighs. 'Where are we going to get one of those?'

60. Sian

She's just thinking of it as any other party. Not a big deal. Not a big public declaration of their love. Not a big smokescreen. Just drinking, dancing and having a good time. She's chosen her outfit. A silky crimson maxi dress that's somehow fitted and flowy at the same time. Spaghetti straps. Cut low at the front and back.

'It looks like a nightie. In a really good way,' Rich had said when she'd shown him. He'd snaked his hands round her waist. The thing was she still found him attractive. She loved the touch of his hands on her. His breath on her neck. She'd turned round to face him. Twenty plus years and he could still get her going. That was saying something. Not only that, but he could still make her laugh (sometimes – he had a tendency towards the dad joke), was a good father, a good husband. Kind and fair and thoughtful. She treasured their shared past. She was just suffocated by the thought of their shared future.

If you could combine just about everything Rich with John's drive and wealth, that would be her perfect man right there.

Now that she had a long-term plan, she felt better. Calmer. Just as she had when Andrew was the goal. She had hope.

The party – the vow renewal – was the band-aid that

would hold her life as it was together until she could leave the whole thing behind.

The clock is ticking to lock John in for a date after his course finishes. She has his details, obviously, she could simply phone him a few days later on any made-up pretext, but she doesn't want their flirtation to lose momentum. It's a fragile being, existing so far only in the confines of her living room. On Saturday – lesson seven – she worried she almost blew it. As they did their usual finger touching, almost hand holding, that has become a ritual as they say goodbye at the front door, she had tilted her head and leaned up, lips parted. He'd almost met her halfway, eyes part-closed. Then he'd sighed and pulled back, leaving her hanging.

'Not yet,' he'd said. 'Not in his house.'

She was such an idiot. She'd worried all night that she'd frightened him away. She'd almost sent him a text apologising if she'd pushed things too far too soon, but she knew leaving that kind of a trail could never be a good idea. This evening, though, he turned up as usual and produced a bunch of vibrant red poppies tied with string from behind his back as soon as the front door was closed.

'They made me think of you,' he said. The relief was overwhelming.

He's an easy student, a good learner, so it's not hard to get through the lesson, with just a few little in-jokes and compliments thrown back and forth.

'Say something about yourself.'

'*Estoy enamorado.*'

She'd laughed. 'Now say something about me.'

'*Eres hermosa.*' You're beautiful.

As he's getting ready to leave, he tells her about an excruciatingly boring function he has to go to at the weekend, for work. 'I wish you could come,' he says.

'Well, you haven't exactly sold it well, but yes. Me too.' She has a boring do of her own to go to, she tells him. 'I'd rather be doing something fun with you.'

'Would you like to have dinner? After my course is over? We can go to a Spanish restaurant, and you can watch me try to order.'

She wants to punch the air.

Yes!

'I'd like that,' she says.

'What would you do if you could do anything?' he asks her on Wednesday. They're by the open patio doors again, the sun hot on their legs. She's wearing a romper suit, her long, pale legs stretched out in front of her.

She squints at him. 'Workwise?'

He nods.

'That's easy. I'd paint all day and sell enough paintings that galleries would vie to have me.'

'Why don't you?'

She stretches up, arching her back. 'Let's see. Within a couple of months or so we'd stop being able to pay the mortgage, a few weeks later someone would come and repossess the house and then we'd end up living with Rich's mum and dad in their spare room. Reason enough?'

He laughs. 'I didn't realise teachers earned so much.'

'You mean you didn't realise me and Rich combined

earned so little.' She laughs a fake laugh. 'It's out of the question, sadly. And that sucks to be honest.'

'If a fairy godfather appeared and said they'd fixed it but Rich couldn't come along for the ride, what would you say?'

'I'd bite their fucking arm off.'

'Ha! And Rich would be OK? What would he do?'

'I don't know. Get a lodger in to pay half the mortgage? I mean, he'd miss me. But you can't stay in a relationship you're unhappy in just because you feel bad about the other person.'

'Agreed.'

'But, you know, I'm not in a situation where I can just walk out.'

'Not yet,' he says, and Sian has to stop herself from diving across the room and hugging him. She's almost starting to find him attractive at this point.

She gives him what she hopes is a seductive smile. 'Not yet.'

61. Sian

There's a definite buzz in Ashdown Close. Julie stops Sian on her way to the park with Dante to tell her in detail what she and Pete are going to be wearing this evening. Vernie and Malcolm appear on her doorstep with two twenty-pound notes, 'For the drinks fund', because they didn't understand what the QR code was or what it had to do with anything. Even Betty shouts across the street to tell her how much she's looking forward to it. Sian nods and smiles and tries to enjoy being the centre of attention.

The truth is that guilt has caught up with her big time. Listening to Rich excitedly planning playlists with Felix on the phone earlier and running through the final wording for the vows with the celebrant has rammed home the cruelty of what she's doing. She's not sure she can go through with tonight.

And Rhys. Shit. What will Rhys think of her when she walks out on a perfectly happy, functioning marriage? His life. His stability. His home. It would have been entirely different if Rich had been shown to be the bad guy, cheating on poor innocent Sian with evil Lottie. She would have had everyone's sympathy and support.

She hasn't thought this through.

She just has to keep putting one foot in front of the other. Let whatever is going to happen, happen.

She gives herself a pep talk as she walks round the

perimeter path. Runs through what she has to do this afternoon in her head. Planning always calms her down. She's had her nails done – hot-pink shellac to clash beautifully with the dress. She needs to wash her hair. Shower, exfoliate, moisturise. She and Rich are planning to arrive at the venue around seven to check things over. They need to eat before they go to line their stomachs. So, cab at twenty to seven, eat at six latest, in the shower by, what? Four thirty to be safe. Give herself time to mess up her hair and make-up and have to start again. She thinks of random other things: put gel pads in her shoes, shave her armpits, feed Dante, book the cab to bring them home. She turns back towards Ashdown Close. She needs to get on with it.

Rich holds her hand on the journey down. He looks dapper in his wedding suit, already altered by Lottie when all hell broke loose. He's doing the no-sock thing, which is not a trend Sian has ever been able to get on board with. Where does the sweat go? What about chafing? She smiles at him, nods at his ankles. 'Aren't you going to get blisters?'

He raises an eyebrow. 'No, because . . .' He undoes a lace and whips his left shoe off. 'I'm wearing these passion killers.' On his feet are tiny nude-coloured socks, made from the same sheer material as tights.

'Oh my god. I can't . . .'

He waves his foot at her, stroking it. 'Is it doing it for you? Can you control yourself?'

Sian snorts.

He places it on her thigh, snaking it around.

'No! Get it off!' She laughingly bats it away. The cab driver catches her eye in the mirror and smiles. She's going to miss him. Rich. If it all works out.

One minute they're standing in an empty room beautifully decorated with high displays of red, yellow and orange flowers – Seraphine and Felix's gift to them as well as a very generous donation to the drink fund that has allowed them to add on nibbles – anxiously sipping glasses of Prosecco and looking at their phones wondering why no one has arrived yet, the next they're surrounded by laughter and chatter and love, a whirl of hugs and kisses on the cheek and being told they look amazing and aren't they cute and where did you get that dress? It's impossible for Sian not to get caught up in the fun of it. She spots a friend from college, a cousin she hasn't seen for years, Rich's mum and dad, beaming with anticipation. Felix is playing a 1960s mix he's painstakingly put together: Donovan, Dylan, Joni Mitchell, Cat Stevens. It's perfect. She knows he's going to do some godawful set later where he'll guffaw out banter over the top of songs that don't deserve it, but it'll be funny if nothing else. It'll get the drunk-dancing going.

She has half conversations with what feels like hundreds of people. Promises to catch up properly soon. She hears scores of tiny fragments of news: *Ophelia had her baby! We're relocating to Dubai! Remember that girl Georgia? In prison. Drugs!* Later she'll mix them all up in her head and forget what's happening to who.

She tries to drink slowly. The vow renewal is at nine and she doesn't want it to be a car crash. She catches sight of Rich here and there, in his element. She's happy for him. She knows he's taking the loss of his friendship with Andrew hard. That he can't understand why Lottie has turned on them too when it's her husband who betrayed her, not him.

As evenings go, it's pretty perfect.

Which, she thinks, is weird, but she'll take it.

At ten to nine she fights her way to the ladies to check her hair is still where it should be – she's piled it up in a loose bun with a few soft waves escaping round her face – and she doesn't have eyeliner on her cheek. It takes twice as long to get there than she'd anticipated because every other person stops her for a chat, and then twice as long to get back. She spots Rich frantically looking round, and realises it's her he's looking for, as if she might have disappeared on him.

'Thank god,' he laughs when he spots her. 'I thought you'd stood me up.' He leads her over to a raised area where the celebrant – their friend Sky with her long grey hair and a nose ring – waits, and a cheer goes up around the room.

It's short and really rather sweet. Sky says a few words about how Rich and Sian met, their wedding, Rhys, the Brodie's Notes of their life together and then asks them to repeat the words they've chosen. They had agreed no schmaltz, no romance tropes, no clichés.

'Twenty years is a long time,' Rich says. 'But I'd do it all again. Maybe on fast-forward because those years when Rhys was a baby were tough.' There's a ripple of laughter around the room. 'You know how much I love you, so

I'm not going to tell you now. You know you're my best friend, so I won't say that either. I'll just say this . . . I'm actually looking forward to growing old with you. I won't care when you have wrinkles and a moustache and gout and varicose veins, and those weird moles that sprout up out of nowhere with black hairs growing out of them . . . Actually, I might need to rethink this . . .' More laughs. 'Seriously, without getting soppy, you mean the world to me. Let's go for another twenty.'

A cheer rips round the room. Rich gives her a beaming smile. Sian pushes away a feeling that she's the world's worst human being.

'Sian?' Sky says.

Sian clears her throat. 'Twenty years is a long time. But I'd do it all again . . . Shit, sorry, wrong one . . .' Thankfully she's getting the laughs too. It helps. 'Rich, I never could have imagined when I first saw you trying to rap along to "My Name Is" by Eminem at Maggie and Jim's wedding and realised that you knew every single word, that all this time later we'd still be here. And now, ladies and gentlemen, he's here to perform it again . . .' She waves an arm at him with a flourish. 'No, seriously, thank you for being my constant, my confidant and my comfort blanket. You're a triple threat. Now let's celebrate with everyone we love the most. Apart from Rhys, who thought this whole thing would be a huge cringe.'

More raucous cheers. Someone proposes a toast. It's done. She hasn't promised him a future or her eternal devotion. She hasn't promised him anything.

Of course there are speeches. Rich's dad, Ray, heckled by his mum Barbara. Felix, slightly worse for wear, Vita braying through a list of mutual acquaintances no one else in the room has ever heard of, Celine, who manages to somehow make her tribute an advert for her own website. Just as Sian thinks they're all over and they can get the dancing going, Betty – Mrs Martin – the self-appointed queen of Ashdown Close by virtue of being its longest resident – takes the stage.

'I've been asked to speak on behalf of your neighbours,' she says in a confident voice. Sian sees Vernie and Malcolm, Julie and Pete, Sam and Linz, Mr Millman all nodding along.

'You were the only one who volunteered,' Pete shouts. Sian offers up a thanks that at least it's not him paying tribute. They'd be here all night. She just hopes Betty won't call Dante out as the phantom pooer. He's not, by the way. She knows it's Sam and Linz's dog, Muffin, when Linz takes her out for a late-night vodka-fuelled toilet break, but Sian is no snitch.

Betty ignores him. 'It is safe to say that the street has livened up since Rich and Sian moved into number eight. They've brought a much-needed injection of fresh, youthful air to us old codgers . . .'

Vernie and Malcolm both chuckle.

'. . . and some fun for the other youngsters, I'm sure. They have fitted in seamlessly with their friendly, warm and caring personalities and hospitality. Although some of us are still recovering from their housewarming party. It's always a pleasure to see a happy couple spending time together . . .' She starts a sort of round of applause that the guests latch on to enthusiastically.

'So, it was a surprise when I was walking round the park

a couple of months ago and I overheard Sian confiding in her friend and our neighbour, Kitty from number ten . . .'

Alarm bells start to go off in Sian's ears. What's happening? She grabs Rich's arm and whispers in his ear. 'Shall we go round the back and have a quickie?'

He laughs, but turns his attention back to Betty, ever polite.

'. . . found out that Rich, her beloved husband, was having an affair . . .' There's an audible gasp from the crowd.

'OK, I think Mrs Martin might have taken advantage of the free bar,' Sian shouts as loud as she can to drown her out. Everyone has turned to look at her.

'What the fuck?' Rich says.

'And that the woman he was sleeping with was her best friend, Lottie, who many of you know. I heard it clear as day. I'm sorry, Rich. I'm sorry to your parents who I know are here. But your wife started those rumours about you, not Kitty Harbinson. And everything else that happened after, happened because of that conversation. Kitty was telling the truth.'

There's an avalanche of chatter. Sian can't look at Rich, but she can feel his eyes boring into her. 'She's making it up,' she says. 'She's a fucking nasty gossip, you know that.'

'What's going on?' he says. 'Why is she doing this?'

Sian ignores the questions raining down on her from other people and grabs Rich's arm. 'Come and talk to me . . .'

They turn towards the door. She just needs to get out of there. Her mind races as she tries to work out what she can say to convince him that Betty is lying. She pulls him towards the exit just as a man – John, what the fuck? – comes striding through the door towards them, closing it behind him and standing in front of it. For a second she thinks maybe she invited him, but she knows without a doubt that she didn't.

She stops dead and Rich half bangs into her.

'Sian!' John says, a big smile on his face. His voice is so loud everyone stops and looks round. 'Fancy seeing you here.'

She notices he's holding his phone and what looks like a small Bluetooth speaker. Whatever is about to happen she knows it's not going to be good.

'Let's go.' Rich doesn't move. She could make a run for it, but what? Would she have to wrestle John to get past him? For all she knows he's a certified maniac. Beyond what he's told her, she only has the few details she found about him on Google to go on. His place of work. A couple of official-looking headshots. Or does he think he's her knight in shining armour come to save her from her unhappy marriage? It crosses her mind briefly that the latter wouldn't be all bad. Humiliating, yes, but it would just be a fast-forward to the result she wants.

'John . . .' She gives him a hopeful smile. 'What are you doing here?'

'Everyone,' John booms. 'As someone who's become a good friend of Sian's over the past few weeks, I wanted to play you all a little something. If I could just have your attention for a moment.' He presses a button on his phone. The guests have all gone quiet. They know this isn't scripted. Sian catches sight of Barbara and the upset on her face almost floors her. She sinks into a chair as John's own voice blasts from the speaker.

'*What would you do if you could do anything?*'

Shit. She knows exactly what's coming.

'*Workwise? That's easy. I'd paint all day and sell enough paintings that galleries would vie to have me.*'

'*Why don't you?*'

'*Let's see. Within a couple of months or so we'd stop being able to pay the mortgage, a few weeks later someone would come and repossess the house and then we'd end up living with Rich's mum and dad in their spare room. Reason enough?*'

'*I didn't realise teachers earned so much.*'

'*You mean you didn't realise me and Rich combined earned so little. It's out of the question, sadly. And that sucks to be honest.*'

'*If a fairy godfather appeared and said they'd fixed it but Rich couldn't come along for the ride, what would you say?*'

'*I'd bite their fucking arm off.*'

'*Ha! And Rich would be OK? What would he do?*'

'*I don't know. Get a lodger in to pay half the mortgage? I mean, he'd miss me. But you can't stay in a relationship you're unhappy in just because you feel bad about the other person.*'

Every mouth is open. Every pair of eyes is on her. He taped their lessons. Everything. Every stupid little flirty comment she made. She has no fucking idea what is happening. There's a click. An edit. It's her.

'*I don't want to do the whole "we live separate lives" bit, but we kind of do. I think he would coast along forever for an easy life. But I don't know if I can do that.*'

'*I'm not the sort of person who would break up a marriage.*'

'*It's broken already. We're going through the motions. But I get that it makes you uncomfortable. Trust me, I'm not a cheater either. We can take it slowly and see what happens.*'

'*I'd like that. Do you think you'd ever leave him?*'

'*Yes. God. It's just the practicalities, you know. I'm only still here because I haven't worked out how to get by if I do.*'

There are gasps around the room now. Sian forces herself to look at Rich. He's not even angry; he looks as if his world has been devastated. Shattered. Barbara and Ray lean on each other like two survivors of a train wreck.

'I'm sorry, Rich,' John says. 'This gives me no pleasure, but we thought you should know the truth.'

Rich doesn't take his eyes off Sian. He shakes his head. 'We? Who's we?'

'For those of you who would like to hear, I have some friends here who can explain everything.' John reaches behind him and opens the door. Kitty – of course it's fucking Kitty – strides in like Boudicca, nostrils ·flared. Behind her is Grace, her loyal shadow. And then . . .

'Lotts? Really?'

Lottie gives her a steely stare.

'Yes, Siany. Really.'

'Didn't he do brilliantly?' Grace flings her arm round Alasdair. The artist formerly known as John. 'I'm so proud of you, honestly.'

'You know she tried to kiss me?' He grimaces. 'I fought her off. Actually, I told her I wanted to wait. My morals wouldn't allow me to commit such a sin in Rich's house. John is very moral.'

'Good,' Grace says. 'He'd better be.'

Kitty studies her for any signs of suspicion, of the old Grace and all her distrust of men and their motives, and sees none. She reaches out a hand and squeezes Alasdair's arm. 'Thank you.'

'Best fun I've had in years. And I can speak Spanish now. Well, *un poco* at least. I almost left that on the tape to show off.'

The plan had been to make a swift exit after their revelation, but Sian had stormed out immediately, gawping as Grace planted a kiss on John's lips as she passed them. Rich had followed soon after, accompanied by his parents. Kitty had wondered whether to try to speak to them, but it seemed insensitive. Give them time for it all to sink in. She had no idea where any of them had gone.

The friends who were still there had surrounded them. No one, it seemed, had any doubts. The neighbours all hugged her and apologised for allowing themselves to be deceived. She was sure that if she stayed on in Ashdown Close they would embrace her back into the community. Sian would be the pariah for as long as she remained. But Kitty would never forget how quick they'd been to disown her. And besides, the woman who'd moved to Ashdown Close no longer existed. She was a different person now.

Rather than telling the story over and over again, someone – Seraphine, she thinks – decided that everyone one should listen while they each told their part of it. Kitty hadn't been sure she could do it – the bald confession about her and Andrew would sound too harsh, too cold, to a room full of people, but Grace held her hand and, when it came to it, Lottie reached out and held the other one, and then they all started crying, but they got through it somehow. They actually got a round of applause.

'God,' Vita said when it died down. 'If she'd just asked me, I'd have made my dad give her some made-up job as his resident artist or something.' Which, Kitty thought, pretty much summed up how life was for these people.

'But, who's he?' Pete said, jerking a thumb at Alasdair.

It was Alasdair who had volunteered. Who had come up with the idea of John in the first place. After the meet-up at Kenwood and the realisation that what they had was too flimsy, too easy to write off as hearsay or gossip or misunderstanding, Grace had brought him up to date while they were lying in her bed one night – one of the things they had bonded over was his love of her stories and this ongoing one in particular. He liked that his suggestion of Magda contacting Sez had been taken on board and had worked. He felt invested, he told her.

Besides, he was bored at work, and creating a few fake webpages for a hedge funder called John Wright (a friend who was cursed with a surprisingly common name) who didn't exist gave him something fun to do while he worried about whether the residents of Hounslow would find it more user friendly to click through three times to identify the exact type of parking permit they needed to order, or whether they would prefer to fill in a form spelling out their needs and wait for someone to get back to them. It wasn't really up to him, to be fair, the council had very set ideas, but he felt it was important he tried to humanise the consumer in his thought processes.

'She wanted Andrew because she thought he'd indulge her desire to give up work and paint more or less full-time, correct?' he'd said to Grace.

'And to stick it to Lottie in the process. But yes, correct.'

'So, it's not as if I'd have to make her fall in love with me. I'd just have to be rich, single and interested, and then get her to come on to me, say a few mean things about Rich, and record it all on my phone. Then, if I get anything, you can play it in front of Rich and all their friends after Betty's done her big speech.'

'You'd do that?'

He'd shrugged. 'I've always wanted to learn Spanish.'

'What if she doesn't say anything incriminating? What if she's a really professional teacher and she would never mix her personal life with her work?'

'Then we can go to Barcelona for a weekend, and I can impress you with how bilingual I am. Besides, I saw what she did to you and Kitty. I never want to see you that sad again.'

Grace had propped herself up on one elbow. 'Are you for real?'

'Not for the next few weeks if we do this, no. But generally, absolutely definitely.'

'It's only just over a month till the party. I don't know.'

'I'll book three lessons a week. I'll lay it on thick. She won't know what hit her.'

'I love it,' Grace had said. 'But let me talk to the others.'

It was desperation and lack of any other viable option that had made Kitty agree. After all, what was the worst that could happen? Sian busted Alasdair somehow and they'd be back where they'd started.

Grace had told Kitty that for the next couple of days Alasdair had bombarded her with questions. *Should John have glasses? What about a hedge funder? I have a cousin who's one (stinking rich, awful git) so he could give me tips. Has he been married before?*

'He's loving it,' she'd said.

So, they'd given him the go-ahead and he'd messaged Sian and booked a course of twelve lessons. Three a week in the run-up to the vow renewal, paid for by his friend John Wright who also agreed that Alasdair could wear his fake Rolex and use his PayPal, so long as he reimbursed him.

Now they're in Betty's living room, the five of them: Kitty, Grace, Alasdair, Lottie and Betty, of course. Mr Millman – she can't bring herself to call him Eric yet – is in the kitchen making tea. No one can face another drink yet. They're wired.

'You were brilliant too, Betty,' Lottie says. She has some of her bloom back. 'We listened from outside.'

'You were,' Kitty and Grace say at the same time.

'I love him,' Kitty says later, while they're sitting on the sofa, as Alasdair brushes his teeth in Grace's bathroom. 'He's perfect for you.'

'I think I might too,' Grace blushes. 'One day. He got new shoes.'

Kitty lies down and leans her head on Grace's shoulder. 'I noticed. Did you choose them?'

'Too right I did. He was very nice about it.'

'He's very nice full stop.'

'He really is. Are you OK about him staying over? I mean, you were here first.'

'I love you too. You know that?'

Grace angles her head on top of Kitty's. 'Course. We're besties.'

63. Four months later

Grace's stomach enters the room first. For someone so small and only four months gone she's carrying an impressive bump, although Kitty is convinced she's enhancing it by pushing out her stomach because she's so excited for people to spot her condition. It just happened. Blissful in the first flush of love, she and Alasdair got careless, and now here they are planning a wedding and with a miracle baby on the way. Alasdair, it seemed, was as thrilled as she was. Kitty – godmother in waiting, maid of honour to be – could not be happier for them. This week Grace is moving into his flat and Kitty is going to be renting hers. She's finally leaving Ashdown Close for good.

Her house still hasn't sold, but she's found a tenant to cover the mortgage. Anyone who came to view hers had also viewed Sian and Rich's, and theirs – a better layout, a more loved interior, on for the same price – inevitably sold first. She hasn't seen Sian since the night of the party. (She's still teaching at the same school, Kitty knows that from Linz, whose eldest started there in September, but no one's sure where she's living.) Rich moved out last week. They're friends again, Lottie, Andrew and Rich. He's coping. He's started seeing someone, but it's early days and he's cautious.

'She's nice,' Lottie tells her. 'You know. Not a psycho. Not trying to ruin my life.'

A month after the vow renewal, Kitty accepted an invitation for her, Grace and Alasdair to a party at Vita and Bertie's, knowing that Andrew would be there. She had to face him sometime, Grace told her. She'd checked with Lottie first that it was OK. Lottie's sweetness, her kindness, her noisy love of food were all genuine, it had turned out. She didn't have the capability for meanness any more than she had the capability to play basketball.

'Of course. God. Come. It'll be lovely to see you,' she'd said when Kitty called her.

Kitty hadn't seen Andrew since the afternoon he and Lottie came round so that Lottie could hear her and Grace's side of the story. She still thought about him, still compared every other man she met to him and found them lacking, but that's all he was, a fond memory, a huge regret. She wasn't sure how she would feel.

There was no sign of them when they first arrived at the majestic Georgian terraced house and showed their invitations to the black-suited man waiting at the bottom of the candlelit steps.

'Are we really underdressed?' Grace had stage-whispered. 'I wasn't expecting it to be this posh.'

Grace's rigid fashion etiquette rules had relaxed considerably since she'd found happiness. Kitty had accompanied her to buy her first pair of jeans last week and she was wearing them now with an oversized tailored white shirt and chunky sandals. She'd ditched her glasses for contacts. ('Alasdair misses them. He said he liked my "Sexy Secretary" act when I whipped them off, so I said, "It's 2025. I don't think you can say stuff like that any more, and anyway, I'm an administrator, not a secretary. Besides, I can't see a thing without them, so when I take them off I might as well be having sex with the postman, which isn't ideal for either of us," and he said, "Or the postman," which made me laugh even though it strictly speaking didn't make any sense . . .') She was growing out her bixie and had ditched the hairspray for salt spray so her hair fell in beachy waves almost to her shoulders. She looked like a woman who was having a lot of good sex.

'Absolutely not.'

Alasdair – big, burly, sweet, kind Alasdair – had put an arm round Grace and said, 'You look absolutely gorgeous,' and Grace had blushed scarlet. Kitty had wanted to stuff the pair of them and keep them on her mantelpiece they were so cute.

It was unlike any house party any of them had ever been to. Waiters circulating with trays of canapés and bottles of Bollinger. A string quartet in one room. Kitty didn't really know anyone except the hosts and Seraphine and Felix, and she recognised a couple of women from the Salon – Xanthe and one of the beret wearers – but she was no longer intimidated by these people; she no longer yearned to be one of them. She'd rather be in a corner with Grace and Alasdair taking the piss.

She spotted them as they walked in. Rich first. Then Lottie. And then, bringing up the rear, Andrew.

She knew she was staring, but she couldn't look away. It was almost as if she'd forgotten he was a real, living, breathing person. That her heart might remember him, whatever her head was saying, and start pounding. She gripped Grace's arm.

'Ouch. Oh.'

Rich saw them first. He waved. The first evening that Kitty had been at home after the party – having camped out at Grace's until Betty let her know that she'd seen Sian overseeing the loading up of a van and she had, apparently, moved out for good – Rich had rung her doorbell and apologised profusely. She had done the same. They'd both been quick to believe the worst about each other. There was no atmosphere. Rich was his usual uncomplicated and open self. When they'd agreed there was no reason they couldn't be friends, Kitty knew he'd meant it.

Lottie and Andrew both looked over. Kitty kept her eyes fixed on Lottie and smiled warmly. Lottie hared straight over, grabbing the three of them in a hug in turn, Kitty first. 'It's nice to see you all.'

'You too,' Kitty said. 'Are you OK?'

Lottie smiled. 'I am. Can I borrow you for a second?'

'Sure.' She followed Lottie back across the room where, to her horror, Andrew was still standing talking to Bertie. Kitty hesitated and shot a look back at Grace who gave her a slight grimace in return. Lottie took hold of her hand and Kitty felt she had no choice but to follow if she didn't want to cause a scene. Andrew, Kitty noticed, looked just as uncomfortable as they approached.

'Hi . . .' Kitty mumbled.

'So. You two need to talk,' Lottie said.

Kitty's mouth fell open. 'No. Lottie, what?' She couldn't even look at him.

'For all our sakes. Mine too. Bert, will you help me find a drink?' She left before they could protest, taking Bertie with her.

'I had no idea she was going to do that,' Andrew said quietly. 'We don't have to.'

'It's probably the grown-up thing to do,' Kitty said. 'I just don't know . . .' She stopped as she saw a man she didn't know approaching and grinning at Andrew.

'Let's go outside,' Andrew said. 'Back in a sec, Marcus.'

She followed him through a small study and out through the double doors into the stunning garden. She remembered Andrew telling her once that he had redesigned Vita and Bertie's outdoor spaces last year.

'This is beautiful. Is this you?'

He still hadn't looked her in the eye. He nodded. 'Yep.'

They walked over to sit on a low wall.

'Listen . . .' she started to say as he spoke too. 'How are you?'

'OK. Better now the truth is out there.'

He half laughed. 'Grace's boyfriend, eh?'

'Yeah. Genius. They're really happy. It's lovely.'

They both stared out at the other guests for a moment.

'I'm sorry,' he said eventually. 'That things turned out like they did.'

'Hardly your fault.'

'I mean, that I chose to stay with Lottie. It wasn't choosing her over you . . .'

She looked at him. 'I know. I know it was hard. But it was the right thing to do. She didn't deserve any of it. Sian . . . us.'

He finally looked back at her. She almost looked away, but they had to get through this awkward stage somehow, so she forced herself to hold eye contact for the briefest of seconds. Any more and she thought she might lean in for the kiss and everything else be damned. Think of it as aversion therapy, she told herself. You look at a picture of a spider and eventually you can hold one in your palm and feel nothing. 'Exactly,' he said. 'And I couldn't . . . I would never, you know.'

'I do.'

'However much I wanted to.'

She couldn't respond to that. She just wanted to cry. She let out a sigh.

'She's lovely, Lottie. Really properly lovely. I wish Sian hadn't made me think otherwise.'

'Yeah. It's not like it's hard to be married to her.' He rubbed his hand over his head, hair neatly cropped again.

'You'll get there,' she said.

'I will,' he said. 'I'll make sure I do. You know, Lotts really wants us to be friends.'

Kitty exhaled loudly. 'Well, we can. Let's just decide we're going to do it. Awkwardness gone. No more talking about what happened. No more apologies. New start right now.'

He smiled at her. A warm, genuine smile. She knew how grateful he was that she was trying as hard as he was. 'Done,' he said. 'New start.'

'Can we get a drink? I'm desperate.'

415

'Let's go,' he said, standing up.

It was over.

And she felt OK.

Grace stuffs a couple of things into a holdall. She's been moving gradually for a week, and it doesn't look as if anything's changed. Kitty has agreed she can leave whatever she wants in the spare room for now. 'That's where you'll be sleeping whenever you stay over, so you're the one who'll be looking at it all.'

'Shall I stay here tonight? Just the two of us?'

'Aren't you and Alasdair supposed to be going bowling?'

Grace shrugs. 'He wouldn't mind. If you need me.'

'I know he wouldn't because he's basically perfect.'

Grace's phone beeps. She holds it out to Kitty. 'He says ask if you want to come with us.'

She had worried that maybe Grace and Alasdair had started to think of her as a charity case. If they'd made an agreement to make sure she got out of the house now and then, like she was their old, lonely aunt. But then she'd realised they just liked hanging round with her. That they had fun, the three of them. And Lottie sometimes when she wasn't on set. No Andrew so far, but Kitty thought the day would come and she would be absolutely fine with it. They had decided not to move away, Lottie had told her. Now that Sian had gone.

'OK. I will.'

Grace writes a message back. 'OK. I'm almost done. Oh . . .' She pulls out the rescued fat plushy frog from behind a cushion. 'Shall I take him, or do you want to keep him?'

'You take him. You're frog woman.'

Grace looks at it. 'I think he should stay here with you. So you're not on your own.'

'Oh my god. Stop.'

'I'll put him on the bed.'

Kitty laughs. 'I love you, you know that.'

'I do, because you keep telling me. I love you back too. Obviously.'

'You're having a fucking baby, Gracie. You're marrying the nicest man in the world.'

Grace plonks herself down on the sofa. 'I can't quite believe it.'

'Will you adopt me? You and Alasdair. When you get married.' She sits beside her.

'Absolutely. You're never getting rid of me.'

Kitty laughs again. 'I don't want to.'

She leans in and Grace lifts an arm to put round her shoulders.

'I'm going to be happy here, I think,' Kitty says.

'If you're not, you can move in with us.'

'Don't say that because I actually will.'

She rests her head against Grace's. They sit in silence for a moment.

'You know, you're very clingy these days,' Grace says. 'I like it.'

Acknowledgements

Firstly, I'd like to thank Sez de Courcy, whose family member won a bid at an auction raising money for Freedom From Torture for her name to be used in one of my books. Sez, I think you should always go by Sexy Corgi from now on. https://www.freedomfromtorture.org

As ever, I owe so much to everyone at Penguin Michael Joseph: my editor Maxine Hitchcock for all her brilliant support, Gaby Young, Emma Plater, Stella Newing, Beatrix McIntyre, Nina Elstad, Vicky Photiou, Rachel Myers, Laura Garrod and, of course, the amazing Louise Moore. Sarah Bance, I promise I will learn the rules of when to write 'fifty' and when to write '50' one day.

Huge thanks to Jonny Geller, Viola Hayden, Natalie Beckett and everyone in the translation team at Curtis Brown.

Peter MacFarlane and all at MacFarlane Chard, I can't quite believe we have a musical touring Europe.